Lights Out

Louise Swanson is the pen name of bestselling author Louise Beech, who has published eight novels with Orenda Books, and a memoir, *Eighteen Seconds*, with Mardle. Her books have previously shortlisted for the Romantic Novel Award and the Polari Prize. She won *Best*'s Book of the Year with her 2019 psychological thriller *Call Me Star Girl*. Louise blogs regularly on louisebeech.co.uk, and is on Twitter under the name @LouiseWriter and Instagram as @Louise_Beech_Swanson

Also by Louise Swanson

End of Story

LIGHTS OUT

LOUISE SWANSON

HODDER &
STOUGHTON

First published in Great Britain in 2024 by Hodder & Stoughton Limited
An Hachette UK company

1

Copyright © Louise Swanson 2024

A CIP catalogue record for this title is available from the British Library

Hardback ISBN 978 1 529 39614 0
Trade Paperback ISBN 978 1 529 39615 7

Typeset in Bembo MT by Hewer Text UK Ltd, Edinburgh
Printed and bound in Great Britain by Clays Ltd, Elcograf S.p.A.

Hodder & Stoughton policy is to use papers that are natural, renewable and recyclable
products and made from wood grown in sustainable forests. The logging and manufacturing
processes are expected to conform to the environmental regulations of the country of origin.

Hodder & Stoughton Limited
Carmelite House
50 Victoria Embankment
London EC4Y 0DZ

www.hodder.co.uk

This one is dedicated to . . . *me.*
I worked so bloody hard on it.
Also, after a million books, I've run out
of people to devote them to.
All writers should do this, just once.
Because you're great.

(Also it's dedicated to Laurie Ellingham's dog, Rodney, and Janet
Harrison for the 'tea at the Ritz'. These things matter too.)

'We can easily forgive a child who is afraid of the dark; the real tragedy of life is when men are afraid of the light'

Unknown

It's dark.

Not just dark. It's like light never existed. Like it got gobbled up by a great, hulking, greedy monster. She's trapped in here with it; and it knows her deepest fear. It knows that bad things happen in the shadows. Children chanting outside in the place where it's bright. They forced her in here. They knew. They laughed and pointed and *knew*.

Scaredy cat, scaredy cat, scaredy cat.

She is; she hisses and pants and claws at the edges of her prison, a feral creature. Feels for walls, a door, the handle, escape. Twists at a knob but it doesn't budge. Kicks in the hope of breaking it. She's going to die; she can't breathe. The air is stagnant, clogs her throat with the kind of dust that never sees daylight.

Never let her out, never let her out, never let her out.

They must. She can't survive this. Warmth trickles down her leg. The stench of piss. She collapses in a puddle of her own waste. No energy now to fight. She resigns. Wishes she might pass out. Oblivion would be a mercy.

No such blessing.

It's to keep you safe.

Her dad's voice.

Nothing bad will happen while it's on.

But she knows he's not here.

She screams and screams and screams.

I

Welcome to UK GOV The best place to find government services and information

Lights Out Announcement – 10 December

A state of emergency has been declared concerning UK electricity. To ensure that we get through winter without major disruption we must put in place a complete night-time switch off. It will begin on 5 January. Every night, between 8 p.m. and 7 a.m., energy supplies will be switched off by providers, except for those to essential services such as hospitals, hospices, care homes, and supermarkets.

Climate change and growing consumption have forced us to ensure that our supply chain does not break down. We have done this before: in 1974 a period of electricity rationing lasted for two months, with a three-day working week, but we, as a country, came out stronger the other side. This year, as part of our Greater Green Plan, the One Day Power Off scheme reduced energy consumption significantly. Lights Out will build on that success.

This is a temporary measure and will prevent the need for a complete blackout. The government will continue to find ways of securing greener electricity supplies and will update you on a weekly basis. Further advice is available from your provider, from this government website, and from your local MP. Remember: the government's first priority is always the safety of our country.

Households can prepare for this by reading our comprehensive leaflet, which will be sent to your mobile device tomorrow or you can click **here** for more information.

NIGHT ONE

I

Death Favours the Dark

Death calls most frequently at night. He sneaks in while the lights are off and his victim sleeps, vulnerable but not always oblivious. Hospice residents are mostly taken by him between three and four a.m. Some victims are ready, welcome him; some, recognising his icy grip, ardently resist.

It makes no difference.

A serial killer on a mission; when he enters a room, Death won't leave until the deed is done. If it's time, it's time.

Grace had been waiting for Giles's death for hours.

She spoke softly to him while she did; it was her way. Conversation was one-sided. But still, as she did with all of them, Grace asked Giles questions, queries that lingered in the air, never to be answered.

Despite working in a hospice, she didn't always get to *see them out*, as she called it. But she was there in the lead-up. End-of-life carers try and anticipate the moment of death, but it's futile. Patients sometimes look deceased, perk up unexpectedly, and then flag again. There's a papery translucence to the skin, like they've adopted a premature ghostly form, and their breathing slows, slows, *slows*.

'Shall I sneak you a gin and tonic later?' Grace joked, knowing it was Giles's favourite tipple.

Quiet.

After a while, she said, 'It's happening now. Lights Out. Can you believe it?'

Quiet.

'I'm nervous about it,' she whispered.

She couldn't imagine it. Didn't want to. What would it be like, swinging a torch around the house, trying to illuminate every dangerous dark spot? Because, for Grace, darkness was always danger. Without light, there was peril.

After a while, Grace slipped out of the room to strip empty beds for new patients.

When she returned to Giles his facial muscles had slackened and his jaw had dropped, full surrender. His breathing was shallow, irregular. There's rarely the romantic, movie-esque last scene, no wailing around a tidy bed, no delicate, poetic sigh from the one passing over. The dying prefer to go alone; they'll wait until husbands and wives have gone home to rest, until siblings pop out for a cheese baguette, until children have said they need to make a call, they'll be back in a tick. Death loves an empty room.

With little fuss, Giles passed. Grace had witnessed many deaths in her five years here and, in her experience, most people departed in peace, features softened as pain ended. Death at the end of a long and dreadful illness was a relief.

And this was why Grace loved being a health-care support worker at the hospice, providing both palliative and end-of-life care. Palliative care is when no further treatment for your illness remains. End-of-life care is provided when you're closer to death. 'Why would you do such a job?' her husband, Riley, asked when she first applied. But Grace didn't feel that 'job' was the right word for it. If you were drawn to something, it was more. A vocation. People found it morbid when she told them where she worked, asked if it was horrible, traumatising. But she could honestly say that it wasn't. Life might sometimes be those things, but death was kinder.

'Sleep well, Giles,' said Grace. 'Glad I got to see you out.'

She made a note of the time. Three thirty-two.

Then she got Claire, the nurse on duty – the person in charge on that shift – who would be able to verify the death. After leaving the body for one hour as a mark of respect, they commenced with last offices. This was a procedure where the deceased was positioned, arms by their sides. They were then washed, dressed in clothes chosen beforehand, and labelled with an ID bracelet on an ankle in preparation for transportation to a mortuary.

As they worked, Grace wondered, as she often did, where humans went when they died. Giles's body was empty, a disintegrating vessel, but where had his soul gone, his essence, the vibrancy that had lit up his eyes? How could it disappear after a life of animation?

When they'd finished, the night had settled. Claire suggested Grace leave her duties and sit with another patient, Gloria. 'I know you've got quite attached to her,' she said.

There wasn't always time to sit with patients, though extra effort was made if they were feeling low or had few visitors.

Gloria, a delicate lady in her late eighties, had no one.

Grace went to her room and pulled a visitor chair up to the electronic hospital bed with protective sheets on the mattress. There was a huge clock opposite the bed so patients could easily see the time and date, orient themselves, keep track when long days blurred into one. The room was dressed to appear homely – lilac curtains, matching cushions, a smart TV, coffee table and a lamp, now on low so carers could see, and patients didn't wake afraid. Grace often thought of *Changing Rooms* episodes where a tired room got 'transformed' into a boudoir with a bit of gold stencilling, but you knew it was still just an old bedroom.

She entwined warm fingers around Gloria's chill hands as though to infuse her with life. She slept most of the time now, even during the day; strong pain medication meant patients were often drowsy near the end.

'It's dark and it shouldn't be.'

Grace jumped.

Gloria's words were clear when her throat must be dry, and she had been unconscious a while. The lamp was low, but the room wasn't dark. Grace would never have gone in if it was. Of course – Gloria's eyes were shut.

'It's bright here,' said Grace.

A croak then that she couldn't make out.

Quiet again.

Another croak.

Grace squeezed Gloria's hand. 'I'm right here.'

'Why is *he* here?' Gloria's words were weaker but still Grace started.

'Who?' she asked.

'*Him.*'

'Who?'

'The man in the corner.'

Grace spun around, heart hammering. But when she faced the wall, there was no one. She unclenched her fists. The dying often hallucinated, but Gloria seemed lucid.

'Don't let him come any closer,' she begged, eyes still closed.

Grace tried to breathe slowly, not panic.

'It's just us.' She squeezed Gloria's hand, heart staccato despite her efforts. 'You're safe with me.' Was she remembering someone terrible from her past? Patients often spoke to someone the carer couldn't see.

'He wants . . .'

'Yes?'

'He wants to tell me . . .'

'*Yes?*'

'A message for you . . .'

'For *me*?' Grace let go of Gloria's hand in surprise. She picked it up again, quickly. Perhaps Gloria thought she was a family member and Grace should remember these words, pass them on. But there was no family.

'Something . . .'

'Yes?' Grace felt sick.

'Something terrible is going to happen when the lights go out.'

'*What?*' Grace shivered.

'Something . . .'

'*Yes?*'

Grace waited for Gloria to finish. But she said no more, leaving

Grace alone with words crawling over her skin. She looked towards the corner of the room again. For a moment, a man, grinning. Grace gasped, shook her head.

Nothing. No one.

Perhaps Gloria had been voicing the things heard in recent weeks, she reasoned to herself. After all, the Lights Out scheme had been discussed a great deal.

Then the lamplight sputtered.

Something terrible is going to happen when the lights go out.

Grace didn't want to be in the room any longer. If the lights went out – suddenly, violently – she wouldn't be able to breathe. She would collapse, she would scream until her throat was on fire. She would *die*.

She ran into the corridor and didn't look back.

2

The Feather Man

Just before dawn Grace dropped into a threadbare chair in the staff-room. It had been hard to concentrate since she fled Gloria's room in a panic. Tasks that usually took minutes tied her hands in knots.

Now, she surrendered to exhaustion.

An open sweet tin full of empty wrappers sat on the coffee table. The newspaper nearby was a week old. The headline said: *Are you ready for the big switch off?* Below, two smaller ones: *Nurses threaten first strike in seven years* and *Big Freeze Coming.* And below that: *Feather Man Targets Fifth Victim.*

Grace skim-read the Feather Man article. An unidentified man was breaking into homes in the Leeds area, dazzling the occupant with a torch, and blindfolding and tying them up. Then he disappeared into the night, leaving a single white feather near his victim. It was all anyone could talk about. Fear was building. His activities had become more insidious recently. The first three victims he just held captive and sat nearby, calling them despicable. The last two women he had burned with cigarettes, leaving them scarred for life.

Grace shuddered: it was her worst nightmare – the idea of someone creeping around the house at night, blinding you with a torch. Thank God she slept with all the lights on. She worried momentarily for her son, Jamie, who lived in Leeds, but as the article pointed out, so far only single, generally older, women had been targeted. But what if he widened his crime spree? What if he headed east, closer to Hull?

'Weird, isn't it?'

Grace jumped. Claire, in the doorway, a steaming mug in each hand.

'What is?'

'That it's happening right now, and we're oblivious.'

'The Feather Man?' said Grace, confused.

'Lights Out.' Claire handed Grace a mug, sat opposite. 'Mum messaged earlier, after she'd got the kids to bed, said they'd enjoyed it, the camping lamps, snuggling up for a story, but I reckon they'll tire of it in a few weeks.'

Grace tried not to think about it.

'No one else wanted to work,' Claire continued. 'They all wanted to experience Lights Out. God knows why. What's to see? Loads of dark streets and windows. It's gonna be an inconvenience and the longer I can avoid it, the better.'

That was not Grace's choice of word: inconvenience. When talk of the scheme began a few months ago, she'd felt sick. She'd told herself it wouldn't happen. Something that extreme would be averted. Riley had agreed, said he'd heard that it was only talk, a device to scare people into conserving energy. Now she realised that this was a foolish hope, one she never really believed, telling herself it was the way we tell children fairy tales to soothe them.

'It'll be dangerous,' said Claire. 'They predicted this freezing weather weeks ago, the government *knew*, yet they've *still* gone ahead. People will die in these temperatures without electricity. It's criminal.'

Grace nodded. 'Makes you wonder what their true intentions are.'

'Well, this Greater Green Thing is just to win votes next year. Since when do *they* care about the planet? Last week, the Prime Minister went from London to Glasgow, to some green meeting, in a bloody private jet. The irony!'

When the government announced that street lamps on quiet – *poor*, many said – streets would be part of the switch off, thousands complained that these lights reduced crime at night, that this was yet another scheme where those on the breadline paid the price.

London would remain lit, however. The Distribution Network Operators would still supply localised power to the city. MPs hadn't backed down when criticised, instead suggesting a Night Watch scheme where residents could take turns guarding residential areas. In Grace's postcode they had already formed one, before Lights Out had even started – Riley was on duty next Friday.

'Are you in tonight as well?' asked Claire.

'No.' Grace had wanted to be, but she wasn't back until Wednesday for a day shift. She thought about tonight – about the absolute darkness beyond these walls – and had to exhale slowly.

'You OK?'

Grace nodded, too fast. 'Just tired.'

Claire yawned as though the admission had freed her fatigue too.

Exhaustion was a killer here; they all worked long hours for not enough pay, and Claire had three children at home, no husband, just an elderly mother to help with childcare. Twice, Grace had walked in on Claire using the red-cloth-covered Grateful Table (they avoided *food bank* to lessen any humiliation), filling her bag with beans and pasta. Grace quickly left the room so as not to embarrass her. She had been so upset that she secretly slipped a twenty-pound note in Claire's purse while Claire was catching up on admin. Grace knew well what it was like to want more for a child than you could give, the guilt when you couldn't supply it.

'Maybe we'll sleep better with dark nights,' said Claire.

Grace didn't say that she slept with the lights on. That Riley had to wear an eye mask in bed because it drove him mad. That she avoided the camping trips he loved because of how dense nights were in the country. That she much preferred a night shift so she had to sleep during daytime hours. She tried to smile in response, but in truth, she feared an eternity of it. What if the country adapted to it? What if it became the norm? After all, long ago, they lived without electricity.

'Imagine all the Lights Out babies in nine months.' A joke was easier.

'Oh, God, *no thanks*,' cried Claire. 'Though I wouldn't mind a hot man in my bed right now – not that there's room with my entire household in there!' Pause. 'Are you prepared then?'

Grace washed her cup in the sink. 'I guess.' She had read every leaflet and website on how to prepare for the imminent dark. But she knew that nothing could ready her for this moment. Facing her worst fear.

Handover between night and day staff was quick for once. Just after ten past eight, Grace walked into the dawn glow. Curls of marmalade-coloured mist bounced along rooftops. Cold snatched her breath. Blades of grass crunched underfoot as she took the shortcut through the park. Grace blew hot air into her cupped hands. Claire was right; this chill was lethal.

One after the other, lights came on in windows, soft yellow against the dawning sun. Homes had survived the dark first Lights Out – they could finally shine again.

At home, Riley was dressed for the office – half-smart, half-casual, a grey shirt with jeans – and looking for something, every bulb in the place glaring without need.

The house was pretending to be a home. Much like the hospice rooms made less clinical with soft furnishings, it had the appearance of being dressed up to add cheer. They were renovating – extending the kitchen and ripping out the living-room fireplace – and so the decor was a mishmash of the previous owner's style, bare brick and a new skylight that Grace loved.

'How was it?' she asked, kicking off her black trainers.

'How was what?' Distracted, Riley patted his pockets as though to search for something.

'The first Lights Out.'

He shrugged. 'Oh, fine. Hardly noticed. I took the camping lamp when I went to the toilet, though I did stub my bloody toe. I guess we'll learn where everything is, like the blind have to. It was bloody cold by eight thirty.' He finally looked at her. 'How was work?' She knew him well enough to know he only wanted a brief answer, so gave that.

'Yeah, fine.'

Something terrible is going to happen when the lights go out.

The recollection of Gloria's words hit hard, suddenly.

How long did Grace have until the lights went out tonight?

She shook her head, buried her fears.

'What've you lost?' she asked.

'My keys.'

He riffled through the kitchen drawer they called Shit and Stuff and held them aloft. His smile punctured her heart, always had. She remembered when they met.

She had been walking along the path that ran parallel to the river when out of nowhere – or at least from a thin passage hidden by overgrown foliage – he appeared. Typing furiously into his phone, he didn't see Grace, and almost knocked her into the river. She swore; he apologised. Then, she looked at him properly, felt that subtle *oh* when we see someone we like. He had given her his estate agent's card so she could 'call him if she wanted to sue'. She hadn't dared, but when they crossed paths again on the same walk two weeks later, he asked her out.

'I'm not the only one who's forgetful, eh?' Grace couldn't help but say now, despite her nostalgic thoughts.

'*Sorry?*'

'You. Not knowing where your keys are.'

'It's not as bad as *you* last week,' Riley said, snide.

'What do you mean?'

'Going to work when you weren't even on shift,' he said.

'I got muddled.' Grace was defensive.

'And your phone?'

She had lost it two weeks earlier. Found it eventually in the bread bin.

'Well, *you're* distracted all the time,' she sighed. 'I feel like . . .'

'What?' Riley spoke harshly.

'I feel like you're never here. And when you are, you're not.'

He smiled. Touched her cheek. She savoured it. 'That doesn't even make sense, Amazing.' His nickname for her, after the song, *Amazing Grace*, was one he only used in rare affectionate moments, when he wanted to either reassure or seduce. Or act as though he hadn't just been cold. She could never be cross with him for long.

'Gotta go,' he said, cold again. 'See you tonight.'

He leaned towards Grace's cheek but kissed the air. Ten years together and he still kept her on her toes. Perhaps it was that he could be cool, wasn't always as affectionate as she was, and this kept her yearning to access that private, held-back part of him. But now, with the darkness of Lights Out looming, she *needed* him.

'Tonight,' she said softly as he hurried out of the house.

Tonight.

The second Lights Out.

Don't think about it now.

'You'll be on time won't you?' she called after him.

'Huh?' Riley paused at the open door.

'You promised,' she said, urgent. She had asked him over and over to be home before the electricity went off.

He finally looked at her, said impatiently, '*Yes*, I'll be home before lights out.'

'Thank you.'

She hated her weakness. She wasn't needy. She had been a single parent for fourteen years, budgeting carefully while on benefits for half those years, surviving where many might have gone under. But every vase had an invisible crack; every rose had a hidden thorn.

'Later,' he said.

When he'd gone, she opened the fridge to grab milk and make Horlicks and wasn't hit with the usual chill air. Of course – it had been off all night. Riley wouldn't have opened it to keep the cold in, though. She noticed now that he had insulated the gap between its bottom and the floor with blankets as recommended, and had stuck a note to the door, reminding her not to open the freezer for at least two hours after the electricity was back on.

She heated milk, made her drink and took it upstairs. Sometimes, if it was a weekend and Riley got up later, the bed was still warm. Today, a Monday, it had cooled; his smell lingered though, excess aftershave. She drank her Horlicks, had a shower, got into bed, and put on the morning news. An MP was assuring viewers that despite reports to the contrary, those on life support in hospitals would be safe during Lights Out. 'The switch off,' he insisted, 'will not be a danger to anyone. The vulnerable who depend on electricity will be cared for.'

Grace's phone buzzed.

A message from Claire:

Sorry to tell you, but as I was leaving, Gloria passed away, out of the blue. It was dead odd. She said that something terrible was going to happen when the lights went out and that was it, gone. Creeped me out.
X

Grace wished that she hadn't seen the words before trying to sleep.

She switched the device off. Tried to pretend Lights Out wasn't looming, that this was a routine daytime nap, that she was safe because she would be bathed in sunlight as she slept, and would wake to a house where the flick of a switch illuminated each room.

But the feelings she had tried to bury since the announcement now ran riot.

How was she going to get through not one, but multiple nights of blackness?

How dark would it *really* get without any electricity?

What if she lost her mind?

She ran to the toilet and threw up.

Welcome to UK GOV
The best place to find government services and information

Lights Out – Tips for Adapting to the Switch Off

Warmth during the winter nights will be a concern. Emergency battery-operated heating devices are available for the vulnerable and elderly who live alone. Click **here** to apply.

The elderly should move in with family for this period. Bed-share to keep the very young and the very old warm. Go to bed earlier. Make bedtime fun for children by reading stories and playing board games in torchlight. Click **here** to learn about the Bed Early Scheme.

To avoid using your fridge/freezer, buy only what you want to eat that day and stock up on shelf-stable foods. Click **here** for some shelf-stable food recipes. However, if you still prefer to use your fridge/freezer, most appliances will remain chilled if you adhere to the following:

1) Keep appliance doors shut from 8 p.m. onwards. Duct-tape them if you need reminding.
2) Insulate the exterior and the space between the base and floor with blankets.
3) Use the fridge food the following day, freezer food within a week.

If you have any further concerns, read the Frequently Asked Questions **here**. This is a temporary measure. Remember: the government's first priority is always the safety of our country.

NIGHT TWO

3

In the Dark, Everything Waits

Something terrible is going to happen when the lights go out.

Grace woke with a strangled gasp, clutching her throat, the remnants of the dream fading, just out of reach. Had she spoken the words aloud? She had dreamt of Gloria. A ghostly Gloria in white robes who wandered the house, pointing wordlessly into shadowy corners where bloated spiders with frightful blood-red bodies writhed in a nausea-inducing mass. Grace sat up, still shaking.

Daylight. Thank God

It was almost one. She got up so she would be able to sleep tonight. That was her switch to a day-shift routine. Night shifts messed with the body, made her feel she had died and been brought back to life. Still, she preferred where possible to do them, and sleep during natural brightness.

The house was frigid. Grace always tried to keep the heating off until evening, unable to justify warming an entire house for one person, with the excessive cost. Now, she may as well use it, despite government advice to be careful during the day so it didn't counterbalance the purpose of Lights Out. Home workers who had been economical, typing while wrapped in blankets, might now have the heating on all day since they couldn't later.

Maybe if electricity use soared during the day, the switch off would end.

Grace cranked the heating up.

She made a strong coffee, wondered what to do for tea later. Riley usually got home by six, though recently, despite the housing market slump, he had been working longer hours; the poor man, doing all he could to keep them going.

As had been suggested, they had stocked up on shelf-stable foods, rice, pasta, bottled sauces, tins and vegetables, and had minimal products in the fridge, just milk and margarine. Grace had read the recipes that came through the door, shaking her head at the ridiculous ingredients it was unlikely average working-class households would stock in their cupboards. It had also been suggested that people eat their main – *hot* – meal at lunchtime, but this was easier said than done when most were working long hours to pay the growing bills, barely taking long enough to stop for a sandwich.

Grace would keep it simple.

Tonight, she would make a vegetable pasta bake.

Tonight: the word alone held dread. She knew she was kidding herself this was a day like any other, to avoid thinking about the imminent enforced darkness.

A sound, upstairs. A floorboard?

Grace put her coffee down and went into the hallway. Glanced upstairs, chest tight. Another creak. What the hell? Was someone *there*? She waited. Breath held. Nothing more. Maybe just the wind, the house settling, her own anxiety about eight o'clock and the lights going off.

She couldn't help but think of the Feather Man. Someone creeping around a house, unseen, with rope and a blindfold, belonged on a cinema screen, not in Leeds.

She scrolled to Jamie's number in her phone, wanting to check how he'd coped last night, ask if there had been more strange break-ins in the area, craving some company. But as her thumb hovered over the green call button she realised he'd be at work. She smiled at the old picture next to his number: Jamie, six years old, hair mussed, smile cheeky.

Grace had found herself pregnant at nineteen, to a man who didn't hang around, and so she had gone it alone. Jamie, now twenty-four, lived with his boyfriend, Harry, over in Leeds, and she didn't see him as much as she wanted. Being his only parent until she met Riley ten years ago meant they had a tight bond. Even when Riley did arrive, Jamie was fourteen and, understandably, not ready to accept a new dad in his life, so their relationship had always been more that of mates, not fatherly.

She put her phone away.

Silence upstairs still. Thank God.

Grace went into the half-finished – or half-started, depending how you looked at it – living room, perched on the flabby brown sofa that would be going to the tip soon, unable to relax.

On the coffee table her two goldfish – Jennifer and Brad, named for her favourite *Friends* episode – swam around their bowl. As she approached, they switched direction, perfectly in unison, and swam more vigorously. Riley always laughed when she said they knew she was in the room. But it was true.

She should check how her mother coped last night.

'My milk doesn't smell right, dear,' answered Catherine, not even a hello.

Catherine would have liked her daughter to call her by her first name, but Grace refused. If she could have got away with being called Lady Catherine, she'd have demanded that. Born when working-class women were expected to answer to men, she didn't want a relationship and trained as an actress in London. It hadn't led to the glittering career she hoped for, so she returned to Hull in her thirties and married. She had Grace as late in life as Grace had had Jamie early, at forty-two. Now eighty-five, she arose early and applied full make-up no matter what. Every day was a stage performance to her now.

Grace smiled. 'Well, did you keep the fridge door shut all night?'

No response. Then: 'You took your time calling me.'

'I was on a night shift. I've been asleep. Have you got your heating on now?'

'I'm a bloody Yorkshire woman,' Catherine cried, and – expecting this response – Grace mouthed the words at the same time as her mother said them, 'I don't need the heating on until at least teatime.'

'How did you get on last night?'

'Absolutely fine. Though Annabelle next door was a pain in the bloody arse, ringing every hour, panicking about everything. My mother survived the Hull Blitz, for God's sake. They had to go into freezing air-raid shelters in the middle of the night. We just have to wrap up and go to bed early.'

Grace couldn't argue with that. She had suggested Catherine move in with them for the duration of Lights Out but her mother wouldn't hear of it. 'Why would I leave my home for your draughty, dilapidated house?'

She'd had a point. Riley's mum and dad were much younger and also happy to stay in their own nearby house.

'Do you need anything?' Grace asked. 'I'm home tomorrow, I can drop by.'

'No. I'm meeting Gillian from the over-fifty-fives acting group. They really want me to join but I hardly have time with all my other groups.' She paused. 'How are you doing with this switch off?'

'I haven't experienced it yet. Tonight's my first.'

'You'll have Riley there, won't you, dear?'

'I will.'

Thank God.

'Gosh, I remember what a state you used to get in when there was a power cut; a teenager and wanting to sleep in my bed.'

Grace remembered too. One minute she would be doing home-work or reading a book and the next, total blackness. She would freeze, a wicked story-book character turned into stone. Catherine would return to find Grace sobbing and frantically searching draw-ers for the torch, spell broken, body unfrozen now. It was so bad she slept with the lamp on every night.

Perhaps realising she had been blunt, Catherine added, 'It's understandable, though I would have hoped that you'd have grown out of it by now.'

Grace heard shrill voices of taunting children. Scratching against wood. Absolute blackness. Damp. The smell of urine. Endless dark before, finally, blinding light. Cruel laughter. 'It's . . . it's hard,' she managed.

'Anyway, I've got to peel the potatoes,' Catherine cut across, having clearly lost interest in the subject. 'Talk soon.'

And she hung up, as she always did when she was done.

Grace stared at the darkening phone screen; even that started a sinister churning in her gut; in the dark, everything waits for you; it is weighted with your worst fears.

She should charge the device while she could.

It was almost three. Five hours until everything went off. Five hours until full dark. But Riley would be here. It was being alone as much as the blackness itself. This was why she shared her mum's bed during a power cut, even aged eighteen, why she'd hated living alone. Perhaps even why she got pregnant young, so she never would be. She let Jamie sleep in her bed when he wanted and, even when money was tight, always had a lamp on in the bedroom at night.

A dull thump against the window.

What the *hell*?

Grace dropped the phone. Approached the glass. Peered through it. A tiny brown bird on the ground, hobbling amidst the dying leaves. Poor creature. Must have hit the pane. She was about to go outside, make sure it was OK, when it flapped hard and flew away. Thank God.

She looked up into the sky. It might not be noticeable to anyone who didn't care about the dying day, but Grace saw that it was beginning to change, imperceptibly. Sunset would be four-ten. She had checked. Always did. Smoke-grey clouds scurried as though escaping the forthcoming night. The sun sank from its regal spot towards the rooftops. She reached out as though to push it back to glory at the top of the sky.

Please don't sink, please don't sink, please don't sink.

Grace moved away from the window and started turning the

lights on – *flick, lit* – as was a regular task undertaken long before darkness descended. They had been told to turn everything off before the electricity was cut so there wouldn't be a surge when it resumed at seven, but Grace ignored this advice for now. With this threat looming, she relished the brief illumination. Riley joked that she was the sole cause of the fuel crisis. She knew having all the lights on wasn't right, but it was a compulsion. And she rarely had the heating on in the day to compensate for this overuse.

Flick, lit.

She was lit.

For now.

4

Nothing Bad Will Happen While It's On

At five thirty, when dusk made a mirror of the windows, Grace prepared pasta bake. By six thirty it was ready to serve, but Riley still wasn't home. Grace didn't want to reheat it; pasta went rubbery when you warmed it up. Should she eat? Let him make something else? No, he'd be here, he promised. Probably just traffic.

At seven she ate alone.

At seven forty she scraped his into the bin.

Then she called him, pacing the uneven kitchen floor. No answer. She rang again and again, leaving message after message. *Has something happened? Where are you? You promised you'd be here.*

No response. She hurled the dirty plates in the sink then stood, gripping its rim, glaring at the froth.

She would have to get ready for the switch off alone.

Fifteen minutes to go. She couldn't move.

Thirteen minutes to go.

Eleven.

She *must* do it or she would sail into murky waters without the lifeboat of a lamp.

At seven fifty Grace ran upstairs.

Where the hell had Riley left the camping lamp?

She found it in the bathroom. She switched it on, cranked it up full. It had a max output of 490 lumens, which Riley had assured her was enough to see what you were doing when camping. But an average living room needed more than a thousand lumens. Shops had recently sold out, and many hiked the prices up before that.

Grace's main concern was the strength of the beam, but she was afraid to turn the lights off and test it. They had been instructed not to use candles due to the fire hazard; any household caught doing so would be fined a thousand pounds. It didn't really matter to Grace; candles weren't bright enough for her anyway. Small flames more fitting for romance or remembering the dead.

Five minutes to go.

Where the hell was Riley?

Still chance for him to make it.

Shit.

Grace needed to turn the sockets and switches off before eight. The former, not so much a problem; the latter, she simply couldn't do. One finger hovered over the bedroom switch.

Start here, work down, take the lamp.

Get a grip of yourself, you're a forty-three-year-old woman, for fuck's sake.

Click. Done. Relief. The lamp was reasonably bright. But the landing light was still on. She would only know its full strength in pitch black.

Three minutes to go.

Holding the lamp out, Florence Nightingale checking her wounded soldiers, Grace turned off the landing light, breath held. Dormant shadows woke. The lamp's output was soft, didn't dispel the gloom of far corners.

Two minutes.

She hurried downstairs where brightness still shone. Which one to turn off first? The kitchen, then finish in the living room, a smaller space so should be better illuminated by the lamp. She hit the switch in the kitchen and scurried into the hallway.

One minute.

Still no Riley.

This was it. She was alone.

She went into the living room, hallway floorboard squeaking underfoot. Table lamp off first. Big light remaining. She couldn't do it. *Can't, can't, can't.* Thirty seconds. Let it go off at their command. She could not be the instigator.

Ten seconds.

No, no, *no.*

Grace closed her eyes.

Waited to hear shrill peals of children's laughter.

When she opened them, the room was dimmer but not completely dark. She put a hand over her chest until her heart slowed down, the other still gripping the camping lamp. She was OK. Nothing bad had happened.

She went to the window.

No street lamps, no house lights. She had never seen a world like this. In windows, hazy ghosts moving around with similar lamps. Opposite, upstairs, two children with a torch bounced on the bed, its beam swaying like a sci-fi sword. Stacey and Jack. She said hello to them in a morning if she passed them going to school. When she and Riley first moved here a year ago, Stacey had come over with a welcome pack she had prepared herself – complete with raisins, home-made gingerbread and a single rose on top – and said she did it for all the *new people*, but only Grace got a flower.

Grace looked up at the sky again.

What was the saying?

I know that only when it is dark enough can you see the stars.

Martin Luther King.

On a cruise once with Riley, they had dimmed the lights for some proper stargazing on deck. Without the light pollution an average city emits, the sky was a blanket of silver morse-code dots telling a beautiful story. She had never forgotten it. Now, perhaps the sky was still adapting to this darker world. Maybe it was cloudy; she couldn't see a thing.

Out of the blue, she thought of her dad.

Was it because of the lamp in her hand?

All she could see was the lamp on her childhood bedside table. It was made of stained glass with little stars cut out so a tiny galaxy of them hit the ceiling, and could be dimmed or turned up as required. At bedtime, when she was done reading, her dad would come in and say goodnight, his hair flecked with grey, his glasses mirroring her sleepy face. Though her dislike of the dark was merely a child- ish fear back then, he had bought the lamp to help her sleep.

He always said, 'Nothing bad will happen while it's on, Maisie.' Maisie had been his nickname for her, short for Amazing. She found it profound that Riley used the same moniker.

Feeling sad, Grace pushed the memory away.

She had spent most of her adolescence and adult life pushing them away. Pushing away the absent man whose departure she blamed herself for; she was a bad daughter to make him disappear. If she opened her heart even a tiny crack, she would break in a way that could never be fixed. Memories invaded though; his warm presence, his deep voice, silly sense of humour, the stories he made up for her.

But she pushed, pushed, *pushed* them away, all of them.

Otherwise the darker, hazier, memories of him would rush in; the dad he became later in her childhood, as though someone else had invaded his body.

'I'm sorry,' said a voice.

Grace screamed.

Jumped back from the window.

Dropped the lamp.

5

Halfway Through a Bloody Murder

'Jesus, don't break it.' Riley retrieved the lamp from the floor.

'Where the hell *were* you?' she shouted.

He tutted. 'Showing a house at seven,' he cried. 'I couldn't turn it down, it's big, it'll be a huge commission.' She didn't know if it was the dimness but Riley looked pale; maybe she should be kinder, work had been busy recently. But he had broken his promise.

'Why didn't you let me know? You *knew* how anxious I was.'

'It was all last minute. I was going to call and then I got wrapped up in the client. He was pretty demanding. Oh, for God's sake, come here, you're shaking.' He pulled her into a rough embrace, into his smell, and she felt safe.

'Why would anyone do that so close to the switch off?'

'Do what?'

'View a house so late.'

'I don't know, but I wasn't about to lose a sale like that.'

'There's no tea. The pasta spoiled.' She wanted to stay in his embrace but he pulled away. 'You won't be able to cook now. You can't even ring for a takeaway, they'll be shut.'

'I'm fine, I had a big lunch. I'm trying to do that, like they suggested.'

'So what do we do now?' Grace looked around the living room. 'It'll get cold. What did you do last night?'

'Went to bed, watched that new series on my laptop.'

'You won't be able to have a shower.'

'I'll wait until morning.'

'I love your real smell anyway.' Grace kissed his cheek. She needed his attention, his affection.

Upstairs, Riley put the lamp on the bedside table.

'Will it last all night?' Lead in her chest.

'It should do.'

'*Should?*'

'When I'm camping it's only on a few hours. Get the torch if you're that bothered.' He shook his head, irritated. 'It's in my drawer.'

After they had cleaned their teeth – Riley with the torch because Grace couldn't let him take the lamp – they got into bed. He opened his laptop, found the new crime drama.

To Grace's surprise, despite the tension of the evening, exhaustion from the night shift hit and she fell asleep halfway through a bloody murder. She woke to the lamp still glowing on her bedside table, and Riley asleep, eye mask in place, laptop shut at his side. She took a moment to be grateful. She had a good husband, a good life; maybe the switch off wouldn't be as terrible as she anticipated.

The next time she woke it was seven a.m. The lamp had survived the night. She got up after the heating had been on ten minutes and flipped the bedroom light switch, despite the sun tiptoeing into the room. Riley didn't stir. She made tea in the kitchen. She wasn't at work until tomorrow for a day shift. Today she would do very little.

She went into the living room.

It took a moment to notice, it was that subtle.

Brad and Jennifer. Her fish.

They weren't alone.

What the actual . . .?

Grace put her mug on the coffee table and leaned towards the bowl. A smaller fish, blueish grey, whereas Brad and Jen were orange, swam alongside her pets. She must be seeing things. But after shaking her head, closing her eyes, opening them again, it remained, longer tail disturbing the water vigorously.

How? *Who?*

This wasn't a hallucination, this fish was very much there, and he very much hadn't been last night. It could only be Riley. But why, when? He must have sneaked down in the night to place it in the bowl. But that made no sense.

And then she saw the small note, behind the bowl.

She picked it up, read the tiny, neat handwriting, hand trembling and throat dry. She dropped it. Screamed for Riley.

I have you in my sights.
Love,
The Night.

6

We All Smile in the Same Language

Tom was the kind of man to apologise if he bumped into you, to give up his seat on a bus, and to hold a door open for men and women alike. He was a man with distinct likes and dislikes; he liked his job in the cemetery, liked the rain, and liked the moonlight. But at the moment, he really disliked arriving home.

He never knew what he would find there.

Now, nowhere near that home, he dreaded entering the brick building sitting in the middle of a car park like the last square of stale cake in a tin. Inside was an equally dull, empty waiting room where two tired sofas and a glass table piled with magazines formed a square. A receptionist had him sign some forms – he barely read them – and then motioned to the sofas with a half-hearted smile.

Tom couldn't sit. He was too nervous to stay still, to skim through pages he wouldn't register. He studied the room; the faded print of Monet's *Water Lilies*, the stained paper cup next to the bin, the lightning-shaped crack in the ceiling.

After five minutes, a door opened and a woman in a powder-blue suit with hair cut in a sharp bob glanced at the empty sofas, frowned, and then looked towards the window where he stood. 'Tom Clarke?'

'Yes.' He jumped.

'Is it just you?' Understandably, she was surprised.

Tom looked around as though to check he was alone, paused. 'She had to go away. Last minute. Couldn't get out of it.' He paused again. 'Should I leave?'

'No, not at all.' She had a folder in her hand with their names on it. He wondered what was inside. 'Some people come for one-on-one sessions, though it works best when a couple attends together. Will your partner be able to come next time?'

'Yes.'

'Great. I'm Carole. We can do some groundwork today. Come in.'

Tom followed her into a pleasant room where three modern chairs created a tight triangle, a plant thrived in a pot, a row of black-and-white prints lined one wall, and a filing cabinet dominated the one opposite, above which was a picture of children holding hands beneath the words WE ALL SMILE IN THE SAME LANGUAGE in garish rainbow letters.

'What kind of groundwork?' He hated tests, got nervous that he would score poorly.

'Take a seat.' She took a chair opposite where she gestured for Tom to sit, and opened the folder.

'What does groundwork mean?' He remained on his feet.

'We'll get to that. First, can I check some things? Did you sign the forms with Jenny at reception?' Tom nodded. 'And you've agreed your allocated payment per session?' He nodded again. 'So, before we proceed . . .' She paused. 'Would you like to take a seat?'

'Yes.' He did.

'Before we proceed, I must make sure you're aware that this is strictly confidential. What you share is shared only with relevant staff here, but there *are* some instances where I'd involve the police. People get worried about that but it's only when I have reason to believe a person is a danger to themself – or to another.' Carole spoke as though she was placating an injured animal.

'A danger? Like . . . *how*?' Tom looked at the door, feared the type of clients she might have waiting outside the room.

'Suicidal tendencies. Or domestic violence.'

Tom shook his head. 'Oh, no, I've never . . . never would. Neither of them. And my partner . . . she's normal.

'We don't say normal here.'

Tom felt judged. 'Don't we?'

'No.' Carole paused. 'Of course there's terrorism too.'

'*Terrorism?*'

'If I've reason to believe any person is involved in terrorism, it's my duty to report that too. But otherwise, everything is confidential.' She smiled and it briefly lit up her face. 'Do you have anything to ask me?'

'Don't you ask *me* the questions?' Tom wished he could pace the room.

'It's more talking than questioning. I want to make sure you're comfortable.'

'I wonder . . . can I . . .?'

'Yes?'

'I'd feel better if I could walk around.'

'Walk around?'

Tom fidgeted in his chair; he knew how he must look. He wasn't the most handsome man, though people said he had a kind face. But who wanted that? Where did that get you in life? He kept his mousy hair clean and styled it as best he could, he wore the clothes Harper bought him, more stylish garments than he might have chosen, and he ate healthily. 'Not the whole time,' he said. 'But can I get up? I do unnerve people sometimes. I had a job interview, didn't realise I was doing it.' He sighed. 'I didn't get the job. So I just wanted to check it's OK.'

'Should we talk about *why* you need to move around, Tom?'

'No, I'd just like to be able to do it. I can't sit for long. I can only compare it with getting carsick.'

Carole nodded. 'Would you like me to get up and walk *with* you?'

'No need for that.' Tom stood, and moved behind his chair.

She looked thoughtful. 'Like being carsick, you say. Tell me, were you ever locked in a car as a child?'

'*What?* Mum was *wonderful*. My father . . . not so much, but I'm not here to talk about that. You're a relationship counsellor. That's why I chose you.'

'*You* chose me? Did your partner agree?'

'Of course. I meant . . . well, I mean . . . *we* did.'

'Tom, why don't you just tell me what made you come here?'

He walked to the filing cabinet. The window looked out onto the car park. It was the most depressing view – leaden concrete, overflowing bin, dead rose bush. Night would fall in a few hours, and with it the second switch off. He loved the dark, but for the first time in his life he feared what it might bring tonight.

'Shall I just blurt it out?' asked Tom. 'Is that what everyone else does?'

'There are no rules here.'

'Not that I know what I want to blurt out.' Tom did know but was afraid. Some things were hard to say. They hurt too much.

'Why don't you tell me about you and your partner.'

Tom paused.

'Harper. OK. We're very different. I bet lots of people come here and say that, don't they?'

'This is about you, Tom. There's only what *you* feel. Tell me how you met?'

Tom moved from the window and walked towards the door, stopping halfway and turning back. 'We met in a bowling alley. You could say she bowled me over.' He laughed weakly; Carole didn't. 'Anyway . . . I was there with work colleagues, a team-building exercise, it was silly. And she was with friends. When we chatted it made things interesting, you know, us being different. She's confident, you see. She approached *me*.' He laughed, shook his head, saw her as she had been then: red hair like fire sparking away from an oval face dominated by the most glorious smile. 'We'd never have met otherwise. I'm not very good with women. Or people. I mean, women *are* people. You know what I mean. I was flattered. She's attractive and I'm . . . well . . . I'm just me. Now I think we're *too* different.'

Carole twisted to look at him as he walked towards the window again. 'So would you say the thing that initially drew you together is now driving you apart?'

'I suppose. She's a flirt. Always has been. I didn't use to mind, because it was with *me*. Men love it, don't they?'

'I don't know – you tell me, Tom.'

'They do, they love a beautiful, vivacious woman.'

'Tom, you say *they*. But *you're* a man. Do *you* like that kind of woman?'

'I don't know,' he said softly, sitting back down, slumped.

'How long have you been together?'

'Three years, living together for one. It was the cost of living.'

'What was?'

'Why she moved in.'

'Oh. Tell me about some good times?' suggested Carole.

'If there were only good times, no one would come here, would they?'

'It's about balance. By looking at the good we can consider how it affects the bad.' She shook her head. 'Though bad is the wrong word, really.'

'We've had good times. You don't stay if there aren't, do you? Of course, you can't answer. It's about me. I don't like it when it's about me. I feel . . . exposed.'

'Why do you think you feel that way?' asked Carole.

'Doesn't anyone who's in the spotlight?' Tom sat back in his chair, drumming his fingers on the arm. 'I've been off work.'

'Why is that?'

'Anxiety.'

Carole nodded, solemn. 'I'm sorry to hear that, Tom. Is this related to Harper?'

Tom shrugged. He began to wish he hadn't booked these appointments. What had possessed him? What was he hoping to achieve? He had never been for counselling before. But then his life had never been as strange as it was now.

'The world is changing, isn't it?' he said.

'How so?'

'Lights Out is huge.'

Carole nodded. 'How do you feel about it?'

'I don't mind.'

It was true. Being organised meant he was ready. He had purchased three camping lamps, a small fridge that ran on recharge-able batteries, and downloaded a variety of films to watch. He had hoped he and Harper might get close again.

'I feel for those who are alone,' he said. 'But I feel safe in the dark. I read once that the dark is a canvas on which you paint your worst fears. That we pin to it our demons, that we face our worst memories there, see our real souls. We only look inward when we can't see anything else, and this is our greatest fear – the truth, us.'

'Profound.' Carole nodded. 'We should do counselling without the lights on.'

'We're all equal there, aren't we?'

Carole appeared to consider it. 'Can we go back to your anxiety. Is it a recent thing?'

Tom stood and paced again; sometimes he counted his steps but that was when he didn't have to concentrate on a conversation. As a kid, he had always avoided the cracks in the pavement, fearing bad luck. 'It's all different now. It could be *me* that's different. But I'm not. No, I think *she's* different. Yes – that might be it.'

'Different is vague. Can we look for a better word?

Tom stood behind Carole's chair. She twisted to speak to him. 'Tom, might you not stand there. It's a little unnerving.'

'I'm so sorry.' He moved to the cabinet.

'Another word?' she said.

'Another word what?'

'We're trying to analyse exactly what *different* means.'

Tom walked around the chairs. 'Oh. Different is . . . change. Is that right?'

'Tom, it's whatever you say it is. This is your session.' She uncrossed and crossed her legs again. 'So how would you say Harper has changed?'

'She hasn't.' He stopped and looked at Carole.

'So she hasn't . . . and *you* haven't?'

'*Something* has.' He returned to his chair, stood behind it again, gripping it now. 'Strange things have been happening.' He closed his eyes to block it out.

'Strange things?' Carole spoke softly, her expression somewhere between fascinated and nervous. 'Tell me about that.'

A shrill fire alarm suddenly sounded.

'I forgot to say,' cried Carole over the intense blast. 'It's the monthly fire drill today. We have to go outside. Please, come with me.'

She guided Tom out of the door and into the car park, the receptionist following them with her mobile phone, which she then used to film video selfies while saying that there was a fire at her workplace and it was 'all drama'.

'It'll only be a few moments and we can go back inside.' Carole shivered.

'I want to leave,' said Tom, itching to pace, fidgeting.

'We have another twenty minutes of our session left. Are you sure?'

He nodded. He didn't even know if he would come back, in truth. He felt exhausted, though that could be from the sleepless nights recently.

'You have another session in two days,' she said.

Why had he booked so many? Other couples generally went once a week. 'Yes,' said Tom, though he wasn't sure if Harper would go.

And then he walked away.

He should go home. He should prepare for Lights Out in five hours. But home had become a place of dread. It wasn't the imminent dark. To Tom that was a living entity, a comforting friend, as familiar as anyone he knew. It might be scary to some, but when you got acquainted, let it wrap its thick arms around you and pull you in tightly for a hug, there was safety there.

No, it wasn't the switch off.

It was that the house he and Harper had built together, the rooms they had chosen their cream fabrics and white paint for, the walls they had hung their lives on, was now *different*, and no, he couldn't think of a better word.

Tom stopped in his tracks. Yes. *Yes, he could.* The word was unwanted.

Or was that just how *he* felt?

FIGHT FOR THE LIGHT!

Tired of doing what the police should be doing? Scared of the rise in shop looting and house burglaries? Join us for a peaceful protest and let's get our lives back!

Meeting point: **Date:**
Victoria Square, Hull.   **11 January, 2 p.m.**

Police are NOT patrolling your area! This government promised that every crime mattered with its Beating Crime Plan – now WE are patrolling our neighbourhoods at night while THEY sleep in their beds safe, and still have round-the-clock electricity!

LET'S TAKE BACK OUR NIGHTS!   **#FightForTheLight**

NIGHT THREE

7

Ghosts Don't Put Fish in Bowls

Grace screamed again for Riley.

In the living room, strange note still between her fingers, alien fish in her bowl, she was in a living nightmare. Riley was grumpy when he finally entered the room, hair stuck up on one side. Grace had moved away from her beloved fish as though distance might dissolve this invader. She cowered in one of the corners she hated at night; she was her own shadow.

'What's wrong?' he asked.

She pointed to the bowl. He approached, studied it for a few seconds, and then looked at her, confusion creasing his brow. 'What's wrong with it?'

Grace left her corner, went into the ring for a fight. 'Are you *blind*? There's another fish.'

He looked again. 'Oh, yeah. When did you get it?'

'Why would I yell for you at this time in a morning to show you one I'd bought?'

'I don't understand.'

'Someone *else* must have left it.'

'*What?*'

'Whoever did, left this.' She gave him the note, hand trembling. 'I have you in my sights,' she said as he read it, the narrator to his silent, moving lips. 'Did you do it, as a joke? I don't mind if you just *tell* me.'

'Why would I?' laughed Riley.

'To wind me up.'

'Well, I didn't.'

43

'So who did? Who the hell is *The Night*?'

Riley turned the note over as though the answer might be on the back. 'I don't—'

'And the fish. Where did it come from? It's madness. Call the police, right now.'

Riley peered into the bowl where Jennifer and Brad tried to outswim their new housemate. 'Maybe it's Angelina,' he said.

'*What?*'

'Angelina Jolie. You know, here to break them up . . .'

'That's not funny,' said Grace quietly. 'How can you joke? Someone must have been in the house. Go and check the doors!'

Riley studied her. 'Maybe you bought it and forgot.'

'*What?* I'm not crazy. And even if I did, what about the note?'

'Maybe you wrote it in your sleep.'

Angry, she grabbed it and held it in front of his face. 'It's not even my handwriting. Why aren't you being more *serious*? Someone has been in and done this and you don't seem outraged.'

'It's just . . . *odd*, isn't it?' He looked around. 'Has anything been taken?'

'I don't know – you should check, see where they got in.'

Riley left the room.

'The so-called Night Watch man wasn't any good, was he?' she called after him. 'Wait – what if it was him?'

'Ben from number seventeen? I doubt that,' called Riley from the kitchen, 'and you can't go randomly blaming people.'

'Well, we need to ask him if he saw anything.'

Even though the heating had been on a while, Grace was chilled, felt she might never thaw out. She had got through the dark. Now this. She listened to Riley going around the house, in and out of rooms, feet heavy, an estate agent checking a house rather than showing it.

He returned to the living room; she hadn't moved from her spot. 'Everything looks fine. There's no way anyone has been in, all the doors and windows are locked, the chain is across the front door, and nothing seems to have been taken. There's just . . . *that.*'

'It doesn't make sense.' This should have soothed her but it was somehow worse. It meant that one of them *must* have placed the fish in the bowl and written the note – that was logical. 'You *definitely* didn't buy that fish?'

Riley looked annoyed. 'Why would I? I don't like them. I have to get ready for work.'

'You can't *leave* me.'

'What, with a killer fish?'

'It isn't funny.'

She had been petrified of the dark, of something vague – this was real, here, odd.

'Listen,' he said. 'Hear me out and don't get annoyed. What if you *did* buy that fish and forgot?' She stepped back from him. 'No, listen to me. You've been really stressed about the Lights Out. You've been a state, not sleeping well.'

'Not so much that I don't know what I'm doing,' Grace cried.

But doubt crept in.

'Maybe,' he continued, 'you bought it, put it in the bowl, and put it out of your mind.'

She resisted his logic. 'Even if that's true – which it isn't – I didn't write that note. Why would I write such a thing, call myself The Night?

'As I said, maybe in your sleep. You were sleepwalking last week.'

'*Was I?*'

'Scared me to death. Standing at the other side of the bedroom smiling at me.'

Grace shivered again. 'But the note . . . it's not my handwriting.'

'Wouldn't your hand move differently in your sleep? And . . .'

'Yes?'

'Well, you once told me . . .' Riley faltered.

45

'*Yes?*' pushed Grace.

'You said your dad . . .'

'What?'

'You said when you were small he liked to leave you little cryptic notes around the house.'

'*Did I?*' Grace had no idea what Riley was talking about. No memory of this. But then she had pushed so many recollections down over the years. 'When did I tell you that?'

'Oh, ages ago. Just once. You'd been drinking.'

Grace couldn't respond. Was it true? 'Well, it's more like *your* writing,' she said eventually.

Riley shrugged. 'I don't have answers. Clearly no one has been in the house.' He studied her; she glared back, feeling betrayed, even though he hadn't done anything. What he was saying was rational. 'Maybe you're like the Feather Man,' he said. 'But you leave fish.'

'Don't say that.' Grace thought of the masked intruder attacking women in their homes. 'Why did you bring *him* up?' He was too close, too real. Leeds was only an hour away. What if he tired of that area? What if this had been him? It made no sense. She hadn't been tied up, hurt.

'Maybe it was a ghost,' she said quietly.

'Ghosts don't push fish in bowls.'

'Go to work then,' she barked.

'Don't forget, the kitchen guy's coming to measure up. Tell him we want white units, extra gloss. Also, charge the batteries for the camping lamp. And this . . .' He tore the note into small pieces. '*Gone.*'

When he had gone too, Grace made another cup of tea.

It went cold while she paced the room, wringing her hands.

What if Riley was right? What if her paranoia about Lights Out had led to nocturnal wanderings with a pen, unconsciousness making her scrawl alien? What if she *had* bought the fish and forgotten? If she let the idea in, it became a memory. She could see herself in the pet shop. She *had* got her days muddled last week, turning up for the wrong shift. She forgot to put the bin out so now it was overflowing. And apparently she had been sleepwalking.

It was possible. It *could* be her.

She couldn't settle. Couldn't focus on reading or watching TV. Wished the house renovations were done and the house wasn't dusty, half-complete, unhomely. The chaos meant new shadows, surprise shapes to unnerve, things forgotten there to shock. In the end, she got a pen. Was about to write the creepy words, check how she might form them.

Luckily, the phone interrupted.

Jamie.

'Are you OK, Mum?' he asked, without bothering to say hello. He knew her fear of the dark.

Grace smiled. She saw him suddenly, aged five, bringing a worm in from the garden, saying he thought it 'was poorly' and could they help it? Jamie wanted to make a bed and feed it Coco Pops. Another time Grace was reading him a book about tigers, explaining how they were rare in many parts of the world, and asked if he knew what that meant. 'Not cooked properly,' he said.

How her heart had melted. Her clever, funny, unusual boy.

'I'm just tired,' she lied, trying to sound convincing. She hated worrying him.

'Sure? We can come over at the weekend.'

'No, you and Harry should be out having fun. How is he?' Grace then smiled as Jamie told her about their trip to IKEA, arguing about colour schemes: real-life, everyday stuff that grounded her, reminded her that the world was good.

'How were you with the dark?' Jamie asked then.

'OK.'

'Really?'

'Yes, really.'

It's what was here afterwards, she wanted to say.

47

'If you're sure.' Jamie paused. 'Have you seen this Feather Man in the news?'

'I have,' she admitted, hoping not to talk about him. She preferred to keep it distant, pretend it was a fictional crime mystery on a streaming service that couldn't touch her. Now, glancing at the curious new fish, Grace felt the story had more resonance, was coming closer.

Could there be an intruder who left . . . *fish*?

It was ridiculous.

'Oh, my God . . . one of the women he attacked . . . Eileen at the office, she knows someone who knows her.'

'*No*. The poor woman. How *is* she?'

'She's physically OK, but I can't imagine the mental trauma. She lives alone, her husband died a few months ago. She woke in the night and he was just *there*. In the room. Blinded her with a torch. Then . . . well, he . . . *burnt* her. God, can you imagine?'

'No,' said Grace quietly. 'That's *horrible*.'

'He was there for three hours, apparently. Jesus. It must have felt like three days.'

'Did he leave a note?' Grace asked suddenly.

'Not sure.' Jamie paused. 'Why?'

'Doesn't matter.' Grace felt foolish, tried to sound casual. 'Nothing.'

'Maybe I shouldn't have mentioned it when you're anxious.'

'I'm fine, sweetie. I should . . . I have things to do.'

'Call me if you need me, won't you?'

Grace wouldn't. She would never burden her son. 'Stay safe. Keep your doors locked, even when you're in the house, OK?'

After Jamie had hung up, she tried to avoid the fishbowl, but that proved impossible. She went into the kitchen, the bedroom, anywhere else, but was drawn back again and again. Each time, she almost expected its blue-grey resident to have disappeared. But no, still there, weaving between Jennifer and Brad, oblivious to the anxiety he had caused. Should she flush it down the toilet? No. She didn't have the heart. Couldn't kill a living creature. And what if she *had* bought him? That she could almost believe, but . . . the note. Those words felt too concise to be something she had written while asleep.

Eventually, she fell asleep on the sofa. There was a dream, vivid, the kind that as it unfolds is more real than your waking life. Grace's dad came into the living room, sat by her feet. 'There's nothing to be afraid of,' he said with a cheeky wink.

'But I am.' She feared that if she spoke too loudly he would disappear.

'Just go into it fearless.'

'Into what?'

'The dark.'

'But I—'

'It's warm, inviting . . .' Then his face contorted, and the smile melted like heated wax into a shocking grimace. Grace gasped, pulled back. He reached for her with clawed, blood-stained hands.

She woke, heart hammering.

Since his disappearance when she was ten, Grace had looked for her father. She had never mentioned that she did this to her mother, who she knew would tell her to stop trying to bring up the past. It should have been easy, but searches yielded no results. In some ways, she hoped he had died: a concrete reason that prevented him finding her. Otherwise, he could never have loved her, not really.

She saw them now – a memory – in the garden together, a place he loved to be, identifying new birds, cultivating his many flowers, checking the greenhouse. He was showing her how to tell if the tomatoes were ripe, his thick hand over her small one, his words patient and encouraging, the sun blessing them both.

Then a grey cloud came over and he was . . . *the other dad.*

The dad he became, just before he left.

The strange man who washed his hands over and over in steaming hot water, who repeated random phrases that Grace couldn't make sense of, that scared her a little. In other rooms she would hear, *Don't let them in, don't let them in, don't let them in.*

And that was why it was so difficult to think of him.

A sharp knock on the door. Grace froze, stock still on the sofa where she had fallen asleep. Didn't want to answer. Another rap, sharper. *Shit.* She got up and approached the front door slowly. Opened it with the chain on. Just the kitchen man. Grace could barely remember which units they wanted, and after he had gone she forgot when he said he'd be starting work. Riley would have to call him; he really *was* going to question her sanity now.

But far more worrying than that; outside, the day was dying.

The dark beckoned again.

I love a house when it sleeps. I love that I'm part of the shadows. The quiet is alive. I buzz. I exist. I come to life. No one knows I'm here. She doesn't know I'm here. She. It's the she that I'm here for.

I'm here.

I'm here.

Does she dream? Does she sense in those escapes my presence? Does she know that I'm here, in her world now, part of the air she breathes? That I'm here to show her who I am. That this is my house now.

That I've waited all day for this . . .

8

Haunted As I Am

Just before ten past four Grace approached the window to watch the sky.

Today had been cloud free; a carpet of leaves crisped in the sun like sugar browning atop a warm dessert. The sun hurried down, burnt out after all that shining, desperate to retire early.

Grace glanced up at the opposite window. As though lit by an invisible spotlight, a face emerged – Stacey. She lifted a hand and waved. Grace waved back, cheered by the gesture. It was like looking at herself, long ago. She had thought that when she first saw the girl on her doorstep, Welcome Pack in hands. They shared the same straw blond hair, the same pale skin. Grace realised now that if she'd had a daughter she might look like Stacey. This incited a sudden affection for the girl across the street, shining in a window.

Blackness descended.

But not before Grace had switched all the lights on.

Flick, lit.

She could relax. For now. Don't think about eight o'clock.

To keep busy, she rummaged in the cupboards, thinking of the evening meal, and realised Riley hadn't said if he would be home on time. Once upon a time, Riley would never have thought of letting her down when she had asked him to do something. Was her fretfulness driving him away? Would she have to turn all the switches off alone again or would he be home to do it? The not knowing was as difficult as the dark.

But at six, Riley arrived. She was stirring noodles, vegetables and soy sauce in the wok, the perfect Lights Out meal.

'Any more fish?' He hung his coat up.

Normally Grace would have laughed, but it wouldn't form.

'Be glad it wasn't a white feather.'

'Stop talking about that creep,' she muttered, more to herself.

'Maybe there *isn't* a Feather Man – maybe it's a load of paranoid women, scared of the dark.'

Grace stirred the food vigorously. Riley nudged her to show he was joking, but she wasn't amused.

'Smells good. Just gonna grab a shower before the electricity goes off.'

'Did you speak to Ben?' she called after him.

'*Ben?*'

'From number seventeen. About if he saw anyone loitering around the house.'

Though she had nearly managed to convince herself that she must have bought the fish, had been sleepwalking with a pen at night, Grace couldn't let go of other possibilities.

'What's the point? It's obvious no one came in.'

Riley disappeared and she heard the shower start up. When it stopped, she served the food. They sat at the table, ate in silence. She hated it. Wanted to laugh, bitch about his more demanding clients like they often did. It was her fault. He'd been jokey earlier and she ignored it. She wanted the smile that punctured her heart back. Was he sulking? He often did, playing the victim if she didn't laugh at his joke or if she responded less than enthusiastically to something he wanted her to agree with.

But what had she done tonight?

Still, he was here. He turned out the lights before eight, while she followed him with the camping lamp, gripping his arm. The dark wasn't as scary with company. They went to bed when the house grew cold. Riley wanted to read his Kindle – Grace did the same but found that she was reading the same line over and over: *haunted as I am, haunted as I am, haunted as I am.*

In the end, she snuggled up to him, kissed his neck; the persistent but gentle clue that she wanted more. He ignored it. Reluctantly, she set him free, turned away and said good night.

She remembered when they met, Riley said he loved that she was a lone parent, had created a stable home, held down a job too. She told him then she hated the dark, blushing, explaining her flaw to him the first time he stayed over. He asked where this fear had come from, but she glossed over it, saying the 'usual childhood fears'. 'It's cute,' he'd said with affection. 'I'll keep you safe.' Clearly, it wasn't cute now when it meant he had a wife who might have lost her mind.

They had later married, promising love in sickness and in health.

Surely that meant in darkness and in light too.

In the morning, the camping lamp had again lasted all night.

Thank God.

Perhaps it was a good sign. Perhaps she and Riley would be fine.

He had turned everything off eleven hours ago and now she switched it back on. She willed positivity: *flick, lit; flick, lit.* She had work at eight, wondered if there was time to make Riley eggs for breakfast, an apology for being grumpy. After showering, she went to the kitchen and grabbed the eggs from the shelf where she now stored them.

And as she did, she saw . . . *something.*

On the remainder of the old worktop, between the spice rack and the fridge, two items that had not been there last night. She dropped an egg on the floor.

'*No,*' she whispered.

It was a pair of ivory candles. Identical, both tall, carved with delicate gold swirls, pretty, standing as though guarding their corner.

'No,' she said again.

She had *not* bought those candles, no matter what anyone tried to tell her.

Then she saw it: nearby, a piece of notepaper, folded once.

Grace knew she could not possibly have sleepwalked a second time in a row and scribed a strange message onto a page.

Burn me and I will fire.
Love,
The Night.

She threw it on the worktop. The words evoked something. A memory. A person. A man she hadn't thought of in years.
    Steve.

NIGHT FOUR

9

Four-year-old Stars

Tom sat in the waiting area with a small box on his knee.

It was a different receptionist today, a man who barely looked up when Tom entered, and then took a call on his mobile. Until an hour earlier, Tom wasn't even going to come. After another night without sleep, he had napped until noon, and then woken feeling sick. This was how his anxiety manifested itself normally: restlessness, lack of appetite, and the sureness that he was the only person in the world who felt like this.

Carole's door opened.

The subtle odour of cigarette smoke crept past her as though trying to sneak out unseen. She wore the same suit as she had for the previous session, and held the same folder; it made Tom feel no time had passed in between, that the lightless nights had blurred into the monotonous days.

'Oh.' She looked around the waiting area. 'Just you again?'

'Yes – she, um, broke her leg.'

'Oh, dear, that's a shame – where?'

'In Grimsby.'

'No, which part of her leg.' Carole suppressed a smile.

'Around the shin. She's in a bit of pain. We may have to loan a wheelchair.'

'We have disabled facilities; I can arrange for a ramp to—'

Tom stood. 'There's no need, thank you.

Carole gestured at him. 'Come in anyway, Tom.'

He followed her into the office and took the same seat as last time, sniffing the air. She wafted her hands, found a can of air freshener in the cabinet, and sprayed it dramatically. 'The cleaner was smoking earlier.' She avoided Tom's face. 'Would you rather rebook these sessions for when your partner has recovered?'

'No. The other day was helpful. I think it might be good for me. I didn't feel well before. Talking to you, I tidied things up in my head. I might again. Does that sound crazy?'

'Crazy is a bad word, Tom. I don't use it here.'

He frowned. 'I thought *bad* was a bad word.'

'Sorry?'

'Last time . . . you said . . . doesn't matter.'

Carole finally sat opposite. 'Can I ask you, does Harper *really* know you're here?'

'Of course.' Tom gripped the box in his lap.

'I feel like you *want* to come alone. That's fine, but we should address it.'

'She'll be here next time.' Tom wanted to stand and walk but tried to remain seated for longer. When he moved, it calmed his brain. He glanced at the WE ALL SMILE IN THE SAME LANGUAGE picture. It irritated him and he wasn't sure why. The sickly sweet sentiment? The fact that he hadn't felt much like smiling recently and it mocked him?

'But her leg?' said Carole. 'Won't it be weeks?'

'She might feel less self-conscious by next week. You get used to these things, don't you?'

Carole looked at the box, concern creasing her brow. 'What's that?'

'Harper bought me a gift. I wanted to know what you thought it meant?' At least he *thought* she had. It had been on the bedside cabinet that morning when he woke late. He could have called her at work to ask but felt it was something only *she* could have chosen.

Wasn't it?

'Tom, it's not my place to analyse a gift someone bought you.'

'It's not sexual or anything.' He paused. 'Can I say sexual?'

Carole waved her arm as though to dismiss the box. 'Yes. Look, I think we should just talk. Shall we continue from where we were the other day? You told me strange things had been happening. Would you like to talk about that?'

Tom paced the room, box in hand. 'But the gift is important,' he said. 'It's a nice thing. I want to know what it means. Does she love me or is it all going to start again?'

Carole watched him. 'Is what going to start again?'

Tom paused in front of the door. 'You can only do so much, can't you? You can be a good listener . . . and you can be patient . . . and you can give all the attention in the world . . .'

'Yes, those are *good* things. Would you say you're patient and attentive?'

'I try. But I must have gone wrong somewhere. It takes two, doesn't it?' He looked at Carole, knowing she wouldn't respond, that she would wait for him to go on. 'Then she buys me this.' He paused. 'At least I *think* she did.'

'You think?'

'There have been . . .' Tom shook his head, changed tack, didn't want to talk about *that* yet. 'It's . . . full of hidden meaning that only she could know.'

'Right, Tom, I can see you need to tell me about the gift.'

Relieved, he started to open it.

'I don't want to see. Did she buy you it while she was away?'

'I guess.'

'Before she broke her arm.'

'Her leg.'

'In what circumstances did she give it to you?' asked Carole.

'What do you mean?'

'Had you just made love for example? She might find that difficult now, with the leg. What I mean is, was it during a nice moment or was it while, say for example, you argued?'

'I don't know. It was . . . well, it was just on the bedside table when I woke.' Tom came back to his chair and sat down. 'I'll show you.' Before she could object, he removed the lid from the box and took out a vibrant Russian doll painted all the blues of a summer ocean, with a petite face, and long eyelashes, and yellow hair the colour of sweetcorn. The nested set of wooden canisters opened in the middle, revealing another identical smaller one, and then another, and another, until there were seven, each decreasing in size. Tom lined them up on the chair's arm, a large family.

'It could mean many things,' said Tom. 'I should explain.'

'Please do,' said Carole.

'On our first holiday we went to the Lake District and stayed in a little B&B with goats in the back garden. I bought her one a bit like this from a gift shop on the lake. Unusual item to find in an English store. But it was so pretty.' Tom swallowed sadness as it rose in his chest. 'Pretty like Harper. I told her that, said even more inside. I know, I'm a sap.'

'It's a lovely gesture.' Carole's face softened momentarily.

'But then during an argument – about wheelie bins, would you believe – she threw it out on the patio; all the bigger ones smashed up and the little ones were scattered everywhere. It was . . . bedlam. It looked like there had been a mass murder of dolls. So we had to get rid of the broken ones. I kept the tiniest one. I've got it still, in a drawer. I'm daft that way.' Tom could see it now, wrapped in blue tissue. He wasn't a hoarder, but he kept special things, tickets for concerts they had been to, cards she had bought him on Valentine's Day, doodles she had drawn on restaurant napkins.

'And then this,' he said. 'It must *mean* something.'

'Maybe she simply saw it in a shop and thought, Tom would like that.'

He packed the dolls up, put them back in the box. 'Carole – can I call you Carole?'

'It is my name.'

'The thing is, Carole, she rarely buys me gifts. That's why I was shocked to see it on the bedside cabinet like that. I'm scared it's a . . . parting gift.'

'Only she can tell us that, Tom.' She studied him and he wondered how much of what he was saying she could see through.

Probably a lot: she was a counsellor, she had probably been trained to see the unshown, hear the unsaid. He didn't want to speak ill of his beloved Harper. 'When Harper joins you, we can talk about that, can't we?'

'I suppose.' He stood again, put the box on the chair and moved around the room, back and forth, retracing steps as though to find where he had come from.

'I think we're skirting around the true issue.' Carole watched him. 'I think you brought the dolls to avoid what you'd really like to talk about. It's a common occurrence here. Sometimes people don't know what's bothering them until they start talking. But I think you know, Tom. I think you don't want to look at it. I understand that. It's frightening. We fear that if we look at something, it becomes real. But if we *don't* look, it's more terrifying. The unknown. So – together – shall we try and look at it?'

'I think I . . . can we take a break?'

'Do you need to use the bathroom?

'No. Yes. Maybe.'

'Well?' Carole prompted gently.

'I . . . this is only our second session.'

'You want to take things more slowly?'

Tom wondered again why he was really here. Was he going to tell Carole about why he dreaded going home? What would she say? Would she even believe him? He imagined telling her what had been happening recently, felt the words form in the back of his throat. No. They would sound ridiculous.

'I've heard everything,' said Carole.

'Sorry?' Had she heard his thoughts? He dropped back into the chair, tried to read her face.

'There's nothing you could say that might shock me.'

I bet you've never heard this, he thought.

'And everything here is confidential.'

'I know. You said. Except terrorism.'

Carole didn't appear to know what to say. He suddenly felt sorry for her. Maybe he should give her something, so she felt she had got somewhere, helped him, even a small bit.

'I'm grateful to you,' he said.

'Why is that?' Always the professional response.

'You've listened to me.'

'I'm just not sure that you've really talked.'

'It's all I've done,' he said.

Carole studied him, waited.

'How have you found Lights Out?' he asked.

'Why don't you tell me how *you've* found it,' she said.

'It's my favourite time of the day,' Tom said, quietly.

He closed his eyes for a moment, as though it was that time now.

'Did you know that the beam coming from the stars takes about four years to get here so you're witnessing the past? Whatever you were doing four years ago is hitting you in the eyes.' He was rambling, he knew, spouting anything to avoid thinking about why he was really here. 'Harper is often out at night.'

'Where does she go?'

Tom stood. Walked to the window. It had begun raining; he loved the rain. There was nothing better than walking in a downpour, cleansed, face up to let it wash away tears.

'Where's Harper at night, Tom?'

'I want to leave,' he said, heart tight, unable to face such pain.

'We have fifteen minutes.'

'I need to go.' He grabbed the box from the chair.

Carole nodded. 'I'll see you again . . .' She looked at the notes in her folder. 'In two days. Will you both come?'

Tom didn't know what to tell her. He might not have shared his full story here, been absolutely honest, but he found it hard to lie outright. Better to say nothing, as he often did. So he closed the door softly behind him and headed out into the rain, which he embraced as he did the dark.

10

Burn Me and I Will Fire

Grace ran from the house, heart pounding, leaving in her wake the strange note, the two ominous candles, a broken egg, and a still sleeping Riley. The words in the note wouldn't leave her head; they stuck there like a yellow Post-it. *Burn me and I will fire.* She had to escape them, run hard.

She crashed into Stacey, walking alone to school, knocking the poor girl over on the ice.

'Oh, my word, I'm *so* sorry,' gushed Grace, helping her up.

'It's OK,' said Stacey breezily.

'Are you hurt?' Grace knelt down to check. A hole in Stacey's black tights revealed a bloody scrape. 'Oh, gosh, you *are*. We need to clean it, get a plaster on you.'

'Oh, I can do that at school.' Stacey shrugged, not fazed. Grace remembered all the tumbles Jamie had as a kid, how as he grew older, they came harder but he cried less. Kids were resilient.

More than I am, thought Grace. *I could learn something from Stacey.*

They had to part ways at the end of the street, Stacey going left and Grace going right. 'Can I walk you to school?' asked Grace. Thinking of it, she asked, 'Where's Jack?'

'He's ill,' said Stacey. The girl looked sad for a moment. For her brother? Something else? Should Grace ask? Did she know her well enough? The look passed, and Stacey smiled. 'And it's OK. I'm meeting my friend Abbie on the corner.'

Grace watched her go, suddenly protective. It was a dangerous world, and not all those perils lurked in the dark.

She hurried on to work, cursing herself for not driving, and arrived, back sticky with sweat despite the cold.

She would *never* have read a report that the Feather Man had struck in Hull if someone in the staff changing room hadn't left a newspaper open. She skim-read the piece, barely noticing other staff getting changed into their uniforms. An elderly woman had been targeted but her son intervened, chased him away.

No. He was in *her* city now.

It reignited anxiety about the words in the note: *Burn me and I will fire.*

Steve.

He had always bought candles for the bedroom, spoken heatedly of his desire.

Put him out of your head. He's history. It's not him.

But there in the staff changing room, newspaper in hand, a flashback came hard. Eyes as dark as her fears. In her kitchen, a basic room back then when life as a single mum meant budgeting carefully. *What kind of mother are you?* Words he often said, making her believe she was a failure. She had sent Jamie to school with a sparse packed lunch, having run out of bread. The guilt was acute. Steve played on it. Promised life would be better with him.

Then you'll be a better mother . . .

'Grace?'

She jumped, dropped the newspaper. Claire. Face concerned.

'You're as white as a sheet.'

'I . . . yes . . . I . . .' Grace tried to focus.

'What is it?'

She gathered the pages from the floor. 'This Feather Man. He's here, apparently.'

Claire looked around. 'I can't see him.'

'Ha.' Dark humour was the way of staff. 'I didn't know you were working today.'

'I'm covering. Can't refuse when I'm still paying off Christmas.'

The morning was busy, kept Grace from thinking. She stripped beds, aided those who couldn't feed themselves, and helped a patient called Sheila into the small garden so she could enjoy the winter sunshine and the snowdrops blooming in large tubs, despite the chill. Grace listened, letting Sheila get worries off her chest about how her family would cope when she passed; patients often offloaded secrets.

She returned to the room that had been Gloria's.

It was unnerving to go into the space where she had said those curious things. Where she had imagined a man in the corner. It was impossible that she could have foreseen the notes and gifts left in the dark, but odd that she seemed to have predicted an intruder with her dying words.

Something terrible is going to happen when the lights go out.

There was a new patient in the bed. Musical beds – as they referred to it – was part of the job; they were on loan like library books, read and returned for someone else. Some slept for six months in them, some just days. There were twelve in total, enough for 'each of the disciples' a nurse called Sam often joked.

Martha was in Gloria's bed now, fifty-one, with advanced lung cancer. Grace introduced herself cheerfully and listened when Martha got upset that no one would be visiting until the weekend. Visitors were welcomed all through the day; patients' families were as much at the heart of the hospice staff's care. Unlike in a hospital ward, these residents were on limited time, so structured visiting hours didn't exist. Grace always rustled up tea and biscuits if families wanted them, and if there was a birthday or anniversary, extra treats would be found.

Later that morning, Grace and Claire took their lunch break in the staffroom. There was a new tin of biscuits – probably a gift from a family member – but the Grateful Table looked bare. Sadly, few had much to donate. Grace had some tins and nappies put aside but had left them at home in her rush.

LOUISE SWANSON

'God, Richard, the new guy in Room Four, he certainly hasn't lost his sex drive!' Claire was chattering away happily while eating a sandwich she'd brought from home. 'He might have days left, but he finds the strength to leer down your top when you lean over.' Claire paused when Grace didn't respond; they often shared inappropriate jokes as a way to cope with long shifts and sad deaths. 'You sure you're OK?'

'I forgot to bring any lunch.' Grace avoided answering. She liked to listen to problems rather than share them. It had always been her way; was why she enjoyed this work so much.

'Have one of my sandwiches.'

'Then *you'll* be hungry.'

'For God's sake, it's just a cheese and onion bap,' cried Claire, passing another sandwich over to Grace, who took it gratefully.

'Anyway, I should marry him. He's loaded,' continued Claire.

'Who?' Grace frowned.

'Richard in Room Four.' Claire sighed, shook her head.

Grace tried to think up a jokey response but couldn't. 'Did you sleep any better?'

'Have you been raiding the drugs cabinet?'

Grace laughed now. 'You said the other day that we'd sleep better with Lights Out.'

'No. It's so bloody cold. We daren't leave the bed. I've got all the kids in with me. Ralphie has a cold, bless him, and then Mikey threw up. Not his fault, but it was a pain in the arse cleaning up with a torch. And try heating baby formula without electricity! I managed to get a battery-operated warmer but I know a few mums who are having to give their babies cold milk. It's barbaric.'

Grace tried to concentrate on what Claire was saying but kept seeing the note.

Burn me and I will fire.

Saw Steve, eyes lit by the glow of rows of tiny candles.

'That's terrible about babies and cold milk,' she managed to say.

66

Claire nodded, now devouring a yogurt. Then she stood. 'Anyway, shit to do, and Richard can't leer on his own.'

As they returned to the ward, Grace got a message from Riley:

Why did you leave without saying goodbye this morning?

She saw the candles in their kitchen. She might have picked similar for the living room when it was finished. But she *hadn't*. Whatever Riley might say, she *hadn't* bought them and forgotten.

She. Had. *Not*.

She couldn't admit the real reason she'd been so spooked earlier – about Steve. She never had. What happened back then, she had been too humiliated to admit. Too ashamed to say that she had chosen a man like that, let him into her life, into her son's. Too embarrassed to describe how he slowly made her believe she needed him so much she let go of friends, let him take over her finances, her life.

As she walked along the corridor, Grace saw Steve, a surprise visitor, walking towards her, flowers in hand. *No*. She shook her head. Not him. A family member for a patient. But his face lingered in her mind. Was it possible that after all this time he was back?

She typed a message to Riley:

Talk later. You need to turn the lights out tonight and get the lamp on. Meet me at the door with it. I'll message when I'm leaving. X

Riley responded: *OK*.

The afternoon passed as swiftly as morning had. Grace wanted the clock to slow, to keep her here, afraid of the night.

She returned to check on Martha and found her sleeping, oxygen cannula in place above her mouth like a second smile.

Grace tried to concentrate on her job. On Martha.

'I'm lonely,' Martha said, as Grace sat down by her bed.

Such simple words that had Grace reaching for Martha's hand.

67

'I'm scared of death.'

Poor Martha. It was frightening for many when they first came here, knowing that this was the end of their journey. Some had made peace with this idea. Grace often wondered how she would feel if it were her. Or a loved one. Only if that happened did she think you'd ever truly know; witnessing others going through it simply wasn't the same. Still, she was happy that she got to see them out. That she made some small difference, perhaps, to ensure they passed peacefully.

HULL LOCAL NEWS

Feather Man Mystery Deepens

A woman in Hull claims to have been targeted by the Feather Man. Seventy-one-year-old Ellen Mills was left severely traumatised after waking to a masked man in the bedroom corner. Fortunately she screamed and her son, Felix Mills, who was sleeping in the next room, tackled the intruder. The man, however, managed to escape.

The Feather Man, who has so far only targeted women in Leeds, has been breaking into homes, dazzling the occupant with a torch, then blindfolding and tying them up. He also burned two victims, and strangled another until she passed out. The name has been given to him by police because of the single white feather he leaves behind, though no such item was left in Ellen Mills' home.

Humberside Police are looking further into the case.

Meanwhile, there are concerns about the number of admissions to A&E by those who have had falls or are suffering from hypothermia. These cases are mostly occurring in the elderly, but a worrying number have been children. A boy aged three was admitted on Tuesday with severe asthma due to damp in the flat where he lives. He later died. A housing association was criticised for neglecting properties, resulting in an increase in rising damp.

11

The Lights Out Casualties

At eight thirty, after a long handover, Grace left the hospice.

Outside, a different kind of dark to usual: layered, multiple shades of deepening greys, depending on where you walked. Grace often graded the dark, absolute blackness being the most terrifying, a ten, twilight being tolerable, a six. This one was an eight on that scale of fear. She wished she had driven to work instead of running from the house so she was safe within the confines of a vehicle right now.

She lingered in the security of the hospice hallway's orange lighting. Rummaged for her phone, switched on the torch; it illuminated the immediate way, but this meant even darker patches on the perimeter of light, patches where anything could hide. She switched it off, let her eyes get used to the night. Now it scored a more manageable seven.

It was cold; cheek-numbingly, eye-wateringly cold. Grace braced herself. She would run, not only to escape the dark, but to get warm. Pounding the pavement, stumbling twice over uneven slabs, she stayed on the main roads, hating how few people there were. She was the only person in the world. Pubs, restaurants and supermarkets shut at eight now.

Eventually, it was impossible to avoid quieter streets. Then she could run no more. Her heart was bursting out of her chest. She walked fast, grateful that her black trainers were soundless. But she could have sworn there was a soft footfall a second after hers, like an echo . . . was someone else on the street? Foolishly, she stopped.

Someone standing. A few metres away. Not moving. Grace gasped, shut her eyes.

Opened them.

Still there.

'Hello,' she said, nervous.

Was it Steve? *The Feather Man?*

No, *God*, no.

But of course, nobody answered her. She squinted. The shape hadn't moved. She started running, and didn't stop until she was home. She had never been so glad to see the house, gloomy as it was, a silhouette against the stars.

Except . . . there was no lamplight in the hallway. She had asked Riley to wait there with it. He must still be at work.

Shit.

If the camping lamp was upstairs, she would have to locate it in pitch black. Her phone. She'd *have* to use her phone's torch now, risk those dense, dark shadows beyond the beam. She found it in her bag.

'You OK, love?'

Grace screamed, dropped the phone, scrambled for it.

'I'm sorry, it's just me!'

She couldn't see who, backed away, switched on the torch.

'Ben, number seventeen.' Grace's eyes adjusted to the light that now illuminated his face, seeing the numerous chins, ruddy cheeks and kind eyes of her neighbour. 'I'm doing the Night Watch.'

'Shit, yes, of course.' Grace gulped, tried to pull herself together.

'Need me to help in any way?' Ben's words were gentle, full of concern.

'No, I'll . . .' She paused, then decided to launch in. 'Last night, did you see anyone near our house?'

'No. It was all very quiet. Boring. Hard to stay awake. We might have to pair up in future.' He paused, breath fogged in the chill, then frowned. 'Why?'

Grace knew how silly it would sound if she said that a fish and two ornate candles had appeared, despite no evidence of any break-in. 'I thought I heard something.'

'I walk up and down every half hour, trying not to nod off. But if you're concerned, I'll keep your house in my sights.'

Grace flinched at the words.

I have you in my sights.

The first note. Surely a coincidence; a commonly used phrase. She had questioned Ben's hand in the break-in, but it was ridiculous. A person keeping watch wouldn't be so foolish. Besides, didn't she now think that there was a much likelier culprit out there?

'Thank you,' she said.

'To be honest,' said Ben, perhaps glad to have someone to talk to. 'I'd rather be out here tonight. My water pipes burst in the early hours. It's this freezing weather, and the heating being off so long. My kitchen is a mess, but I can't get a plumber – they're so busy with similar problems caused by the switch off.'

Grace nodded, sympathetically. 'I saw this ridiculous suggestion by the government that we should wrap duvets around the pipes – but we need them on the beds so we don't die of hypothermia.'

'Well, I'll let you go,' he said.

Grace finally headed for her front door.

With Ben watching, she tried to overcome her fear of the shadowy hallway and enter, phone torch showing the way. In horror films, women alone in a house were easy prey, but the clichés of such movies were so overused that they weren't frightening anymore. Besides, Grace thought, what would a director make of candles and a fish appearing in a house during a Lights Out situation – surely that would be more the stuff of comedy?

Grace crept up the stairs, phone light shivering in her hand so that waves of blue rays swept a dizzy ocean over the carpet. She caught sight of one of the pictures on the wall; Riley and her at some black-tie work function. His face was fiendish in the gloom. They stared into each other's eyes, and then he growled at her.

She shrank back with a scream.

She was seeing things.

Find the lamp, find the lamp, find the lamp.

Thank God. On Riley's bedside cabinet. She switched it on, waited for her heart to slow.

Then she heard the front door open.

It would be Riley, she *knew* it, but the tension of the evening had her waiting, breath held. This was what the dark did to her.

For a moment, no one spoke. Grace froze as she heard the foot-steps downstairs. What if it wasn't him?

'It's me,' he called then. 'Where are you?'

She went down, lamp in hand, relief weakening her knees.

'Sorry,' he said, 'crisis at work, the system was down and some-one had to wait for the engineer. Of course that was me.'

'It's always you,' said Grace, annoyed.

She kissed him anyway, smelled him; melted. She wanted to pretend it was the old days.

'You alright?' he asked.

She nodded; brief in her response so she didn't irritate him. 'You?'

He responded at length, describing the house he had seen earlier. Grace's tummy rumbled; she suggested they get some dinner. 'We only have the gas hob now.' He usually started the meal when she did a day shift. 'We can boil pasta, warm a sauce.'

'OK.' Riley took the lamp and headed for the kitchen.

'Wait.' Grace put a hand on his arm. 'This morning . . . the reason I ran. There was . . . another item. *Two* items.'

Riley studied her. 'More fish?'

At any other time, she'd have laughed. 'Two candles.'

'*Seriously?*'

'In the kitchen. You didn't notice this morning?'

'I had a shower and went straight to work.' Riley shrugged.

'And I did *not* buy them and forget, before you say it.'

He didn't respond.

Grace paused.

Tell him about Steve, whispered her unconscious.

But that story was so long, so dark, so past. What if she shared the shame of her disastrous relationship with him, and then they discovered someone else had been leaving the items? No. She would keep quiet for now.

She followed Riley to the crime scene; it *was* a crime scene, in every sense of the word. On the worktop, abandoned like a piece of sail from a storm-ravaged ship, the note. Between the spice rack and the fridge, two ornate candles, sentinels keeping watch. And on the floor, the broken egg, putrefying.

'You left *that* there?' tutted Riley.

'I was scared. Someone has been in the house. You can't deny it now.'

He grabbed a piece of kitchen roll, gathered up the egg, and put it in the bin. 'I can't check the doors now because we've been in and out.' He sounded annoyed. 'Was it all secure when you left this morning?'

'I guess.'

They looked at one another. 'I don't see how they got in,' he said.

An idea struck Grace – one that chilled her to the bone.

'What if someone has a *key*?' she said, as much to herself as to Riley. 'For the back door, like Mum.' It would have to be the back door since they put the chain across the front one last thing at night. The back door was an old one, not the most secure, needing to be replaced, like so much else in the house.

When Grace was a child, her mum said that Santa Claus had a magic key to get into all the houses – an idea that caused Grace nightmares. She always wrote on her festive list that he should ignore their house. On Christmas Eve, she'd lie awake, dreading the sound of a door handle squeaking. No child could have been more relieved to discover he was a myth.

Steve couldn't possibly have a key though – they'd only bought the house recently, and it had been years since she'd seen him. Surely there was no way he'd be able to get in?

She realised Riley looked distracted.

'What is it?' she pushed. '*Does* someone have a key?'

'Not that I know of.' He touched a candle. 'These're illegal goods, you know.' Then he picked up the note, read it. 'Fire me and I will burn,' he said. He appeared to think of something. 'Hasn't that Feather Man been burning his recent victims?'

Grace couldn't believe that it hadn't occurred to her. She had been so wrapped up in memories of Steve. She was chilled to the bone.

'Why would you say *that*?' she cried. 'Now I won't stop thinking of it! Do you think it *was* him? Is that what you mean?' She grew more hysterical.

'No, of course not,' Riley insisted. 'It doesn't fit, does it? He targets women alone, and he breaks in, and we haven't been broken into. Also, no feather.'

'But there was an article, he was in Hull, didn't leave a feather!' Grace's voice was shrill.

'Stop it.' Riley grabbed her shoulders. 'They're all older women.'

'I *told* you we should have sorted a house alarm,' she cried.

They discussed getting one a few weeks ago but Riley said that with Lights Out and the government recommendation that people should have fully charged back-up for them, it would be a pain in the arse. And what if it kept going off, woke them? Riley said with the new Night Watch scheme they were safe. She had been comforted by that but now, not at all.

'I want one,' said Grace, still shaking.

'I'll ring around tomorrow.' He said it finitely, ending the conversation, instead starting to rummage in cupboards. 'Right, which pasta sauce do you want?'

She stared at him in disbelief. 'How can you sound so . . . *not bothered*?'

'What else can I do right now?' Riley shrugged.

'Aren't you *scared*?' She couldn't get the Feather Man out of her head.

'Tell me what you want me to do then,' he said, exasperated.

'Call the police.'

He sighed. 'But Grace, nothing's been taken, there's no sign of a break-in . . . they'll think you're crazy.'

'Me? Why *me*? Am I imagining those candles?' Her voice was tight, the hurt deep.

'OK, they'll think *we're* crazy. Don't you see that?' Riley sighed. 'Do you want me to sleep down here?'

'No. Stay upstairs with me.' She *hated* her insecurity.

'Whatever you want.' He looked at her. 'Maybe it's someone who fancies you.'

'What do you mean?' She frowned.

'A man likes you and is leaving you gifts.' His voice had an edge as he spoke. *What was he implying?*

Grace closed her eyes. Saw Steve. Saw a wrapped gift outside the door of her tiny flat, heard three-year-old Jamie singing 'Baa Baa Black Sheep' behind her. Saw her trembling hands open it, reveal a photograph of them both when they had been happy, smeared now in red paint, like blood. That had been weeks after they ended.

But this *couldn't* be him. Why now, out of the blue, after almost twenty years?

It made no sense.

'Just teasing.' Riley laughed, making her jump.

'I don't know how you can be so casual,' said Grace quietly, to which Riley had no response.

Instead, he made pasta and sauce which they ate in the kitchen with their coats on; it might have been romantic in the soft lamp-light if the two strange candles hadn't looked on from their corner, a gift from a sick-sense-of-humour Santa Claus.

'Are you leaving them there?' asked Riley.

'Shouldn't we, for the police?' She looked around. 'We should set cameras up.' Then she would know for *sure* if it was Steve and could deal with him herself, never tell Riley about that horrible time, the guilt she felt at upsetting Jamie.

'You'd need ones that see in the dark,' said Riley. '*And* that run on batteries.'

'Maybe if we get a house alarm fitted, they can do that too?'

'Let's think about it tomorrow.' The conversation was over.

The house grew too cold to stay downstairs. Riley led the way to the bedroom with the lamp, Grace clinging to his shirt. The chill sheets were as unwelcoming as a grave. It took an age for her to get warm while he cleaned his teeth. Once they were settled together, he opened his laptop and loaded up the crime series. Although he was there, beside her, Grace had never felt more alone. But she was afraid to kiss his neck in case he didn't respond again.

How long had she felt this insecure with him? Was the switch off exacerbating it? Was it something deeper?

She was afraid to consider that.

'Goodnight.' She curled up in her sleep position.

'They'll say we're a Lights Out casualty,' said Riley suddenly.

'A *what*?' Grace opened her eyes.

'That's what they're calling people who have suffered as a result of it. I was reading on Twitter about the rise in suicides this week.'

A lump rose in Grace's throat. 'That's so sad.'

'Anyway, goodnight,' said Riley, as though he had just told her to remember the bins.

She felt morose. Many had it much worse than she did. Patients were dying at the hospice. Parents had to choose between food and heating for their children. The cold that took Grace's breath away on the walk home (*run*, Grace, you *ran* most of the way) could kill people. Could make people feel compelled to *die*. She stifled a sob.

At least a twelve-hour shift was a blessing when you wanted oblivion; despite vivid images of Steve being taken away by police officers, screaming her name, and of the blue-grey fish swimming around the bowl, and two candles flickering angrily, Grace drifted off.

I move quietly through the house. I don't want to disturb her.

Not yet.

I like to fill the rooms, know them, own them. I touch the fabric of the cushions and sofa and curtains. I smell the chill air. I make myself at home. My eyes take time to become accustomed to the blackness. It doesn't take long. I'm a patient man. Imagining. Preparing. My mother said I'd never amount to anything but she isn't here anymore. I am.

I'm here. I'm here.

A movement. Upstairs. Is she awake?

Has she sensed me finally?

I don't want her to come down here and find me.

I wait. Wait. Wait.

Nothing else.

Soon it will be time . . .

12

I Am Here

Grace was trapped in a tight, dark, airless space. She couldn't see anything beyond her own nose, not the hands she held out, not her surroundings. She scratched at wood, her nails snagging and pulling. *I've been here before.* She had. *I can't do it again.* She couldn't. The dark. Too much. Too endless. *I can't, I can't, I can't.*

Then someone opened a door. Joy, at first. Steve. With flowers, roses and calla lilies. His favourite gift. She reached for them, cried out in pain. A thorn. Blood. Steve kissed the injury. *I didn't mean to upset you.* But he had. He had played his watch-the-clock game. *It's about being able to trust you, Grace.* If she popped to the corner shop, he timed it; more than ten minutes and she'd been flirting with the assistant. When she got ready, he timed it; more than five minutes and she had too much make-up on, was going to flirt with men at work.

The roses and calla lilies burst into flames.

And Grace was back in the dark, airless space, screaming, screaming, *screaming.*

Riley's voice from afar.

She followed it. Emerged into the real. The glow of the camping lamp. The safety of their bedroom.

'It's me,' he mumbled, still half-asleep. 'You were screaming . . . scared me . . .'

Grace thought her heart would jump out of her chest.

'What did I say?' she asked.

He responded, but at first she couldn't quite hear. When she asked him to say it again, he was snoring. Only as she began to drift off did she realise what he had said, the words appearing as they often do when the brain has put the unheard vowels with the more audible consonants, and gifts you their meaning.

She had screamed, *I don't want to die.*

She didn't.

But the dark always made her feel she would.

In the morning, because they hadn't switched off the lights yesterday, they all came on at once with the return of the electricity. Grace welcomed it. Riley's alarm went off and he shuffled into the bathroom. She lay in bed a little longer, enjoying the warmth, not wanting to go downstairs. She was at work tonight so should get up, take a morning walk, and then nap in the afternoon to get through it.

'Can you check the house?' she asked when Riley emerged.

He sat on the bed, studied her; she couldn't read his expression. 'You OK?'

'Yes,' she lied. That was what he wanted.

Riley nodded slowly. 'Do you ever think . . .?'

'What?'

'Nothing, it doesn't matter.'

'No, *what?*' insisted Grace.

'Well, maybe . . .' He couldn't look her in the eye. 'Should you speak to someone?'

'What do you mean?'

'A counsellor,' he said quietly.

Grace wasn't sure how to take the suggestion. She knew she'd been erratic. But surely Riley knew her too well to write her off as a lunatic?

'It was only an idea.' He headed downstairs.

A counsellor? She didn't need that.

'Anything there?' she shouted after a while, still annoyed with him.

'Can't see anything.' Her relief was immense. Maybe – just maybe – she *had* put those candles in the kitchen. 'Right, I'm off.'

'Remember to ring someone about a house alarm,' she called.

But he had gone.

She got up, made coffee, took it into the living room, and switched on the TV to catch the morning news. Shook her head at the MP lecturing a distraught guest whose father was in hospital because he had fallen in the night.

'I feel for him,' the red-faced MP blustered, 'but a man of eighty-nine could fall in daylight. What we gain from this scheme far outweighs the few casualties.'

'But it isn't a few,' cried the woman. 'What about the crippling cold that's put ice on the *inside* of people's windows at night? Ten degrees is the average temperature people are living in when the heating's off. It sounds mild but it has a severe impact on the heart, lungs and brain.'

'We've been giving advice,' tried the MP, 'and we've offered t—'

'What on earth can you offer to a frozen eighty-five-year-old woman in a damp flat? To my dad? Aren't you one of those MPs who has moved his entire family to your second home in London so they all stay warm there?' The woman was on a roll. 'It's disgusting that the capital gets electricity while we freeze! It's even worse in Scotland – my aunt said her water pipes have frozen so she can't even make a cuppa. You lot have no idea.'

The blue-grey fish flip-flopped as though applauding her.

Grace headed back upstairs to dress for a walk and halfway, something made her stop. Had she sensed rather than seen it? Her eyes were drawn again to the picture of Riley and her at the black-tie work do.

Except it wasn't.

What the *hell*?

They no longer smiled their way out of the gilt frame. Behind the glass now was a painting of a gold dragon, immense mouth agape, not breathing fire though smoke lingered on the air, red sky raging behind him, hell in the heavens. The details were meticulously etched. Grace could see the ripples of skin as though it moved, hear breath like it lived, smell ash like there had been fire.

Then it turned and looked at her.

She gasped, stepped back, nearly fell; almost another Lights Out casualty. When she blinked, it was back in position, motionless, not real.

And then she saw the note, tucked behind the frame. Fingers clumsy, she opened it.

I am here.
Love,
The Night.

Welcome to UK GOV
The best place to find government services and information

Lights Out – The Night Watch Scheme

TIPS FOR A SAFE NIGHT WATCH:

1) Create a shared rota using a preferred app.
2) Let those who are able to do more shifts do so if those who work full-time can't.
3) Wrap up warmly, prepare a flask, and check the streets every hour. Working in pairs will alleviate tiredness.
4) If you see something suspicious, do NOT deal with it yourself. Call your local police station and report what you have seen. An officer will be sent to you as soon as possible.
5) Make extra time for homes where the elderly or vulnerable live.

Remember: the government's first priority is always the safety of our country.

NIGHT FIVE

13

Deterring Ghosts and Devils

Tom went to the cemetery in the rain.

He wasn't generally a morose bugger, but he needed to get out. He was a cemetery caretaker, but he had been signed off due to acute anxiety. Some days he missed it, wished the doctor hadn't given him a sick note. Maintaining the grounds on his own was therapeutic, suited his solitary nature.

Harper had often said that he must be morbid to 'measure and mark out grave spaces'. But doing such a thing felt . . . honourable. He made sure that a person's last resting place was perfect. The dead deserved that.

As Tom walked through puddles, it was tempting to check the bins and pick up soda cans from the pathways. Instead, he sat on a bench beneath a yew tree; such a cliché. These evergreens are common to graveyards because of their ability to thrive in all weather and soils. Their branches are supposed to deter ghosts and devils, though Tom wasn't sure about that. Of course, he couldn't sit for long. So he walked the circuit again, returning to his spot beneath the yew tree.

He had almost been dragged into a protest earlier, so came here to decompress. He hated large crowds, loud noises, the simmering chance of violence. Trying to get through Victoria Square, he had been hit in the face with a placard; FIGHT FOR THE LIGHT almost knocked him off his feet. He didn't want to fight for it. He liked the dark. He had run from the chanting and yelling.

Here, there was peace.

He looked to his left; frowned.

On the bench, a single flower. He moved closer. A black rose, made of silk. He looked around. The place was empty.

You must have put it there.

No, he hadn't.

Black roses symbolised mourning and tragedy, though few people used them on coffins or at funerals, preferring brightly coloured, hopeful flowers. Had someone left it to say something? If so, what? Had it been there earlier, and he hadn't noticed? Not likely. Had someone dropped it when sitting here while he walked the grounds earlier, perhaps from a bunch intended for a grave? But Tom hadn't encountered a soul since arriving here.

He shivered. The rain had stopped. It was time to go.

He headed home, avoiding Victoria Square.

Even though home was a place he dreaded going.

14

His Name, the Unmentionable

Grace found Riley's number with trembling fingers but it went to the message service. She tried again, wandering the house, checking the windows and doors; all intact; chain across the front door. Then she rang the local police station. A woman took some details, said they were much busier than usual but someone would come by the end of the day.

Despite the horror, Grace couldn't tear her eyes from the gold dragon.

She shook her head, forced herself to walk away, paced the landing and then went back, imagining the original picture back in the frame, all being well again. She reached out to tear it down, but realised she should leave it for the police. It could have fingerprints on it and she might disturb them.

Who the hell did such a thing – removed a photograph and put a garish artwork in its place? *Why?* Was there a coded message she couldn't see? Steve had harassed her after they broke up, left gifts, but this just didn't *feel* like that. And the note from The Night. Why would Steve call himself that?

She put it in the 'Shit and Stuff' drawer with the one from yesterday and slammed it shut. When she couldn't get hold of Riley after multiple tries, she called her mother.

'Hang on,' said Catherine brusquely, 'I'm polishing my nails. Let me put the lid on.' Grace waited. 'I don't want it to clag. I want to look nice for my audition.'

'Your audition?'

'For my over-fifty-fives acting group. They're very amateur, think they're Judi Dench when they're more Punch and Judy, but it'll do me. I'm playing Lady Macbeth in their upcoming production.'

'You already got the part? Why the audition then?'

'I don't have it yet, but I will. How are you, dear?' Catherine blew on her nails.

Grace paused.

What stopped her answering? Knowing how it would sound if she told her? Or was it that mostly they talked about the surface stuff, the everyday things, the topics that were easily digested and just as easily changed if needed. It had always been that way. Grace was sure it began around the time her father left. Catherine had spoken of it only when it happened, then never again, refusing to answer Grace's questions.

Eventually she had given up asking and blamed herself for his disappearance.

As she recalled it – and this could be hazy, change with her mood – he had been there for a bedtime story, and gone the next morning. No explanation. She had often analysed that last evening, seeking answers for the sudden departure that followed, but time and distance were the midnight mist that swallowed any remnants of that evening.

Now, his name was the unmentionable.

At the thought of him, Grace felt someone behind her.

Didn't dare turn.

She pictured him, hiding some treat or surprise behind his back as he often had then, a Kinder egg or a plastic pink watch with the time stuck forever on noon. She saw him asleep in an armchair – blue plaid, his favourite – snoring softly, then farting as he often did, waking at the sound and blaming another item in the room. 'It was the curtains,' he would say. 'It was the door.'

It wasn't that she feared him (*you did, Grace, sometimes; later on, at the end, before he left*) but that she feared turning and him *not* being there. Why were these memories so rich in colour, so easily evoked, when she rarely let them in? Was it the situation now? And were her fears evoking the man she'd rather not look at; the one she was sure only filled the house in the months before he left; the strange, scary Dad.

The one who ranted. *Don't let them in, don't let them in, don't let them in.* 'Who?' she had wanted to ask, but been afraid to. And besides, the glazed look in his eyes meant he often didn't even see her there. Now, someone *had* been in. Now, *she* wanted to yell these words.

'Are you there, dear?' Catherine interrupted her train of thought.

'Yes.' Grace's word was a croak.

'How are you?'

'Not good,' admitted Grace.

'Are you coming down with something? Do you want me to make you som—'

'Nothing like that.' Grace wanted her mother to listen, not find solutions. 'I . . . something's been happening.'

'Like what?' Catherine was impatient; she wanted answers, fast.

'Someone has been coming into the house and leaving strange items.' There. Grace had said it.

'What kind of items?' Catherine spoke more softly now.

Grace described them, realising how odd the collection sounded when put together. She shivered when she told her mother what the three notes had said, and that despite these peculiar additions, nothing had been taken.

'I hope you've called the police,' said Catherine.

'I have. Someone should be coming today.'

'Do you have any idea who might *do* such a thing?'

Grace shook her head, then quickly added, 'No idea.'

Her mother had never known how bad things had got with Steve so there was no point sharing his name as a possible suspect. The shame she had felt at how much she let that man control her when she should have been putting Jamie first was not something she found easy to share. She would look for him on social media later though, see where he lived, what his life was now, if it was possible he might have done this too.

'There's been no sign of anyone breaking in,' she continued. 'That's the strangest thing of all.'

'Dear, there are only three possibilities then.'

'Yes?'

'It's either you . . . or Riley . . . or someone who has a key.'

The obvious conclusion, unless you blamed something ghostly, but how would anyone from another realm put a picture of a dragon into a frame? And Steve couldn't possibly have a key.

'You're right. I *know* it isn't me.'

'And Riley?'

'Why *would* he?' Grace paused. 'And only you have a key.'

'Somewhere,' said Catherine vaguely. 'Please let me know what the police sa—'

Grace's phone flashed; Riley was calling. 'I have to go, it's Riley and I want him here for the police.' She hung up and pressed green. 'I rang the police,' she told him. 'They're coming at some point. Can you get home?'

'I'm not sure . . .' He sounded as though he hadn't registered what she was saying.

'Please try.'

Grace sounded desperate, she knew, but who wouldn't? She mediated a constant internal battle between independent Grace and needy Grace. Once upon a time, as a single mum, she had done it all – changed plugs, plumbed washing machines, decorated rooms, and built wardrobes. She was an embarrassment now, depending on Riley. How had it happened? She was like a cotton reel that had unspooled, until the empty bobbin was bare and helpless. When support was there, you took it, got used to it, forgot the days when you'd survived – *thrived* – without it.

'I could do with the support,' she admitted.

'I'll try.' Riley was obviously irritated. 'Didn't they give a time?'

'No. Did you get hold of someone to fit a house alarm?'

'Grace, I'm at work,' he cried. 'Why don't *you* ring around?' And he hung up.

A police officer arrived two minutes before Riley did. PC Littlewood had feathery hair flattened by his hat and a face that looked as though he would rather be anywhere else. Riley hurried into the house.

'Sorry,' he said. 'Busy morning. I've got fifteen minutes.' Grace brushed it off. At least he was here.

'So you've had a break-in?' PC Littlewood asked, his expression bored.

'It's not that simple,' said Grace.

They went into the living room. Grace didn't drink the tea she had made for them all. She put her mug next to the fishbowl; the glass steamed up, so the curve was a toothy grin, as though the fish had been involved in the tomfoolery. She pointed to it. 'There are three fish now.' She blinked thrice as though to confirm the existence of each one.

PC Littlewood watched the gentle undulation of waves caused by the fish swimming back and forth. '*Now?*' he repeated.

'We only had two,' explained Riley. 'Grace came down the other morning and the grey one had been added. Angelina,' he added, with a small, wry smile. Grace nudged him. It wasn't the moment for jokes.

'Sorry?' PC Littlewood frowned.

'Doesn't matter.'

'Someone came into your house and added a *fish?*' PC Littlewood couldn't hide his disbelief.

'Yes,' whispered Grace. She glanced at Riley who finished his tea with an irritatingly loud gulp. 'That's not all . . .'

'Oh?' said PC Littlewood.

Grace found that she couldn't voice the curious additions to her home; instead, she led him to each violated area. To the pair of candles guarding a corner and to the fierce dragon artwork on the stairway wall. Riley leaned in to study the print; of course, he was seeing it for the first time.

'That's *hideous*,' he said.

PC Littlewood looked at it with equal distaste, then at his notepad, and then at Grace. 'And you're absolutely sure this isn't your painting?' he asked.

'You think I don't know what's hanging in my house?' she cried. 'I've never seen it before in my life. Yesterday there was a picture of me and my husband in there. He'll tell you that.'

Riley nodded. He reached for it.

'No,' said PC Littlewood. 'Fingerprints.'

'I wanted to see if our picture was still in there.' Riley looked at Grace. Of course. Had the pictures been swapped or did the other remain?

'I need to make absolutely sure what has been . . .' PC Littlewood coughed. *'Added.'*

'Just what we've shown you,' said Grace.

'Has anything been taken?'

They came downstairs and he scanned the rooms, an expert eye looking for something out of place.

'That's just it.' Grace's *it* came out as a sob. 'Nothing's gone.'

'Was there any sign of forced entry?'

'Not that I could see,' said Riley. 'I checked each time.'

'Does anyone have an emergency key?'

Grace shook her head. 'Only my mother, but Jesus, it wasn't her.'

'Have you fallen out with or upset anyone?'

'Not that I can think of,' said Grace.

'Anyone you can think of who might do such a thing?'

Was now the time to mention Steve? Tell Riley she had not only been stupid enough to get pregnant at nineteen, but three years later she had been blinded by the passion of a man who promised a better life and then ruined it with insidious control and gaslighting.

Grace saw Steve as though he had come into the room to assess the crime scene too. She had always felt his arrival before she saw him. It was a mixture of fear and love and of having to assess his mood to prepare for how she should *be*. He didn't speak. His silence was always the worst. In it, she would panic, worry what she'd done wrong, add up how long she had taken to bathe or talk to a friend. Now, the ghostly Steve finally spoke: *Remember what I told you, Grace? You are mine, and you always will be, and I'll never let you go.*

'Grace?'

She jumped. PC Littlewood was studying her.

'Sorry . . . I . . .'

Riley shook his head. 'I can't think of anyone who'd do this.' His words were firm.

Grace repeated them, if only to make herself believe.

She didn't mention Steve.

PC Littlewood's radio crackled; voices overlapped, spirits fighting for attention at a séance. 'I'll send someone to brush for prints,' he said. 'I can't say when; we've had a huge rise in calls since Lights Out. People thinking they've seen an intruder. This Feather Man in Leeds has really unnerved people.'

'I read that he broke into a house in Hull,' said Grace.

'I can't talk about that,' said PC Littlewood.

'But what if he was responsible for *this*?'

'This isn't his MO.'

'Can you be *sure*?' Grace pushed.

'I'm sure PC Littlewood knows more than we do,' said Riley.

'Anyway,' said the police officer, 'breaking and entering is a crime, and if these items aren't yours, someone has been in. Once I get back to the station and log it, you'll be given a crime number.' He studied them both. 'In the meantime, I'd recommend a house alarm.'

Grace looked at Riley.

He looked away.

'Don't destroy these items,' said the PC. 'We might be able to lift prints.'

'From a *fish*?' Riley said, and Grace shoved him.

PC Littlewood looked around the house one more time before leaving, clearly as baffled as they were by the intrusion.

Riley said, 'You never told him about the notes.'

'Neither did you,' she snapped.

'I just thought of it.'

'Me too.'

Her knees suddenly felt weak. It was all too much. The switch off, the idea that someone had been in the house, a police officer having to come, the past chasing her.

'Who the hell is The Night?' She paused. 'I think it's someone who knows my . . . *fears*.'

Steve had known about them, mocked her for it.

'Tonight I'll sleep downstairs while you're at work,' said Riley. 'Keep an eye out.'

'Oh, *thank you*.' Grace was grateful.

'Right, I have to get back to work,' he said.

When he left, Grace tried to sleep, ready for her shift, but she tossed and turned and, in the end, got up. It would be a long night.

She got her laptop, opened Facebook. Typed in Steve Tudor. Thankfully an unusual surname. It brought up ten options, four without a picture. And there he was. Black hair thinning now and flecked with grey. Eyes narrow, like a rat's. She felt sick. All those feelings of worthlessness, there again. All the things he had said to undermine and belittle her.

Ever wonder why your father left, and then Jamie's father too? Ever thought it must be something to do with you? But I'll never leave you. Ever.

Still, she clicked on his profile, and then on his About. According to this, he lived in Lincoln and was married. In pictures, he and his wife looked happy. She was blonde, slight, eyes bright. Did that light hide fear? Her joy looked real – in holiday snaps on a beach she looked at her husband with unadulterated adoration.

Why would he come all the way to Hull every night with weird items and leave them in her house?

Had he changed? Did people like that *ever* change?

She thought about messaging him, but resisted. If it wasn't Steve, she'd be opening up a past she would rather avoid. Leave it. See what happened. What the police found.

Just after four, Grace went to the window to face the dying day. She looked up at the opposite bedroom window, feeling that if she saw Stacey there, all would be well. But the black glass stared back, vacant, dead eyes. She should check Stacey was OK after knocking the poor child over on the street. She made a note to herself to stop by tomorrow.

The sun fell, shrouded in cloud, a festive orange wrapped in tissue paper. She hurried around the house switching everything on, *flick, lit*.

At least, with work, she would escape the dark tonight.

15

I'm Watching Over You

Grace left the house at seven fifteen, went across to Stacey's house, and knocked on the door. Martin, her dad, answered, tea towel on shoulder, steam rising from a large pan in the kitchen behind him. Probably making the most of the remaining forty-five minutes of electricity. She knew he was a single parent.

'Just checking on Stacey,' she said. 'I bumped into her yesterday, knocked her right over. I feel *terrible*. I tore her tights.' Grace went into her bag, took out the pair she found in her drawer earlier. 'They might be a bit big, but here's another pair.'

Martin smiled. 'That's kind, but she's fine. Never even mentioned it. She's in the bath, but I'll give her these. Thank you.'

And he returned to his evening meal.

Though she sometimes walked to work so that she could enjoy the sunrise walk the next morning, tonight she was too nervous, and got in her car. The temperature was a painful minus two, and she was glad of the heating.

Claire wasn't on shift. Sam was the nurse in charge, a no-nonsense man who worked hard and expected the same from his staff. A lack of funding meant too few carers. Tonight was no exception. There was no one to cover the second nurse being ill, and the bank carer hadn't turned up. Strike talk had started again. Grace wasn't a nurse but knew she would stand with them.

Handover done, she was allocated her duties and got on. She had six patients to check through the night; she repositioned them when needed, made sure they were comfortable, and did anything else that arose, making tea, lending an ear.

It was a hard slog. Grace felt close to tears at inopportune moments. Melody – a too-young woman with advanced cervical cancer – talked sleepily about the Venice trip she was missing, her words weighted with drugs, dragged out between dense pauses. A bunch of dusky pink chrysanthemums sat on the cabinet; Melody handed Grace a single flower before falling asleep. She wished she was somewhere else.

It wasn't often she did.

She loved this role, but tonight it was a burden that bit too heavy. Then she felt guilty for feeling that way when she had the luck of being alive. She had requested these night shifts to avoid the darkness of home; now she was complaining.

A man called Raymond died suddenly just after four thirty. He would never again have the insomnia he had cursed. He hadn't been in the hospice long. To Grace he seemed too well to be there, though she knew he had HIV, which had been controlled by antiretroviral drugs, and had developed AIDS after a cancer diagnosis.

Sam verified the death, and they gave him his hour.

Then they took a break; they were supposed to have half an hour, but she knew it would be ten minutes. Sam put some packets of pasta on the Grateful Table. Damn. She had forgotten her tins and nappies again.

'You OK?' He devoured a cheese baguette.

'Yeah,' she lied. 'Just tired.'

'How are you finding Lights Out?' he asked.

'I'm getting on with it.' Grace knew this simple sentence belied her anxiety. 'I don't agree with it, but what can you do?'

'Me neither. It's bullshit that the government is trying to be green. They don't give a shit about reaching net zero by 2050. This is to appease us, get votes.' Sam paused. 'But you *can* do something. There was that big protest this afternoon. Wonder how it went? My brother went. Have to ask him.'

'That was *today*?' Grace had seen it on posters but felt curiously distant, as though it was happening in another world, another place.

'It has made me think how grateful I'll be when we have electricity around the clock again,' said Sam. 'There are apparently about seven hundred *million* people in the world who don't have it, and we're grumbling about a few hours at night.'

He had a point.

She should be thankful.

In the morning, Grace drove home, sad to miss the sunrise on her face, but glad to avoid the chill. School children, out early, swung book bags; a wild breeze whipped frozen leaves into a frenzy, and some chased them. She saw Stacey and Jack on their street and pulled up alongside them.

'Thanks for the tights,' cried Stacey. 'They're a bit big, but dead warm.' She pointed to her legs.

Grace smiled. 'That's good. You need them. How's your scrape?'

'It's a scab now,' said Stacey. She seemed distracted; looked tired.

'She picks at it,' piped up Jack.

Grace laughed. Then she spotted the dusky pink flower Melody had given her on the passenger seat. Remembered the lovely rose Stacey had included in her Welcome Pack. Held the chrysanthemum out for her. 'For you,' she said.

'Oh, that's pretty.' Stacey sniffed it, cheeks flushed. 'Thank you.'

'You're welcome.'

Grace watched them go and then drove to the house. It was going to be OK. Riley had stayed downstairs so no one could have got in without disturbing him. And she would sleep well because she'd been awake for over twenty-four hours now. Plus, it was daytime.

She let herself in, found Riley in the kitchen, eating toast.

'I think this milk's gone off,' he said, sleepily, hair mussed. 'We'll have to just get a pint every day, I reckon.'

She kissed his cheek. 'Well?'

'Well, what?'

'Was everything OK?' She glanced around the kitchen, fearful of new candles or strange artwork, but it all looked the same.

'I guess.'

'Did you manage to get much sleep down here?'

Riley didn't respond, avoided eye contact.

'You *did* sleep downstairs?' she demanded.

'I meant to but I fell asleep while I was on the laptop in bed.'

'*What?* You promised.' She wanted to cry.

'It's the warmest place in the house. I woke at four but fell asleep again. Listen, I looked around just now and I can't see anything unusual.'

Grace was afraid to check; Riley wouldn't notice if she painted the bedroom walls brilliant cerise.

'If you're so bloody scared,' he said, 'why don't you *do* more?'

Grace was hurt. 'What do you mean?'

'Well, if you hate Lights Out so much, get out there, go on a protest, *do* something.'

'I . . .' Grace didn't know what to say. Maybe he was right. Maybe she should find out if there would be another one. But her shifts were long, and life was hectic. Excuses? Maybe. It might do her good to get involved in such a thing.

'Don't forget I'm doing Night Watch tonight,' he said.

She *had* forgotten; she would be alone in the dark.

'You'll be fine,' he sighed, as though hearing her thoughts. 'You'll be safe because I'm watching the house.' He paused, bit his toast. 'When are you next at work?'

Distracted, Grace had to think. What day was it now? Friday morning.

'Sunday,' she said. 'A day shift.'

'I've got to go. See you later.'

'Will you manage Night Watch after a day at work?' she asked.

'Sure. Tomorrow's Saturday – I'll sleep then.'

When he left, with the sun on her side and no murky corners to catch her unaware, Grace checked the house. Still the blue-grey fish in the bowl, but nothing else in the living room. Still the gold dragon gracing their stairway wall, but nothing else nearby. She made Horlicks without milk and carried it upstairs to get a shower. Then she climbed into bed.

The camping lamp sat on Riley's bedside cabinet.

And on hers, a lady.

A lady without arms.

A white figurine, perhaps porcelain, Grace wasn't sure. A recreation of the Venus de Milo statue. A beautiful piece of artwork that stabbed her in the heart with a blunt knife. A graceful item whose poise mocked her.

'No, no, *no*,' she said softly.

And beneath it, a note.

I'm watching over you.
Love,
The Night

HULL LOCAL NEWS

Search on for Women in River Humber

Four women were spotted walking into the River Humber late last night. Humber Rescue were alerted and searched the area but without success. Hayley Morris, 36, who lives along the riverfront, said that she couldn't sleep and that something drew her to the window at midnight. 'It was an eerie sight,' she said. 'Four women walked along the beach, holding hands. I thought, what a time to be out, especially with Lights Out, and the bitter, bitter cold. Then they walked into the river, in a row, still hand in hand.'

There has been an increase in the number of people jumping from the Humber Bridge this week, with one of the employees patrolling the bridge reporting that she had spoken to and prevented at least five people from climbing over the railings. 'We are always on duty,' she said, 'on foot and in patrol vehicles on either side of the bridge.'

The search will continue for the four unnamed women. Concerns have been expressed by local residents that these incidents are due to the big switch off. 'There are people alone in the dark,' said Esther Shaw, 48. 'The government haven't thought this through. Those who are depressed now have freezing, dark nights to deal with too. I think it'll get a lot worse.'

I'm here.

It's like I'm always here. Even in the day, before darkness falls, I'm here. In this house. I hold my breath. Let it out slowly. Again. Again. It means I leave a part of myself here after I've gone. My breath, there, with the other molecules, part of this place.

Now, to her.

Her.

Shhhhhhhh.

Stop it. I'm not listening to you, Mother. You're not here anymore. You can't scare me now. I'm in charge.

Shhhhhhhh. You're disturbing me.

You're making me mad . . .

NIGHT SIX

16

Something That Wasn't There Before

Tom was empty-handed when he entered the reception area for the third time, nodding at Jenny the receptionist because he couldn't quite muster a smile, and then sitting on the sofa, upright, near the edge. The way he felt.

He had thought about bringing something he wanted Carole to help him analyse but decided against it. She hadn't been particularly helpful last time. He was early and knew he would have to try and sit still for ten minutes.

Then – as though sensing his agitation – Carole opened her door after a few minutes. He expected her to say, 'Just you again,' and he couldn't have coped with that, not today, but maybe he looked such a wreck that she simply said, 'Glad you came back, Tom. Come in.'

He followed her inside and they settled into their unspoken sitting agreement. The scent of cigarette was absent this time. Perhaps she only smoked when she was stressed. Maybe she had found Lights Out difficult. He continued to find it the most reliable part of his day; whatever else happened, the dark came at eight.

'Did you find out if it was from Harper?' asked Carole.

'*Sorry?*' Tom was confused.

'The Russian doll.'

'Oh.' He hadn't. There had been so much else going on, he had forgotten to bring it up. 'No.'

'OK.' Carole looked disappointed. 'How are you today then, Tom?'

'Not good.'

It was the truth. No point hiding it. He knew how he looked; if he usually made effort with his hair, today it was wild; if he wore clothes Harper had chosen, today they were creased; if he showered each morning, today he hadn't bothered.

'Tell me about that,' Carole said kindly.

The words choked him. He wanted desperately to pace but had decided he wouldn't.

'If you need to pace, you can.'

'It's hard not to.'

'I think you do it to avoid other things,' she said softly. 'You employ the physical to ignore the emotional.'

'If I sit here – and I don't move – I get . . .'

'Yes?'

'*Agitated.*'

'I don't mind that. I see plenty of agitation in here. You can express anything, so stop worrying and talk as freely as you want to.'

There were two things that threatened to burst out of him, rather like the creature in the *Alien* film. He felt that the carnage might be as bloody and painful. One thing was what he had been bottling up all week for fear of being laughed at – the curious occurrences since Lights Out started – and the other was a new development.

'How about you start by telling me why Harper *really* isn't here?' asked Carole.

'She doesn't deserve to be.' The words came out harshly. Tom was surprised at their strength. They had potency he didn't feel.

'Why would you say that?' Carole leaned forward, unable to hide her interest.

'Maybe if she *had* been . . . at the start of the week . . .'

'Yes?' Carole was quite literally on the edge of her seat.

'She won't come now.' Tom's voice broke. 'It's too late.'

'Why is that, Tom?'

'I'll tell you, but I can't sit still. It's claustrophobia inside my head.

If I walk, my head clears.' He stood, strode with purpose, as though he had some important destination to reach. Maybe that place held all the answers.

'I'll just say it, shall I?'

Tom realised how manic he sounded. Carole must think she was about to witness a confession of criminal proportions but he had never so much as stolen a pen from work.

'Take all the time you need,' she said slowly.

He stopped in front of the WE ALL SMILE IN THE SAME LANGUAGE print. He tried to speak calmly. 'She had an affair.' He turned, looked at Carole. 'That's what she did.'

Carole nodded. 'I see.'

'It's over now.' He shrugged. 'She ended it a few months ago. I mean, she *told* me that, but she could be lying. And now . . .'

'Yes?'

'She met him through our friend. Pam. I really liked Pam. She took notice of things. Asked about my hobbies. She smelled of the perfume my mum used to wear. She didn't introduce them; it wasn't her fault. But Pam knew him, and they were out one night . . . and that was it.'

'How long have you known?'

'Five months . . . maybe a month into the affair.' He paced again.

'How did you find out?' Carole asked.

'I keep thinking of those poor smashed-up wooden dolls.' Tom shook his head to free pain that surged in his gut. 'I was broken up too. I thought about nothing else. She said she would end it when I confronted her. Said she loved me, that she'd been depressed and he cheered her up.' Tom increased his pace. 'But other things have . . . been happening.'

'What things?'

'This week . . . since Lights Out.'

'What things, Tom?'

He circled the three chairs. Carole twisted to watch him pass by. If there had been a song playing, it would have been like a childhood game of Musical Chairs, and he might have been compelled to sit, try and win. If he told Carole about the items, she would think he had lost his mind.

He went back to talking about Harper. 'It might not've been the first affair. She could have been with ten men. She's a flirt, there's nothing wrong with that. Some people love to be the centre of attention. It's when you take it further, isn't it?'

'Tell me more about how you *felt*?'

As though the music had stopped, he sat. 'Like I'd been hit by a ton of shit. Can I say shit?'

'Yes.'

'I sat up all night. Kept thinking what had I done wrong? Not done? Why didn't I know? My head span.'

'It's natural to blame yourself. It can take two people to cause an affair in some ways, but self-blame is futile.' Carole paused. 'Have you both talked about it?'

'At first. Then she got annoyed, said I should drop it, it was over.'

'I see.'

'Do you know what the most painful thing was?'

'Tell me,' Carole said kindly.

'She loved him. It wasn't a fling. During an argument she admitted that he completed her Sudoku puzzle. She's never been poetic but she talked that way about him. She said we were together out of habit, *he* had opened her eyes. That hurt. Sex is just sex, but she *loved* him.' Tom glanced at Carole. 'Am I allowed to say sex?'

'Of course.'

'I could forgive sex but when you don't have their heart your own dies a bit.'

'Is that how you feel? Like you've died?'

'Just my heart.' Tom's voice cracked. 'I tried to take my mind off it with hobbies.'

'What hobbies?'

'I tried to learn Russian at a free town hall class. Then I tried swimming lessons, but the chlorine gave me a rash. Then I got lost in books. I read about the Vikings but they were cruel creatures, so I stopped. I tried to fill my head so I wouldn't think about her affair. But then she talked about it. It was like she wanted to relieve her guilt by putting it on me. She expected me to comfort her. I said, you want my *sympathy*? And she did! She thought I'd be grateful it was over.' Tom held his head in his hands like it might fall off and smash if he didn't. He looked up. 'And I *was* grateful. Am I pathetic?'

'No. It takes great bravery to talk about this. Not everyone chooses to, but you did. That's positive, Tom.' She held his gaze; her eyebrows met like thin magnetised caterpillars.

'Maybe I'm weak, but I still wanted her. I said we could rebuild things. She said OK. I said to make a real go of it, perhaps we should see someone.' Tom looked at Carole. 'You. She wasn't having it. She said, "People in my family don't take their private business to perverts."'

'Perverts?'

'Her words, not mine. She said that anyone who wants to sit and listen to people's problems must be a pervert.'

Carole clearly wasn't offended by this. 'Is there something else you need to say?'

'I do . . . but . . .'

'Take your time.'

'Now . . .' Tom had to take a breath. 'Now, she's leaving anyway.'

'When did she tell you that?'

'This morning,' said Tom, anguish crushing the words.

'And when does she plan to go?'

'Today. She's packing now. I couldn't stay and watch. I'm too tired to beg anymore.'

'I'm sorry, Tom.'

'Me too.' The words were insufficient; he was desperately sad.

'Is she going to . . . the lover?'

'She said not. That she no longer wants to be with me.' Saying this was agony. 'But . . . I don't know.' Tom stood again, sure that Carole supressed an irritated sigh. He must be the most annoying client she had ever seen.

Maybe he should leave, never come back.

'Shall we come back to the other thing you want to talk about? I feel that this is more pressing somehow than Harper's imminent departure.' Carole said the last two words in a hushed tone, like she was either respecting them or didn't quite believe them. Tom frowned. He sensed a shift. As though Carole had realised something, and he wasn't sure he wanted to know what it was. 'Shall I ask you some simple questions?' she continued. 'Might that help?'

'I guess,' he volunteered, unsure.

'Did you do something to her?' Carole spoke softly, studied him. '*Sorry?*'

'Did you d—'

'No, I heard you, I'm not sure what you mean.'

'Did you kill her?' She could have been asking if he had washed the pots earlier.

'*What?*' Tom had reached the window and stopped abruptly, as though the glass was some sort of repellent. He turned towards Carole. 'Where did that come from? Of course not! I thought you meant subtle questions that would relax me, not accusations.'

'I had to ask. It wasn't an accusation, it was a question to get things out in the open.' She sighed as though this was obvious. 'A few months back I had a session with a chap who behaved like you are. He was agitated, paced back and forth. Turned out he had killed his wife and left her in the bath for two days wearing only her favourite pink shoes.'

'I thought these sessions were confidential.' Tom felt sick.

Carole looked momentarily shamefaced. 'I didn't tell you his name.'

'I *know* his name – that story was all over the papers.'

'Exactly. I've not betrayed his confidence. When I saw the story in the paper afterwards, I felt terrible. I could have *done* something.'

'Not if she was already dead.' Tom realised he sounded flippant and felt bad; that poor woman. 'Harper is alive and well and deciding what to take as she leaves me forever.'

'I'm sorry if I was blunt. I just don't want to make that mistake again.'

'I haven't killed *anyone*,' cried Tom. 'I'm no predator!'

'Good.'

'I'm not my father.'

'Your *father*?' Carole studied Tom like she had struck gold.

'He didn't kill anyone either but . . .'

'Yes?'

Tom shook his head. He regretted bringing his father up. It was history too painful to talk about now. 'Look, things *have* been happening, but nothing like murder.'

'That's what you need to talk about to me.'

'I really want to tell *someone*.'

'It might feel like a weight has been lifted.' Carole leaned forward in her seat again; it squeaked, as though glad to have reprieve from her occupancy.

'I'm not sure anyone would believe it.' He came back to the chair but refused to sit, on principle. She had thought him capable of murder. He would not take her seat now. 'I'd be mocked the way . . . the way my dad used to mock me . . .'

'I won't mock,' said Carole. 'We can try and make sense of it together.'

'You have to take notice of everything.' Tom spoke to himself. 'Otherwise you could miss things. Things . . . not there before. Like being a small animal in the jungle. If you don't know your surroundings, you get eaten.'

'You feel like life has eaten you up?'

'No. You don't see it at all. But that's fine. You've helped me think straight. I know that I need to talk about what's been happening.' Tom glanced at Carole. He knew she hadn't been entirely professional. It didn't matter now. 'But it won't be to you.'

'Because of the question about killing Harper?'

'I should report you for that.' He wasn't angry, just put out.

'I didn't mean to cause offence.'

'Who *wouldn't* be offended by such a question?'

'Perhaps if you just tell me straight out, we might get some-where.' She was curious now, Tom knew it. She didn't care about him. She wanted to know about the things.

The things.

But that wasn't a story she deserved to have.

'I'm going home,' he said softly.

It was a place unfamiliar now. A place that had changed. A place that might now be empty, at least of human company. Could he face that? If she was still there, could he face that, the pain of seeing Harper when she was no longer his?

All that he had tried to do to save them, it hadn't worked. Was there any point now?

'I hope you get help elsewhere,' said Carole.

Tom headed for the door, every bone in his body weighted with lead. He paused, turned back. 'What would you do if you found . . . something . . . strange in your house?'

Carole didn't respond; he realised that the question sounded like some sort of threat. 'I'm sorry, it doesn't matter, I didn't me—'

'What do you mean *something strange*?' she ventured.

'Something that wasn't there before.'

'I'm not sure I understand the question. Can you give me an example?'

Tom regretted the rash question. 'It doesn't matter. Goodbye, Carole.'

And he left.

Outside, it wasn't raining, and he wished it was. It wasn't dark, and he wished it was. It wasn't over, and he wished it was.

17

Gifts For a Woman

Grace needed to sleep. She would go insane if she didn't. She had been awake for more than twenty-four hours now. But how, with an armless woman watching her? She didn't want to touch her but had no choice. Grimacing, as though she was holding a wasp's nest, she moved the figurine to a drawer in the cabinet, along with the note, and slammed it shut.

She ran downstairs, checked both doors and all the windows. Nothing amiss. That was it; later she would ring for someone to fit a house alarm, maybe some cameras too. From now on Riley would sleep downstairs. And they would think of a way to block the doors so even if someone *did* have a key for the back door, they would be unable to open it.

Grace returned to the bed, curled up in a ball, shivering despite the heating being on.

I must sleep, I must sleep, and then I'll deal with everything.

She didn't.

I'm watching over you.

Her mind raced. Who was? If it wasn't Steve – and she still couldn't be sure it wasn't – then *who*? She thought again of what Riley had said, the word burn in the note with the candles, and its possible link to the Feather Man. What was happening here felt different to how his attacks had been reported, but could he be doing *other* things? Things they hadn't linked to him yet? *This?*

No. *No.* She couldn't let that possibility in.

Grace had assumed that these items had been left for her, but maybe Riley had an admirer. Maybe she was searching for the wrong kind of suspect. Did that make her feel better? No. She would hate some woman chasing him. And someone had been in the house, whoever the target, and this time they had been in the bedroom. How had Riley not even woken?

Didn't he say he had, at four?

Perhaps he'd been unconsciously disturbed by the intruder but not seen them.

Sleep, sleep, sleep.

Somehow, she got a few hours, broken by nightmares that had her gasping for air, scratching at wood, clawing for escape, finally waking, relieved to see open curtains, lazy sunshine collapsing into the room. Her breath came in sharp rasps. It was light.

It was OK.

She got up after two. There were numerous missed calls from her mother, so she made coffee, took it into the living room, and rang her back.

'Where *were* you?' demanded Catherine, no hello as usual.

'Asleep.' The coffee hadn't kicked in yet. 'I did a night shift.'

'I was worried. Did you call the police?'

'We did.'

'*And?*'

'Someone's coming to brush for fingerprints. No idea when. They're really busy. I can't imagine my new fish and a couple of candles are the highest priority.'

'They should be,' cried Catherine. 'It sounds like you have a stalker and in those crime dramas these things *always* escalate.'

'Maybe Riley has the stalker.'

'A fish? Candlesticks? A drawing? Those are gifts for a woman.'

I'm watching over you.

'There's been something else.' Grace described the sculpture, realising she hadn't told Riley. She dreaded bothering him with it. He had seemed more annoyed by it than afraid.

'The Greek Goddess of Love,' said Catherine. 'That's *definitely* a gift for a woman – and it was on your side of the bed, which means . . .'

'*What?*' The blue-grey fish chased Jennifer around the bowl.

'They know which side you sleep on.'

Grace felt sick. 'I wasn't here. Maybe they put it on the empty side to avoid detection.'

'Should you come here? I don't have much on. I sailed through my audition yesterday. They were very impressed.'

'I'd be no company,' said Grace. 'And it's fine, Riley won't be late because he's doing the Night Watch duty tonight. Mum . . .'

'Yes?'

'I've also been . . .'

'Been what, dear?'

'I'm not . . .'

'What?'

Grace remembered the sad piece she'd seen in the paper yesterday at work about four women who had walked into the River Humber. She was anxious, afraid, but was she in the same sad place as those poor women? Did she want to walk into freezing water and sink?

No.

'I've been very anxious,' she admitted.

'It's the dark. I know. That incident.' Catherine spoke more kindly now.

The incident.

The sound of shrill laughter on the other side of a door, echoey, too cruel.

The darkness. The claustrophobia. The fear.

Grace knew what her mum was referring to. She knew what thing had amplified a childish fear of the dark into an absolute dread of the night, a fear reinforced by the sudden departure of her dad not long after. She knew that after heartless kids locked her in a school cupboard, she had needed light at all times. But, as always, she brushed the memories away, like rubbish that gathers at your step after a storm.

'It's not just *that incident*. You know it's not. It's also about my dad leaving.'

Grace was surprised at her words. She had mentioned *him*. They never did. Hadn't for years. He was the unspoken loss they shared. But she didn't care. She needed to. It was time. Something about the culmination of the past few days had opened a chasm, and he had crept in. She had been thinking of him, more than in a while.

'I know you won't say his name,' she said. 'But I need to.'

Silence.

'Say it, Mum. Say his name.' Grace was exhausted and it made her overly emotional. 'I know it hurt you when he went, but it hurt me too. I know you never met anyone else after him, that you weren't interested, and I know this must be because he had your heart as he did mine. But not discussing it doesn't work. He's still in my head, in my heart, smashed as it is. Look at the state of me.'

'You're not a state.' Catherine was clearly put out by the suggestion.

'But I *am*. Inside. Show me a grown adult who sleeps with the lights on.'

'You're a wonderful, strong woman,' insisted her mum. 'Look at what a marvellous single parent you've been to Jamie.'

'I managed that *in spite* of it. That was a battle, every day.'

'And you fought and survived.'

'Maybe I'm tired of doing that. Look at me now. I depend on Riley. My fears are getting worse, not better.' Grace ran out of steam; she put her face in her hands. She had shared her shame; she wanted to cry.

'Let's go out and do something next week,' said Catherine. 'We can talk properly.'

Grace suddenly felt great affection for her mum. She was a tough old boot and had a healthy, in-your-face ego, but this hid, from those who didn't know her well, a very decent heart. 'That would be nice.' Grace paused. 'Sorry for being miserable.'

'You've a lot on your plate. These strange gifts would scare anyone. You need to get to the bottom of it, then I think you'll sleep better.'

Grace knew that it was as much – perhaps *more* – the Lights Out scheme that was the problem. 'I know,' she sighed. 'Talk tomorrow. Oh . . .'

'Yes?'

'Did he . . . did my dad . . .?'

'Yes.' Catherine was guarded.

'Did he ever leave strange notes around the house for me, when I was little?'

Silence. 'I don't know. I don't *think* so.'

'OK.' Did Grace believe her? She wasn't sure, and hated it. If she closed her eyes, *pushed*, Grace could see a tiny, folded note, her small fingers finding it under a cushion, the words . . . *what words?* She couldn't see. 'Doesn't matter,' she said. 'Tomorrow then.'

She hung up to a message from the kitchen workman. She had forgotten about his visit the other day, his promise of getting back to her with a date to begin proper work on the kitchen. It would not be for at least three weeks, he said. Damn. More time living in this halfway house. And yet, Grace found she was relieved. She didn't need a stranger – *another* stranger – in the house right now.

Police Report

Case number:	Date:
2333429987FB	11 January

Reporting Officer:	Prepared by:
Sgt B. Sparrows	DC Y. Cooper

Incident/Issue: At approximately 3 p.m., Sgt Sparrows was one of twenty officers notified via radio of a 999 call to Humberside Police that there was a serious disturbance of the peace occurring in Victoria Square, Hull. Ms Vanessa Smith, who had placed the call, was concerned that protesters were 'threatening to burn down City Hall because local MP Scott Brady had been spotted going inside'. Brady said on BBC Radio Humberside this morning that Lights Out has been a 'huge success so far'. Assumed that protest is in reaction to this comment.

Description of Accident/Issue: An extremely large crowd had filled the square to protest against Lights Out an hour before I arrived with PC Littlewood. Other officers were at the scene already. A male with a megaphone was telling the crowd they should 'get Brady out here and make him listen'. A small group were throwing bricks at the City Hall doors, others had begun destroying street lamps, shouting 'fuck their light'.

Action taken: I spoke to one man, claiming to be a Colin Pembleton, who had the megaphone, asked him to tone down his language and keep this a peaceful protest. He cooperated, told the crowd they were 'fighting for the light, not here to destroy it'. Arrested three men and two women for criminal damage.

18

A Metal Suit of Mania

At four fifteen – soon it would be four twenty, then four twenty-five – Grace went to the window to watch the day die, willing the planets to defy the season's rules and dance across the sky, swap places, the sun kicking the moon into submission. How she longed for spring, long days, bright nights. Her favourite month was June when the sun didn't set until gone ten and woke again at four.

She looked up at the bedroom window opposite for Stacey but the curtains were closed. In front of those drapes, on the window-sill, a small shape. A flower in a vase?

Yes. Grace was sure of it.

The chrysanthemum that had made Stacey flush and smile.

She smiled too.

Before it was fully dark, she hurried around the house, fingers conjuring the sparks, *flick, lit*. Safe now. Full light.

She wanted to make something special to send Riley out fully fuelled for his night duty, so warmed cheese sauce and pasta, his favourite, and he surprised her at five thirty.

'How'd you sleep?' He leaned in to kiss her cheek, missed.

'Fine,' she lied. She didn't want to ruin the evening, tell him about the figurine on her bedside cabinet. Just one meal without thinking about it. Just one meal like they used to have.

He showered and they ate in the kitchen. He was quiet but Grace didn't mind. It was nice. Life was good with less to discuss. The most romantic meals were the silent ones, eyes across a table, anticipation. But she realised Riley was distracted rather than relaxed. A million thoughts fought for attention behind his eyes; she had no idea what they were.

'You OK?' She put her knife and fork on the empty plate together; two metal hands entwined.

'Yeah.' He didn't sound it.

'How was work?'

'Fine.'

'Something's wrong, clearly,' she said. He used to be so chatty.

'It's nothing.' He pushed his plate roughly into the centre of the table, left the room. She stared at the spot where he had been, still seeing him there the way you do shapes in front of the sun after you shut your eyes. In the hallway, the sound of the understairs cupboard opening, the floorboard squeaking near the living-room door. Was he starting Night Watch already? It was only seven forty.

She found him putting his coat and hat on.

'You don't have to start yet,' she said.

'May as well.' He shrugged.

'I was thinking . . . we should somehow block the doors in case someone is getting in with a key, or they're undoing the lock somehow.'

'I might need to be able to get into the house tonight,' he snapped. 'And I'll be watching the place, for God's sake.'

She was hurt by his brusque tone, but still tried to be kind. 'I'll make you a hot flask.'

'I'll come in when I want anything. I need the torch.' He started up the stairs to get it.

'The *torch*?' Grace gulped. He returned with it. 'Do you have to take that?'

'How can I see out there without street lamps or house lights?'

Grace knew it was true but her anxiety soared. She grabbed it from him.

'What the hell?' He took it back.

'Please stay while we turn all the switches and sockets off,' she begged.

'For fuck's sake,' he growled, eyes blazing. She stepped back, shocked. 'You need to get over it. You hate the dark, I know that, but it's time to grow up. It's getting ridiculous.'

Grow up?

Grace couldn't speak. They glared at one another.

'I know it's all tied up in your childhood,' he said, less angry. 'I get that, but lots of kids go through trauma and they're not in this kind of state. No wonder Jamie was such a fussy kid, afraid of his own shadow, following you around everywhere, needing reassurance.'

Now Grace came to life; she wouldn't tolerate criticism of her son. She had let Steve make her feel she was a bad parent, but no one would do that again.

'Don't you fucking talk like that about Jamie.' She pushed Riley into the wall, enjoying the shock that drained his face of colour. 'Say what you want about me, but not him. This has *nothing* to do with him.'

'Why can't you get this angry about your *own* problems?' Riley said quietly, still against the wall. 'Maybe you could help yourself. I told you earlier, get out on a protest, do something, but you're pathetic.'

'Fuck you.'

She was breathing hard.

Then he opened the front door and stepped outside. She watched him walk down the path, devoured by the blackness, stolen from her, it felt, before closing the door. She leaned against it.

Jamie *had* been a sensitive kid – artistic, his teacher had said – but that was his nature. Wasn't it? Was she to blame for him being shy, preferring to stay at home reading while others boys rode their bikes up the street? No, she'd encouraged him to mix, taken him to toddler groups, but he always wandered back to her, happier to sit on her knee and watch the world from that safety.

Maybe she *had* been overly protective, but she believed that children shouldn't shoulder the worries of their parents. That wasn't their duty. Grace had kept her history from Jamie. She had never said bad things about his grandfather – never said much about him at all, only that he had gone, and that was his choice. Because the truth was that until he left, he *had* been wonderful.

Mostly, whispered the child, Maisie. *Mostly. Later on, in the months before he went, he changed. He changed . . .*

She could have shared with Jamie that his grandfather didn't read bedtime stories, he made up his own, the darker the better, the way she loved them. She could have shared that he always left his study door open a crack to say that she was welcome anytime. She could have shared how they laughed at his constant wind, blaming anything else for the 'trouser noises' as he called them.

But would she have shared that there was another man?

A man he slowly became, slipping into a costume, like armour – a metal suit of mania was the phrase that came to her now. What had happened? Why had he changed?

Grace had also excused Jamie's dad, said they were young when she got pregnant, and it must have been scary for him. She had tried to be Jamie's mother, his father, and his grandfather, and that had been hard; so many empty seats at so many Sunday dinners that she had to fill.

Maybe she had been a fussy mum, maybe she should have learned long ago to switch the lights off, but it was done now. Jamie was grown up, had made a good life for himself, and that was all that mattered.

Still, how *dare* Riley say such a thing about her child?

Grace needed to find the camping lamp, get prepared. It was just her tonight. She found it in the bedroom. As she turned to bring it back downstairs, a man, in the doorway. Not Riley, too bulky. She screamed.

Darkness, suddenly.

Thick, absolute.

No, *no*. Not now. It must be eight. Grace screamed again. Fell to the floor. Dropped the lamp. Curled in a ball.

Your eyes will get used to it. Breathe slowly.

But her heart wouldn't comply. She couldn't move. Was frozen. *There was a man, there, you saw him . . .*

Still, she couldn't move. The world settled around her. The heating clicked as it went off. Had he gone? Had she . . . *imagined* him? With trembling fingers, she groped for the lamp and turned it on. No one there. What if he was in the house?

Dare she go downstairs?

Riley was outside, Grace could yell for him. She moved slowly onto the landing, lamp aloft, shadows flickering, jumping at every movement. No one there. The same in the living room and kitchen. Maybe she *had* imagined a figure. She *must* have done. There had been no footsteps to announce him, and clearly there was no one in the house.

She longed to get Riley back, insist they talk. No; let him calm down, talk in the morning. His cruelty had stung. Some of his words, she had to admit, had been peppered with truth. She *did* need to get over this fear. It dominated her life now.

But how?

It was too late for a shower. Grace couldn't concentrate on her Kindle so she crawled beneath the duvet, shivering. Get through the night, and she and Riley could work it out at dawn. The lamp was an ally, on the bedside cabinet; she wouldn't think about what was inside the drawer beneath it. Somehow, she slept, waking regularly, confused about Riley's absence, remembering, clouds of grey suffusing her heart.

She woke to full blackness.

The lamp had died.

She was all alone.

She screamed.

Never let her out, never let her out, never let her out.

'Help me,' she whispered.

She rolled over to Riley's side and reached for the torch. Not there: *he* had it. New batteries for the lamp. Where *were* they? Did they have any?

127

Her phone said it was 3.45 a.m. She realised – she could use her phone's torch.

Then, a sound downstairs.

Grace froze.

Maybe Riley coming in for a snack. He had said he might. She had to remember that she was safe with him patrolling the street, giving their house the most attention. But what if it wasn't him? She would *never* go downstairs, face an intruder; she wasn't one of those fools in slasher movies who met a messy end after doing so.

She listened,

Prayed for quiet.

There were no other noises. Perhaps she had imagined those too. She grew drowsy.

When she next woke, it was past seven; gentle waves of dawn warmly welcomed her, and the lights she hadn't turned out last night were on, full glare. Riley would be back soon. He would need to sleep. It was Saturday. She wasn't at work until tomorrow, so they could talk later, fix things. She would admit she needed help with her fears. It couldn't go on.

But *he* needed to apologise for criticising Jamie.

Downstairs, she made coffee, but couldn't settle until Riley returned. She ended up in the living room, wishing it was finished, the walls smooth and painted the soft grey they had chosen, the planned bookshelves built, the new fireplace fitted.

Instead, another unwelcome addition.

On the remaining brick hearth of the old fireplace, plugged in and switched on, an ornate lamp. Tiffany, the shade coloured glass, patchwork squares of amber and tan and gold, with an ostentatious gilt stand. This arbitrary item did not feel random. This felt personal.

It was exactly like the lamp she'd had as a child.

A lamp her father had bought her.

And when it had gone out, everything went wrong.

'Who left this here?' she screamed into the emptiness.

She didn't pick up the note that was slipped beneath. Couldn't.

She backed away, coffee swilling from her mug, muttering, 'Who left it?' again and again. Where the hell was Riley? His shift finished at seven. He needed to be here, see this, know her fears had substance. She ran to the window, looked up and down the street. No sign of him. Damn. Maybe he was already in the house. She went into the hallway.

'Riley? Are you home?'

No answer.

What if something had happened to him?

She ran upstairs, grabbed her phone, sent a message: *Where are you?*

Maybe there had been an incident. Maybe he had caught someone leaving their house, apprehended them and was at the police station. Then she noticed that Riley's wardrobe door was slightly open. It had been closed last night.

Was someone in there?

She glanced at the bedroom door, ready to run, scream.

Suddenly her father was at her side. Torch on, promising there was no monster inside the wardrobe. *Nothing can hurt you while I'm here.* Except he wasn't there, he hadn't been for over thirty years. She was alone, facing her greatest fears.

She heard his voice, telling one of the made-up stories he created just for her: *Once upon a time there was a brave girl who had eyes that could see through the dark. She could shine them where darkness fell, get rid of all the monsters in the wardrobe with her bravery . . .*

She opened the wardrobe – empty. Riley's T-shirts, his jeans, his hoodies, all missing. It made no sense. Had the person who left the odd items finally taken something? She riffled through his drawers – half empty, socks and pants gone. What the hell?

The room blurred around the edges, replaced with a memory, vivid; *that* night.

The childhood lamp on her bedside table, dimmed but warm, the stars cut in the glass casting a galaxy on the ceiling, sending away wardrobe monsters. Her dad had turned it down low earlier, saying the same thing he always did: 'Nothing bad will happen while it's on, Maisie.' Before the child Grace closed her eyes, it died. Evil shadows gobbled the room up.

She screamed for her father until she lost her voice. Dad, Dad, *Dad*. But he didn't come. And in the morning he had gone.

Now, the phone pinged in Grace's hand.

Riley.

I think we need some space. I packed a few things while you slept, I'm staying with a friend for a while. I can't do this anymore.

My mother told me, you're nobody. You walk into a room and no one sees you. You speak and no one listens. So I never spoke. I watched. And this is good. Because you see everything when no one knows you're there. You see all that people are trying to hide. You learn what every expression and tic and movement means.
    But still, I like the shadows.
    I like to surprise.
    I've waited my whole life for this.
    I'm here. I'm here.
    And now it's time . . .

NIGHT SEVEN

19

The Uninvited Lamp

Grace read again the final line of Riley's message: *I can't do this anymore.* She gasped back a sob. Sank to the floor, pulling the duvet from the bed as she did. Do what? Live with her?

He said he thought they needed space.

But didn't they have plenty already?

Her job meant she was absent at night. In the morning they crossed paths for ten minutes before he went to work, and she slept. No couple had more distance. Over the years Grace had worried it would be their undoing. Now it was the thing he wanted. Which was why she felt that wasn't quite the truth. She recalled how distracted he had been when they ate in the kitchen. How often he'd had a faraway look in his eyes recently. There were things Riley wasn't saying.

Upset dissolved into anger; he had left her, like a coward, in the middle of the night. Just like her dad. Grace called Riley. It went to the message service. She hung up, refusing to leave a message, then dialled again. How could he sneak into the house, get his things and go, without a word?

Why hadn't she heard him when she was so restless?

No: she *had* heard a noise at 3.45 a.m. Riley or whoever left the lamp. Remembering it, she went downstairs. Still on the hearth, bulb shining through multicoloured glass squares, note tucked beneath. She knelt down, intending to turn it off, but her fingers froze.

All she could see, once again, was the childhood lamp on her bedside table. Her dad turning it low, saying, 'Nothing bad will happen while it's on, Maisie.'

Grace shook her head.

This couldn't be that lamp. *That* lamp lasted another few years and then her mother binned it while Grace was at school, saying she would buy her a new one, a nicer one. But, God, it was just like it. She should switch it off, hide it away, call the police again. But what was the point? They hadn't come to brush for fingerprints yet. *She* had to figure it out. Was the lamp a coincidence or had it been put there by someone who knew its significance?

Steve had known about it.

He had taunted her fear of the dark, made it worse, mocked her.

But he couldn't possibly have a key to the house.

Riley, of course, knew about her fears, as did her mum, a few select friends.

She rang Riley again. Still the message service. Was he at work? Should she call him there? Was she the kind of wife to cause a scene at his office? No. This was private. She rang the message service again and this time she spoke. 'What on earth have I done to deserve this? Why couldn't tell me you were going? Where *are* you? Call me as soon as you get this.'

Then she sank into the flaccid sofa. What the hell would she do with the hours that loomed? The three fish chased one another around the bowl; it appeared that Jennifer and Brad had simply accepted this new, blue-grey resident. Grace couldn't, yet she also wouldn't hurt it by moving it or flushing it down the toilet.

The phone rang; she almost dropped it, trying to answer.

Her mother.

'How are you, dear?' she asked.

Grace was tempted to lie but the truth fought harder. 'Not good,' she admitted.

'Another strange item?'

'An ornate lamp. Multicoloured.' She paused for effect. 'But tha—'

'A lamp?' interrupted Catherine.

'Yes.'

When Catherine didn't speak for a moment Grace knew that she too had seen the significance; she too was remembering her daughter's long-ago starlit bedside comfort. 'It sounds like this intruder knows you,' she said.

'It could be coincidence. The other items don't mean anything personal, not that I can see. But, Mum, that isn't all, last night Ri—'

'Has anyone been to brush for fingerprints?' Catherine demanded.

'Not yet, but I'll call soon because of the lamp.' Grace took a breath. 'Riley's gone.'

'Gone? What do you mean *gone*?' She sounded confused.

'He left in the night.' Grace's voice broke. It hurt so much that he had chosen to do it in such a way.

'But where? *Why?*'

Grace couldn't answer either question. She walked into the hallway, looked up the stairs, glanced at the dragon artwork. She continued back into the living room and went to the window. Outside, the street was deserted. The wheelie bins were still out, spilling debris onto the path. Was it strikes again, the switch off?

Who knew? The world waited with the rubbish for what the night might bring.

'Grace, are you there?'

'Yes. Mum, I don't know why. I've been . . . upset recently. Not just because of these break-ins but the whole Lights Out thing. I've been overly emotional at times.'

'But that's no reason for him to abandon you. How *dare* he. I swear, when I get my hands on him.' Catherine paused, switched tactic, perhaps feeling for her daughter. 'He'll be back. This isn't like . . .' Her voice trailed off.

Grace knew what she had wanted to say. 'This isn't like my father?'

'I wasn't going to say that. Riley'll be back. He's a good husband.'

Is he? Grace wanted to say but was prevented by loyalty. *Would a good husband creep off in the night without even explaining why?*

'Look, Christine at the over-fifty-fives acting group called earlier,' said Catherine in her usual brusque way, 'and I'm going to meet them all soon. But you could come this evening?'

Grace longed to say yes. But she needed to stoke that new fire in her belly, face her demons. Deal with what she would do without Riley. 'No, it's fine, honestly.'

'Are you sure, dear? You sound so . . . sad.'

I am, thought Grace.

'I'm fine,' she lied again. 'I'm probably overreacting and Riley'll be back for tea.'

'Will you let me know?' asked Catherine.

'Yes.'

'And let me know what the police say.'

'I will.'

Grace hung up, found the saved number in her phone for the local police station, and dialled, but it rang and rang and rang; she imagined a deserted reception area with WANTED posters fluttering in a ghostly breeze nearby, like a scene in a sci-fi movie. She tried again but still no answer. She had read that the switch off had meant more accidents, more crime – and it had only been a week. How did the old world seem so long ago already? How quickly she had accepted a change so huge that the government were giving more updates than they had during the Covid-19 pandemic.

Grace googled a number for a local home security systems company and rang them too. A friendly receptionist said she would have someone call back, but that they were very busy and it might be weeks before anyone could assess her house. Grace realised afterwards that such a system might not even work without electricity.

Where *was* everyone?

No police, no bin men, no one to fit a house alarm, no husband. She must face the night alone.

And it was already early afternoon.

20

In the Mariana Trench

At four fifteen Grace went to the living-room window to watch the day pass away with dread as thick as treacle. The resolve she'd had all day dissolved. The sky was overcast so no sun to watch fall, no gold to dismiss. In the opposite bedroom window, Stacey, in the windowsill, eyes upward, dusky pink chrysanthemum still in a vase next to her. Grace waited, hoping to catch her eye, but the girl was lost in thought, miles away.

Grace hurried around the house, *flick, lit*, making the place safe before closing the curtains.

The day was over.

Sadness for a moment replaced the earlier fire, and she sent another message to Riley: *How can you ignore me? It's cruel!* Two blue ticks showed he'd seen the previous message.

Where was the man she loved?

Did he have a shadow side?

Like her father.

Eight o'clock approached; panic squeezed her windpipe with a killer's hands. She stood at the sink for five minutes until nausea passed. On TV earlier there had been a quiz question asking what the deepest point of the ocean was; it was Challenger Deep, within the Mariana trench. That was where Grace was; the bed of the sea. No deeper to go. She had hit the bottom. She must swim to the top.

At seven fifty, she began.

She had briefly thought earlier she should stay in a hotel, escape the house, be safe, but they were closed. Now she thought, *no*. This was *her* home and she would *not* be driven from it. So she put recharged batteries in the camping lamp and looked for the torch. Then she went around the house turning off the sockets and switches.

She finished near the uninvited Tiffany lamp. Couldn't switch it off.

Seven fifty-eight.

It was going to go off, but she couldn't be the one to do it.

Seven fifty-nine.

Grace closed her eyes.

When she opened them, the light had gone, except for the camping lamp's determined beacon. Her heart pounded. But she had survived.

Next, she needed to stop the intruder getting in. They *had* to be coming in the back door because of the chain over the front one. She could leave the key in the lock so that no one could use one on the other side. At the back door, she slotted the key into its hole. Put the table in front of it too? No point; the years old door opened outwards, so they could climb over.

Grace shivered. She couldn't help but think that she was alone. And that the Feather Man had targeted solitary women.

She hurried up the stairs, crawled into bed. She had to be up early for work so she set the alarm for 6.30 a.m. Tried to sleep. Woke often, every creaking floorboard and groaning tree seeping into her oblivion and dragging her from the depths of the sea to the surface of consciousness.

Ten minutes after four she woke yet again; the kind of awake that wouldn't easily shrug off. What had disturbed her? Was someone downstairs? If so, what could she do? Nothing but lie here, eyes squeezed shut, praying they left. Then – when the house had been silent for a while – Grace opened one eye.

And screamed.

Someone else. In the room. A shadowy figure by the wardrobe where the camping lamp's beam didn't quite reach.

'*Please* . . .' said Grace, not knowing what she was asking for.

The figure stepped forward. She gasped, pulled the duvet over her face. Heard heavy breathing. No, no. *no*. Did he have a torch? A piece of rope to tie her up? No, no, *no*. After a while, nothing. She dared to peer out.

No one. Her imagination. Again.

No wonder.

She tried desperately to sleep. But it was a long, torturous night that she thought might never end.

HULL LOCAL NEWS

Search Ends for Women in River Humber

Two bodies have been recovered from the River Humber four days after a search of the area. Coastguards were called to a stretch of water near Hessle yesterday and discovered them.

The tragedy comes after a search for four women on Thursday around the Humber Bridge area, involving a helicopter, coastguards, and RNLI crews. They had to contend with the highest tidal swells this year when waves over-topped defences. 'It's a great tragedy,' said Billy Raymond from Humber Rescue. 'We're accustomed to searching for one person, but four, it doesn't bear thinking about.'

It's thought that these women knew each other through a support group for those who have experienced domestic abuse. This has been on the increase since the switch off with more women needing to find shelter elsewhere.

Police are in contact with the family of the two discovered women, who have not yet been publicly identified. Despite the potential of two bodies still to be found, the search has been called off. The Humber Bridge has been the site of several tragic incidents recently, prompting calls on authorities to take action. With the big switch off, and the lights on the bridge down to a minimal few, local residents fear a long, dark winter of searches.

NIGHT EIGHT

21

Alone Like This

Night Eight. Tom sat in his favourite armchair in pitch black, alone.

Harper had been gone two days. Not that he was counting. The dark counted for him; the Lights Out nights were numbered by every excited newsreader and hashtag and gossip in the supermarket. Were they all going to be spent alone like this?

Harper had already left when he got home after his final single-person relationship therapy session. The bed was cold, and her drawers were empty. The fridge was lukewarm, and the TV remote was all his.

All he had now were the unusual items she had left behind.

The items that had caused so much strife between them.

The candles. The ornate lamp. The crystal.

But he wouldn't be going back to Carole to tell her anything.

Tom wasn't sure what to do with his life now.

He only knew he would sit here until he knew oblivion.

22

I'm Here

Morning mercifully arrived and, exhausted, Grace switched the alarm off before it sounded at 6.30 a.m., and got up. With no heating until seven, the house was deathly cold; her breath was a ghostly mist on the air. She boiled water on the hob for coffee, shivered in her dressing gown. She couldn't shake off the horror of thinking she had seen a shadowy figure in the bedroom by her wardrobe last night.

No sign of Riley, still no message either.

Fuck him.

Because she hadn't turned them off last night, the lights came on at seven. The uninvited lamp shone on the hearth, launching luminous layers across the brick. She looked around for new items, heart tight. Went into the hallway, intending to go up for a shower. *Something.* Next to the front door. In a glass vase, six red roses. The kind of gift a lover gave. There was a small note beneath. Grace opened it, praying it might be a heartfelt apology from Riley, but knowing this wouldn't be what was waiting. She read it, gasped, stepped back; the faulty floorboard squeaked as though it too was shocked.

I'm here.
Love,
The Night.

HULL LOCAL NEWS

Feather Man Mystery Deepens Further

A woman in Selby claims to have been targeted by the Feather Man. Sixty-eight-year-old Donna Roberts called the police after finding a single white feather and a note in her kitchen. The back door was broken. 'I didn't hear anyone come in though,' she said. 'And no one came into my bedroom as far as I know. But I'm very shaken and will be staying with my mother for the rest of Lights Out.'

The Feather Man has been breaking into homes, mostly in the Leeds area, dazzling the occupant with a torch, then blindfolding and tying them up. Recently his torture has escalated with two women being burned and another being strangled until she passed out.

North Yorkshire Police are looking into this more unusual case. 'Though the white feather has been left,' said PC Brian, 'it is the first time a victim has not been tied up or hurt. And the note is new. It could be a copycat intruder. We urge everyone to be vigilant, and contact the police if they see anything suspicious.'

23

An Instance of Something Happening

Grace kicked the roses over, ran to the back door. The key was on the mat, had clearly been pushed out by whoever got in. She backed away, shaking her head. Ran upstairs, showered, the hot gush merged with chill tears. Dressing in a dash, she hurried out to work, hair still wet, not caring. She barely acknowledged a cheery hello from Stacey and Jack across the street, Eskimos in chunky coats, cheeks ruddy.

Just as she arrived at the hospice, realising too late that she'd walked so would have to walk home in the dark tonight, her phone pinged. Riley. A message.

Sorry I didn't respond yesterday, was at work. Staying with mate, talk soon.

No kiss, no affection.

Sadness and anger fought a half-hearted battle.

In the staff changing room Claire looked as preoccupied as Grace felt. Her hair was stuck up on one side and she had a discount supermarket bag in each hand. 'I won't have time later,' she explained, lifting one. 'I'm always rushing to do everything before the switch off, planning for tea because I can't rely on the freezer. I bet whoever thought this scheme up didn't have three kids.'

Suddenly, despite it all, Grace missed having a small child despite how frazzled Claire looked; it had been tiring at the time, but good to be needed. 'If I can help, just ask,' she said. Spending time with Claire's kids might cheer her up right now.

'Thanks, my love. Just having someone say that is nice.'

'I mean it.' They headed down the corridor.

At the nurses station the handover was complex, with a couple of incidents on the night shift. Claire gave Grace her duties, and she got on with them, efficiently and with zest, despite how she felt, vigorously cleaning rooms and greeting a nervous new patient called Zelda with warmth.

It was Sunday so there were more visitors than usual. Late morning, the family of an elderly man called Brian brought in his pet dog, Oscar. This was something the hospice encouraged; pets were welcomed since they were as much a part of a patient's family as relatives were. Oscar didn't bother exploring. He sat in Brian's lap – obviously delighted to see his dear friend – and they watched TV together.

Grace and Claire grabbed fifteen minutes for lunch; Claire suggested the bench in the small garden at the centre of the building. They shared a checked blanket over their knees, necessary against the chill, wind tugging the tassels, so they shivered in unison. Grace had forgotten lunch again and shared Claire's baguette, apologising, and insisting she would bring a whole picnic next time.

'Something's going on, isn't it?' said Claire. 'You're not yourself.'

Where should Grace begin? She couldn't bring herself to admit that Riley had walked out, feeling it was her fault, and knowing that Claire coped with three small children and no partner. Also, he had said they would talk tomorrow. Grace hoped that would mean he then came home.

'You'll think I've lost my mind,' she managed finally.

'We work here, we already lost them.'

Grace smiled. 'No, but really.'

'Try me.'

'I'm . . . I'm really scared of the dark.'

'Aren't we all?'

'No. Not like other people are.' Grace paused. 'You've seen me overreact, must have thought me insane.'

There had been a night when Grace was in one of the rooms and Claire, not knowing she was there, switched the light out.

Grace screamed, much to Claire's distress. Claire apologised profusely. Once she calmed down, Grace made up a story about how the other night a man followed her home, and she was still shaken up.

'I'm not coping,' she said now, taking a big breath. 'I think it all started with this . . . *incident* . . .'

Incident was an interesting word. It was mostly used to describe a harrowing event even though it simply meant an instance of something happening. Newspapers used it when they talked about four women walking into a river. Lifeboat rescue workers used it to describe saving someone from choppy waters. Staff here used it for all kinds of occurrences. Grace used it to avoid talking about the details of what happened.

'I . . .'

If she let it in, she would be trapped in that eternally dark space. Be able to see absolutely nothing in the blackness, be scraping at whatever her hands found, screaming and screaming.

'Sorry. I never talk about it normally.'

'Try,' said Claire gently.

Grace looked at the time. They only had ten minutes left of their break.

Claire suggested, 'If not now, some other time?'

Grace couldn't commit to that. It made her feel pressured, anxious.

'Do you think Lights Out triggered your fears?'

So obvious. She nodded. Claire didn't push. Instead, she put a soothing hand over one of Grace's.

'That isn't all.' Grace felt safe enough with Claire to share the other incidents, for want of a better word. 'Someone has been coming into the house and leaving strange items.'

'*What?*' Claire looked aghast. 'What kind of items?'

'You'd never believe it. Such random things.'

'Like what?' asked Claire.

'Candles, flowers, a lamp . . . a picture of a dragon.'

'A *dragon?*' Claire laughed and quickly said, 'Sorry, I'm not laughing but that's insane. Have you any idea who's doing it?'

'No, none,' lied Grace.

'All at once or——?'

'One each day for the last week.'

'Don't you have a house alarm?'

'No,' sighed Grace. 'I called to get one fitted but they're booked up.'

'Can't you set some cameras up to capture who it is?' asked Claire.

'I wanted to, but how? You need professionals to do that. Plus, I'm not sure they run on batteries.'

'What does Riley think? Have you called the police?'

At his mention, Grace's heart hurt. 'He's as baffled as me. And yes, the police came the other day, said we'd get a crime number, that someone would brush for prints, but we've heard nothing. I tried calling again yesterday but there was no answer. I know how busy they are, how many are in much more urgent need, but if anything is left again, I'm going to the station in person. What if it escalates? What if this person does something . . . *worse?*'

'Absolutely,' agreed Claire. 'There's that bloody Feather Man still on the loose, isn't there? Do you think it could be him?'

Grace felt sick; saw again the shadowy figure in her room last night. 'I thought of it, but it's nothing like that . . . *is it?*'

'I suppose not. He broke into a house in Selby the other night. Didn't hurt the poor woman this time, thank God. He just left his usual feather . . . oh, and a note.'

Grace froze. 'A note? What did it say?' She had seen another newspaper article in the staff changing room earlier but ignored it, knowing it might only stir up more fears.

'They never said. Why?'

Grace ignored the question.

'Selby you said?'

'Yes.'

This meant he really wasn't sticking with Leeds now. She needed to find out what the note had said. But how? PC Littlewood? He likely wouldn't share such information.

'Do you want me to come to the police with you?' asked Claire.

'No, it's fine, honestly.'

'Riley'll come, won't he?'

'Yes,' said Grace softly.

'I bet they're busy.'

'Who?' Grace was distracted, still thinking of the Feather Man leaving a note. She thought again of the one about *burn me and I will fire*, and Riley linking it to what he had done to those poor women.

'The police,' said Claire. 'They've got more crime to deal with now, and that Fight For the Light protest the other night – it got a bit out of hand.'

Grace nodded. 'So busy,' she repeated softly.

Claire looked at the time. 'We should get back.'

'I know.'

Grace suddenly felt exhausted. Wanted it to be home time, even though it would be dark, and she hadn't prepared. She would have to eat soup for supper, drink black tea boiled in a pan, go to bed alone, cold.

They returned to their duties. The rest of the shift was without incident, but inside Grace's head there were plenty; she saw a masked man climbing into her bedroom window, leaving a feather and a note on her pillow while she slept.

It was hard to concentrate.

On an afternoon coffee break, she looked again at Riley's message. She had been too busy to respond, was glad this had delayed her; he made her wait, let him stew. She began typing and then deleted it. He'd suggested they talk tomorrow. What else was there to say until then?

Let him worry as she'd had to.

★ ★ ★

At twenty-five past eight Grace loitered in the safety of the hospice hallway lighting, looking out into the night, afraid to join it.

The clear sky beheld a thousand stars, a midnight blue carpet that a child had dropped glitter on during a Christmas card-making session. Grace felt insignificant at their magnitude. The universe didn't care about a government scheme to 'save the planet'. It didn't care about who was cold and who was alone and who was hungry.

It didn't care that she was terrified.

She set off, walking briskly. If someone knew where she lived, then surely, they knew where she worked too. What if they were watching? Following. She ran then, into her street, bumped into a man, screamed in his face.

'It's me, Martin,' he cried.

Stacey and Jack's dad.

'Sorry,' she said, out of breath. 'I didn't see you.'

'It's a bloody nightmare, isn't it?' he said. 'Night Watch duty. God knows how the others lasted, but I've had to work all day and I have to go in tomorrow. The government didn't think of that, did they, when they expected us to do the job of police officers? Didn't get much sleep either cos our Stacey has a terrible cough.'

'Oh, no, bless her. So much of it about with this freezing weather.'

'The house is arctic after eight. We can't get warm. My mum's in there with the kids now but I fear she'll be an icicle when I get back in the morning. I had to tell her off though for putting the gas oven on to keep Stacey and Jack warm.'

'Why?' asked Grace, confused.

'That poor old dear in Manchester died, didn't she? It was on the news. Had her gas oven on all night and ended up dying of carbon monoxide poisoning. It's been happening a lot. People desperate for warmth, especially the elderly.'

Grace thought immediately of her mum; she must check *she* hadn't done that. Gas hob in mind, she asked, 'Can I make you a flask of warm soup? Do anything for Stacey?'

'Nah, don't worry, she's a sturdy little one.'

'Give her my love.' Grace felt a pang of concern that she was ill during this cruel season.

'I will.'

Turning to go up her path, she stopped, said, 'Would you keep an eye on the house tonight?' Then she regretted it, knowing Martin might ask why.

But he didn't; perhaps he thought she was just an overly worried woman. 'Of course,' he said. 'Don't you worry about a thing. I'm here.'

She frowned. Familiar words. *I'm here.* One of the notes.

Burying her paranoia, she unlocked the door, glancing up at the opposite window. Curtains shut, no Stacey. Probably in bed, after all it must be nine o'clock, and she'd been unwell. Still the shape of the vase and flower; a tiny beacon of hope.

There was no welcome with a cold, dark house; it gave a deathly hug. Fumbling around, heart pounding, Grace knocked something over. Damn. She felt about in the gloom – those bloody red roses left that morning. She made her way into the living room – speaking aloud to self-comfort, *It'll be OK, it'll be OK, Martin is outside* – found the camping lamp on the hearth and switched it on.

She held it to her chest, absorbing its glimmer.

This was it. Just her. Alone in the house. All night.

You used to do it.

But that had been as a single mum, and Jamie had been some solace, a warm body, another soul. And there hadn't been all of this going on.

Still in her coat and scarf, she took the lamp into the kitchen, opened a tin of soup, and warmed it on the hob. While it bubbled, she messaged her mum quickly, warned her not to use the gas oven for warmth if she had been.

Then she stood at the back door. She knew now this was how the intruder had got in. She needed a chain on it. Maybe tomorrow she could buy one, fit it herself. For now, despite its failure, she pushed the key into the lock. Maybe they wouldn't get lucky pushing it out a second time.

To save washing extra dishes with cold water, she took the pan and a spoon and the lamp upstairs, and climbed into the icy bed to eat her soup there. She had no heart to watch anything on her phone, no mind for her Kindle, so when she was done, she cleaned her teeth and lay down, pulling the duvet up to her nose the way a child does to ward off the monsters. Then she got up and dragged the wooden drawers in front of the door; they might get in, but they wouldn't get in *here*.

The night settled with her, oppressive, too close, too clingy.

She prayed for the lamp to last.

She prayed for the back-door key to stay in place.

She prayed for the morning to come faster.

She prayed for sleep.

By a miracle, it came.

She dreamt of the *incident*. She was back there, more alone and afraid than she had ever been before. When you've been in the dark that long, your sense of time evaporates and the solitude is utterly unbearable. That's what gets you the most. In that moment, you call for the ones you love. You plead for them to come. Sometimes, in these dreams, *he* did, and Grace escaped, returning to the light.

This time his voice united with the shrill cries of cruel children.

Never let her out, never let her out, never let her out.

Why was her dad willing her to stay in that terrible place?

She screamed and screamed until her throat was fire.

Woke with those cries lodged in her throat. Thanked God the sun was crawling up over the distant rooftops. It must be seven. The heating kicked in; she listened to the clicking radiators before braving the house. Gratitude for that warmth was primal – she had been cold in her single parent days, wearing a coat in the house in

December while Jamie was cosy at school, to save money on the bills.

After pushing the wooden drawers back into their place, Grace went downstairs, mindful of her surroundings, studying every picture, windowsill and corner, expecting the unexpected.

In the hallway, the red roses were scattered across the rug, a water patch surrounding them. In the kitchen, nothing out of place. She made coffee and took it into the living room. As far as she could see, everything was as she had left it yesterday. She switched the TV on to a debate between two politicians and a teacher who was describing how Lights Out had affected her children. Many arrived at school cold and miserable, and there had been more coughing in the classrooms, which meant mood was low, and concentration was zero.

At the thought of their red noses, Grace felt morose. It was Dickensian.

Then she saw it.

She had been distracted by the screen, not looked beyond. In the corner, a tiny pink object. She approached, the way you might a spider. It was a crystal. Possibly a rose quartz. Lovely in any other circumstance except this one. And beneath, a note.

Tiny, but powerful.
Love,
The Night.

Grace leaned behind the TV, picked the crystal up, hurled it at the wall. It remained intact: infuriating. She didn't care about keeping it as evidence or for fingerprinting. She tried again. Still intact.

'Fuck you,' she cried. 'Who *are* you? *Why me?*'

She saw a flash of pink, a small wink; a memory; a gift. From Steve. A thin, gold ring with a rose quartz at its centre. Tiny, but powerful. Too big, having to be altered, thrown back at him as he left.

That was it; she was messaging him.

It *must* be him. Who else could it be?

And then she was going to the police station. If they wouldn't come to her, she would go to them directly. She couldn't let them ignore her anymore.

Tonight I feel different. I'm not sure what it is. I almost didn't come to the house. I almost turned and went home on the approach. But then I remembered why I'm here, at the back door, shivering despite my heavy night attire. I remembered who I am. What I'm here for.

I'm here. I'm here.

And I went inside.

I've been hearing my mother's voice all day.

I wanted to scream.

Coming here silences her.

Coming here is all I have.

I'm glad I came. Now, to begin . . .

NIGHT NINE

24

A Raw Response

Unable to destroy the crystal, Grace turned her rage on the fish-bowl. She plunged a hand into it, grabbed the blue-grey fish, carried it – flipping and flopping wildly – to the kitchen bin, threw it in, and slammed the lid shut. A moment later, regret. It was a living creature. She retrieved it, speaking soothingly to the weakly flapping fish, and hurried it back to the bowl. Sadly, it was too late.

Her phone rang. Riley's name flashed.

She found herself sliding the green icon, sniffing back tears.

'Hello?' A question, clearly gauging her mood.

'I'm *here*,' she shouted, angry.

'Oh.' Meek now. 'OK. How are you?'

'How do you expect?' she cried. Adrenalin still coursed through her veins. 'You leave in the middle of the night, no explanation, after ten years, and you think I'd be *OK*?'

'No, of course not. I . . . I had to . . .'

'I know, you wanted *space*.' Sarcasm now.

'It all got too much,' he sighed.

'What did? I don't understand.'

'Your anxiety, pressures at work, the house renovations . . .'

'So you abandon it all.' Grace could barely get the words out in her rage; she was appalled. 'Leave me in a house that someone is breaking into. Can't you see how selfish you're being?'

'I wasn't thinking straight. Look, I'm sorry for what I said about Jamie.' Riley paused. 'Has anything else been left?'

'Yes,' snapped Grace. 'I'm surprised you didn't trip over the red roses in the hallway when you *sneaked* out yesterday morning.'

'I didn't see anything. It was dark.' He paused. 'And today?'

'A crystal. And another note.' She paused, tried to calm herself down. 'When you said I mentioned once that my dad wrote me little notes . . . what exactly did I tell you?'

'Oh, I can't remember now.'

'Well, that's not an acceptable response. I need to know,' cried Grace. The whole thing was horrible and she didn't need Riley being vague, not when he had buggered off leaving her here.

'Maybe I got it wrong. Maybe you were just drunk.'

'Did I tell you what he wrote in them?' pleaded Grace.

'I can't remember!'

'Well, the blue-grey fish is dead,' she spat, not sure why she needed to say that now.

'You *killed* Angelina?' Riley was teasing but Grace wasn't even slightly amused.

'It was an accident.'

'What are you going to do?' he asked.

'What can I do? It's *gone*.' Grace stood at the window, watching the day awaken, curtains opening, cars starting up. Tears welled now the anger had subsided a little.

'I mean about the crystal and the note.'

'What am *I* going to do?' she cried. 'Why is it all on *me*?'

'I meant, what are you going to do today? Want me to call the police again?'

'Well that's very big of you, of course, thank goodness for *you*,' Grace spat back, her tone dripping with sarcasm. 'No, I'm going to the station this morning. This can't go on.'

'Well, is there evidence of a break-in?' he asked. 'The doors, windows?'

'They're getting in the back door.' Grace went there – the key was on the mat again. 'I put the key in the lock but they've pushed it out.' She paused, suddenly feeling vulnerable. She was tired. She wanted to lean on her husband, she wanted him to be there for her, despite all he had done. 'Will you come to the station with me? Are you coming home?'

Silence.

After a moment, quietly, Riley said, 'Not today, Grace.'

When? she wanted to ask, but pride muted her. What had gone so wrong? *Call me Amazing*, she wanted to say. *Where has my Riley gone, the man whose familiar, warm smell has sustained me all these years?*

'Not today,' she repeated.

'We'll talk tomorrow,' he said.

'I'm supposed to be grateful for that?'

'I'm at work, but I said I'd call, and I did.'

'Apologies for disrupting your day,' snapped Grace.

She hung up, returned to the living room.

Emotions fought for dominance; sadness at this new solitude, rage at his indifference, and fear of what another night might bring battled until the victor was sadness. She watched the dead blue-grey fish floating in the bowl, only moving when Jennifer passed, resurrected in her watery wake.

Grace got a plastic sandwich bag from the kitchen drawer and put the blue-grey fish inside. It deserved some sort of send-off. She would free it into the River Humber after she had been to the police station. She put the sandwich bag next to the crystal and the latest note from the night in her bag and went for a shower.

When she arrived at the red-brick police station building surrounded by chipped metal railings, her mum rang. Grace declined the call; it would have to wait.

Inside, the receptionist sat behind an ugly, purpose-built desk with a glass window protecting her from visitors. A name badge announced her as Kate Rawlings, and a telephone headset flattened her frizzy hair. She was speaking to someone as Grace approached, trying to calm them down. She hung up, took a breath and immediately the phone started again. She ignored it, perhaps happier to deal with a human.

'Can I help?'

'Could I speak to PC Littlewood? He came to our house a few days ago. We've had some break-ins. He said someone would brush for prints and that we'd get a crime number, but no one has been.'

'Let me see if I can find him for you. What's the name please?'

'Grace O'Neill. Tell him that we've had another break-in. Multiple break-ins, actually.'

Kate nodded, disappeared through a door. Grace took one of the five uncomfortable plastic chairs beneath a busy noticeboard, in a row like they were queueing for the nearby toilet. A man entered, slight but somehow solid too, hair windswept; he approached the counter without seeing her. He waited, leaned closer to the glass to look behind it, and then waited some more, running a nervous hand through his hair.

'She went somewhere,' said Grace.

He turned, clearly surprised to see someone. Opened his mouth but didn't seem to be able to speak.

'The receptionist, I mean,' Grace clarified, the man seeming so confused.

Maybe he was here to report a crime too, and it had affected him. Grace's heart melted. Maybe he was traumatised; he looked it.

'She was here a few minutes ago, she's gone to get someone.'

'Oh,' the man managed.

'I'm sure she'll be back any minute.'

'Oh,' he repeated again.

He loitered by the desk, looking then at the door, appearing not to know whether to stay or go. Then he sat, as far away from Grace as was possible, three chairs dividing them. Neither spoke for a while; he was clearly uncomfortable, fidgeting.

'Never a policeman when you need one, eh?' Grace hoped to ease the mood.

'No.'

'Or woman.'

'Sorry?' He finally looked at her; his eyes were soft blue, sad.

'Doesn't matter.'

'Oh.'

'I'm here about a break-in – a few actually.' Grace wondered if she might make the man feel better if she shared it, in case he'd experienced it too.

'Oh.' He looked distressed; like he *had* been through the same.

She didn't want to push, so just said, 'It's hard . . . unsettling.'

'You don't deserve that.'

'No one does, do they?'

'No, they don't,' he said, earnestly.

'Is that why you're here? There've been a few since the switch off.'

'It's . . . I . . .' Abruptly, he stood and began pacing, stopping to look at the noticeboard, then the desk, and then walking back again. Grace watched, fascinated. It was as though he had forgotten she was there.

'These waiting areas are never very enticing, are they?' he said suddenly.

'I suppose not,' she agreed. 'They're not exactly hotel foyers. Some flowers and a cushion or two might be nice.'

'I'm sorry.' He stopped in his tracks.

'For what?'

'This. Me. I pace when I'm . . . I pace.'

'No need to be sorry,' said Grace. 'We all have our thing. I guess I . . . I'm . . . I don't like . . .'

Why was she almost telling a stranger that she was terrified of the dark? Before she could finish the sentence, her phone rang again. Rummaging in her bag, she dropped it; half the contents scattered across the tiled floor. She knelt to retrieve them, grabbing tampons and keys and the crystal, cursing, finally finding her phone.

It had been her mother. Too late.

The man approached, cautious. He knelt down opposite Grace. Studied the sandwich bag in her hand.

'It's a dead fish,' she said, flustered, knowing she must seem crazy to have such a thing in her bag.

He stared at it.

She shook her head, felt immense sadness again. 'It's . . . *she's* Angelina.'

'Angelina?'

'*I* didn't call her that. My husband did.' Grace touched the sandwich bag. 'I killed her. I didn't mean to. I feel terrible now.'

'Will you get another?' The man looked anxious, or maybe his expression was one of grief, she couldn't be sure. Maybe he had lost a pet, was remembering that pain, empathising.

'She's not part of the family,' said Grace. 'It's a long story.'

'I love long stories. What's she doing in your bag?'

'I . . . no, you'll laugh.'

'Try me.'

'I'm going to put her in the Humber. Have a little send-off ceremony. Silly, I know. Maybe I shouldn't bother. I . . .' Grace shook her head. 'But it's not really Angelina I'm sad about.'

'It's never about anything that simple.' His face softened with sympathy. 'You don't deserve to be sad.'

'How do you know I don't?' Grace laughed. 'I could be a psychopath who deserves all the misery on earth.'

The man smiled, slightly, and it was lovely. 'I mean, no one deserves to be sad.'

'I guess.' Grace's eyes teared up again; this was ridiculous – she must be hormonal, on top of everything else. 'Sorry, it's been a rough few weeks. If someone had told me two weeks ago I'd go to a police station with a dead fish in my bag . . .'

'I don't like police stations.'

'Must've taken a lot for you to come then. So were you broken into as well?'

He hesitated. 'It's . . . more . . . *complicated.*'

'Isn't it always? Definitely with marriage.' Why had she said that? It was like when she had almost opened up about her fear of the dark – the words arrived neatly in her mouth, ready to march out. 'Sorry. We're . . . me and my husband . . . we're having some problems.' Her knees began to ache now from kneeling on the cold floor, but she feared that this odd, intimate moment of confession with a total stranger would end if she stood. 'I don't know why I'm telling you this.'

'I bet it wasn't your fault.' He studied her, eyes kind.

'What wasn't?'

'The problems in your marriage.'

'I could say that, in anger. But aren't we all a bit at fault? I'm not easy, I have my issues. Maybe I could've been a better wife.'

'I bet you're a wonderful wife.' He spoke without looking at her.

Grace had to swallow in order to respond; the emotion at having this stranger tell her just what she needed to hear right now was intense. 'Maybe not,' she managed.

Finally, she stood, her knees unable to remain in that position.

She sat back down. The man did too, one seat closer as though he was more reassured now. For a brief moment, Grace hoped the receptionist wouldn't come back; it was good to talk to someone who had no idea about her life, no judgement. Friends were great, but they came to your confessions with preconceived ideas and knowledge, with old war wounds that the relationship might have caused, and with words they knew you needed to hear. This man sat here with none of that. With nothing but a raw response.

'Are you married?' she asked.

He seemed to think about it, studying his upturned palms as though he was reading the lines there to determine the answer. 'No.'

'Do you have a partner?'

'Yes. *No.*'

'You're not sure?' She smiled.

He looked at her. 'It's complicated.'

She nodded. 'An overused word, but one that often applies.'

The man listened intently and then spoke so quietly that Grace at first wasn't sure what he had said; it took her brain a moment to decipher the rhythm of the words. 'I dread going home.'

She didn't know how to respond. He sounded desperately unhappy.

And yet she knew this feeling too.

She knew that a cold, empty house waited, one that needed renovating still, that had items in it she didn't want. But he likely meant to an unhappy partnership; maybe difficult children or huge debts.

'Me too,' she said.

He nodded.

'What is it you dread about going home?' she asked softly.

'I dread what will b—'

Kate returned to the desk. 'Sorry I was so long – I couldn't find PC Littlewood. I think he must have left the building.'

Grace was annoyed at the interruption to their conversation. The man now hunched over again, looked at the floor.

'Can anyone else help?' asked Kate.

'No, he knows about it.' Grace approached the desk. 'He saw the scene, and I don't want to have to explain everything to someone else.' She hadn't told him about the notes, and she needed to. Needed to ask if it was true that the Feather Man had also left one in a house. 'Can he call me as soon as he's back?'

'I'll ask him to.' Kate spotted the man, then, still in his seat. 'Can I help you?'

He came to the desk. 'It's . . .' he tried.

Grace realised that he might want some privacy; whatever had happened to him might need an audience of one. 'Nice meeting you,' she said, hoping to catch his eye. But disappointingly, he refused to look at her.

When she got to the door, she looked back. He still hadn't spoken. Kate must have been well trained because she waited.

Grace realised as she walked home that she hadn't even asked his name.

25

Solace in the Samaritans

Tom still hated going home.

He had been afraid of what he would find there but now he dreaded seeing what wasn't there: Harper. It had been three days since she left, taking most of her clothes and many of the things Tom had always thought were his. Three days since his last session of solitary relationship counselling with Carole. Harper had insisted she was not going back to her lover, that she wanted what she'd never had: herself.

Now, Tom leaned against the metal railings outside the police station, unsure what to do next. He had been in there for twenty minutes, but when it was finally his turn to speak to the receptionist, he had been mute. The many words he had been able to find at Carole's sessions dried up.

Eventually he managed, 'I don't know where to start . . .'

'How about with a name,' the receptionist had said.

'Mine? Oh. Yes. Tom.'

'Tom?' She was after a surname. When he didn't respond, she said, 'And do you wish to report a crime?'

'Yes.'

'Would you like to give your statement more privately? I can arrange for a room if there's one free, and—'

'A *room*? I don't want to go into a room.'

And then he had come outside.

Tom had gone to report the break-ins but found he couldn't. He didn't trust the police. As a child, he had witnessed his mother asking for their help each time Tom's father left her black and blue. No one ever came, nothing ever changed.

How would they help him now?

What would they do? The only people who listened to Tom's mum had been the Samaritans.

A flashback overwhelmed him; he was sitting at the top of the stairs, frozen because the meter had run out again, his mum's dressing gown on because it was the warmest in the house, listening to her sob in the hallway below as she unburdened her sad tale with a listener on the end of the telephone. Tom's father was at the pub – they were the clichéd kitchen-sink drama couple, a worn-down woman stuck at home, dreading drunken footsteps on the garden path, while their little boy cowered under the covers upstairs each night. That boy became a restless adult who paced, found safety in the darkness that had embraced him when he needed it, and did everything he could to make his girlfriend happy.

And now, despite that, that woman had gone.

A light-bulb moment then.

Maybe *they* could help: the Samaritans.

Yes.

Tom knew where the building was. He'd passed it many times coming home from the cemetery, a lanky, white-terraced building with an unkempt garden, the infamous green words on a sign above two of the long windows. But they must be overwhelmed now. They wouldn't want him there, whining about his life.

Tom had seen on the local news that Lights Out meant the place shut now at eight p.m. and those who needed to call late at night – people who were lonely, cold and scared – were all the more desperate. But it was daytime now; it was open. Tom knew the Samaritans did face-to-face chats because a workmate at the cemetery had been there following his divorce, but whether you could just turn up, he wasn't sure.

He drove there anyway. Sat in the car outside the building, feet twitching because he couldn't pace. The place didn't look welcoming with its dark windows, like stretched, hellish eyes, but he parked around the corner, walked up the uneven path to the midnight-blue door, pressed the buzzer, and waited.

'Samaritans, how can we help?' came a broken-up response after so long that Tom had been about to leave.

'Oh.' He didn't know what to say. He was tempted to turn and run but something rooted his usually twitchy feet to the stone step. 'I didn't book or anything.'

'Would you like to speak to one of our volunteers?'

'Yes. No. *Yes.*' He got so anxious when he thought about opening up.

'I'll come down to you.'

After two minutes the door opened and a young man in dungarees with long blond hair knotted at the back of his head smiled warmly. Sharply contrasting this welcome, the smell of damp emanated from a dank hallway that seemed to stretch for miles into nowhere behind him; thinly carpeted stairs ascended into an unseen place.

'People usually book an appointment,' he said, 'but we never turn anyone away.'

'Is it OK if I already tried relationship counselling?' asked Tom. 'It was silly because I went alone, and it wasn't really for me, but does that mean I can't speak to you?'

'We see everyone. Come in.'

Tom followed him inside.

'Our face-to-face room is up here.' He led the way up the stairs and onto a large landing, off which were five doors; one was open and showed a dated, well-used kitchen and another opened onto a toilet with a broken seat. Beyond a third door, Tom heard a chorus of voices rising and falling. That must be the telephone room. That must be where they listened to the helpless, the desperate, the broken.

His mum.

'Just in here,' said the blond man, opening a different door onto a small room with two chairs set close to one another, clearly to encourage intimate conversation. It wasn't unlike Carole's room in that way, but there must be less funding here because the pale blue walls were chipped and the coffee table – upon which a box of tissues sat – was obviously a refugee from some even sadder place. 'I won't be a moment.'

Tom was left alone.

He stared at the chairs, unable to sit. A muffled conversation in the hallway pulled him back to the door, but he only caught the words *walk-in* and *don't mind* and *back soon*. On the wall, a placard read: *Every seven seconds, we respond to a call for help. No judgement. No pressure. We're here for anyone who needs someone.* He wondered how often the calls came now, following the switch off. Maybe he should leave. Others had bigger problems, and he was abusing this system.

Too late: the blond man returned with a folder – always the folder – and smiled. 'I'm Karl,' he said. 'Please, sit.'

Tom forced himself to take one of the chairs, and Karl took the other one. 'Thank you, I'm Tom.' He had occasionally found himself attracted to men, not as much as he was to women, but there was something, a quivering warmth, a curiosity. Karl had an ease in his own body that Tom didn't, so maybe it was envy rather than attraction. In women Tom found comfort, safety, passion; with a man he imagined fight. And that scared him. That was down to his father, he knew it.

'Everything you tell me is confidential,' said Karl, kindly. 'I'm not here to give advice, or make suggestions, or judge – only to listen, and to encourage you to talk about your feelings.'

Tom nodded.

'Take all the time you need.'

Tom nodded.

'Would you say you're feeling suicidal?' asked Karl.

'Where did that come from?' Was that the state Tom looked in? He had made more of an effort this morning, knowing how dishevelled he'd been that last day with Carole, when Harper left. 'Should I be?'

Was that what was required to be here?

'I'm sorry,' said Karl, ruffled now, the quiet ease disturbed. 'It's a question we ask. I maybe rushed it, I've only been here three weeks, I'm still—'

'Oh, that's OK.' Now Tom felt bad. This poor man was new and here was Tom upsetting him. He returned to the chair, determined to help Karl back to his previous calm. He should give him something, make him feel he was doing a great job. 'My partner has gone,' he admitted.

Karl nodded.

Tom found he could fill that space.

'It was three days ago. She'd had an affair, though she insists it's over and that isn't why she left me. Weirdly, I believe her. Maybe I'm just a fool.' Tom paused. It was odd to have someone simply listen, without interruption and without judgement clouding their face. This must have been why his mum found solace in the Samaritans. 'But now . . . I know she went back to him.' Tom paused. 'Initially, the affair lasted a month. The night I . . .'

Karl still didn't speak. Somehow, it was more encouraging than Carole's continuous questioning had been.

'The night I caught her, I'd been out under the stars,' continued Tom. 'My favourite place in the world.'

He remembered running outside when his parents' fights got too much, finding consolation in the heavens above, in the hug of the shadows. How could anyone be afraid of the dark when the horrible things you could see in the light were far worse?

'On a clear night you can see an ever-changing display of fascinating objects, you know,' he explained, 'from stars and constellations to bright planets, often the moon, and sometimes special events like meteor showers. You don't even need special equipment to see it, although a sky map can be useful, and good binoculars help too.' Tom paused, expecting Karl to ask him to get back to the affair, but he just listened. 'Anyway, that night I went into the street for a more panoramic view. Harper's car was parked at the top of the street, which I thought odd because she always parked outside the house if my car was on the drive. Something – an instinct maybe – had me approach the car on the opposite side of the road so she wouldn't see me.'

Tom stood.

Karl looked surprised. 'Do you need to leave?'

'Can I walk around a bit? I know I'm strange, I didn't mean to alarm you.'

'Of course.' Karl looked relieved now.

The room was small, so Tom walked around the chairs. 'She was in the car with a man,' he said. 'At first I thought, well, he's probably just a friend I haven't met before and she's given him a lift. She'd been out with her mates, you see. But then . . .'

Karl waited.

'Then they kissed. Properly, you know.' Tom circled the chairs faster; he saw it now, felt again the pain he had experienced seeing Harper lean in and hold this man's face as she devoured him; that was the word that had felt like an apt description.

'How did it make you feel?' asked Karl.

'Insignificant.'

Karl nodded.

'Like a white dwarf.'

Karl frowned.

'Those are stars that are very, very small, and they emit a lot of their light in the ultraviolet part of the spectrum so they can be hard to see in our skies.'

'OK.'

Tom stopped by his chair. 'When Harper went out four nights after that, I followed her. She was all dressed up, said she was meeting her friend Briony. She walked, which she doesn't usually, and I kept far back, trailed her quietly. I found it so easy. I'm kind of invisible, you see. At least, I feel that way at times. Anyway, after we had walked for about half an hour, she went into a house. The man who opened the door was the one in the car.' Tom sat down. 'And I knew. It wasn't a one-off. It was an affair.'

'How did you feel?' asked Karl again. Tom realised that must be part of the training. To ask how a person felt.

'Defeated.'

'OK.'

'Later I was angry. How *could* she? Then sad. I felt a whole range of emotions.'

'Very understandable.'

'I sat in the house and watched her go out a few more times in the following weeks, all dressed up again, saying she was meeting this friend or that friend. Then, after a few weeks, I told her I knew. She didn't deny it.' Tom shook his head. 'But that's not really it,' he said. 'It's what's been happening since.'

'Tell me more about that,' said Karl. Tom wondered if the volunteers had a book of specific prompts that they had to memorise.

'I'm scared it's going to happen again tonight,' said Tom.

'The affair?' asked Karl, despite himself.

'That fear's a given. But, no, I mean . . .'

Why was this so hard to talk about? He had just shared the pain of having his heart broken. Nothing had been worse than that since witnessing his father attacking his mum, though escape from those scenes eventually came when his father died of a sudden heart attack. No, sharing what had been happening recently, Tom feared not being taken seriously.

'If it's not the affair, what are you scared is going to happen again?' Despite his previous demeanour, Karl looked concerned.

'I'm afraid of being at home alone and that . . .'

'Take all the time you need, Tom.'

'Do you know what dragons represent?' he asked.

'Um . . . I need some context.'

'If you found one, in your home too.'

'An actual dragon?' Karl's face was a picture. 'Aren't they mythological?'

'No, sorry . . . I didn't mean a real creature, I mean, say, a piece of art that depicted one.'

174

'Um . . . just randomly in my house?'

'Yes. Hanging on the wall.'

'I guess I'd be freaked out,' admitted Karl. 'I'd wonder why. How?'

'And how about if you found red roses?'

'Red roses? I guess it depends. Roses are a nice gift, but if some-one had put them in my house without me knowing, I'd find that odd.' Karl seemed to remember that this was Tom's session. 'Has this happened to you?' he asked.

'I went to the police about it but I . . . there's a history with them. I couldn't.'

'Can you tell me then?'

'Will you take me seriously?' asked Tom.

'I will.'

'It's be—'

Karl's face drained of colour, so suddenly that Tom stopped speaking.

'Are you OK?' He leaned towards him.

'I . . . just . . .' Karl's words fell clumsily out of his mouth. He slumped forward in the chair, and Tom leapt up to stop him falling out of it.

'Help,' he cried, not wanting to let go of Karl in case he fell, hit his head.

In the end Tom had to abandon him and go onto the landing. He knocked on the door that sounded like it led to the phone room. After a moment, a young woman opened it, face full of query.

'It's Karl,' said Tom. 'He doesn't seem well at all.'

'Oh, he's diabetic.' She hurried to the kitchen and grabbed a can of Coke from the fridge, and then went into the small room. 'Come on, Karl,' she said briskly, 'you need to drink this.' He shook his head at first, but the woman clearly knew how to deal with his hypo and held the can firmly to his mouth. He shook his head a few times but then drank. Tom felt useless, in the way. 'He'll need twenty minutes to feel OK again,' the woman said to him.

'I think I'll . . .' Tom didn't even finish.

'It's been awful,' she said. 'Because Karl depends on a fridge for his medication, and this bloody government haven't given him a battery-operated one, his insulin went off and now his blood sugars are all over the place. Poor, poor, Karl. Come on, finish your Coke.'

While she spoke, Tom quietly left the room, headed back down the stairs, and departed the building. He sat in his car for a few minutes. The sky was beginning to darken, just at its boundaries, a crisp sheet of dark-blue paper burning at the edges. His favourite time of day. Tonight would be the ninth Lights Out, his fourth one alone.

He thought about her then.

Not Harper. He was tired of thinking about her, of listening for the door, hoping she had changed her mind, of checking for new messages, of starting to type a desperate plea to her and then deleting it.

No, he thought about the woman at the police station; about her sad face. The way she had kneeled for so long like a small child saying her prayers. The way she spoke about the fish called Angelina.

Other people were hurting too.

26

The Shadow Father

The River Humber was at its most majestic.

Often ugly brown due to sandbanks and sewage, today it reflected a brief blue sky and appeared like an ocean. The tide was far out so Grace walked down the stony, coarse beach to the water's edge where the chill stole her breath. She stood on a large slab rock to avoid sinking into the mud, and balanced carefully to bend down and empty Angelina into the estuary. The fish disappeared, sucked away by the perilous currents of this most dangerous river.

Grace couldn't help but think of the four women who had walked into its vicious swirl, hand in hand, in the middle of the night, when it would have been as chill as an ice queen. She waited a while, not just mourning the little fish, but those four victims of the dark.

Then she walked along the river, the same path she had been on when she first bumped into Riley. She saw him, younger, surprised, back then. Saw them collide. Her heart ached. Crisp leaves tickled by the river breeze brought her back to the present.

It was time to go home.

Once home, Grace went on Facebook and found Steve's profile again.

Hesitantly, she typed:

I have no choice but to message you out of the blue – some strange things have been happening to me and I need to know that it has nothing to do with you.

She pressed send. Regret, immediately. Panic. Could she undo what she had done? No. Too late. It was sent.

Late afternoon, the countdown to darkness began. It was customary now, a familiar dread that had triggers – the subtle change in the light outside, the slight drop in temperature, and the lengthening of shadows. Grace sent a message to her mum saying it had been a busy day, she had been to the police station, and had heard from Riley; she knew this would cheer her up, though Grace was conflicted about what she wanted now.

His absence forced her to look at life in a different way. With the rug pulled away, her feet got used to a colder floor. She was angry, couldn't stop replaying the image of him moving around quietly in the night, gathering his stuff together, creeping away while she slept; the ultimate act of cowardice.

Just as her father had done.

She saw him then, a dark shape, hunched over, pulling drawers from cabinets, wrenching wardrobe doors open, hair wild, eyes wilder. Fear was rarely the emotion that swirled around him; laughter, yes, the warmth of story-sharing, yes, safety, yes. But this memory evoked terror.

You remember the shadow father, whispered adult Grace.

No, I don't want to, whispered Maisie.

What had been happening then?

Why did the image dissolve the more she tried to look at it?

It had been later on, when Grace was older, close to the time he left, she was sure. If she pictured herself younger than about nine, he was laughing, cheeks wrinkled, eyes bright; if she pictured herself aged ten, that man still existed, but was joined by a darker twin who confused and scared her.

When had he left little notes around the house?

When had that been?

Was it even true that he had?

★　　★　　★

178

At four twenty Grace was at the window. No matter how she tried to be positive, anxiety always surged. Today, it was the heaviest of blankets. Today she feared she wouldn't see the morning again. It was irrational but as real to her as shivers after being submerged in icy water.

She looked up at the window opposite for her hope: young Stacey. She was there, looking right at Grace in that moment. It felt like a sign. She waved and Stacey waved back, grin visible. Obviously she was in good spirits, despite being ill. And the dusky pink flower – perhaps wilting, it was hard to tell from this distance – was still in the vase.

Grace closed the curtains.

She hurried around the house, on autopilot, *flick, lit.*

The uninvited lamp was the final stop on the illumination tour. She paused, unsure about letting it shine. It could have belonged to anyone – it could have been in hands that hurt or abused. *Steve.* He might have responded. She switched the uninvited lamp on and found her phone. The message icon at the top.

Steve: *Oh, look who it is. How are you?*

This wasn't what she wanted, nice chit-chat. She needed answers, and then she would block him.

Grace: *I'm only messaging because I need to know something. Do you ever come over to Hull?*

Steve: *No, but I could.*

Did she believe him?

Grace: *Were you in Hull last night?*

Steve: *No, but I can come tonight . . .*

She wondered if the restraining order she had taken out back then was even valid now. Was she breaking it by getting in touch after all this time? This had been a mistake. She closed the app and ignored further messages from him.

As eight o'clock approached, she did the slow switch off. The camping lamp's beam had become a familiar friend, one who steps up when you least expect them to. She went to the back door with it, key in hand, but what was the point? She inserted it anyway.

Upstairs, she cleaned her teeth, pushed the wooden drawers in front of the door, and tried to read her Kindle. The wind howled; every scraping branch and rattling bin had Grace reading the same line again and again. In the end, she lay down. Though this room was bright, knowing the others were shrouded in shadow had Grace whispering to herself, 'You're safe in here,' over and over.

But was she?

The dark had its own response: *Something terrible is going to happen when the lights go out.*

At three a.m. she was still awake.

A sound downstairs.

Someone was in the house.

The floorboard near the living-room door creaked. Heart pulsing, Grace waited. Were they coming up the stairs or going into the living room? What the hell was she going to do?

What if it was Riley?

No, he'd make himself known.

Another sound. The same creak. Had someone gone into the living room and come back out? What if she heard that fourth stair creak she knew well? Where would she go, what would she do? Who was on Night Watch duty? Maybe she could open the window, shout, try and climb out.

The same anger she had felt earlier at Riley creeping away in the night surged now – sudden rage at someone coming into her home, uninvited. Would she lie up here, useless and terrified if five-year-old Jamie was in the house? No. She would have fought to the death to protect him.

Before she could change her mind, she got up, shivering but determined, and approached the bedroom door. It would be noisy moving the drawers back to their spot, but she did it anyway. On the landing, she paused, listened.

'Who's there?' she called, voice shrill with nerves. 'I've got a weapon and I've called the police.'

No response. What had she expected?

Then, a familiar sound: the back door closing.

Grace raced downstairs, into the kitchen. No one there. The door locked again. Their key on the mat beneath.

She wasn't about to check for new items in the dark and hurried back upstairs, hands blue now, teeth chattering. It took an age to get warm again.

She opened her messages while she thawed out; ten more from Steve, the last one an hour ago. He asked if she missed him, if she thought about him, because he still did her. Was there a way to find his location, to know if he had been here tonight? She remembered Riley once saying you could trace anyone on such apps but she had no idea how. If she could work it out, she would know.

Grace tossed and turned the rest of the night.

When the sun finally kissed the walls, and the heating clicked on, she had barely slept for an hour. She went downstairs.

This time, she knew which room to look in.

The living room.

The floorboard squeaked as she entered.

At first she couldn't see anything new. Then she saw it. On the windowsill.

What the hell?

It was the photograph that had been removed from the frame on the stairway, the one that now contained a dragon. It was Riley and Grace at a work do, re-presented in a black ash frame. She moved closer. A love heart had been drawn around Grace's face in red sharpie. Such an amorous symbol but it chilled her to the bone. Why *her* face? Why nothing around Riley?

Then she saw the note, folded beneath.

She opened it.

I will protect you.
Love,
The Night.

All of the previous notes flashed before her eyes: *I'm watching over you; I'm here; Tiny, but powerful; I've got you in my sights.* Loving phrases when taken out of this context, sinister and unnerving when left by a stranger in the middle of the night.

Did the words hold clues? Was it the language of a lover?

Or the language of someone who wanted to take care of her?

Someone fatherly?

A *father?*

It's cold. But it won't stop me. I'm tired. But it won't stop me. They're not taking me seriously. But it won't stop me.

I'm here.

I'm here.

HULL LOCAL NEWS

Warm the Body Not the House Doesn't Work

Local plumber, Bob Snithely, warned that if a house isn't adequately heated during winter, it can cause problems for the residents, exacerbating issues with damp and mould. 'I don't care about government advice to warm the body not the house,' he said. 'It doesn't work.'

'In an average household,' he explained, 'the water vapour released into the air from bathing, cooking, washing, and even breathing is eighteen litres per day. When the heating is on, the air is warm and has a higher capacity to hold moisture. Cooler temperatures lead to the air holding less moisture, creating condensation on walls and windows.'

Plaster on walls then crumbles, wooden window frames rot, and electrical equipment can be damaged as the water causes corrosion on components.

Teacher, Sarah Giles, has noticed an increase in the number of children off school ill. 'Many don't get home until after six if their parents work,' she said. 'Then the heating is only on for an hour or so and the house doesn't get fully warm after being cold all day.'

Local hospital trusts warn that they expect a higher admission this winter of children with serious chest infections as a result.

NIGHT TEN

27

My Lid is Unscrewing

Grace called Riley. 'I'm not ringing about us,' she said before he could speak. 'I need to ask if you're absolutely sure you *don't* know who's doing this to us?'

'Doing what to us?' He sounded distracted.

'Leaving these fucking items!' She tripped over the fireplace corner. 'Last night I *heard* someone. I even came onto the landing, heard the back door close! And this morning, the picture that was on the stairs is on the living-room windowsill, and someone drew a red heart around me.' She slammed the frame face down.

'Shit,' Riley said quietly. 'You need to get the locks changed.'

'Thanks for that.' Sarcastic. 'I will.'

Why hadn't she? Life. Everything going on. But she needed to.

'Can't your mum come and stay so you're not alone?'

'My *mum*?' cried Grace. 'Have you heard yourself? How will it help to have an eighty-five-year-old woman with me, when my *husband* should be here?'

'Sorry I—'

'Do you know how to find someone's location on a Facebook message?'

'*What?*'

Grace was incensed now. 'Never mind. I'll work it out for myself. You enjoy your space, and I'll deal with all of this.' She hung up. 'Fuck,' she said to the room. '*Fuck.*' Anger was better than fear and she clung greedily to it.

She made coffee and stood and glared at the returned, defaced, photograph. In the daytime, it was easy to be outraged. The sun made everything safe. No one could hurt her while it shone. When it sank . . .

Grace remembered she was doing a night shift, which was some solace. But first, a long day to get through. She found the number for a locksmith and called them; just like with the house alarm fitters, they were fully booked for two weeks.

She made toast, sat on the sofa, feet curled beneath her. MUM flashed on the phone screen. She should answer, she had ignored a few calls.

'Sorry I didn't get back to you yesterday,' Grace said, mouth full.

'I wish you wouldn't eat on the phone, dear. It's crass.' She couldn't help but smile. Her mother's predictable response was a comfort. 'And I *never* use the gas oven for warmth.'

'*Sorry?*' Grace was confused.

'Your message. Telling me never to use it to stay warm. I'm not stupid, Grace, I've seen the news. And anyway, I'm a tough old boot. I can cope.' She paused. 'Is Riley back?'

'No,' admitted Grace.

'*No?*'

'I've spoken to him. He reckons he needs . . . *space.*'

'That's better than . . .'

'Disappearing and never coming back?'

Catherine didn't speak but Grace knew what she was thinking.

'Mum, I want to talk about my dad.' The words came out before Grace even knew they were there. Maybe they had been there for days. Maybe since the Lights Out scheme began. And maybe even more so since Riley had left.

'*Now?*' Catherine acted like Grace wanted to talk about bowel cancer.

'Not right now, but I need to. I don't think it's helping me that I can never express how I feel about what happened.'

Perhaps evoked by her mention of her father, violently, Grace remembered something.

She was ten, sitting on the stairs, open door blasting a gale around her ankles, billowing her thin, lace nightie. It began raining; water came in, splattering the tiled floor with glacial drops. Then her mum was there, dressing gown pulled tight around frail body. 'What are you *doing*?' she cried, slamming the door shut. 'The house is freezing. Isn't it bad enough that you leave the lights on in every room, now you're letting the heat escape. What on earth is *with* you?' Grace couldn't respond. Not only because her teeth were chattering ferociously, but because she wasn't allowed to say his name in case her mum got upset.

Dad.

The one she was waiting for that day. The one she wished would come home. The one she felt that if she kept the door open, he might walk through it again. She'd thought she'd seen him on the street the day before, had come home in tears.

But who would he be if he did return? Which dad?

The *other* one, the one who in Grace's later childhood washed his hands until they were red in steaming water, who stomped around the house, muttering strange phrases, hair wild. *Don't let them in, don't let them in, don't let them in.* Or the one she loved, knew, who still made up bedtime stories for her, and kept the light going.

Her mum's voice. Now. Back in the present. 'I'm sorry you feel you can't express yourself. But I was . . .'

'What?' Grace put her empty plate on the coffee table. Brad and Jennifer swam slowly as though they had just woken up.

'I was protecting you. Back then. I wanted us to make a new life together, make sure you knew I would never leave you like he did. So I never spoke about him again.' For the first time, Catherine sounded all of her eighty-five years. Grace felt desperately sad for them both, for the wife whose husband left, and the child whose father did. But wives can find new husbands. Children can't find another father. And Grace had constantly wondered what flaws *she* had that had sent hers packing. 'I put a lid on the whole thing and screwed it tightly shut,' finished Catherine.

189

'Well, my lid is unscrewing,' Grace said softly.

Catherine sighed. 'I find it hard to go back and look at it, now I've shut it off.'

'Look, you said we should do something this week. It's already Tuesday and I'm doing a night shift tonight but I could sleep in the morning and meet you in the afternoon?'

'I've got a rehearsal.'

'How about Thursday? I'm working the day shift Friday.'

'I'll juggle things.' Grace had to smile; her mum always made out she was making an extra effort to give up her time.

'Thursday then,' she said. 'Mum . . .'

'Yes?'

Grace suddenly wanted to make her mother feel better. 'I don't blame you for finding it hard to talk about my dad.'

Silence on the line.

'Let's talk on Thursday then,' she said, tired.

Catherine was brisk and business again. 'Will you pick me up and we go for lunch?'

A knock on the door then. 'I have to go,' said Grace.

'How did you get on with the police?' asked Catherine.

'I'll tell you when I see you.' Grace went to the door, opened it with the chain across. PC Littlewood. *Thank God.* 'Bye, Mum' she said. 'The police are here, I have to go.'

'I'm sorry no one got back to you,' he said, 'but I was just in the area. I have five minutes. My colleague said you came into the station. Has there been another break-in?'

'Yes. Come in.' He stepped over the threshold. 'Multiple, in fact. And some other items have been left. It's every night now. Every night since Lights Out started. I actually heard them last night. But by the time I tried to chase them, they'd gone. They're getting in through the back door.'

'Can you stay somewhere else?' he replied, ignoring what Grace thought were really the key issues on the matter. She didn't tell him that she refused to be pushed out of her house. 'Can you ask whoever's on Night Watch duty this evening to pay particular attention to your property, tell them what's gone on?'

Grace had no idea who it was tonight, but she felt helpless at the futility of it. People *had* been watching. Riley himself had been there one night; and she'd asked Martin to watch over the house. She wanted to scream at PC Littlewood – and would have done, if she hadn't thought this would get her nowhere.

Why wouldn't anyone take her seriously?

She realised it might be Riley's turn at some point and neighbours would want to know where he was. Hiding her true thoughts, she simply said, 'Is anyone coming to brush for prints then?'

'Hopefully this week.' He didn't sound convinced, remained in the hallway as though to make clear he wasn't stopping long. 'If it's any consolation, something similar happened elsewhere in the region.'

'What do you mean?' Grace's heart constricted.

'An . . . unusual break-in.'

Grace remembered the nervous man at the police station, his pacing and unkempt hair, his intense gaze. She took her plate into the kitchen. 'Did a man report it yesterday in person?' There might be others going through this, strange as it was. Didn't criminals in TV dramas often target more than one person? Would she feel better knowing she wasn't alone in this nightmare?

'I can't disclose that, I'm afraid. All I can recommend until we get back to your house again is that you get a good alarm system fitted and speak to your Night Watch volunteers.'

'I *have*,' sighed Grace. 'But this other break-in . . . how was it unusual?'

'I can't share that I'm afraid.'

'Have they caught that Feather Man yet?' she asked. When the PC didn't respond, she pushed with, 'I heard that he left a note with his white feather the other night. What if his note is connected to *my* notes?'

'*Your* notes? You've had notes?'

'Oh,' Grace said, 'yes. I meant to . . .'

PC Littlewood watched her. 'I'm afraid I can't talk about the Feather Man,' he said.

So he did *leave another note,* thought Grace.

'I understand your anxiety,' said PC Littlewood, 'and I will push for them to brush for prints next week.'

'And until then?'

'Speak to the Night Watch volunteer. Have family members stay with you.'

When he had gone, every bit of Grace's energy departed too. It had been a long, sleepless night and she was working this evening. The house settled around her, its daytime sounds less ominous than the nocturnal creaks. She should try and sleep. In bed, she stuck to her side; she had read once that divorced people often did, even after many years. Would she sleep better in Riley's spot?

Contemplating it, she drifted off, unable to move, exhaustion stronger than the many thoughts that whirled around her head.

28

A Genre That Doesn't Fit Easily Into a Box

As eight o'clock approached on the tenth switch off, Tom sat in his favourite armchair that had sagged to perfectly fit his body and waited for the day to die. This was his new routine. He loved that abrupt moment when it all went black, as though a magician had clicked his fingers.

'Lights out,' Tom whispered when they expired, as if he had commanded it.

Then he waited, let the gloom wash over him.

It had been a crazy few days.

He couldn't stop thinking about Harper's message earlier: *I want half of our savings.*

Did he still miss her? Yes. When she had still been home, for the first five Lights Out nights, she had gone around the house switching everything off and setting up the camping lamps he'd purchased in the downstairs rooms. Now, Tom rarely used those lamps, preferring to feel his way around the house, to leave all the curtains open so that the only illumination was what the moon gave.

He was living life *his* way now, and yet still, she haunted him.

Her message flashed again in his head.

I want half of our savings.

Tom had always been a good saver, careful, keeping a handwritten log of what he put away. He had opened the account in both their names, said they should save together for the future, but really, he had invested far more than Harper had. Was that all that mattered to her now? Getting the money?

Her demand had hit him like a plank of wood. He hadn't even been thinking of how they might divide things. Would it be a horrible case of *that's mine, that's his, that's mine, that's his*? They weren't married and the house was his, she had simply moved in, but he would never withhold money – she could have it all, he didn't care.

He hadn't seen her since she left.

Weren't you at least supposed to *try* before you went into such a final mode?

To *talk*?

Tom recalled when he was reading about the Vikings in a failed quest to keep his mind off the affair, learning with surprise that Viking women enjoyed a higher degree of social freedom than men. They might not own the properties, but they were in charge of the farms and homesteads, they handled the finances, and they always made sure they had a far larger portion.

Harper was quite the Viking woman.

He shook his head.

Enough is enough.

Time to do what he had been thinking about all day.

He went into the hallway, listened. The house didn't speak, it slumbered heavily in the absence of electricity. The thing that now kept him going was this house. He loved the place. He had done more with it than Harper had.

Tom climbed the stairs and then stopped halfway.

He couldn't quite make out the middle picture of three on the wall but he knew what it was; if he closed his eyes he could see it coming to life. He also knew that it had replaced what was originally a photo of him and Harper on a holiday in Bali.

That said everything.

Harper's response to it at the time had been repulsion. 'It's ghastly,' she'd cried. 'Get rid of it right now.'

Maybe that was in part why she had gone?

Maybe he *should* have thrown it out immediately.

Why had he kept it?

This image of a golden dragon, great mouth agape, not breathing fire, though smoke curled from one nostril, with a raging red sky behind, hell unleashed.

He moved along.

In the bedroom, even without light, Tom knew it was tidy now Harper's underwear and hair products weren't all over the floor. He felt his way across the room to the bedside cabinet. Picked up the heavy ornament there, feeling the gentle curves of the Venus de Milo sculpture, seeing them the way a blind person must see braille beneath their fingers.

He would finally follow Harper's instructions to 'get it the fuck out of here'.

He should have done that weeks ago.

He carried her down the stairs, his feet easily finding each step in the dark, grabbing the dragon picture on the way past. Back in the living room, he felt for where the Tiffany lamp sat on the shelf. All the colours of the rainbow, it was now a grey silhouette. When she first saw it, Harper had refused to touch it, said Tom should unplug it, and 'bin the fucker'.

Now he did; he carried it with the other items into the kitchen. In there, he grabbed the two creamy candles from next to the bread bin.

Enough is enough.

He went out of the back door with them in his arms. The garden was an unused guest room shrouded in ashen blankets. Yes: he should have done this days ago. He should've listened to Harper. No point leaving them there in case he went to the police. He was too afraid to.

Tom threw first the Venus de Milo onto the patio. It cracked with a dense thud. Not entirely satisfying. Next he hurled the dragon artwork against the ground; it broke with a substantial crack. The candles barely made a sound but the lamp smashed with all the gusto of a piano being dropped.

'What the hell's going on over there?' came a voice.

Tom jumped, paused.

Kevin next door, probably having a sly cigarette by the bins, as he often did. 'You OK, mate?'

'Yes, sorry, just . . .' Just *what*? What the hell was he doing? Smashing up the things that had plagued him for weeks. 'Just having a clear out.'

'You could wake the bloody dead,' grunted Kevin.

A door slammed.

Should Tom leave it all there, dark shapes on the ground, small lifeless bodies? What had possessed him? Why not put them in the bin like a sensible human?

He had needed destruction.

To hear it. To end them. To be the one who decided when it was time. Now he felt flat, like the air had been let out of him.

He wondered if his father had felt that way when he was done raining blows down on his poor mother. When he finally stopped, panting hard, and stormed off to the shed or the pub or his bed. Tom had never been violent; never raised a hand to another person, barely even raised his voice. Where had it got him though? Not that he would ever hurt anyone. But had he fought so hard against the fear that he carried his father's destructive DNA that he had become a pushover, someone who let things go, gave up easily, didn't fight back?

He looked up at the sky.

Lights Out had given him the gift of clearer heavens. The waxing, gibbous moon was positioned to the celestial south of a small speck that Tom knew to be Jupiter. The duo would remain together all evening and set in the west after midnight. By then the diurnal rotation of the sky would shift Jupiter to the moon's left. Much fainter, Neptune was positioned a palm's width to Jupiter's right, though the moonlight made seeing the distant planet more difficult.

Tom was always calmed by the thought of a vast universe that didn't give a shit about what happened here on earth.

Enough is enough.
Now, the items were gone.
It was over.
But why didn't it feel like it truly was?

29

Head or Heart

Work beckoned. Grace finally remembered the nappies, tins of beans and soup put aside and added them to her rucksack. Ignoring government instruction, she left everything switched on as she departed so that when she returned in the morning she'd be greeted with light. If an intruder came tonight, she wouldn't be here.

Though she loved the morning stroll at the end of the shift, she was not up to walking there in the dark now, so she drove. She glanced around the street for torchlight from a Night Watch volunteer, but all was deathly quiet. Perhaps no one was surveying the area tonight – a news report earlier said that people were tiring of it, exhausted from losing sleep and then having to work all day.

She stopped to buy snacks for Claire on the way in.

But in the staff changing room, no Claire. Sam arrived, out of breath, unwrapping a striped scarf. 'I'm covering,' he explained. 'Claire's daughter Lily has a nasty chest infection. Lights Out has another casualty.'

'Oh, no. Hope she's OK.' Grace thought of the teacher on the TV debate talking about how ill children had been since the switch off started; a fist of unease curled about her heart. She must try and call Claire on the first break.

'I'm sure she'll be fine.' Sam sighed, hurriedly changing. 'I was supposed to be on a date, but it is what it is. Right, handover.'

Grace put her items on the staffroom Grateful Table before following him to the nurse's station where Hillary, the nurse in charge, passed on essential information. It had been a quiet shift, relatively incident free, and with one admission in the afternoon.

Grace hardly took any of it in. Her phone buzzed against her thigh; she wondered if it was Steve again. She would ask Sam to show her how to look up the location of a messenger, find out once and for all if he was the intruder.

Then Hillary said the name of the new patient.

And all of that went out of Grace's head.

Her knees gave.

Sam frowned, asked if she was OK, but Grace's throat was stuck shut. She nodded dumbly. The words Hillary said after the patient's name buzzed around her head: *bowel cancer, end-of-life care, carer breakdown, no family, damp house, Lights Out, Lights Out, Lights Out.* Grace squeezed her right hand inside the left, and then swapped, feeling dizzy, wanting to run.

No, she wanted to *stay.*

Go and see them, right away.

She was pulled and she was pushed, an indecisive tide.

She tried to breathe, in, out, in, out.

Handover ended and Sam allocated Grace's duties; she tried to concentrate. The new patient was on her list. The words blurred before her eyes.

Maybe it was another person with the same name. But it was so unusual, a surname she had never met anyone else with, and an uncommon first name. It wasn't possible. Now was the moment to disclose what she knew because she wouldn't be allowed to care for this patient; it would be inappropriate, ethically wrong, wasn't done in a hospice. If Grace shared their identity, Sam would allocate her a different patient, and she would have to avoid that room.

Was that what she wanted?

She didn't know, had to think fast, process a million imagined scenarios at once. What to do? Head or heart? Ethics or emotions?

'Sure you're OK?' asked Sam. 'You look very pale.'

'Yes,' said Grace, too quickly. 'I haven't been sleeping.'

'It's strange times,' he said with sympathy. 'Are you OK to get on then?'

'Yes.' That was it. Chance gone.

She had a new patient.

His name was Bailey Brighthead.

Before she got married, she had been Grace Brighthead.

He was her father.

30

They're Coming

Grace went to the room Bailey Brighthead had been allocated, a small square corner space, both windows giving a different view, one lovely, of fir trees, and one dull, of the car park. The usual cushions and curtains attempted to make the place more home than hospice.

He was asleep – understandable, it was after nine. Grace approached the bed quietly; the only noise was the sound of the air mattress and his grunted breathing. Because he was here for end-of-life care, there was no life-sustaining equipment, only a discreet syringe driver, which is a small battery-powered pump that delivers a steady stream of medication through a small plastic tube under the skin, and a catheter bag.

The dad she had known had fat fingers that traced 'Round and Round the Garden' on Grace's upturned palms as a child. These hands were thin, pale, this body was gaunt, barely anything but a sliver beneath the sheet. The dad she had known had presence, filled a room, sometimes too much, too loudly, a little scarily, but she wouldn't think of those times now.

This man was small. Small and silent.

Maybe there had been a mistake.

Then she looked at his face. Though the skin was sallow – a side effect of the final stages of bowel cancer – and hung loose in places, it was him; she knew the contours of that jaw, the shape of those thick eyebrows, even after all this time. The hair she remembered as thick though, was now thin, almost white.

She hadn't known he lived in this area, but why would she? Why would he tell her that when he had never been in touch before?

There was a lamp on the bedside cabinet, not lit. She longed to switch it on, bathe them both in warmth, but it might unsettle him. He stirred. She backed away. Waited.

Approached again.

This could *not* be him. Maybe there had been a mistake. How old would he be? God, at least eighty.

And he was dying.

How did she feel? Sad. Small. Angry. Needy. Resistant. What was she going to do? Tell the hospice who he was and then not be able to care for him, or keep quiet and get to know the man who disappeared over thirty years ago when she was ten? She needed time, space to think about it. But that wasn't possible.

She left the room, got her things and escaped, breathing hard as she ran through the frosty car park to her vehicle. She messaged Sam, said she had been violently sick so left immediately. For the first time, she didn't notice the night; she got home with no recollection of the journey. The house was a cavernous mouth that swallowed her with a gulp. Once inside she sank to the hallway floor, sobbing, unable to remember where the camping lamp was.

It was that day again.

The day her father left.

The stained-glass lamp shone brightly, scattering stars on the ceiling. Wardrobe monsters cowered in its light, evaporated like morning mist. Grace read in its glow, eagerly turning the pages, devouring C.S. Lewis's words. Just before eight thirty – as he always did – her dad arrived for *proper* story time. There were no tales like the ones he told. Grace often wondered how he came up with them so easily.

That night, he sat on the bed, said in a sleepy voice, 'Right, Maisie, what will it be? The tall tale of Mr Tall?' Grace giggled. He had been telling that one since she was five, and she was way too old now, but didn't care. 'Or something scary?'

'Oh, something scary,' she said. Her favourite. It made no sense when the night beckoned, and when she knew her fears would escalate in his absence, but the thrill of huddling up and sharing ghost stories was too addictive.

He yawned again.

'Are you OK, Dad?' she asked.

'I . . . it's the medication.'

'What medication?' She was confused. She wondered if it had something to do with him whispering to himself in the bathroom earlier: *Don't let them in, don't let them in, don't let them in.*

He appeared to regret his mention of medication. 'Oh, just a little something to help me sleep,' he said, yawning again.

'Bailey!' Her mum's voice from the kitchen.

He ignored it. Opened his mouth to speak – or maybe yawn.

'*Bailey!*' Louder now.

'Time for you to go to sleep anyway,' he said to Grace, turning the lamp low.

'Oh, stay a bit longer,' pleaded Grace, suddenly – inexplicably – desperate for him to remain. 'You haven't even started your story.'

'Nothing bad will happen while it's on, Maisie,' he said, glancing at the lamp. Then he closed the bedroom door after him.

Just before Grace shut her eyes, the bulb died. She gasped. Evil shadows gobbled the room up. She screamed for her father until she lost her voice. It was the suddenness that shocked her. The absolute blackness. Her lack of being able to prevent it.

Dad, Dad, *Dad.*

But he didn't come.

And in the morning he had gone.

Her mother was sitting in the kitchen, smoking a cigarette, something she rarely did. 'He won't be coming back for a long time,' she said. 'We'll get through it together, Grace. We don't need him. We won't speak about it. It's the best way.' Catherine put her free finger over her lips to say shush. 'We won't speak his name again.'

We won't speak his name again.
And they hadn't.

Now, Grace waited for her tears to subside.

Then she crawled up the stairs like something savage, back door forgotten, intruder not at the front of her mind now. The camping lamp sat on the bedside cabinet; she fumbled, switched it on. It was ten thirty. She would never sleep after napping this afternoon but the house was too cold to stay up.

He's back, she thought. *I willed it. I've been thinking about him, and he's back. I told my mum I wanted to speak about him. I let my lid unscrew. What strange twist of fate brought him to the hospice? Is it remotely possible he left the items in the house? Wanted to let me know he was here? Surely he would have been too weak. Surely it can't have been him. Now, should I ignore this chance to care for him or acknowledge and seize it?*

Riley had left to make room.

But what the hell was Grace going to do now?

It was a long night. Dreams merged with consciousness. Grace was in the garden with her dad, trimming pink roses, the sun a halo of gold, her small hands clipping next to his large ones. But then those tiny hands clawed at the edges of a space she couldn't see, alone, no bigger ones to help. When she woke, they were curled into fists. She fell asleep again; this time her dad's voice, a raging storm gusting up the stairs.

They're coming, they're coming, they're coming.

Grace cowered in the dark until it subsided with the dawn.

They're coming?

Who?

At one point, half awake, she felt a presence in the bedroom. Perhaps it was the ghost of her dying father. Perhaps the remnant of another nightmare. Perhaps Riley. She didn't turn towards him. Perhaps it was The Night. She found she didn't care anymore in that moment.

In the morning, she was alone.

Except for a single red rose on the bedside cabinet.

Grace screamed and shuffled away from it, into Riley's cold, empty spot.

The intruder had been *in the room*. While she slept.

She had forgotten to pull the drawers across the doorway.

She didn't look at the note next to it. She didn't want to hear from The Night. She ran downstairs, searched the rest of the house. Nothing else. Nothing moved. No evidence that a stranger had climbed her stairs while she slept and placed what was classed as a romantic gift by her slumbering head.

And yet they had.

I watch her sleep. My favourite part. I think she knows I'm here. She's restless. What does she dream of? I love her. I hate her. I don't know her. Yes, I do. I do now. I've never had a girlfriend. Never had a lover. But I know her. And she will know me.

I'm an expert watcher. Until it's time to stop watching.

My heart speeds up.

This is what I've come for.

This . . .

And then my gift . . .

31

An Unspoken Act of Absolution

Fifteen minutes later, Grace was still glaring at the single red rose, like a lover's apology on the beside cabinet. Steve often gave her flowers to say sorry for the things he did. He felt roses were apology enough for smashing her phone because she had been 'flirting with a work colleague'. Apology enough for hiding the keys so she couldn't leave the house for two days.

Grace remembered the note, opened it.

Roses with thorns last longer,
Love,
The Night

Last longer? What did *that* mean? Was Steve poetic enough to come up with such a cryptic, creepy phrase? Desperation compelled her to work out if there was a connection between the notes and Steve's messages, so Grace finally looked at the new ones from him. *You obviously still think of me.* Four times. *Still there?* Twice. She tried to figure out how to locate where he was but couldn't and threw the device on the cabinet.

She screamed her frustration at the walls.

They didn't care.

She should check the doors but that would be futile – she knew they had come in the back door. She should call the police but that would be pointless too. They didn't give a fuck. No one seemed to.

She stomped down the stairs, ignoring the dragon and going into the kitchen to make coffee. The milk was off so she drank it black. The fridge hadn't juddered to life, despite the electricity being back on. It had finally given up, too.

One more thing to think about.

She wasn't going to bother Riley with it.

Fuck him.

Let him have his space.

Grace went into the living room. Brad and Jennifer circled the bowl in response. She stood by the window, the coffee's steam fogging the glass. What was she going to do about her dad? She was back at work on Friday, in two days, so would have to decide by then. Had he *known* she worked at the hospice and made sure that was where he ended up? It didn't seem likely. Grace tried to recall the details from yesterday's handover. Hillary had said there was no family and a damp house. Wherever her dad had gone, he had not replaced her. And he hadn't mentioned to any of his carers that she existed.

However his disappearance had impacted her, for some reason Grace still couldn't bear the thought of him being alone, living in poor conditions, suffering with the pain of cancer.

'Dad,' she said quietly, as though to practise saying his name.

A soft tap on the front door then. Grace frowned. Nervous, she approached the hallway cautiously. She was tempted to ignore it. *Get a grip.* She opened the door onto the back of a checked jacket, onto a man with fine hair cut short around his ear, who was much taller than Grace but still just a kid in her mind. Jamie, her son. She breathed a sigh of relief.

'Mum,' he smiled, turning around.

'What are you doing here?' she cried.

'What kind of welcome is that?'

'Stop it, I'm happy to see you.' She hugged him, inhaling his still boyish scent. She loved to sniff his cheek like she had when he was little; if he was in a good mood he indulged her, if not, he shooed her away. 'Aren't you at work?'

He came into the house, hung his coat over the banister. 'I've got the morning off and Harry's away at some conference.'

'You won't be able to stay long then. Coffee?'

'Yes.' He followed her into the kitchen. 'I just got up and drove here. I had this . . .'

'What?' She paused, kettle in hand.

'This really strong feeling you were upset.'

Grace didn't speak. They had often had a sixth sense about one another's feelings in the past, perhaps because it had just been the two of them.

'You haven't sounded like yourself recently, but this morning, I was sure you needed me.'

She switched the kettle on and bolstered herself to be brave, to lie, to gloss over what was going on, but suddenly found that the tears she stubbornly fought were flowing down her cheeks.

'Mum, what is it?' Jamie hugged her.

She couldn't speak, tried to sniff away her pain against his warm chest. This wasn't right; you weren't supposed to burden kids, you were supposed to be the strong one.

'Tell me,' he urged, panic creeping into this voice.

The kettle clicked off and she pulled away, wiping her face. 'I'm a state,' she said, making coffee. 'It'll have to be black.'

'I don't care about that. Are you gonna tell me what's wrong?'

Which nightmare do you want to know about? she thought. *The strange intruder? The notes? Riley being gone? Or my dad – the grandfather you've never met – being back?*

'Let's go in here.' Grace went into the living room.

They sat side by side on the saggy sofa.

'Talk to me, Mum,' said Jamie.

How to say it? *Out with it*, her mum would say. 'When I was at work yesterday, we had a new patient.' She paused. 'It was . . . it was my dad.'

Jamie put his coffee down next to Brad and Jennifer. 'Your *dad*?'

'Yes.'

'The one who—'

'Left? Yes.'

'I don't know what to say,' admitted Jamie. 'Is he . . . dying?'

'Yes.' It hit Grace then. There was a time limit on her decision. There was an expiry date.

'How long does he have?'

'I don't know. You can never tell. I wasn't really concentrating, I was so shocked. I went to look at him . . . and then I ran, like a big coward.'

'You're not a coward. This is huge.' Jamie looked at her. 'What are you going to do?'

'The thing about my job,' she explained, 'is that you can't ethically care for someone you know. Even if it was just a neighbour, or a friend, you wouldn't be permitted to. So if I tell anyone who he is, I'll be allocated a different patient on every shift.'

'You sound like you *want* to care for him?'

It did sound that way, but she still felt conflicted. 'I guess the fact that I didn't tell anyone yesterday is me trying to give myself more time to decide what I really want to do, isn't it?'

Jamie nodded. 'If you nurse him, and you're found out, will you be in trouble?'

'Possibly,' said Grace. 'I'd worry about that then. *If* I did it.'

'How did he look?' asked Jamie 'Did he see you?'

'He was asleep. They mostly are near the end. He looked . . . old.' Grace's voice broke and Jamie wrapped a hand around hers, the way she had his so many times when he was small, enclosing it tightly. 'Whatever he did, no one deserves to die alone, do they? I've waited my whole life for this moment. I imagined all kinds of scenarios where he turned up, sorry, saying he had missed me, thought about me every day. But I never imagined it this way.'

'What about Grandma? Have you told her?'

Grace shook her head.

'This is about you,' said Jamie. 'He's your dad, and Grandma never wants to talk about him anyway, so you do what you have to do. I'll support that.'

'You're the best.' Grace kissed his cheek.

'So you're going to care for him?'

'Yes. *No.*' She shook her head, frustrated at the indecision. 'I don't know. I have no idea if he'd even recognise me or what I'd to say to him.'

'You recognised *him.*'

'Yes, but he was an adult when he left. I was a child. I don't look anything like I did when I was ten, whereas he's just older.'

Grace realised then that if he didn't recognise her or know who she was, she wouldn't have to tell him. That kind of thing might shock him, cause immediate deterioration. Should she make sure he spent his final days or weeks in as little discomfort as possible? What if she did and Jamie wanted to meet him? He hadn't had a father or a grandfather, didn't he deserve the chance to meet one of them?

'Whatever I do, I'd be quiet about who I was,' she said. 'But then I . . .'

'What?'

'Do *you* want to meet him?'

'It's a bit of a shock to be honest.' Jamie sighed, paused for a moment. 'I need to think about it. But I guess there wouldn't be a whole lot of time for that, would there? And if you *did* care for him and kept quiet about your identity, how *would* I meet him?'

Grace shook her head. 'I don't know.'

'Do your next shift, see what happens. When is it?'

'Friday. And tomorrow I see Grandma.'

'Oh.'

'Yes. *Oh.*'

'You're not obliged to tell her anything,' said Jamie, finishing his coffee.

'I know.' She gathered the empty mugs up, the clash making Brad and Angelina swim more frenziedly. 'Are you hungry?'

'I got a McDonald's breakfast on the way here.'

'How long have I got you for?'

'An hour.'

Grace made herself some toast. When she headed back to the living room Jamie was looking at the unfinished decor. 'We're further on than you,' he said. 'Only one room left to do. Doesn't it annoy you? Doesn't Riley want to get it finished?'

'He . . .' Grace decided to keep quiet about his disappearance. There were bigger things now. 'He's letting me sort it. I'm still waiting on dates from my workman.'

'That's nice.' Jamie motioned to the Tiffany lamp on the hearth. 'New?'

'Um, yes.' That wasn't a lie; it was.

'Just need the loo.' She heard him pause on the stairs. 'What the fuck is *that*?'

'What?'

'That dragon artwork.'

What was she supposed to say? 'Riley's idea of a joke. Don't ask.'

'Whatever.' Jamie continued upstairs.

For the remaining hour, they caught up on general life; Grace was reminded of the uncomplicated and lovely relationship they shared, one formed because for fourteen years there had only been the two of them, and that kind of bond is solid. If she now decided to care for her father she would, essentially, be forgiving him, because that's what caring for him would be: an unspoken act of absolution. Grace knew she would never understand why he had left because there was nothing and no one that could have taken her away from Jamie.

'Have you heard any more about the Feather Man?' Grace asked Jamie, shaking free of the past and changing the topic.

'Only that he'd broken into a house in Selby.'

Grace shuddered. 'I don't like that he's . . . spreading his wings, for want of a better phrase.'

'And wasn't there a report about an elderly lady here in Hull?'

'Wasn't she confused?' But could Grace be sure? 'How is that poor woman you know who was . . .?'

'Not good apparently. Who would be?'

Not me, thought Grace. *Not me.*

When Jamie had to go, her heart constricted. She hated good-byes; no matter the circumstance, she feared loved ones leaving and not returning again. She would prepare, mentally, emotionally, pull back, detach. But that never worked with Jamie. She kissed his cheek on the doorstep, watched him walk to his car.

Come back, her heart yelled. *Stay a bit longer.*

But he left.

And she was alone again.

Day lumbered towards nightfall. Grace tried to occupy herself, ignore the oncoming dark. She remembered Claire's daughter Lily was ill, felt bad that she hadn't called, so sent a message: *How's Lily? I meant to message yesterday but came home from work sick. X*

She considered asking Claire how to find someone's location on Facebook messenger, but it wasn't right to bother her with it. She couldn't ask Riley; he'd wonder why she needed to know. Plus, she didn't want to engage with him. She googled it, but when she tapped the four dots it suggested in Messenger, the option didn't appear. There were no more messages from Steve, and for now Grace wanted to leave it that way.

If it *was* him, what could she do right now?

Soon it was time to undertake her safety procedures. Grace went to the window at four twenty. A puddle reflected the failing sun; both disappeared below the rooftops. In the upstairs window opposite, just a black square of glass staring back. Then, after a moment, a silhouette. Stacey looked out, doll in arms, straw hair wild. Grace waited to see if she saw her so she could wave.

But she didn't.

The dusky pink flower had gone. Died?

Grace felt morose. She switched the lights on and closed the curtains.

When eight approached, dread clung to her clothes like evil pollen as she wandered the house, camping lamp in hand, going through the switch-off process, put in mind of last offices after a patient died and was positioned for the mortuary. She paused, mouth parched, stomach queasy; with new fire in her belly could she turn the lights *and* the camping lamp off? Endure the dark?

She covered her eyes. Turned it all off. Waited. Opened her eyes. With the curtains shut, the blackness was thick, absolute. No. *No.*

She was back there. In that enclosed space. Trapped. No air. Voices on the other side. Scratching, scratching, scratching.

One voice, louder than the others: *her dad.*

But he hadn't been there that day. She was *sure* of it.

Desperate to quash the memory, she fumbled for the camping lamp again, knocked it over, scrabbled around, found the switch.

Light; blessed light. She devoured it the way flowers do sunshine.

She *couldn't* face the dark alone.

She went to the back door. Studied it. Should she break the lock so the intruder couldn't get in with their key? Surely that would mean *anyone* could get in? There was still the option of going to her mum's, but with the difficult decision to make about her dad, she needed her own space. There was nothing else to do but go to bed, like others across the land, a mass exodus of evacuees deserting downstairs for the duvet.

The single red rose was still on the cabinet.

She opened the window, chucked it out. Doubtful it could be fingerprinted.

Her phone pinged. She jumped.

Riley.

I know our chat didn't end well yesterday, but I want to talk. How about Saturday? I could come home? X

Saturday seemed so far – it was only Wednesday – who knew what might happen between now and then. She thought about ignoring him, as he had her, but couldn't play tit-for-tat games.

Grace replied: *Yes.*
Then she tried to sleep.

The house was quiet. No creaking. No tapping branches. No squeaking floorboard. The absence of sound was unsettling. Unexpected. Grace woke often, straining to listen. Still nothing.

In the morning, peace. But was it the lull before a storm? Had the intruder learned how to avoid noisy areas? She lay a while. Today, she would see her mum. Grace had insisted a few days ago that she wanted to talk about the past, but since then that past had found its way into a hospice bed where she worked. Perhaps it was more important that she got answers now. It might help with the decision about her dad. But, until she made it, Grace wasn't going to tell her mum about Bailey's arrival.

Grace waited until the radiators had thawed the house out, then she went downstairs.

It seemed just as she had left it last night.

No new candles, crystals, fish, dragons or lamps.

No note from The Night.

She searched the house twice.

Nothing.

It was eerie. Like someone had freeze-framed her life. And despite everything – despite the horror of it, the mystery, her fears – the oddest emotion unfurled in Grace's gut. One that made no sense for this moment. Utterly ridiculous.

She felt abandoned.

HULL LOCAL NEWS

Assault on Local Neighbourhood Night Watch

A woman 'screamed out' when she was sexually assaulted by a man on a major Hull street. The attack is reported to have happened near a convenience store in North Hull. Police are appealing to potential witnesses to come forward.

It happened on Tuesday 16 January at around 10.25 p.m. In a statement, Humberside Police said: 'We are appealing for help from anyone else who was in this area at that time.'

The woman was on Night Watch duty alone, despite government recommendations that people pair up. This advice came after incidents where volunteers felt unsafe on shift. A national survey shows that the number of people keeping guard has fallen dramatically.

'You wouldn't get me out there again,' said Emma Murphy from North Hull. 'Sending young women out alone in the dark to keep an eye on things, it isn't right, is it?'

We are appealing for anyone who witnessed the assault to come forward. If you saw anything that could help with our inquiries, please call us on the non-emergency number. Local MP, Scott Brady, said, 'The government's first priority is always the safety of our country, and I am very distressed to hear about this senseless attack.'

32

Not a Place For Children

Grace's phone buzzed in her dressing-gown pocket. She scrambled to open the message.

It was Claire.

Hi love, it's been hell, thought I'd have to take Lily to A&E, she was coughing until she was sick but then she got better. The house is so cold at night, but what can I do? X

Grace wrote back, sending her sympathy, but in truth felt hopeless. There was nothing really she could do either.

There was also another message from Steve: *Playing shy now, eh?*

She ignored it. Went around the house a third time, half-expecting a plant in the bathroom or a new fishbowl on the landing.

She was picking her mum up at eleven. At the thought of Catherine, Grace saw the slight figure in the hospice bed. The lack of movement, as though her dad's spirit had left his body already. Did she want to go back to him? It might bring closure. Or pain?

She was back at work tomorrow.

Today she must decide.

At ten forty she approached her car just as a police vehicle pulled up. *Thank God.* Maybe they finally had some answers. She would have to cancel her mother, and Catherine hated being let down, but it would be worth it.

She was about to call out, invite them in, when she realised that the police car was parked outside Stacey's house, not hers. Martin opened the door to them almost immediately; he looked a wreck, as though he had been in a war zone. Unease unfolded like forgotten dirty laundry in Grace's gut. She loitered, couldn't hear what was said. What on earth had happened?

A fishbowl? Candles? Dragon artwork?

'It's terrible. She's missing.'

Grace jumped. It was Ben from number seventeen. He put a hand on her arm, apologised for startling her.

'Who is?' she asked.

'Stacey.'

'*No.*' Grace felt sick; she had only seen her last night, in the window. 'When?'

'Apparently she went to bed last night, as usual, but wasn't there this morning. Martin called me in a right state. It's not like her at all. Sweet little thing she is, quite shy.' Ben was clearly distressed.

'This is terrible. What can we do? Should we knock, offer help?'

'Maybe wait until the police have gone,' suggested Ben.

Grace nodded. 'Yes. Right. I'll go later.'

'Gotta go, but I'll keep you updated.'

'Please do, thanks.'

Grace couldn't move. A little girl, *gone.* A little girl who had shared her enjoyment of the sky, missing. A little girl she had knocked off her feet, lost. A little girl no longer in her window. A car horn blasted. Grace swore, jumped out of the way. Went to her car, got in. There, she felt numb. No item in the house today, now no Stacey. Had the intruder got bored of her, and simply moved next door instead?

Suddenly, an image of a box popped into her head.

What the hell?

It was a rectangular box, perhaps big enough for toys, dark wood, heavy-lidded. Inside, thudding. A muffled voice; a child's voice. Then scratching. It was the scratching that drained the heat from Grace's blood.

The image dissolved like dew in the sunshine.

And yet she had felt abject fear at the vision of that box.

Grace suddenly saw her dad again.

Not lying in a hospice bed, but young, working in his garden, stomping around the house, leaving mud everywhere to her mum's annoyance, breaking wind and blaming the walls, the doors, the curtains. Maybe he'd had bad moods, maybe there were dim memories of him stomping around the house at night, shouting and throwing things, but Grace was sure – *are you?* – he had never hurt her.

She couldn't stay away from him.

She knew now: she would return to his bedside.

Finally, she drove to her mother's house, parked outside, honked the horn. After a few minutes, Catherine got into the car. 'Sorry, I'm late,' Grace said.

Catherine looked at her, added, 'You look terrible.'

'Do I?' She realised she was shaking.

'What happened?'

'A little girl on our street . . . she's missing.'

'Oh, my word. What happened?'

'I don't know, only that she was there last night and isn't now.' Grace shook her head. 'Martin must be worried sick. Her dad, that is. It's just him, so he doesn't have the support of a partner.'

'We've both been there,' said Catherine.

'We have.' Grace paused. 'I'm wondering if her being gone has anything to do with what's been happening to me?'

'But, dear, *how?* Was something left behind at Martin's house?'

'I don't know. You're right. I'm being ridiculous.' Grace exhaled, knowing she needed to be assertive, drive this conversation towards her father now. 'Lunch then?' Would she even be able to eat? 'How about that nice place at Raywell?'

Grace drove there, relieved that her mother was rattling on about her new acting group, how she was sick of Lights Out because rehearsals were limited to day time, and how the show couldn't happen until it was over. She kept seeing Stacey in the window; all the Staceys from the last few weeks, all the windows, all the times she had been there, both waving back and not seeing Grace. Was there something she had missed? Something that pointed to where she had gone?

And then a box.

Dark wood, heavy-lidded.

What was inside?

Grace shook her head; she was losing her mind.

They got a window table at Millers near the Yorkshire Wolds, one of their favourite eateries, with views of the sloping gravel drive and fat evergreen trees.

'Is Riley back yet?' asked Catherine after they had ordered food.

Grace shook her head. It was a touchy topic, but less painful to think of than a missing child. 'He's coming on Saturday. To talk.'

'I guess that's something. Sometimes I think you youngsters don't value marriage like we used to, dear.' Catherine being her usual blunt self.

'I do,' said Grace. 'Don't lump me in with everyone else. Considering my childhood, I've done pretty well.'

Catherine looked hurt and Grace felt bad. 'You *have* done well,' said her mum. 'I just meant . . . generally. My marriage was a good one – I cherished it. Yes, there were tough moments like most have but . . .' Catherine appeared to realise she had said more than she wanted about the past, and changed the subject. 'What's happening with the police, then?'

'PC Littlewood – he's our officer – turned up out of the blue, but didn't have any helpful news.'

'Any more break-ins?'

'Yes. This morning, though, nothing. It was odd.'

Her mother leaned forward in her seat, a confused look on her face. 'Surely you must be *relieved*?'

'Of course.'

The food arrived, two steaming jacket potatoes with cheese and salad.

'You don't sound sure.' Catherine nibbled a piece of cucumber.

'I've been terrified, lying awake, not knowing who's in my house, night after night . . . and then suddenly it stops. Is it going to happen again? Will I now spend the rest of my life wondering about it?'

'Keep on at the police.'

'I *am*.'

Grace ate her salad. She imagined blurting out that her father was lying prostrate in a hospice bed, his remaining days numbered. That's what she was here to discuss after all – the past. But it was hard.

'I think,' she tried, 'me being anxious in the dark has made the last few weeks all the worse. My issues stem from . . . not only . . . the *incident* . . . those kids . . . at school . . . then my dad leaving . . . but from not *talking* about it all.'

Catherine didn't respond.

'I know you thought you were doing the right thing when I was little,' Grace continued, 'but when you refused to answer questions about my dad, you made me feel that I didn't even have one. And I did. He was there for the first ten years.' Her voice broke. 'The morning he went, you just said, *he won't be coming back for a long time.*'

Catherine dropped her fork with a clatter, tried to catch it before it hit the floor. The waitress brought another. 'I thought if I went on about him,' she said, 'it would do more damage.' She looked hurt.

'A *long time* isn't forever, but he never came back. Did you know where he was then?' Catherine didn't respond. Grace buried pain, waited too, then said, 'Did you think he might come back still?'

'In truth, I didn't know.'

'But you knew where he initially went?'

Despite the clean fork, Catherine stopped eating, half of her potato abandoned on the plate. 'I wanted you to get over him. Over . . . *it*.'

'Over what?' Grace gulped a too-large lump of potato down.

'Over him going.'

'No, you meant something specific. You *did*. I can tell. Was there something *else*?' Grace grew angry.

Catherine's face softened. She held Grace's gaze. 'I thought it would be kinder in the long run for you to forget it . . . I mean *him*.'

'But children can't get over a parent. It's not the same as if you lose a partner. I was *ten*. He was my *dad*.' She paused. 'Where was he when you thought he *might* come back?'

Catherine looked down, as though ashamed. 'It's not a place for children.'

'What do you mean?' Grace couldn't eat anymore.

'What difference does it make?' Catherine sounded close to tears and that upset Grace. 'After that, he disappeared. You know, I tried to look for him. I tried for years to find him. I thought, maybe I can persuade him to come back. But I've never been able to locate him. You know how hard it is, you've tried in the past.'

Grace had. 'Where *was* he before he left us forever?' she demanded, voice low.

Catherine looked again at her half-empty plate.

'*Where?*'

'A psychiatric hospital.'

Grace couldn't have been more surprised if her mother had said the circus. 'A *psychiatric* hospital? But . . . *why*? He wasn't—'

'*Crazy?*' finished Catherine, eyebrow raised. When Grace looked offended at her choice of word, Catherine tutted. 'Oh, that's how they spoke about such things back then.'

'Such things? *What* things? What was wrong with him?' Grace couldn't take it in; her father had been *ill*.

As though this information had freed the memory, she saw him through a narrow gap in a doorway, red-faced, eyes strange as though nothing lit them, walking in a circle in his study, over and over and over. Then another; him bellowing in the garden late at night, *Stop watching me, stop watching me, stop watching me*. And another where he was washing his hands in steaming water, again and again and again.

'He had what they now call bipolar disorder, back then "manic depression". Medication wasn't what it is now, and he often refused to accept that he was ill and stopped taking it. Eventually because of that . . .'

'Yes?'

'He suffered with psychosis. That developed later, when you were older. He had these . . . hallucinations. Thought government agents were breaking into the house. Thought he was going to be taken away.' Catherine looked frail, sad, and Grace felt terrible that she had interrogated her. But she needed to know. She *deserved* to know. 'It was hard. Even though he was a gentle man, he scared me when he was that way. It's a frightening experience to see someone you love like that, especially when you know they're a good man, a good dad, and it's only the illness that makes them behave that way.' She looked at Grace. 'He scared you too sometimes. Which destroyed him.'

Grace could hardly take it in.

She had cared for a patient once with bipolar disorder who, in his manic phase, didn't sleep for three days. She had found it distressing, but had never quite been able to put her finger on why. Had that been the buried memory of her own father's behaviour? Had it triggered old feelings? 'Why on earth didn't you tell me?' she cried now. 'I'm an *adult* now. This might have helped me.'

Catherine spoke as if she was narrating a story that had nothing to do with her. 'It's hard when you've told things a particular way for so long. Look, a friend of mine back then had had some counselling and she—'

'Yes?'

'She advised me to hide certain things. To keep you in the dark about . . . things that were better buried.'

'What do you mean?'

Catherine paused as though recalling, then seemed to remember that Grace was awaiting an explanation. 'I . . . well, I was trying to help you.'

'*Help* me?' Grace felt queasy.

'You were so distressed. I didn't know where to turn. She was there.' Catherine nodded, as though to insist that she had made the right decision. 'She said I should rewrite what had happened as a better version. To protect you. She said you were only ten, you'd absorb any tale I told.' Catherine paused. 'So I did.' She touched Grace's hand 'Because that's not all . . .'

'What do you mean?' It was too much; Grace thought she might be sick.

Seeming to rethink, Catherine sat up straight in her chair, shook her head. 'Another time. You're in a . . . tough place as it is right now.'

'I don't care, I wa—'

'Listen, all that matters right now is that your dad left because he didn't want to upset or frighten you. Just before he was discharged, that's what he told me.'

'You went there? You *visited* him? Didn't let *me*?'

'You weren't allowed to.'

The waitress appeared at the table then, asked cheerily if they were done – *not quite*, thought Grace – and took their plates, then brought the lattes they had ordered to have after their meal.

'Not allowed to?' Grace repeated.

'No. I agreed – I thought it would be too distressing for you.'

Grace shook her head. 'You said my dad left because he didn't want to upset or frighten me. He *told* you that?'

'Yes. He said that he loved you too much to impose his illness on you. He was afraid it would get much worse, the older he got. It was better he stayed away.'

'And you let him go.' Tears welled behind Grace's eyes.

'What could I do? The next time I went, he had discharged himself. And I never saw him again. I looked, I told you. I tried.'

'What would you do if he ever came back?' Grace wondered then if he had come back to this area to find her, and then got ill before he could. Who knew? He did; *he* could answer those questions.

'I . . . it would be a shock.'

'Yes,' said Grace quietly. 'Tell me what you meant earlier when you said that's not all.'

Catherine shook her head. 'You need to be in a better place, dear.'

'For fuck's sake,' hissed Grace, shocked at her own outburst. She had never spoken to her mother like that. Catherine paled. 'I'm in this place because you deceived me all these years. My head's messed up with all this, so if you're not going to be fully honest, I'm leaving.' She stood.

'Now isn't the time.'

'OK,' said Grace. 'I'm going.'

'But . . . I . . . how will I get home?'

'Call a taxi.'

Grace put a twenty-pound note on the table and marched out, ignoring Catherine's insistence that she wait. It had begun raining so she hurried to the car, reversed hastily out of the parking spot, and sped down the drive, spitting gravel.

Back home, she was tempted to open a bottle of wine, but it would be lukewarm now the fridge had packed in. The phone lit up with MUM but Grace ignored it.

Let her stew.

How can I talk to her now?

Grace tried hard to remember something lovely of her dad. It came, suddenly, a gift she had given him to open on Christmas morning, a handkerchief she had made at school, his initials neatly stitched in the corner, wrapped up in tin foil. 'This is for Christmas morning,' she had said, and he'd responded with, 'What do I get in the afternoon then?' and she joked, 'A kick up the bum,' which made him roar with laughter.

Her father had been ill. It explained so much. The *shadow father*, she called the other dad, the man he later became. That ghostly visitor who looked right through her and spoke in a different voice. It hadn't been his fault. He wasn't *bad*, as the child Grace had sometimes feared. But even knowing that, she also knew that the symptoms of psychosis must have appeared terrifying to that little girl.

Now, she saw the man who told her bedtime stories and showed her how to tell if his greenhouse tomatoes were ripe.

Was that her *real* dad?

Yes. Yes, it was.

Now, that dad stood out, was the one who Grace held on to.

33

Closer to Home

Anxiety about the dark descended as the day bled into evening. No matter what else troubled Grace, she could never shake this fear. Outside the sky was the colour of depression. She hurried around the house, switching on the lights – *flick, lit* – and closing the curtains, unable to look up at Stacey's window.

She had gone over to Martin's earlier, knocked softly, afraid of being intrusive. He answered, face ashen, people in the kitchen behind him – probably family – and shook his head when Grace asked if they had any news.

'Can I do anything?' she asked softly.

The shock must have stolen his words because he closed the door.

Should she go out looking for the girl?

Get her out of the box . . .

It was like someone had whispered the words in her ear. What box? *The dark wood, heavy-lidded box.*

Was it a premonition? Should she tell someone?

No. They would think her insane.

Now, when the clock counted down to eight, Grace went through her habitual procedure with more vigour. Camping lamp in hand, she finished at the Tiffany lamp on the hearth. The house got too cold and she went upstairs.

There was a message on her phone.

Steve: *Why don't we meet? I think you want to.*

Jesus. No, she did not.

She had forgotten about him in the madness of the day's many revelations. She had nothing to lose now; that was how it felt.

Find out once and for all if it was him.

She voice-called him in Facebook messenger. It didn't take long for him to answer. The voice was familiar – squeaky, rough, leering. Why had it ever scared her? Why had she let him take over her life? It was as though she had new strength; knowledge was power; her exposed history fired bravery.

He should be afraid of *her*.

'I won't keep you,' she said briskly, 'but if you've been coming to Hull and somehow getting into my house, it's best you tell me, because the police will find out anyway.'

'How are *you* then?' She could tell Steve was smiling.

'This isn't a social call. You always liked a cryptic note, a game. And the rose quartz was clever. But I don't understand the dragon or the porcelain statue.'

Silence. Unlike him.

'Cat got your tongue?' she said.

'What the fuck are you talking about? What dragon?'

'The one you left,' she said. 'I just don't know how you got in. That's what baffles me.'

'You think I came in your house and left . . . a *dragon*?'

Grace realised how she sounded.

'Cat got *your* tongue?' he mocked.

'No, I . . .'

'Listen, if someone is breaking into your house and leaving weird shit, maybe look closer to home.'

'What do you mean?' She was chilled. Did he know something after all?

'*You*,' he cried. 'You're a fucking nutter. You always were.'

She hung up. Blocked him. Realised she wouldn't be able to find his location now, didn't care.

But the damage was done: the thoughts emerging in Grace's mind were undeniable. She started to panic, all the information she'd received over the past few days compiling in her head, sending her spiralling: what if Steve was right? What if she *was* ill? Ill the way her father had been? Was that why she had been so fraught recently? Was that why Riley had left?

Had she put those strange items and notes in the house after all?

No: the notes were *not* her handwriting.

No: she had definitely *heard* those noises in the house.

She spoke aloud, 'I'm not insane, I'm not insane, *I'm not insane.*'

Then she realised that talking to herself was the definition of paranoia.

Maybe she was.

I'll never be done with this. I've waited a few days. I've relived every second of my night when the sun has ruined it. I think of each exquisite moment once I'm back home, alone, the bare walls pressing in on me. Can I stop? Do I want to? No.

So I'll go back out, into the dark, to show them who I am.

Mother, can you see me?

Mother, can you see me?

Oh, yes, soon they will all see me.

I'm here. I'm here.

Hannah Moore
writing for
the *Opinion*

Lights Out a catastrophic failure by any standard

They might be keeping us in the dark but it's a scandal hiding in plain sight. Employing the oft-used trope of 'we're all in this together' simply doesn't work anymore. We are not all in this together. We, the everyday folk, are fumbling about in the shadows – literally – while this government enjoys full electricity in their homes, around the clock (they have to work into the night), and preaches how we should keep warm and manage our poor, overworked fridges. Not even two weeks in, Lights Out is a catastrophic failure.

We've seen suicide rates increase, car accidents double due to poor street lighting, hospitality businesses fold because they can't stay open after eight and, most tragically of all, children succumbing to illnesses previously not fatal. Hospital admissions are up, crippling our struggling NHS where nurses are threatening to strike for the first time in seven years. What will happen then? Who will care for the elderly when they fall in the dark?

Paul Burch, a Centre Manager at the Samaritans, said that calls have doubled, meaning people often don't reach a volunteer. 'We were not deemed worthy of receiving emergency electricity after eight, so the service has to end until the following morning. Night-time is when we receive most of our calls. It's when people are most lonely and desperate. Now we're having to urge people to call or visit during the day.'

A ChildLine volunteer told me in confidence of the 'horror stories' she is hearing from children as they witness an increase in domestic violence because parents are more stressed than usual by the switch off.

237

In truth, the entire scheme was set up as a vote winner, particularly with the young who are passionate about the planet. That it was to conserve energy is a lie. That it was to help the climate is a lie. That it was to help *us* is a lie. What have they been telling us? *Remember: the government's first priority is always the safety of our country.'* Does anyone truly believe that?

When the switch off ends, we'll be so grateful for the light that we'll turn a blind eye to the truth.

34

A Shell of a Man

Morning followed; Grace rose early for work, glancing out of the bedroom window, hoping to see Stacey in hers. Empty. A sob Grace hadn't known was there escaped from her throat. *Stacey. Are you home yet? Please God, are you home?*

She checked the house over, the thought of a new alien gift appearing terrifying once more, despite the strange feeling of abandonment yesterday when nothing had been left. But even though nothing had been added to their halfway-renovated house, Grace had the clearest of thoughts; a premonition?

The night wasn't done with her yet.

She shook her head – she really *was* losing her mind.

Spotting the Tiffany lamp on her search, she had another thought. Should she take it to work and place it on the bedside cabinet by her dying dad? The thought choked her. She might see him *die*.

Hang on for me, Dad. Wait for me to come.

Before getting in the car, Grace glanced at Stacey's house. The house had looked sad in the morning light, a shrouded funeral attendee. Grace prayed they were all sleeping, Stacey back in her bed, safe. Should she knock? Check? No: it was early, didn't seem right to disturb the family.

She got to work with the Tiffany lamp in a carrier bag, hoping that no one would spot her bringing something unusual into the building. Thankfully, Claire – whose eyes were mostly likely to spot it – arrived late, breathless, hair messily clipped up, and Grace managed to get the lamp to her changing-room locker first, hide it.

Despite her decision, Grace was nervous about seeing her dad again.

If he's still here, she thought. *God, I hope he's still here.*

'You OK?' asked Grace, thinking of Claire's daughter. 'How's Lily now?'

'Much better, thank you.' Claire looked exhausted. 'I dreaded having to take her to A&E, with the crisis, but luckily she picked up.'

'Poor you, it must have been hell.' Grace touched her friend's arm. She wondered for a moment about mentioning her dad, asking Claire not to say anything. No, it wouldn't be fair to put her in that position.

'Right.' Claire was brisk now. 'We'd better get to handover.'

Hillary shared what the day staff needed to know. At mention of Bailey Brighthead, Grace's ears picked up. 'He took a turn for the worse at about two a.m.,' said Hillary. Grace held her breath. 'He had a significant drop in temperature and was very confused about where he was. But this morning he settled and seems more comfortable.'

He was alive.

Grace felt weak with relief.

'He hasn't eaten anything since he arrived,' said Hillary, 'not even ice cream, our usual winner, and he's rejected a water beaker since yesterday.'

Grace knew this was normal for people at the end of their life. In the care of the hospice workers, the patient was the one who led things: if they refused to eat, this was accommodated, because the body was shutting down. It sounded like he was in the period of pre-active dying, which would lead into the active stage of dying. That typically lasted about three days.

Handover done, Claire allocated Grace her duties; Bailey was one of her patients. Once again, she knew this was the moment to admit her relationship to him, but the words disintegrated before they reached Grace's tongue.

Though she wanted to go straight to him, check how he was, even, in moments of emotion, tell him everything she now understood, her other tasks beckoned.

She washed a young woman's hair who wanted to look nice for her family, made tea, plated buns for a seventieth birthday, and turned patients to avoid bedsores.

Finally, she went to the room where her father resided.

The first thing she saw was the cheap, standard lamp that was sitting – as with every other room in the hospice – on the cabinet next to the bed, beige shade slightly wonky, as though someone had knocked it and not rectified it. Grace put it right. She longed to replace it with the other one, let it scatter multicoloured squares of light across the ceiling. But that was going to prove tricky.

Bailey slept, his breathing slow and even.

Last time, Grace had run.

This time, though, she touched his hand, skin cool and surprisingly smooth. As though this connection opened a portal – the way that in films psychic people witnessed bloody visions upon touching a serial killer – she saw them both watching something on the TV. She was about nine. He rubbed his feet and grumbled about getting old. 'How old is old?' she asked him. 'When you groan as you get up, that's old.' He smiled. And she stood, groaning exaggeratedly, and he followed, groaning even more loudly.

Now she knew he might never stand up again.

He stirred, muttered something, perhaps aware of her presence.

'Hello, Bailey, my name's Grace.' Introducing herself always felt like the polite thing to do when she worked with a patient for the first time, and here was no different. As soon as the words left her mouth though, she panicked that this would alert him to who she was, but Grace was a common name. 'I'm going to do your mouth care. Is there anything else you need?'

No response.

'Are you happy for me to clean your lips?'

He grunted, which she took as consent.

'Would you like some water from the beaker first?' she asked.

No response.

He looked so vulnerable. The man who had stomped heavily through the garden, leaving large footprints in the mud, barely made a dent in the mattress now. The man who talked to himself, talked to neighbours, talked to the TV, was now mute. She wasn't going to learn anything about the past from him. She realised she would have to find peace in giving care rather than receiving answers.

'I'm going to clean your lips with a mouth swab and brush your teeth,' she managed to say.

Gently, she mopped up the saliva on his chin, and examined inside his mouth for ulcers or bleeding. Then she applied gel to moisturise his lips.

'Shall we put the TV on? Let's find something you might enjoy.' What had he watched when she was small? It was hard to recall. Gardening shows? Sitcoms? She flicked through channels and left it on an old episode of *Keeping Up Appearances*. 'There you go, a bit of Hyacinth Bucket.'

She tidied the room to stay longer. There often wasn't time to sit with patients, but the fact that Bailey had no family – *he does*, thought Grace, *the hospice staff just don't know it* – gave her a good excuse to linger.

When there was nothing else she could do, she sat in the chair by the bed. Usually she chatted about the news, about something she had seen on TV, but now she struggled.

She realised that she needed him, a thought that took her by surprise.

It didn't matter that she was forty-three, that she was married and had an adult child. Bailey could have protected her from Lights Out, from the break-ins, from feeling alone. If he hadn't left, it could have been so different.

'I hope you've had a good life,' she said softly. She meant it, despite the emotions. 'I hope you found peace wherever you were.'

He croaked a word, but Grace couldn't make it out.

She sat up. Moved closer.

'Yes?' she said.

He tried again but it made no sense. It was frustrating. Sounded like *box*, maybe. Did he mean the TV? Did he want it off? Was his condition making him confused? She wondered if he was on any psychosis medication now; during end-of-life care, only meds that made the patient comfortable were given, unless absolutely essential.

'Catherine,' he muttered.

Grace put a hand to her chest. 'Yes,' she said. Then she remembered she needed to remain anonymous. 'Who is she?'

'Grace,' he whispered.

And she held her breath. Was he speaking *to* her, or speaking *about* her.

'Who's that?' she asked quietly.

'Grace,' he repeated. Then: 'Maisie.'

Grace crumbled.

This often happened with patients – they liked to talk about times gone by. But he said no more.

'Maisie,' she whispered, distressed.

She waited. His breath slowed.

'I imagine your loved ones are thinking of you,' Grace said, voice breaking. 'I bet they send their love and hope that you don't suffer for long.'

She needed some air, felt the walls closing in. She couldn't do it. She couldn't sit there and act as though it all meant nothing to her. Rushing from the room, she crashed into Claire. 'I was just coming to tell you to take your break,' she said.

'Thank you.' Grace stumbled to the staffroom. She flicked the kettle on and put her forehead against the kitchen cupboard's cool surface. This was going to be harder than she had anticipated. She had her dad, and yet she didn't; he was a shell of a man. And he had no idea who she was.

'Need some company?'

Grace jumped. It was Claire.

'I guess,' she admitted.

'Did something happen in there?' Claire motioned back towards Bailey's room.

'No. *Yes.* I mean . . . he reminds me of someone I once knew. It triggered some difficult memories. Sorry.'

'Don't be sorry. Happened to me once. This woman was the spit of my grandma; it made me really emotional.'

Grace made them coffee and they sat on opposite sofas.

'Have you had any more of those break-ins?' asked Claire. 'I wanted to call you but then with Lily being ill . . .'

'She was your priority.' Grace sipped her drink. 'I did, and I went to the police, but they don't have time. But yesterday morning it stopped. Haven't had anything for two nights now. No idea why.'

'So you still have to find out who it was?'

'I'll keep pushing the police.'

Claire studied Grace. 'You've seemed . . . *different* recently. I know you've had these break-ins, but it feels like . . . well, more than that.'

Was Grace so readable? Her mother used to say that every emotion illuminated her face. At the thought of Catherine, she felt sad. The initial anger at her mum's secretiveness had simmered, but had now burnt out a little. Maybe yesterday's new information *was* enough for now. Maybe it *was* better Grace let it all digest before finding out the rest; before knowing it all. She would resolve things with her mum at some point, she just wasn't ready yet.

'*Grace?*'

She realised Claire had been speaking to her. 'I guess it's just the long dark nights too,' she volunteered.

'And we can't even go out and get pissed,' sighed Claire, seemingly happy enough with Grace's response not to push the subject further. 'As soon as the pubs open again at night, we must.' She stood. 'Right, we should get on.'

For the rest of the shift, between other patients, Grace tended to Bailey. She said his name to keep focused, to remind herself that she couldn't say Dad. She dreaded leaving him. She wasn't back until Sunday, the day after tomorrow. What if something happened before then? His inability to eat, his cold feet and hands, meant he maybe had only a week. But it was foolish to guess.

How many more shifts might she get with him?

How many hours?

She spoke calmly as she moistened his lips again, as she held his hand to show that someone was there, as she read the pages of a wartime romance novel from the shelf in the day room. Fate was on her side; a quiet shift permitted her time to do these things before she was called elsewhere.

Bailey didn't speak again. But Grace didn't mind. He'd settled.

'You've developed quite a bond,' said Claire during an early evening coffee break. 'Who does he remind you of?'

'Sorry?' Grace frowned.

'You said he reminded you of someone.'

She let the words form. 'Of my dad.'

Claire knew he had left when Grace was little, but nothing more.

Before the shift ended Grace knocked the beige lamp off the cabinet by her father. Then she retrieved the multicoloured one from her locker and found Claire.

'The lamp in Bailey's room broke,' she said. 'I found this in the staffroom cupboard. I could wipe it over and put it next to him. The light will be softer.'

'That's a nice idea,' said Claire.

Grace thought of something. 'Would you . . .?'

'Yes?'

'If he passes away when I'm not here . . . will you . . .?'

Claire studied Grace; she feared she had revealed the truth. But Claire nodded, said, 'I'll let you know.'

Grace cleaned the lamp, placed it next to her dad's head, and switched it on. For a brief moment, she worried it might trigger memories of the similar childhood lamp, and he would realise who Grace was. But if it did, then so be it.

What did any of it matter?

'Nothing bad will happen while it's on,' she said softly near his ear.

HULL LOCAL NEWS

Police issue appeal as concern grows for missing girl

Police are appealing for help in finding a missing girl from West Hull. Ten-year-old Stacey Reeves was last seen in her home twenty-four hours ago. Father, Martin Reeves (39), said she 'went to bed as usual, but it was empty in the morning.'

She is described as a quiet, sweet girl, with light blond hair, about 4ft 5in tall, and of slender build. Her father said that a pair of jeans, a pink North Face sweatshirt, and Adidas trainers were missing, so she got changed out of her pyjamas before whatever happened. 'This gives us hope that she went somewhere,' he said, 'rather than being taken. Stacey's never done this before, though. We're distraught.'

Local residents have joined the search. Bunches of pink chrysanthemums have been tied to lamp posts after Martin Reeves shared in a TV appeal that Stacey kept one in a vase on her windowsill. Teacher, Jennifer Simpson, said, 'She's lovely, attentive and polite.'

Police said officers are 'becoming increasingly concerned' and want to make sure she is 'well and safe.' Anyone with information of her whereabouts is being urged to get in touch with Humberside Police.

Did 'Feather Man' Fall Asleep in Armchair?

Hull woman, Emily Baker, sixty-four, woke in the middle of the night to a man sitting in the opposite armchair. She had fallen asleep in her living room, describing it as the only place in the house that was warm once the electricity went off. She screamed, waking the slumbering man, who jumped up and escaped before she could see his face.

'I was shaken up,' she admitted. 'Thought I was dreaming. It was terrifying. A strange man asleep in my chair. I'm just relieved he ran away when I screamed the house down.'

Though Humberside Police can't be sure it was the so-called Feather Man, especially considering since he didn't leave a feather, widely considered to be the mark of the serial home invader, they are looking further into the incident.

35

I'm the One

Again, the house was dark when Grace got home; she wanted to run and never come back. But where would she go? As she opened the gate, a sound up the street. She hurried up the path, not daring to look back. Voices then, low, ghostly, approaching. She fumbled for her key, dropping it and panicking.

'Grace.'

She shrieked.

'It's me. Ben. Number seventeen.' He had a torch, shone it near his face, then behind him, illuminating other faces from the street, their iced breath fogging the air.

'Yes. Ben. Sorry.' Grace felt foolish. She just wanted to get inside, get the camping lamp on.

'We've been searching for Stacey. We're going to spread out now, head for the parks, the river.'

Oh, *God*. She was still missing then.

'In the *dark?*' Grace said softly, horrified and also confused about why they wouldn't look when it was light.

'We've been searching all day too,' said Ben. 'Then we had a break. But now . . .'

'We can't *stop* just because it's dark,' said the burgundy-haired woman Grace knew lived at the top of the street, voice leaden with sadness. 'What if we did and we found out . . . I don't know. That she was trapped somewhere, and we gave in.'

Trapped somewhere.

'A box,' said Grace before she could think.

Was she triggered by her own experience, by being locked in

251

that cupboard at school, scratching at the door to escape? The physical similarities she and Stacey had, the curious bond that had developed via their window waves, were possibly why Grace was so distressed.

'Sorry?' Ben frowned.

'Nothing.' She buried the image of the dark wood box once again. 'I'd like to help but . . .'

'*But?*' The burgundy-haired woman glared.

Grace was torn. Of course she wanted to help find the little girl, but in the dark, with a few torches? No. *No.* 'I can do tomorrow?' she offered. She was a coward, a total coward. She was letting Stacey down. 'I just did a twelve-hour shift – I might not be much good to you now.'

'Of course.' Ben looked sympathetic, though Burgundy Hair narrowed her eyes. 'I'm not sure of our plans for tomorrow – we're hoping she's back by then.'

The small crowd moved on.

Inside, safe but feeling horribly guilty, Grace found the camping lamp and sat in the living room, hugging it. She had no appetite and was so tired she could barely move. The chill froze her limbs.

God, *please* let them find Stacey.

Grace spent the rest of the evening trying to think of something else. *Anything* else. Anything other than the little girl, missing and out in the dark on her own.

Tomorrow, Riley was coming.

He had been gone almost a week, and yet she was OK. The thought surprised her. It had been tough, yes, but for the past few days she hadn't felt compelled to reach out to him for support. If she hadn't needed him this week, did she need him at all? But if she thought of how they laughed, stayed in bed all day sometimes, she wanted him back.

How long was it since things had been that way though?

Grace carried the lamp upstairs and got into the cold bed. At first, exhaustion meant she slept. Then, after four o'clock, hunger kept waking her. She should have eaten before going to bed. Her rumbling stomach persisted. She never went downstairs alone at night, always got Riley to, but she felt sick and it wouldn't go away.

Damn.

In the end, she got the lamp, and her phone for extra light, and crept down the stairs, avoiding the creak in the hallway. Ridiculous – who was she trying not to wake? She listened. Quiet. In the kitchen, she boiled water on the hob, made noodles. Heading upstairs with them, she paused.

She was sure she had shut the living-room door.

Maybe not.

But she had *always* shut doors, ever since she read an article when Jamie was small that said closed doors slowed fire down. Maybe she had been so distracted she forgot. It was possible. Unease shifted insidiously inside her.

She looked into the living room.

A silhouette in the chair by the hearth.

She blinked. Must be imagining it. Blinked again. It would be gone now, *it would be gone.*

It wasn't.

Then movement; the silhouette shifted.

'Riley?' she croaked, knowing he wouldn't just sit there, not speaking.

A pause, and then a voice, not his: 'No . . . I was waiting until morning,' the voice said.

'Who . . .?' The word was a dry rasp.

'I'm The Night,' he said.

Grace dropped the bowl; felt the ground dropping away from her too.

'I'm the one who's had you in my sights.'

She screamed.

36

The Night

It had taken three nights for him to get here; on one of them he brought a gift, but on two of them he came empty-handed.

The intention with the red rose on night ten had been different to his objectives with the previous items; he left that single flower as an apology, lingering a moment, wondering if he should give it to her in person. He had written that roses with thorns lasted longer to try and say that those who are flawed are stronger. He wanted her to know that, to *understand* that. Since her husband had left, he had wanted to stay each time, speak to her at last. Tell her she'd be stronger without him.

See her.

But for two nights, he had sneaked out before dawn broke, resolve gone. He knew she was afraid of the dark and it had made him panic. So, instead, he thought it was wise that he wait until morning, or else she wouldn't listen to him. But every morning, exhausted then, he couldn't go back.

He was a failure.

What he had hoped to achieve hadn't succeeded.

Now, he felt she deserved to know what had been going on.

She deserved to know *why*.

Earlier that night, he had let himself in the back door with the key after midnight, made his familiar way through the gloom to the living room, avoiding the creak he knew in the hallway. Every time he arrived, he feared she might have installed some sort of battery-run house alarm, and he prepared to run. But so far, she hadn't.

Anticipating the chill, he had worn his usual night-time fleece, fat gloves, and thick boots. He settled in the chair by the fireplace. In recent nights he had sat here after writing his note. It had been the only time in the day he relaxed.

But once he knew for certain the gifts hadn't worked, he had to surrender.

Admit defeat.

Then the frenzy of his obsession dissolved, a jigsaw falling apart so that each piece became a pointless picture of trees or beans or rooftops on its own.

And he knew.

Knew he should talk to her.

Explain.

Make her see.

He tried to anticipate her reaction. Perhaps he should leave, come back during the day, knock on the door. This was madness, sitting in her house, waiting to talk to her. And yet he was rooted there.

He would wait until morning – it would be less shocking for her in the light.

Then he would tell her everything.

It was not good.

But she deserved to know.

When his eyes got accustomed to the gloom, he noticed the Tiffany lamp had gone. She had got rid of the fish, the red roses too, and the Venus de Milo sculpture was missing. But the candles remained in the kitchen, and the dragon in its frame.

Why?

Eventually, he dozed off and was woken by a sound. He started, sat up straight in the chair. Footsteps, on the stairs. He hadn't expected her to come down in the dark. He hadn't expected this at all. She went into the kitchen. He wanted to sneak out but couldn't while she was there, near the back door.

She wasn't going to like this. She might scream.

Maybe she wouldn't see him.

Then he would leave. This was a bad idea. He would be in so much trouble.

What had he been thinking?

She came back into the hallway. Stopped. Froze. A shadowy statue.

'Riley?' she whispered.

He panicked. 'No.' He should explain. 'I was waiting until morning.'

'Who . . .?' Grace sounded petrified. Understandable.

'I'm The Night.' He wanted to explain that too, then realised the words sounded ominous.

She dropped the bowl with a crack.

'I'm the one who's had you in my sights.' He was referring to one of his notes. But what he had written didn't sound quite the same when he said it aloud.

And then she screamed.

He *had* to stop her . . .

37

Waiting For Her Fate

The scream ripped through Grace like a wildfire.

'I'm trying to explain who I am,' said the man, face in shadow, sitting in her armchair. This should have made him appear less menacing, but it was worse. He had made himself at home. He had no right. 'I'm trying to—'

'Get the *fuck* out of my house,' she screamed.

It was supposed to be fight or flight when faced with your most abject fear; both flared in Grace. She wanted to run and never stop but her feet were stuck. He was here. The Night. Here. *Now.*

'I will, but just hear me out,' he said, voice low, edgy.

Grace wanted to raise the lamp, see him, possibly *know*, but couldn't move.

'Hear you out?' she screeched. '*Hear you out?*'

His presumption did something to her. Fear turned into hot fury. And she went at him, a wild animal, lamp swinging, light frenzied. The chair went backwards. He was trying to protect his body from her blows, but when the lamp hit his head, he cried out, shrill and shocked.

Panting, she stopped. Heaved herself off him. Moved away again.

'I'm not here to do anything t—' he tried, prone in the over-turned chair.

'You *must* be here to do something,' she cried, breathing hard. She still couldn't see his face. Had no idea who this man in her home was.

Who should she call? Who would get here the fastest? Certainly not the police. Her brain barely touched on Riley – he was no longer her saviour.

'If you move,' she said, voice low. 'I'll whack you with the lamp again.'

He didn't respond.

She remembered the phone in her hand, swiped her phone screen.

'*No,*' he cried, and tried to get up, out of the chair.

She screamed again. Fear returned, flooding her body, drowning the rage. She backed away, stumbling, righting herself.

'*No,*' he cried again.

Grace ran from the room, slipping on the spilt noodles. Shit, shit, *shit.* Where to go? Where was safe? She raced up the stairs, regretting it immediately; he would have her cornered now. Dreading footfall behind her, she ran into the bedroom, slammed the door, and clumsily shoved the wooden drawers in front of it.

Then she waited.

Waited.

Waited for her fate.

NIGHT FOURTEEN

38

A Massacre of Noodles

Grace cowered in the bedroom until she heard the back door slam, arms around her body, as frozen as the Venus de Milo sculpture hidden in the drawer, camping lamp close. Her breath came in sharp rasps. She tried dialling 999 but kept dropping the phone. Eventually it went through.

'Which service do you require?' asked a female operator.

'Police,' Grace managed to say.

While waiting to be put through she analysed what had just happened. A man. Sitting in her living room. *The Night*, he said. She should have held him down, forced him to stay. She should have held the lamp up. But she had been terrified. Panic that had driven her into violence initially had then become a more muted, understandable fear. How did she know what he might have done? When he lunged out of the chair, it was no longer fight but flight. And yet now, she wished she had overcome that, found out who he was, had him arrested.

Put an end to this horror.

Someone finally answered. 'Police service, what's your emergency?'

'I . . . someone was in my house.'

'Are you in a safe place?'

'I suppose – I'm upstairs,' said Grace.

'Are they still in the house?'

'No, he's gone. I mean . . . I *think* he has . . .'

'Are you injured?' asked the operator.

'No,' cried Grace. 'But *he* might be. Can you send someone?'

'It might be a few hours.'

'What if I *was* injured?' Grace's voice was shrill with frustration.

'Are you?'

'Well, no, but . . . oh, *fuck* it. I'm fine. Don't worry about me. I'll deal with it.' And Grace hung up. She would ring the local police station at nine, get PC Littlewood to come.

Now all she could do was wait. Wait for the dawn. For the warm. The shocking scene kept playing in her mind. She *should* have done more. Shone her phone torch in his face. It was the mystery, the not knowing, that now churned her stomach. How could she stay in the house tonight? What if he came back? Where could she go?

Eventually, the sun began to infiltrate the room, gentle, shy, and the heating kicked in.

At seven a.m., as the lights sprang back to life, Grace cautiously went back downstairs.

A massacre of noodles waited for her in the hallway, but nothing else. She poked her head into every room, opening cupboards, desperate to be sure. She checked the back door – locked again, as on previous nights. Then she cleared the noodles up, made strong coffee, and ventured into the living room. Chair still overturned; the only thing out of place. Nothing added today, just something moved. She righted it. Felt like a ghost in her own house, like she had no substance, was made of nothing; she was exhausted, traumatised, and she should eat. But she knew she would be sick.

It was Saturday. Riley was coming over to talk later. Despite everything, despite what had happened in here in the night, she realised she couldn't bear to see him today. There had been no urge to reach out to him, and now she surged with a need to push him away. She would *not* turn to him in this time of need. He did *not* deserve that honour.

She sent a quick message: *Change of plan, I'm busy today. I'll let you know when I can see you.*

Grace's eyes were drawn to the window, to the one opposite. Empty.

In amongst everything, she remembered Stacey. Was she back home safe yet? Had the search last night been successful? She should go over and find out, ask if there was anything she could do if not. If there was another search, she should join in, *no matter what*.

That strange image appeared in her mind again.

A child, inside some sort of rectangle vessel, trapped and desperate. And when Grace thought of it, she couldn't breathe. Should she tell someone? Tell the police when they came? *No.* They would think her mad.

Just like her father.

Gradually, Grace started to feel more like herself. She fixed some food and sat down at the kitchen table, forcing herself to eat it. As she finished some coffee, a police car pulled up outside Martin's house. She got her coat and headed across the street, needing to find out that Stacey was safe. Watching from the gate, she couldn't see the faces of the two officers who went up the path to determine their news. But Martin's slumped shoulders and shaking head when he opened the door told her it wasn't good.

Shit. *Shit.*

Retreating back inside, despite her earlier promise to herself, she realised her mother had messaged: *Can we talk today, I really want to. X*

The argument with her mum seemed petty now, long past, old news. This was her mum, a woman who had been there her whole life. Yes, she was difficult, she was stubborn, and she had kept important facts from Grace, but perhaps she'd had good reason. There were bigger things going on, Lights Out, the extreme cold, a little girl missing . . . a man – *The Night* – in her house.

Grace called her mum.

'Oh, light,' said Catherine dramatically when she answered. 'Please take me, I deserve to die. Now take me light.'

'*Pardon?*' Grace was unnerved.

'Sorry, I clicked answer without thinking. I'm rehearsing. Lady Macbeth. Her final line.'

Grace raised her eyebrows. Ever the dramatic. 'You sound good.'

'Of course I do, dear. I've been practising.'

Some things didn't change. Grace wasn't sure what to say, so she said nothing.

'Look,' said Catherine, all business. 'I can let it go that you left an elderly woman with no way of getting home, so can't you let it go that I might have made a few mistakes in the past?'

'You had no right to keep all those facts from me. Knowing about my dad, about him being ill, him not wanting to hurt me with it . . . that might have helped me.'

'You're right. But what can I do now?'

'Say you're sorry,' suggested Grace.

Catherine paused. 'I am. I wasn't in the best place then, you have to understand. I sought advice because I wasn't coping either. Imagine being abandoned with a young child.' She must have realised what she'd said.

'I can,' said Grace quietly. 'Except I was still pregnant when I was left.'

'Yes. You were. And you've been amazing. Better than me, clearly.'

Grace realised she was close to tears. 'And I still want you to tell me about the *that's not all* that you said the other day.'

'I will. In person though.' Catherine sounded emotional too. As was her way, she moved quickly on. 'When is Riley coming?'

'He's not,' snapped Grace. 'I don't care. Don't want to see him.'

'Oh. OK.' Pause. 'And what about the break-ins?'

'I went downstairs in the night . . . and there was a man sitting in the living room.'

'*What?* Are you alright? Who *was* he? What did he *want?*' Catherine took a breath. 'Did he hurt you?'

'No, no, and I am, I am. Please don't stress.' Maybe she shouldn't have told the poor woman; it wasn't fair to worry her. 'He ran away when I said I'd call the police. I rang 999 but . . . well, they couldn't help. So I'm ringing the station in a minute.'

'Who *was* he?'

'*The Night.* That's what he said. The man who's been leaving the things.'

'Well, did you see his face?' demanded Catherine. 'Could you pick him out in a line-up?'

'No. And I don't know if they do line-ups in the real world, Mum.'

'You *must* come here. You can't stay in that house alone tonight.'

Despite her fears, Grace didn't want to go there. Despite her fears, she was angry at the idea of being run out of her own home. She would think of something; maybe invite someone to stay over. Might the police let her have an officer outside? Could she find out if Night Watch was still happening and if so might whoever was on duty watch the house all night?

'I'm going to stay at my friend Claire's,' she lied. 'There's no need to worry.'

'Of *course* I'm going to worry,' cried Catherine. 'Shall I come there now?'

'No, I'm fine, honestly. Yes, I was shaken. Yes, it's not ideal. But I'm calling the police station now.'

'You sound so tired, dear. I'm worried about you.'

'It was a long shift yesterday.' An image of Bailey, lying inert in his hospice bed, flashed like a passing street light over a car windscreen, his face orange in the Tiffany lamp's glow. She felt guilty then – should she tell Catherine about this too? No. This was their moment, father and daughter, no one else. And it was only fair that she told her mum something this big in person.

'I'll let you go call the police,' said Catherine. Her mum paused. 'I thought of something after . . . after our . . . the other day.'

'Oh.' Grace waited.

'About your dad. I thought you might like to know.'

'Yes?'

'When you were born . . . he was the first one to hold you.'

'Was he?' Grace's voice wavered.

'I was exhausted. It had been a long labour, I was an older mum. So, he took you. And he . . . he didn't want to part with you.' Catherine sniffed. 'Said he never wanted to let you go.'

Grace sank into the sofa.

'I'm sorry,' said Catherine. 'For everything.'

'I know.'

'Please, *please*, make sure someone is with you tonight.'

Grace hung up, an image of her father cradling her as she took her first breaths vivid.

Hang on until I get back to you, she thought. *Just hang on.*

She dialled the local police station but the phone rang and rang and rang. Brad and Jennifer swam around and around their bowl.

After a shower, she tried again. No answer.

Again. No answer.

She fell asleep on the sofa, woke to rapping on the door. She opened it, cautious, heart hammering.

Ben at number seventeen. 'We're off on another search for Stacey in half an hour,' he said. 'You're welcome to join us.'

Grace wanted to help, desperately, but she needed to get hold of the police.

'If you're busy . . .' Ben filled in when she didn't respond.

'Sorry.' Grace was still dazed from being woken. 'I . . . yes. I'll help.'

'Great. Meet you outside mine in half an hour. It's only a few of us. Lots work Saturdays.'

Grace tried the police again as she headed out the door, but with no success.

Seven people formed a small group outside Ben's house. He took the lead, said they should split up, suggested that Grace and he search the local parks. They poked stiffened, silver trees, pushed through evergreen bushes, prodded dying shrubbery and rotting piles of leaves. Their efforts yielded nothing. Grace was glad – what horrible find might it be in such freezing weather? Much as she wanted to save the child, she was relieved that the search was a failure.

The word *save* played over in her mind on the walk home hours later; why was Grace suddenly so frantic to rescue Stacey? Of course, she had prayed for her return since the day the girl disappeared, but now, a desperation grew. Maybe it was the act of helping, of physically doing something. Maybe that had made it all so real.

Get her out of the box . . .

'What?' Ben, walking at Grace's side, turned to her.

Had she spoken the words aloud?

'Nothing.' She shook her head. They turned into the street. Bunches of dusky pink chrysanthemums were tied to three of the lamp posts, bright beauty in a grey world.

'Oh,' said Grace, the word a strangled sob.

'I know,' said Ben softly. 'Martin mentioned that she had one in a vase. Loved it apparently. Now, people are tying them everywhere as a sign of hope for her to return.'

'I gave her it,' said Grace quietly.

'Sorry?'

'The original flower. The other day.'

'No wonder they're making you emotional,' said Ben.

Grace nodded, close to tears.

They got to her house. 'Ben,' she said, thinking now of the night ahead, her own fears. 'Are they still doing Night Watch duty?'

'Not every night. People are tired.'

'Tonight?'

'No.'

'Oh.' Grace's heart sank.

'Are you OK?'

If she told him she was alone, he'd know Riley had gone. And if she told him about what was happening, the whole neighbourhood would be in chaos. But what if the man – *The Night* – came back?

What if he had horrible intentions, hadn't fulfilled them last night? She exchanged numbers with Ben, using the excuse of news about Stacey, but feeling better that she had someone close by to ring if she needed.

When she got inside, she called the police station again but it rang and rang and rang.

The Lights Out countdown approached.

Grace went to her usual window spot at four twenty-five, anxiety twisting her stomach. The sun struggled through smoke cloud to give the world goodbye rays. She couldn't bear to look at the opposite bedroom window, so she shut the curtains and went around the house – *flick, lit* – ending where the Tiffany lamp had been on the hearth. She hoped that whoever was on shift had kept it next to her dad.

Eight o'clock loomed. She got the camping lamp and did her usual route, turning the lights off, but this time Grace ended in the living room. She could not look at the armchair in case she saw him there: The Night. She paused, mouth parched, stomach queasy.

Could she try enduring the dark again now?

Would it help her cope tonight?

She covered her eyes and turned the last switch off.

Waited. Opened them. As last time, with the curtains shut, the dimness was absolute. And she was back there. Locked in a pitch-black cupboard. Children jeering on the other side of a locked door. *Try*, she thought, breathing hard. *Try*. But seconds later she fumbled for the camping lamp's switch, soaked up its illumination.

Grace still couldn't do it.

What the hell was she going to do?

She had left it too late, not called anyone to come over, or arranged to go anywhere.

Should she sleep in the living room? Push the sofa against the door so no one could get in, sleep on it? Yes. She dragged the duvet downstairs and got settled, phone beneath pillow, Ben's number there if needed. She feared sleep would be a battle. Thankfully, acute exhaustion won. Nightmares came hard though: dragons leapt out of picture frames, children screamed inside locked boxes, and shadowy figures closed in.

But, as far as she knew, The Night did not return.

The Daily Read

TORY MP INJURED DURING BLACKOUT

Conservative MP Charles Princeton was admitted to hospital after a fall in his Kensington home last night. He is being treated at the private Cromwell Hospital for fractures to his leg and arm. He is comfortable and hopes to return home in a few days. MPs are exempt from the switch off because they work through the night, but Princeton experienced an electricity outage due to a faulty fuse box and fell in the dark.

The MP – who was investigated last year after complaints of sexual misconduct – was a big supporter of Lights Out, saying on the BBC's Question Time that he had faith that citizens would pull together as they did during Covid-19. He had previously said, 'A brief time without electricity is better than a long future worrying about our planet. If there are casualties, that's life. If people die, so be it, and when we win the next election, we'll do more.'

A reported one million members of the public have written to local MPs saying they want Lights Out to end. They complained about damp homes, empty classrooms due to the number of ill children, and essential night-time car journeys ending in accident. NHS directors said that hospitals can't cope with the influx of patients. Chelsea and Fulham MP Jane Green was one of a few ministers who spoke against the switch off, saying it would result in tragedy. 'I can't back this,' she said. 'I see a bleak winter ahead.'

NIGHT FIFTEEN

39

And Who Am I?

Work looming, Grace got up before the electricity resumed, pushed the sofa back, and carried the lamp through the house, shivering, breath staining the air. Though she was sure The Night had not returned, she checked for strange pictures, crystals, flowers. Nothing.

Anxiety overtook then as she dressed.

The day. Work. Her father. Claire had not messaged with news overnight, which meant that hopefully he was still there. Still *alive*.

The street when she left at seven thirty was quiet. Cloud cloaked the sun as though it was struggling to wake after a night of insomnia. The winter solstice had at least passed and the days would now slowly lengthen again. The air was breath-freezing; twigs and leaves crunched underfoot as she approached the car. She glanced at Stacey's house. A light in the kitchen. Should she knock? Was it too early? Maybe she should try Ben, see if there had been any news.

No; she was going to be late. After work.

In the staff changing room, everyone stamped feet and grumbled about the chill. Claire had been on the night shift; at staff handover, she ran through the updates. Grace tensed at mention of Bailey Brighthead.

'Bailey took a turn for the worse at three a.m.,' Claire said. 'Since there isn't any family, and he seemed distressed, Janey's with him now until someone else takes over. I think we sh—'

'I can go to him.' Grace was unable to help herself. She tried to disguise the urgency she felt. 'He was my patient on Friday, I liked him . . .'

'That'll be up to your day nurse.' Claire glanced at Sam. 'That OK with you?'

'That's fine,' he said.

Grace forced herself to hear the rest of the handover, knowing it would seem odd if she rushed off. Once it was done, she went to her father's room, not even staying to say hello to Claire. Janey, a care support worker, sat in the bedside chair, holding his hand. With sun filling the room, the Tiffany lamp was off.

It was all Grace could do not to run over and switch it on.

'I've been allocated my d— um, *Bailey* today.' She tripped over her words. 'How's he been?'

'Not good.' Janey stretched, her bones clicking. 'Restless. Just settled this last five minutes.'

Periods of agitation, confusion and hallucinations were common at end of life when the chemical imbalance of the body was completely upset. Grace had witnessed it many times, but knowing her own father was suffering was a whole new experience. Now she knew why family shouldn't nurse relatives at this stage: it was deeply distressing.

Should she excuse herself after all?

No. *No.*

'Hope you sleep well,' said Grace as Janey left the room.

Then she switched the lamp on, took the still-warm armchair, and her father's cool, slim hand. Was he aware of the gentle lamplight? That his carer had changed? Did he recall her from the other day?

Probably not.

This lodged hard in Grace's gut. But what if he *had* known who she was last time; he had said her name, her mother's name. What if he had been hanging on until she returned? Usually patients waited for relatives to leave before surrendering, but what if that family were new to your life?

Might you wait for them to come back?

The door opened; Claire looked in. 'I'm going home,' she said. 'How are you? I know he . . . reminded you of . . .'

'I'm fine.' She wasn't, but what could she do?

'I don't think it'll be long.' Claire looked at him.

'No.' Grace wanted it to happen another day, another week, another month, but that wasn't fair; he would only suffer. He wasn't about to wake up, feel better, and bond with her all over again.

'I've got a few days off at the end of the week – wanna go for lunch?'

'That would be nice.' Grace needed it.

'Have a good shift.' Claire blew a kiss and disappeared.

Grace sat in silence, watching him. She mourned the conversations they had never had, and now never would. Should she speak them aloud, act them out for him? What might they have talked about over the years? What would he have thought of Riley, of Jamie, of what she had done with her life?

Would he be proud?

She put the TV on last time, but today that felt wrong. She should speak, but didn't know what to say. He hadn't moved in a while. Was he still breathing? Just. His heart rate had slowed. Grace wiped the saliva from his mouth, cleaned his lips and applied some gel.

'It's Grace,' she finally said.

She *had* to say it.

It could be her last chance.

'It's me. Maisie. I'm here.' She squeezed his hand. 'Dad. It's me.'

Sometimes the dying needed permission to go. Grace remembered a lady called Viv hanging on and hanging on, and the family getting more distressed. Claire had told them that Viv might need their blessing. That blessing might be forgiveness for something she felt bad over. Grace had overhead Viv's daughter telling her none of them cared about 'the affair'. Viv had drawn her final breath an hour later.

Was Bailey waiting for such a pardon?

Did he feel guilty for abandoning his daughter?

Did he need someone to release him from it?

'I know you tried,' Grace said, near his ear. 'I know now about your illness. That must have been scary for you.' She choked on the words. 'You were protecting me. I know that too. But . . . what a *waste*. All those years. I missed you so much.' She squeezed his hand but there was no reaction. Maybe he had already gone, if only in mind. This was terrible. She was losing him – all over again – without even having had him.

She reached in her pocket for a tissue to dab her damp eyes and an old receipt fell to the floor. It landed beneath the bed. *Beneath the bed*. A memory then: a note. Finding one of his notes. Yes. Pink paper, neat writing. Hidden beneath her bed.

Love you, Little Maisie.

He *had* hidden them for her. Riley had been right. Sweet missives for her to find when he was away with work. How could she have forgotten such a lovely thing? What other things might she now remember? Had this experience, nursing her dad, opened up a doorway to them?

After a couple of hours, the door opened and Sam put his head in.

'Do you want to take your break?' he said.

She wasn't hungry, but made a cup of tea and brought it back to the room. It was a quiet shift, thankfully, or she could have been called away.

As she sipped her beverage, Bailey let out the longest fart.

'Shush,' he croaked.

'Did you tell your fart to shush?' smiled Grace.

'Wasn't me.'

She put a hand to her chest. His old game. Blame everything else.

'Was . . . *you*,' he whispered.

'And who am I?'

'Grace,' he said.

'Yes.' Tears trailed down her cheeks.

'Maisie.'

'Yes.' Even if he was hallucinating, it didn't matter. She was in there – in his head, his heart.

'The dark.'

'*The dark?*' She held her breath.

'I'm sorry.'

'Don't be. You were the one who brought light.'

'I scared . . . you.'

'You didn't,' she said.

'I . . . I . . .'

'Don't speak.' She inhaled, hard. 'Let go . . . if you . . . if you want to. *Dad.*' Then she sobbed into the sheet, not caring if anyone came in.

And weakly, he patted her head.

She lifted it, kissed his papery cheek.

'The box . . .'

Suddenly, Grace frowned.

What box?

The word sent a cold draught through her bones like they were hollow and winter had climbed in. 'What do you mean?' Grace tried to temper her words. 'What . . .' She paused, not even wanting to say the word. '. . . box?' she finally whispered.

'I . . . never . . . I'm . . . sorry.' Bailey's words were barely audible now.

What box? She *needed* to know.

Something flashed – another memory, freed by this simple, horrible word. Hands roughly pulling at her. *His* hands?

Slowly, her dad's facial muscles slackened, billowing sheets unpegged from a line. His breathing grew shallower, irregular; long pauses in between each breath lulled Grace into thinking he had gone, his sudden, raspy inhales startling her.

How could she disturb his peace now?

Still, she tried. 'Dad, what box? *Please?*'

His eyes were half open, like he was checking she was still there.

Then his hand slipped from hers.

He had gone; she had seen him out.

Bailey had held Grace during her first breaths. She had been there for his last.

But it had been ruined by two words: *the box*.

She took his pulse, to make sure. Then she closed his eyelids.

'I love you,' she said.

But she could hardly think straight as she made a note of the time: twelve forty-eight. She should get Sam so he could verify the death but couldn't leave yet. After this, she would never be alone with her dad again. And now there were more questions, more mystery – more anxiety. She bowed her head. Then turned out the lamp.

Something inside released with this action; undid; unfolded, a scrunched-up piece of paper opening of its own accord. It was grief. Pain held in for so long. The lid unscrewed completely and fell off. When hot tears dried up, in their place was a cool calm.

Then his words came to her again.

The box . . . I'm sorry.

She felt dizzy. Staggered back.

She was in the school cupboard. Suffocating. Clawing at the walls to escape. Except the voices on the other side weren't children; she heard her dad, *They're coming, they're coming, they're coming.* And he sounded terrified. Grace tried to get herself together. She must get Sam. But something was rising, up out of her, a horror film skeletal hand from a grave.

A memory.

No, not now. I can't.

She pushed it down, refused to let it play in her mind. Not here, not where she couldn't be alone.

Instead, she got Sam, in a daze, helped him with last offices, her mind elsewhere.

'Sadly, there's no family to tell,' he said.

They already know, thought Grace.

Quietly, they washed Bailey, as carefully as if he had just been born. They dressed him in a simple white shirt and black slacks; Grace had no idea what his style was, but felt pleased with this result. They straightened his legs, put his arms at his side. His ankle was tagged with an identification bracelet, ready for the mortuary.

The box . . . I'm sorry.

No, think about that when the shift's over.

Too much now.

Many times Grace had wondered, while she did this duty, where humans went when they died. She had always felt that the soul had to go *somewhere*. Now, she hoped it was to the brightest of places.

The rest of the shift passed in a horrible blur.

She wanted to escape. But she did her chores – laundry-washing, tea-making, patient-tending – hands shaking, mind wandering. When the undertakers arrived for Bailey, she went to the toilet, unable to watch him leave.

Sam went off to his other duties, leaving her alone as she stripped the bed her father had passed in, sobbing into the pillowcase; she would never see him again. She would never fling open a front door, sit on the stairs in her nightie, hoping it would bring him back.

That door was shut; this was closure.

Except it wasn't.

What had he meant about a box?

You know, Grace.

Did she? Yes. But she needed help. Her mum. *That's not all,* she had said. Had she meant this? Instinct said yes. Fear said yes.

Grace would go to her as soon as the shift was done.

40

A Lesser Thing

Shift done, Grace hurried to her car, drove too fast towards her mum's house. Once there, she knocked on the door.

A light shimmered inside, a tiny ghost. Her heart raced as she waited; she was about to share a shocking revelation with her mother. Two. Bailey had returned, but now he was gone. And she was also sure, had some kind of inkling, that *she* was also about to find out something terrible. She inhaled, looked up at the deep blue sky, at the fingernail of moon, the cluster of silver dots. Despite her fear of the dark, the night sky with its random glitter wasn't as angst-inducing as the shadows inside. She wished she could just stay here all night, never have to face what waited for her indoors.

The door opened. 'Oh.' Catherine was wearing a woollen hat and wrapped in a thick, burgundy fleece. Then again: '*Oh.*'

'Can I come in?' said Grace tiredly.

Should she have come tomorrow, let it all sink in first? No. She needed answers.

'How are you, dear? Did someone come to the house again last night?'

'No. It isn't that.'

Grace followed her mum inside. A large gold candle burned on the hallway bureau.

'You know we're not supposed to use candles.' Grace was agitated.

'I'm careful,' snapped Catherine, going into the living room where a fat script and another three candles sat on the coffee table, as well as an oil lamp on the mantelpiece. The warm light was misleading; the room was ice cold. Grace felt concern for her eighty-five-year old mum but she appeared fine, cheeks rosy, and eyes aglow. On the windowsill, a vase of dusky pink chrysanthemums.

Following Grace's gaze, Catherine said, 'I'm displaying them for Stacey Reeves. Everyone on the street is.' She paused. 'Did you want to sleep here?'

Grace shook her head, sat on the sofa, glad of her coat and scarf. She felt sick. Where to begin? She couldn't demand answers until she broke the sad news to her mum.

'You might want to sit down,' she said.

'I'm fine. I was going to put a pan on the hob.'

'I'm not staying for that, Mum. I've been at work all day. I . . .'

'Yes?' Catherine loitered by the door.

Out with it. 'My dad came into the hospice.'

Catherine studied Grace like she had met her twice, long ago, and was now trying to place her. 'Your . . . *dad*?'

'Yes.'

'What do you mean? As a visitor? Who was he there to see?'

'No. A patient.'

'Oh.' Catherine now sank into the armchair by the door, burgundy fleece gaping to show bony shoulders and a white cotton nightie and thick cardigan. 'Goodness me.' She paused. 'How is he? Should I . . .?'

'He's gone,' said Grace simply.

'To another hospice?' Catherine's face registered the truth then. '*Oh.*'

'I know. It's a shock.' Grace felt terrible now. Maybe she should have let her mother say goodbye to him after all. But how? She would have had to tell staff who he was. 'You have a right to know.' Grace stared at one of the candles, her vision hazing over. 'He passed today. At twelve forty-eight. I was there. He knew it was me, or at least he was imagining I was there.'

Her mum looked frail now. 'Today? Oh. I'm . . . I . . .'

'Shall I get you a brandy?' asked Grace.

Catherine shook her head, resilient as always. 'How long was he at the hospice?'

Grace shook her head, ignoring her mother's line of questioning. 'Mum, I need to . . . I have to ask . . .' The tears she thought were done, returned, hot but quiet, made of both grief and fear.

Catherine got up with more agility than someone half her age and joined Grace on the sofa. She wrapped the fleece around the two of them, a gesture that spoke volumes; she was rarely tactile. 'It *is* a shock. I wish you'd told me sooner. But, also, I understand. This was your . . . *moment*. And I'm glad you had it.'

'Me too,' Grace managed.

'I'm glad he wasn't alone.' Catherine looked sad.

Grace could feel the many questions her mum wanted to ask, and knew how difficult it was for her to *not* speak them. Another time, she would answer them all. For now, she had her own, and was glad of the thick blanket, the law-breaking candles, and her mother's quiet.

The image of a box, long, wooden, closed.

Who's in there, Grace?

'Mum,' she said from within the confines of the blanket.

'Yes, dear?'

'Tell me about what you meant when you said *that's not all.*'

'Now?' she said. 'Dear, you've had a shock, you—'

Grace looked up, spoke tersely. 'No. You need to answer me.' She gulped. 'When he was dying . . . Dad . . . he mentioned a *box*.' She had to compose herself, spoke with fear. 'I felt terror so raw. Mum, what did he *mean*?'

Catherine nodded but didn't speak.

'Little Stacey who's missing, every time I think of her, I see a box, and feel the terror I had when those kids locked me in the cupboard at school. No . . . I feel terror *worse* than when I think of the cupboard.'

'That little girl is the age you were when . . .' said Catherine quietly, as though almost to herself. 'I suppose that could be it.'

'What do you mean?'

'The association. You see her as you. She even looks like you – I saw her picture in the paper.'

'No, I mean, you said the age I was *when* something. When what? Ten you mean?' Grace let it sink in. 'That's when my dad left.'

'Yes.' Catherine wrung her hands. The candles danced slowly.

But something still wasn't quite adding up in Grace's mind. 'But the kids, at school, that was later. I don't understand.'

'Those horrible children locked you in that cupboard because they knew you were terrified of the dark. *Already.*'

'No, that was what *caused* it,' Grace insisted.

Catherine shook her head. 'After what happened, that day, the day your dad went into the psychiatric hospital . . . I tried to get you to forget it.'

'*Forget what?*' Grace was stunned.

Catherine ignored the question. 'I know it might seem unethical but it felt like the right thing to do. Your dad was in the hospital, I was alone, and you were hysterical. I told you about my friend back then who had had some counselling, who told me to rewrite the narrative, didn't I? She told me to put that memory in a box.' Catherine sounded desperate, as though she was living it again. 'I told you it had never happened. Over and over. But I couldn't erase your fear of the dark. That stayed. And the kids were merciless, teased you for it, locked you in the school cupboard that day. So I used that narrative, it was easy. Let you believe that *that* caused your fear of the dark. What *they* had done. It was a kinder thing. A lesser thing. But, really, it was . . . your dad.'

'Told me *what* had never happened? *What* was Dad?'

'He locked you in a box.' Catherine spoke simply.

Grace shook her head. She had come for this, the truth, but resisted. 'No. *No.* He would never do that.'

'He did,' said Catherine sadly. 'Do you want me to tell you?'

Grace did. She needed to know. But she was terrified.

'Tell me,' she said eventually.

And Catherine did; she shared the story that Grace had been repressing all this time.

But it was exactly that: a story. There was still distance from it. Grace looked at the words, knew their truth, but she didn't fully let it in.

When Catherine was done, Grace staggered back into the night, to her car, to the house. She didn't want to go inside. It was a great box, full of menace. It was the place where strange men came in and scared her.

The door taunted her: *Come in, if you dare.*

Where else could she go?

Shakily, she got her keys in the lock, her phone's torch the only light until she got the camping lamp and felt for the switch. She hugged it. Couldn't bear it, wanted the lights on, all night. She screamed her fear and frustration into the labyrinth of rooms. When the hysteria faded, and acute exhaustion took over, she went to the living room, pushed the sofa against the door and collapsed into it. She had come to terms with her father's illness, knew it was the reason for the complex feelings surrounding her memories of him. Now, more to face. His death. A box.

She cried for what she knew, for what she had lost today.

And for what she *didn't* know – whether The Night would return again.

I'm here. I'm here. I'm here.
Always.

HULL LOCAL NEWS

Fridge Artwork Labelled 'Eyesore' by Mayor

Hull City Council are asking people not to dump broken refrigerators in the River Hull or Humber. The constant switching on and off during Lights Out is destroying their main components. This barrage of broken appliances is causing problems for maintenance work.

Two Orchard Park residents, however, have been more imaginative in their disposal. They have built a sculpture in a field, placing fridges to resemble a white volcano, tomato ketchup on top as lava. 'It came to me, like the man in Close Encounters of the Third Kind,' said Gary Hall, 37. 'I'm not expecting aliens, but I kept dreaming about a white pyramid shape. Then I saw fridges everywhere and built it with a mate. It's Close Encounters of the Fridge Kind.'

Hull Mayor, Teresa Nikolic, said the sculpture is an 'eyesore' and should be taken apart and removed. 'We have enough going on in the city at the moment,' she said.

Leaked government reports suggest that Lights Out might end sooner than was predicted.

NIGHT SIXTEEN

41

Déjà Vu

Nightmares chased Grace with long, tremulous arms into the dawn. She started awake, glad of the sun, confused about being on the sofa.

Think about something else, anything but the gaping box of your dreams, the pull of approaching it, to see if the child Grace is in there, curled up, sweaty, and terrified . . .

She was afraid of the dark. But her real dread was of confinement, of being left forever.

Of a box. All along, a box. Not Stacey in it. Never Stacey in it liked she had been imagining, fearing. Grace. *Little Grace.*

And her father had forced her into it.

Don't look at it. No. Can't. Not yet.

But where was Stacey then? *Where?*

Grace waited until the electricity was on before getting up. Brad and Jennifer swam three times around their bowl. Some things didn't change; a comfort. There were no new items, no evidence that anyone had come in. Still, Grace needed to report the intruder. It had been two days since he broke in, scared her by sitting in the armchair, but one of those days had been a twelve-hour shift watching her dad die. So she *must* go to the police station this morning.

The phone buzzed as she made coffee. A message from Riley: *Are you ready to see me? We really need to talk. X*

There was no point in putting it off. It had to be done.

Grace sent: *Come later, after work.*

Even with all that had happened, a part of her had enjoyed having the house to herself. She had always lived with someone, whether it had been her mother, her son, a husband, and it had been good, but now a sense of excitement grew. With that came choice, reality. She couldn't afford this house on her own. They would have to sell it if they split. Did she care? Was she attached to it? She could as easily attach elsewhere, somewhere smaller, somewhere that was all hers.

Phone in hand, she saw a recent text to Jamie. She needed to tell him about her dad but that didn't belong in a message. She should tell him in person.

She sent: *Do you have a day off this week? I'm off so I'll pop over. Lots to tell you. Mum. X.*

He replied after ten minutes; he was free on Saturday. That was settled. But now it was, she felt sad that she would be delivering bad news. She thought of her father, his last breaths, and her throat constricted.

But there was no time for grief.

She must go to the police station. Though still ice cold, it was sunny, the sky a deceptive madam of blue trickery. Grace could hardly imagine the heaviness of night – the terror it brought – as she marched along, coat pulled tight against the chill.

When she arrived at the red-brick police station building surrounded by chipped metal railings, Catherine rang. It was déjà vu – the last time Grace was here, the same timing. As then, she declined the call. It would have to wait; she felt bad, knew her mum would just be wanting to check in after last night.

Inside, the déjà vu ended: a different receptionist sat behind the purpose-built desk. Her name badge said Bella Smith, and the telephone headset sat lopsided on her head as though it was making a statement about the chaos of the multiple ringing phones and piles of untidy files and empty sandwich packets. Bella was on a call as Grace approached, trying to calm someone down. She hung up, took a breath, and answered another call, ignoring Grace.

She would just wait.

She had no choice.

She sat in one of the five uncomfortable plastic chairs beneath the noticeboard. Stacey's sweet face beseeched her from a large poster: *Find me, find me, find me.* Grace must. She must search again, soon.

Bella answered call after call. Grace had just decided to call her mum back while she waited, when the door opened and a man entered, slight but somehow solid too, his hair windswept. He approached the counter without seeing her.

Déjà vu returned. It was the same man she had seen here last time. He had been kind, kneeling next to her, listening; a strange but welcome respite from the madness. She didn't even know him but felt an odd joy at the sight of him again. He watched Bella on the phone – she ignored *him* too – and ran a nervous hand through his hair.

'Never a policeman when you need one, eh,' joked Grace, as she had last time.

He turned. His face fell.

Did she look *that* bad today?

'Last time,' she tried to explain, disappointed. 'You don't remember me, do you? Dead fish in my bag? Angelina?' No response from him. 'Doesn't matter.' Why was she so sad that he had forgotten her?

All colour had drained from his face.

What was wrong with him? Was he unwell? He looked like he might faint.

'Maybe you should sit down,' she said kindly.

The pallor contrasted an angry bruise on his forehead.

Had someone assaulted him? *Poor man.*

Then time stopped. Grace physically felt it. A vacuum around her. Bella's voice slowed down like a record player at the wrong speed. The ringing phones were a yawning buzz. The cars outside became a deep, monotone moan.

And she knew.

'It was *you*,' she croaked. 'Your bruise . . . I did it . . . me. It's *you*.'

It was him.

The Night.

And everything sped up again: phones trilled full pelt, Bella rambled, cars whizzed.

He ran.

Grace leapt up. 'It's *him*,' she yelled at Bella. 'Stop him, you have to arrest him! Someone has to chase him, now!'

Bella put a hand over the headset microphone. 'It's who?' she asked, lazily.

He was getting away. No time. Grace ran too. She fell out of the door, headed up the street where he had gone. She could still see him. Rage fuelled her. She was not afraid now – it was daylight, the safe place.

She *had* to know who the hell he was, and why, why, *why*?

He was heading towards the cemetery. She followed, panting hard, the chill misting her breath. Why the cemetery? No matter. The dead were her daily life. Loss was her friend.

She had lost her dad, a husband, the little girl across the street . . . what else did she have to lose now?

42

Not The Night Now

Tom ran.

When he saw Grace in the police station, he'd thought he might faint. It was the surprise. A punch in the gut. One he deserved. And though he had planned to admit to the police what he had done, he panicked. Ran. Ran hard. Looked back, just once, and saw her giving chase. His feet took him where they belonged: his cemetery. Grace still followed, gaining on him. Inside the gates, he slowed.

What was the point?

What was he running from?

He had finally wanted to tell the police, admit his crimes, so he could speak to her. This could be his chance, in the place that was as familiar as his own home. This was not her house, in the dark, surprising her. He was no threat here. Just a pale, bedraggled, pathetic man who hadn't slept for days.

He slumped onto the bench beneath the yew tree, unable – despite it all – to resist putting a sandwich wrapper in the nearby bin first. Grace marched up but stopped a few feet away from him, obviously still nervous, panting hard. A man tended a grave – one Tom had measured and marked out – not far from where they were so he hoped that she would feel safe, would know that she could scream for help.

'Who *are* you?' she demanded, arms crossed, protection.

'Tom,' he said, simply.

'So not *The Night* now, eh?' Sarcastic.

He remembered the moment a week ago in the police station reception area when he turned and saw her there. He'd had to hide his surprise, stop himself accidentally saying her name. Before then, he had only seen her from a distance, or in the photographs around the house. She was lovely; Harper was vivacious, brash, but Grace seemed the opposite, cautious, with a gentle air.

Now though, scared and angry, she had an edge, a pulsing energy.

'Why have you been coming into my house? What the fuck were you doing sitting in my living room the other night?'

'I'm so sorry.' He felt wretched now.

'Sorry? *Sorry?* I don't care how you *feel*,' she spat. 'What about how you made *me* feel? You've been terrifying me for two weeks. Invading my *home*.'

'I'll tell you why, I will.' Tom tried to appease her.

'Spit it out then.' She glared at him. 'And then you're coming right back to the police station with me.'

'Where we first met,' he said quietly.

He recalled Grace on the floor, scrabbling for things fallen from her bag. The fish in a sandwich bag. The one he had placed in her fishbowl. Dead now. And he had thought of his relationship with Harper.

'I thought you were there to report a crime that time,' she cried.

'I didn't actually say that.'

She paused, eyes flashing. 'So what *were* you doing there?'

'I wanted to tell the police what I'd been doing. I was hoping they'd stop me.'

'*Stop* you? Why couldn't you just stop yourself?'

'I'll tell you. I went there today to turn myself in so they might let me speak to you, explain it all.'

'Explain it then,' she cried.

His legs twitched; he needed to move, to pace. 'I'll tell you all of it but can I please get up and walk around the ben—'

'No.' The word was sharp, a twig snapping. 'Stay there. If you move, I'll scream like hell.'

'I'll try.' Tom knew he deserved no mercy. He felt wretched. His bottom was cold now, his fingers blue. This open place where the dead slept was always devilishly cold in January. 'I have trouble keeping still,' he admitted.

'Tough.'

'You've no reason to be afraid, I've no weapon, no bad intentions, and I've never hurt anyone in my life.'

'How do I *know* that?' she demanded. 'Coming in my house, leaving those items, it just isn't normal behaviour!'

'I see that. I do. That's why I wanted to tell the police what I'd been doing.'

'And what *had* you been doing? And how did you get in?'

'A key,' he said quietly.

Grace took a step back, and he noticed her voice dropping for the first time, sounding utterly bewildered. 'Who *are* you? How the hell did you get a key to my house?' She looked aghast.

'I'll tell you it all,' he said.

'Tell it then! Tell me why you have a key, why you broke in and why you left those *ridiculous* fucking items!'

'I thought I could improve your marriage,' he said simply.

Grace laughed; it was more of a bark. Then she gathered her hands in a tight circle, a keyhole. 'I don't . . . I don't even know what to do with those words.' She shook her head. 'First, there's nothing wrong with my marriage, and if there was, what the hell does it have to do with *you*?'

He wanted to ask where her husband was then, but he couldn't be cruel to her. Sadly, when he told her his full story, he was likely to cause her pain.

'Improve my marriage by breaking into my house and leaving crap everywhere?' she continued. 'You need help, seriously.'

'I probably do.' He was embarrassed to feel tears build behind his eyes. Embarrassed to be shivering on a bench, foolish. Sorry for the upset he had caused Grace.

Her hands fell open, unlocked. She had seen his vulnerability. He knew it. 'Put the key on the ground in front of you,' she said gruffly. 'Yes, you can get up, but if you come near me, I'll scream.'

Tom nodded, went into his pocket, and then placed the key with a soft clink on the path that separated them. He wished he could pace, but sat back down.

'Where did you get it from?' she asked, picking it up, eyes not leaving him.

'Can I start at the beginning?' he said.

'No. What the hell do you mean, *trying to improve my marriage?*'

'I was trying to do the same for my relationship,' he explained.

'By putting a picture of a dragon in my *house?*' Grace's face was a picture of confusion.

'I put one in mine too.'

'*What?*' Grace shook her head, stepped back. '*Why?*'

'Feng shui.'

'Feng *shui?*' She stared at him, the way he had the dragon print when he first saw it.

'It's the art of where things are.'

'The art of . . .' Her mouth hung open.

'Where you put things. Placement. It's the ancient Chinese art of arranging objects and space in an environment to achieve harmony in your life. Feng shui means the way of wind and water, you see.' He was rambling, but speaking about it calmed him, just as it had when he started it all. 'It's been my passion; it kept me going when I was anxious.' After the Russian, the swimming, the books, all the hobbies he'd tried to start and couldn't make stick, this had been the only one to really take his mind off things. And he'd *loved* it, saw it as a way to help them both. The lamp, for example. He had spent a long time searching for the most beautiful lamp possible, scouring antique and charity stores, delighted when he found the Tiffany one, knowing it would light up an important area.

'You put candles in my kitchen and roses in my hallway because you were *anxious?*' Grace shook her head, as if in complete disbelief. A sudden gust of wind caressed her hair with rough hands. Her cheeks were cerise with cold. The weather made her lovely. The weather and disbelief.

'That's what made me learn feng shui in the first place. I thought it'd help me. And it did! And then I wanted to make life better for you too.'

'You put that blue-grey fish in my bowl to improve *my* life? But, why me?'

He didn't want to answer that yet. 'Multiples of three fish are lucky and symbolise yang energy. The best combination is two goldfish, and one black fish, which represents protection. I couldn't get black though so blueish-grey had to do.' Tom remembered emptying the fish from a bag of water into the bowl, taking a moment to meditate – his teacher had said that each placement should be done with sentience if it was to work. 'I was glad you had the bowl in your living room. You should never place fish in your bedroom or in the kitchen.'

'Okay, I'll bite . . . why can't you have a fish in your bedroom?' Grace seemed annoyed, but she was at least following him for now.

'Bad sleep, overeating . . . and duplicity.'

'So what does it mean now it's dead?'

'You must move on.'

Grace appeared to consider this. Tom was getting restless. He needed to pace. He leaned forward on the bench, hoping to hint, hoping Grace might relent now.

'Stay where you are,' she grunted.

'Sorry.'

'I'll scream.'

He held his hands up. 'I wouldn't blame you.'

'The police will never believe this crap; they'll have you sectioned.' Grace shivered despite her thick coat. 'I think you're having me on.'

'I'd never do that. Feng shui is real, it works.' He paused. 'Or at least it did. A bit. At first. Now I don't know if it does and I've no idea what I'm going to do. I did all the things I was supposed to. I decluttered to get rid of bad energy.'

Grace looked incredulous.

He continued anyway. 'I painted the bathroom blue because it's in the north. I searched hard for the right dragon print. It had to be gold, not too angry, but still fierce, so all the residents of the house would be safe. Most of all, I put a large lamp in the Love Area, and kept it on until the electricity went off.' He realised he wasn't only talking about what he had done to Grace's house anymore. He gathered himself. 'And still . . . she's gone.'

'Who?'

'My partner. Harper. She's why I went to the classes.'

Grace's face softened. He knew she must be empathising; she was alone now too. But then she straightened up, looked serious again.

'The notes,' she said. 'What do *they* mean then?'

'The notes. Yes.' Tom shuffled on the bench. 'That wasn't entirely feng shui related. I wanted to let you know I was looking out for you.' Grace shook her head again. 'But when I spoke some of those words aloud the other day, I realised how they sound. Creepy. I didn't *mean* them that way.'

'You didn't think *I'm here* was fucking ominous?' cried Grace.

'I see now, yes. I don't always quite . . . think the way other people do. I know that. My . . . she used to tell me I needed help.'

'I think you do, Tom.'

She had said his name. He nodded. 'I couldn't sign off with my name so I signed off with what I felt I was part of.'

'Why not leave *no* bloody name?'

'I thought that might be worse. But I can see that calling myself The Night has a serial killer element to it.' Grace appeared to stifle a laugh – or maybe she was upset. 'As I said, I get stuff wrong.'

Out of the blue, she instructed crisply: 'I think you should start at the beginning.'

So Tom did.

He told her everything. While he was talking, she occasionally mirrored his emotions, tears springing into her eyes, quickly wiped away. Halfway through, she sat on the bench next to him.

She might not believe him, or want to forgive him, but at least she was no longer afraid of him.

43

The False Feng Shui-er

Tom got into feng shui quite by accident.

He had initially started a free Learn Russian class at the town hall five months earlier, just after he found out Harper was having the affair. He was signed off work – he loved being a cemetery caretaker but couldn't concentrate – and he was desperate to take his mind off her betrayal. The more taxing the thing, the better. But Russian proved a bit *too* taxing, and he gave up after a month.

Then he signed up for Psychology for Beginners.

That was enjoyable until they moved on to Harry Harlow's work with primates. In one of Harlow's studies, baby monkeys were taken away from their mothers and raised in a laboratory setting. Some were placed in separate cages; in this isolation, the monkeys showed disturbed behaviour, staring blankly, circling, and engaging in self-mutilation. Tom found this unbearable.

He never went back to that class.

On the day he got embroiled with feng shui, he was supposed to be starting an anger management class.

He wondered, as he parked outside the town hall, whether it would be full of social misfits with nothing better to do on a rainy Tuesday evening, and then realised that *he* was one of those people. The sky was loaded with tears. He hurried up the stone steps to avoid the rain. Once inside the shabby building, he was greeted with the smell of poorly maintained toilets and the distant sound of scraping chairs.

A sign declared ANGRY PEOPLE THIS WAY; he wasn't sure whether to follow the fiery arrow. He had put his name down in the hope of *finding* some anger, some strength, not of controlling or diffusing it. That had been his problem all through life – he let people walk all over him, was never very assertive. Perhaps Harper might find him more appealing if he could find some fire.

Beyond the peeling door – in the same room where he had attempted to learn how much childhood up to the age of eight impacts us – humans sat in a ring. Perfectly normal looking, some chatting, some relaxed, hands in laps. Tom had found it hard to sit still during previous classes, and often pretended he needed the toilet, so he could walk about. The other students likely thought he had a urinary infection.

Just before he entered the room, a sturdy man pushed past him, marched to the front of the class and cried, 'Anger is the modern curse.' He must be the teacher. 'It's the silent killer,' he continued, sounding very angry about anger. 'It's the harbinger of cancer, of heart disease, of depression. It's the neighbour whose fifteen-foot hedge overgrows your garden, the secretary who steals your husband while you wash his socks in the sink, the driver who cuts you off at a roundabout. Bottle it up and it'll consume you – manage it, and it's your tool.'

No. That class wasn't for Tom. Too intense.

He needed escape, distraction, not a full nervous breakdown.

He crept away, meaning to return to his car, but a softer voice drifted from beyond another open door. He approached. A woman. Willowy, with wooden beads about her neck, cork sandals on her feet, skirts flowing.

'Feng shui,' she told the eight students sitting on the floor around her, 'is an art so powerful it can get you the job you want, improve your health and wealth, increase your ability to have children, and forge strong relationships.'

Her final words had Tom entering the room.

He loitered by an old Lights Out Could Happen poster with a picture of silhouetted houses against the night.

'Come in,' called the woman. 'I'm Sheila, don't be shy. Join the circle.'

And Tom did, nodding at the others.

'Nine of you now,' she smiled. 'The ideal number.'

Tom was pleased to have completed her quest for perfection.

'Feng shui is the art of placement,' she continued. 'It is the art of where things are, and how that affects your existence.'

She paused.

'Today we will study the Bagua,' she said, after introductions had been made. 'The Bagua is a Tibetan tool where each of the nine segments represent an area of your world. We have the Fame Area, the Family Area, the Partnership Area, right through to Health and Wealth. Via Feng shui, we can enhance these areas in the home, and find out where the energy isn't flowing so well.'

'How do we do that?' asked a woman with pink hair.

'This we shall discover over the next few weeks. First, I'm going to ask you each what you'd like to improve in your lives?'

When it was his turn, Tom lied, said he wanted to travel more.

For the remaining hour and a half, Shelia showed the class a large poster of the Bagua and discussed its directions, ruling colours and elements. Tom listened hardest when she talked about the Partnership Area, which could be enhanced by the use of pink and earth tones and was ruled by the number two.

'Pairs work well here,' explained Sheila. 'Two candles, two crystal ducks, two stone hearts. This will ensure that your love is solid, that nothing divides you.'

Tom wrote this down, intending to buy all of them.

Afterwards, he descended the stone steps, exhilarated despite the rain lashing his skin. He got in the car, waited for his heart to slow down. Water zigzagged down the windscreen. This was it; this was his true vocation. Everything Shelia had said called to him, gave him hope. He could stop Harper having another affair. He could take control of his unhappiness.

★   ★   ★

By session two, Tom realised that for two years he had been storing old newspapers in the cupboard in the Reputation Area – which meant he was a disposable headline – and the pearl mirror reflecting the bed was certain death for one's sex life. It could have contributed to Harper's dalliance. He was to blame, too, really then. When Tom moved that mirror to the hallway, she was furious. It had been her grandmother's and she liked the idea that she was 'watching over them', which Tom found odd in a bedroom. They tussled with it but Harper had the last say; it remained by the bed. And so, nothing improved.

Tom couldn't sleep then.

He considered breaking it, but that would be even worse luck.

'When you place a symbolic object in one of your areas,' Sheila said at the third session, 'it must be done with awareness.'

'What do you mean by symbolic?' asked a bald man called Tim.

'What do you mean by awareness?' asked a woman called Emily.

'Symbolic is . . . let's see. Say you wanted to travel to Sweden, you might put a brochure of this country in your Travel Area. Or if you were looking for a job in the Arts, you might place your art books in that area. Do you see?'

'Yes,' said Tim.

'And awareness is . . . well, for example, you must place the Gold Dragon in your house for protection while also *wishing* to be kept safe. You must do it with intention. Do you see?'

'Yes,' said Emily.

'There are false Feng Shui-ers who think accidental placements will have the same results but pay no heed to them. You have to *believe* in your enhancements for them to work.'

Tom realised he was therefore a False Feng Shui-er.

He kept it to himself, promised quietly to be better.

What else could explain that before he began this spiritual journey, back when he discovered Harper's adultery, there was a broken drill in the Relationship Area? That had been accidental, and yet look at the results.

This was when Tom really began to believe in it.

He thought sadly of his neglected childhood home, of the carpet-less stairs he had cowered on while terrible fights raged downstairs, of the always-overflowing bin in the kitchen, the cat litter that never got emptied, and the bare bookshelves. What might he have been able to change with a few magic touches?

Tom tested feng shui out.

At Sheila's suggestion, he enhanced the Wealth Area with purple cushions on the sofa and the wood element, via a carved wooden elephant, willing them to work. A few days later, he got a tax rebate of eighty-five pounds. He then put a postcard of the London skyline in the Travel Area, and though he was anxious when work took Harper to the capital for a fortnight, fearing it being a cover-up for adultery, he was also blown away by how literally his feng shui cure had made something happen.

He wondered then how it might work in other houses.

One evening, Tom had dinner at his beloved mother's home – a lovely flat, nothing like what she had endured in earlier years. When they had finished their jam roly-poly and custard, he moved her bedside commode on to the landing. He worried that the symbol-ism of water in her bedroom (a terrible thing) would deplete her finances. She rolled it back, saying that peeing all over the floor at night would cost a lot more in cleaning products.

'Mum,' he said, 'at least let me remove the mirror on the cabinet.'

When she told her dear son that he needed to get out more, he hid an amethyst crystal in the corner behind her bureau, and was later delighted when she told him the insomnia that had plagued her for weeks seemed to have eased.

Tom realised then that his cures were working elsewhere.

'Remember this is an art,' said Sheila when he had been going to the classes too long to remember what number session it was. 'And it is open to interpretation.'

'What do you mean by interpretation?' asked Tim.

'Well, you may instinctively feel that a certain item belongs somewhere. Let that in. Follow that instinct. Feng shui is a gift we bestow on ourselves, but one that we cannot inflict on another.'

'What if we *do* try it on others?' asked Emily.

'That would be like marrying them without their permission,' said Sheila. 'Unethical, wrong. We can't presume to know what someone else wants. It's not for us to decide the destiny of their lives.'

'Even if they're making a mess of everything?' asked the woman with pink hair whose name Tom could never remember.

'Even then,' said Sheila. 'They must see the light themselves, in their own time. OK, people, tomorrow we explore more on decluttering and how having too many things in our Health Area can cause irritable bowel syndrome.'

Driving home, Tom thought about how the crystal had worked for his mum. Was that immoral of him when his mum now slept well? Shelia wasn't wrong, she knew her craft, but Tom felt empowered by his actions.

He knew then he should go off-grid.

Do things his own way. He felt confident enough to try. Because since he had placed all the correct items in his Relationship Area, and since he had painted their south-west wall pink one afternoon – much to Harper's consternation – they had been getting on a lot better. She wasn't disappearing to 'see her friends' at night.

But was that enough?

Was there more he could do so that his nerves weren't shredded and he could finally return to work?

Despite them getting along, Harper despaired at his constant rearrangement of things. 'I looked for my floral vase,' she grumbled, 'and you've put it in the bloody bathroom.'

Tom felt that if he wanted to keep her, he needed to make sure her ex-lover was thoroughly feng shui-ed too. Then *he* wouldn't be tempted to stray again either. Tom knew where he lived; he had followed Harper there. At first, she had gone in via the front door, which he answered in his bed attire. After a few weeks, she disappeared around the back. Tom wondered what had changed. Later, when he found out and she admitted everything, Harper told him her lover had given her a key so she could let herself in; he apparently liked her to 'find him in bed'.

'Where was his wife?' asked Tom.

'She works nights,' said Harper.

Poor woman, thought Tom.

'Don't pity her,' snapped Harper, as though she had read his mind. 'She's neurotic. Drives him batty by the sound of it. When she *is* home, she has the lights on all night, and he has to wear a bloody sleep mask. Have you heard owt like it? Plain weird. Scared of the dark like a two-year-old.'

Tom wondered if the wife had ever found out about the affair.

If she had also had a breakdown as a result.

One day, Tom had seen this wife.

He passed their house, walking to the park. She was pulling the wheelie bin onto the street. He almost ran into her, mumbled an apology. She seemed distracted, face tired, subtle lines of sleeplessness beneath her eyes. Working nights took its toll. Once at the end of the street, he glanced back. She was still by the gate, lost in thought. He suddenly wanted to protect her too. She was a casualty of this mess, whether she knew about the affair or not.

But how could he?

Then Lights Out happened.

As with everything in life, Tom prepared well. Though he wasn't afraid of the dark, he was anxious that his cures might fail, that the lamp in the Relationship Area would go off at eight. Harper was nervous, which he was glad to comfort, feeling it brought them closer, cuddling during the long nights.

But she started going out again.

'Where to?' asked Tom.

'My friend's,' she said, sharply. Harper must have asked her friend to lie for her because she backed this up when Tom mentioned it. 'We drink wine. It's fun.'

And he was left at home once more, counting the stars, and adding up his losses. In Harper's absence, he wandered the streets, restless, walking in circles, passing the house of her lover, again and again. All dark there though.

Tom knew he needed to up his feng shui game.

He needed to get into that house and put the cures there, stop the man running away from his wife, help *them* connect too. But how? He remembered that Harper had a key. Did she still have it? If so, where would she keep it? He searched her drawers, her pockets, her jewellery box. In the tiny compartment, a key. He held it up. Was this it? Was it a good sign that she didn't have it with her? Surely it meant she wasn't with her lover.

So as not to alert her to his discovery, he got the key copied. Then, the following night, while Harper was sleeping, Tom left the house with the blue-grey fish he had purchased from the local pet store. Knowing that Night Watch volunteers were about, he approached from the rear, weaving through back alleys, hiding in hedges when he thought he saw someone.

And in he went, through the back door.

What had begun as the once-weekly study of an ancient Chinese art now spiralled into what could only be described as criminal; a series of break-ins.

Tom knew this.

Internally, he justified the offences by his honourable intentions, but he was addicted; it was a compulsion now. Still, he thought of the classes now abandoned, of Sheila. Had Sheila known that Tom was now breaking into a house and had left a Venus de Milo statue on the bedside table to 'bring more love' to the couple sleeping there, she would probably have asked him to leave her class. Had she known that he put a dozen red roses in the hallway to enhance their romance, she would have given him a stern lecture. Had she known he had kept the picture of Riley and Grace when he replaced it with the dragon, drawn a heart around her face as protection, framed it and stood it on the windowsill, Sheila would have undoubtedly contacted the police.

Before Lights Out had commenced, Tom had suggested relationship counselling to Harper. When she refused he went alone to see Carole, needing to talk about ahis plans, his *urge*, but then finding he couldn't, not fully. The same with Karl at the Samaritans, and with the receptionist at the police station. He began to sense, that despite all he had done, Harper had strayed again.

Then she told him she was leaving. She said it wasn't for someone else. She said she wanted half of their savings.

He knew the truth. He wasn't stupid.

When he went into Grace and Riley's house on night seven of Lights Out, and Grace was alone in the bed, he knew. When on nights eight, nine, ten, and eleven he still wasn't in their bed, it further cemented this certainty.

Riley and Harper were back together, and this time they were clearly planning a life of their own. Tom still had no clue if Grace knew any of this but after he had broken into her home, violated the ethical codes of feng shui – and look where it had got him, abject failure – he wanted to make right what he had done wrong.

44

The Masterful Storyteller

By the time Tom had finished talking, his voice was hoarse and the sun was sinking lower in the sky like a tired child heading off to bed. How different the cemetery looked in the dying light – gloomy and ghostly. He liked that vibe, but knew many would avoid the place when shadows fell.

The relief at telling Grace *why* he had done what he had – though still, he hadn't shared the full tale – was immense. He had omitted saying that Harper's lover was Riley. He had been a masterful story-teller, told his tale in such a way that avoided this reveal, leaving out how he got the key, not saying why he chose Grace's house to feng shui. He wanted to protect her from the pain he knew was coming, just a little longer.

But Grace wasn't stupid. She had interrupted a few times, gruffly asking about the key and wondering aloud again and again why *her* house was the one he picked, which he glossed over, saying he would come to that, soon, when the moment was right.

He looked at her. She was on the bench still, shivering, hunched forward. They were alone. She would understandably want to escape him now as the darkness loomed. He sensed the question on her tongue, right there, at the front. She *must* know. What Tom *hadn't* said made it all the more obvious.

'You've explained the feng shui,' she said.

'Yes.'

'But I still don't get *why*. You say you wanted to help me but how could you not see that breaking into my house would *terrorise* me?'

'I see that *now*.' Tom did. He had been blinkered by his grief, by his obsession. 'I don't know what to tell you except that when I get an idea, it consumes me. I don't always . . . see things the way other people do.'

'It's been a living hell for two weeks.' She sounded exhausted.

'I'm sorry, I *am*.' He was; sorrier than he had ever been for anything.

Grace stood, stamped her feet, blew on her hands. 'I'm going now. And I never want to see you again.' Had she changed her mind about taking him to the police? He didn't care – he would go. He had nothing left to lose. 'But first,' she said, 'you need to say it.'

'Say what?'

'What you didn't say during your tale.' Grace crossed her arms, glowered at him. 'Where did you get the key to my house – and why my house?'

'The person my partner was sleeping with . . . it was your husband,' said Tom, no games, suddenly tired of hiding the truth.

Grace nodded and he could tell she wasn't surprised at his words, but that she was struggling to hold back tears. She nodded again, couldn't seem to speak, so *he* did in order to give her a moment.

'It began about six months ago, and then she broke it off.' He was still pained by these facts. 'And then recently, I was suspicious again. She told me we were over, but said it wasn't to do with him. I knew she'd lied when I saw Riley had left you.'

'And you saw *that* because you were breaking into my fucking house!' Grace's resurge of rage was understandable. 'If you wanted to stop another affair between them, you could have spoken to Riley, or even me, during the day, instead of creeping in, terrifying me!'

Tom hung his head. 'It was the feng shui. I felt . . . powerful. Like I was really changing things. I couldn't see beyond that. And I knew if I spoke to you, asked if I could add a dragon, candles, you wouldn't let me. I couldn't think of any other way to do it.'

'How about *don't* do it?' she cried.

'You're right,' he said simply. 'I'm sorry Riley and Harper had an affair.'

There was a pause between them. 'That isn't your fault,' Grace eventually managed.

'But maybe it is. Look at me.'

'What do you mean?' She sighed. Her entire posture was slumped now, a marionette with the supporting strings loosened.

'Hardly a catch, am I?' Tom knew his lack of confidence was down to his shaky childhood, to having a father who told him he was weak, and to feeling guilty for not saving his mother from an onslaught of violence. This self-doubt was probably why Harper had left him too.

'How did you know?' asked Grace, obviously ignoring his question.

'Sorry?'

'About the affair.'

'I followed Harper. Saw her in a car with . . .' He avoided Grace's eyes. 'They kissed. I followed her a few times, she went to your house, at first going in the front door, and then around the back, with a key he gave her. I copied that key, used it myself. When I confronted Harper, she admitted it. It ended. I had to believe that. And now they must be together somewhere.'

Grace nodded, eyes damp. 'How did you get my key out of the door?' she asked suddenly.

'What do you mean?'

'I put my key in the door to stop you . . . and *still*, you got in.'

Tom remembered inserting his key, finding another already slotted in. In that moment, he had been a child again. Locked out of the house. His father often did it, wanting Tom to feel excluded. But Tom had a key for when he got home from school, and he found that if his father's key, on the other side of the lock, was slotted in and not turned, he could very patiently push it out with his. Luck and patience were vital. These two things were in abundance when Tom realised Grace had put her key in the lock too. It took a few slow, careful minutes, but he managed to push it out.

'I just know how,' said Tom, realising Grace was waiting for an answer.

'Wait.' She frowned, as if suddenly realising something. 'When we were trying to figure out *how* anyone had got in, and a key came up, Riley did look odd for a moment.' She paused as though to recall it. 'My mum said it had to be either me or Riley or someone who had a key. He tried to blame me at first. With the fish. Tried to make me think I'd bought it and forgotten. And yet he must have known, now I think about it. He must have known his *lover* had a key to our house. He must have asked her about it.' Grace seemed to remember Tom was there. 'Surely she would have known you did the feng shui, put two and two together, and told him that? But that . . . but that would mean that Riley knew all along that it was you who was breaking in? And he said *nothing*. I can't think straight.' She held her face. 'You know Harper – what do you think?'

'I left her key where it was once I'd made a copy. She must have told Riley it was impossible. I don't know. But I feel that if Riley told Harper about the items, she would've figured out it was me, maybe been nervous to get me into trouble.'

'But surely she'd have contacted you, asked you to stop?' said Grace.

'She didn't. We weren't exactly . . . on good terms.' Maybe she didn't question him because she thought he wouldn't give her half of their money if he knew she was back with Riley? Although Tom didn't mention that to Grace.

Grace sighed. 'I'm too tired to figure anything out right now.' She looked towards the cemetery gates, but didn't move. Tom wondered what held her here.

'The lamp,' she said.

'Yes?'

'How did you *know*?'

Tom was confused. 'What do you mean?'

'What it *meant* to me.' Grace looked emotional. 'It was exactly like one I had as a child. It was . . . *special*.'

'I had no idea,' said Tom. 'Really, I didn't. How could I? I just chose one I thought spread the prettiest light . . .' While he still had her attention, he ventured: 'I'm sorry to tell you this but . . . Harper admitted eventually that she loved him.'

'Love,' said Grace quietly, as though she had never heard the word before.

'That hurt more than the . . .' Tom wanted to say 'sex' but wondered, as he often did in many situations, if that would offend Grace. 'Are you OK?'

'*No*,' she snapped. 'Of course not.' She paused. 'But even though it's a shock . . . it sort of isn't. Riley has been working late recently, distracted, and things weren't perfect. And yet . . .'

'*Yes?*'

'I never suspected.'

'Why would you suspect if there weren't any clues?'

Grace shrugged. 'He's confident, good-looking, but I never had any reason to think he would deceive me. He never has. As far as I know.' She appeared to think of something. 'It could have been me. I have some . . . issues. I'm probably not the easiest to live with.'

'I'm sure that's not true,' Tom said kindly.

Grace looked irritated. 'I don't want to talk about him anymore. Them. *It*. It's time for me to go.'

She was right. He had wrecked her life quite enough. What on earth had he expected by going to her house the other night, by hoping that telling her everything would make her say, *Oh, OK, you're a nice guy really, let's forget it all?* He was a criminal. The thought now of returning to his empty house, with the remaining candles and wall colours that mocked him, filled Tom with misery.

'OK,' he said. 'Do you want *me* to go and tell the police I broke in?'

'I don't care anymore.' Grace sounded totally dejected, limp, all the vigour and anger from a mere half an hour ago sucked from her. A balloon deflated. 'I have . . . bigger things now. I reckon your break-ins were so low on the list with all the Lights Out crimes and protests that they'll be relieved to have one less job. Please, just . . . stop. Stay away from me.'

And she set off down the path, not even looking back.

Tom felt morose.

'I know how afraid of the dark you are,' he said to her back, more to himself than anything else.

But she spun around, eyes flashing. Was it sadness? Anger? *Shame?* 'What does that have to do with *you?*' she spat.

'Just . . . I feel for you.'

'Then maybe don't break into my fucking house!'

Tom looked at her. 'I love the dark,' he said, quietly, 'and maybe, to show how truly sorry I am for all of this, I can help you . . . make friends with the dark again.'

'And how the hell would you do that?' She was still here, still listening, there must be a part of her that was intrigued. 'And why would I even *let* you?'

'Fear is experienced in your mind but triggers a physical reaction in your body. Your amygdala alerts your nervous system, setting your body's response into motion, and the only way to reduce it is repeated exposure to the thing we're scared of. Systematic desensitisation means a series of exposure situations.' Tom paused. 'I took a psychology class before the feng shui one. I think you've started doing the exposure thing without even knowing.'

'What do you mean?' Grace seemed fascinated, despite her defensive body language, and glances towards the gate.

'You work at night, with people who are dying.' She didn't ask how he knew this. 'What is death if not the ultimate darkness?' He paused. 'Where do your fears come from?'

Grace shook her head.

'Until you talk about it, you'll never own it.'

'Who are you to lecture me?' she demanded. 'A few classes and you think you can cure me when *you* made my fears ten times worse by creeping around my bloody house at night!'

Tom nodded. 'But the night isn't scary. It was just *me*.'

Grace studied her hands.

'If you want to do the desensitisation thing, I know a place we could try,' he said, softly.

She didn't respond. Two leaves blew playfully around her ankles.

'You know the tunnel down by the river, that leads into the country park? I walk a lot at night – it's pitch black now they've removed the row of lights. You can't see beyond your own hands on a moonless night. It'd be perfect.'

'For *what*?' Grace looked horrified.

'If you went in there alone, for half an hour.'

'*Never*.' She shook her head vigorously.

'What if I walked down there with you, waited nearby. Timed it for you.'

'Why the hell would I go with *you*?'

Tom held his hands up, surrendered his efforts to make it up to her, to help. She was right. It had nothing to do with him. He didn't know what else to say; he didn't want her to go because that would be it, and he would be utterly alone.

Grace said no more, and headed towards the gates, speeding up as she drew closer, not looking back.

Tom waited a moment, not sure what for. Was he hoping she might return? He raised his face to the remaining sun, inhaled the crisp air deeply. Touched the lump on his head and winced. He deserved it.

Then he headed home. He had wanted to talk, share his story, had felt he was a book that needed to find the right reader; a genre that didn't fit easily into a box. That only when a lover of that unusual category found him would he find his voice. But it hadn't gone how he had hoped. Grace had been a reluctant bookworm. She had listened but been a harsh critic.

That was understandable.

If only she could now share *her* story with this very open reader. If only he could listen, make it up to her, *really* help her. But maybe that wasn't anything to do with him and it was time to go back to his own life now, as depressing as that was.

Once home, he went to the Russian doll sitting on the bedroom bureau. Harper *had* bought it for him, left it to make a point. But it was a cruel gift. 'You're too complicated,' she had yelled, before leaving him. 'I never know from day to day which Tom I'm going to get. Never know which fucking doll!'

Now, he put it in the bin and paced, paced, *paced*.

45

A Real Tragedy

Grace managed to hold back hot tears all the way home. Once there and inside, she turned all the lights on because twilight had swallowed the world. Then she stood in the hallway, put a fist against her mouth; it didn't stop the wrenching sobs. Dropping to the bottom stair, she wept, noisily and messily, like a small child.

She cried for her fears, for her losses, for herself.

Once done – as though this had released enough pain to get on with life – she sniffed heartily and headed upstairs.

She paused halfway, studied the dragon artwork. How shocked she had been when she first saw it, imagining it turning to glare at her. Now it felt so innocuous, like a children's painting.

Did she feel better now she was in full possession of the – *very strange* – facts? No more fearing an intruder. No more dreading a sound in the night.

No, not fully.

She was still angry. She had answers, but the horror of recent nights, of feeling unsafe in her home, of being in the dark, was a raw, unhealed scar. She couldn't take it all in. She finally knew who had left the strange things in the house and, just as importantly, *why*. She had stood in a cemetery and listened to his bizarre explanation. But with that knowledge came a new situation A new pain.

Riley had been unfaithful. *Unfaithful.*

The phone pinged. Catherine.

Hope you're OK after last night? I rang earlier but you might just be resting. I'm glad you got your reunion with your dad. I'm sorry for not telling you more sooner. I'm here if you need me. X

Grace sent a quick thank you, assurances that she was OK, but couldn't concentrate on her mum right now.

Riley was coming over. What time was it? Past five. Damn. She'd had no time to fully process all Tom had told her, and now she had to face him.

Lights Out soon, too.

Grace felt sick. Shouldn't she feel better, knowing the notes and curious items were done?

I can help you . . . make friends with the dark again.

Grace shook her head. Who was *he* to suggest such a thing? She must do that herself. But first . . . deal with her cheating husband.

As though summoned by her thoughts, a sharp rap on the door, and then it opened. Riley. Seeing him was a stab in the heart. He had bags, clearly his stuff. The nerve. He dropped them by the stairs.

She inhaled deeply and came down to him. She watched him lean in, as though to kiss her cheek, but something in her face must have warned him off.

'What's that smell?' He wrinkled his nose.

'Not sure. The fridge?'

She must have grown immune to the odour, living here. She headed into the living room. Riley followed. In the past, they sat side by side on the sofa, her on the left, him on the right, much the way couples have sides of the bed. This time, she sat in the armchair, setting a distance. Riley frowned; anyone else would have missed it, but she knew him.

Or at least she had thought she did.

'Nothing else happening with the renovations?' He looked around.

She supressed anger at his presumption that she should get on with it while he was off gallivanting. 'No idea,' she retorted. 'The builder guy said he'd be in touch, and he hasn't. I've had a lot on.' She paused, asked icily, 'So what did you want to talk about?'

'How are you?' Riley sat opposite on the sofa.

Jennifer and Brad swam faster in their bowl, as though to get away from him. Grace remembered that he had called the new blue-grey fish Angelina. It was such a dark thing to say, in light of what was going on.

'How do *you* think?' she demanded.

She saw Riley glance at the still downturned photo on the windowsill, the one with a heart around her head, that she now knew Tom had drawn to protect her. In doing so had he separated her from Riley, rather than uniting them? Maybe she should stand the picture up again.

'Of course,' said Riley. 'I behaved badly, leaving you this week. But I . . . I found it too much. The state you got in at the switch off.'

Grace didn't respond, just glared at him. He was going to let her think his departure had been *her* fault. She decided her tactic then: let him talk himself into a corner.

'I needed space, and that gave me time. Time where I was able to . . . I realised that there's no one for me but you, Amazing.'

Grace could not have been more surprised if he'd said he too was taking feng shui classes and was installing a garden fountain to enhance their finances. Still, she didn't speak. His use of her nickname grated now.

'All I needed was time away, but that was selfish when you were anxious, and when . . .' He paused; she knew he was wondering what to call the break-ins. 'When someone was leaving these items and notes.'

'The Night,' said Grace.

'What?'

'The notes. They were from The Night.'

'Yes.' He paused. 'Has it still been happening?'

'Surprised you care. No, not for a few days.'

'That's good then. Things are getting better. I saw an article this morning suggesting Lights Out might end sooner than they thought. Some MP is unconscious after falling in the dark, so obviously, they'll rethink when it's one of their own.'

'Probably more that they could lose the next election after the failure of this bloody scheme,' said Grace, irritated as hell with her husband.

He looked at her. 'I want to come back. I'm sorry I messed you about.'

'You're not staying with Harper then?' The words shot out of Grace's mouth before she could decide whether she should hold her cards close to her chest or slam them on the table.

Riley's face was a picture – like the stairway dragon artwork: mouth agape, face red. 'Harp— But she— You *know*? But . . . *how*?'

'I'm not answering your questions. You can answer mine. You were with her, weren't you?'

'I . . .' Riley scratched his stubble, a sign he was uncomfortable. 'How do you . . .?'

'Well?'

'I was. Yes. But, no, I don't . . . How do you *know*?' She ignored the question. 'I don't want her.'

Was this a victory?

It didn't feel like it. Riley had deceived her and now he no longer wanted Harper, he expected to come back. If Grace hadn't known about her, she might have welcomed him. She thought suddenly of her father's unexpected return. But that was different. He left to protect her – Riley left for selfish reasons. She realised that in normal circumstances she would be telling Riley about him. That made her briefly sad, but she quashed it.

'Did Harper change her mind and you have nowhere else to go?' she asked.

Riley didn't respond. 'How do you even know?' he tried again.

'Tom told me it all.'

'*Tom.*' Riley looked both surprised and also not. He would know who Tom was, and what he had done, but he must be wondering how *she* knew.

'You knew Harper had a key and you let me think no one did.'

'Yes, but I knew for a fact no one else could have used that key to get in because she always had it with her.'

'Not always,' said Grace.

'How do you know where the key was?' demanded Riley.

She ignored the question again. 'You must have told Harper what was going on at home, correct? And Harper must have told you she thought Tom was leaving these items, because he was doing the same thing at home.'

Riley didn't respond.

'You knew it was probably her husband doing this and you didn't think to tell *me*, to ease my fucking fears while I was here alone?'

'I knew you were safe. That it wasn't some predator.'

'But *I* didn't know that.' Grace could barely contain her rage. He had known. All along. It was vile. 'The truth is it was because I'd know you'd had an affair. You'd have had to admit *how* you knew it was Tom. You're a coward, Riley. I don't even know you anymore. Your secret was more important than my sanity.'

Riley had the decency to looked ashamed. Still, after a beat, he couldn't help but justify his behaviour. 'It's not as black and white as that. I behaved badly but once I knew it might be Tom, how harmless he is, I knew you were safe.'

'And as I said, *I* didn't know that,' she cried.

'You're right. I'm sorry.'

'And you tried to make me think *I'd* done it. Telling me I was in a state and *I* might have written those notes in my sleep. There's a word for that . . .'

Riley waited, frowning.

'Gaslighting.'

He didn't respond.

'And how *could* you tell Harper about me?' she asked. 'My fears. That's private.'

Now Riley looked truly contrite.

'Did you mock me together?' Grace's voice broke.

'Of course not. Jesus, Grace, I'm not a monster. Anyway, it's over. She wants to be . . . independent.'

'Why another woman?' asked Grace. 'How did it start in the first place?'

Riley paled. He obviously didn't want to share this. Grace waited. 'It was at Pam's – you know, from work – it was at her fiftieth birth-day party.' Riley couldn't look at her. 'You couldn't come. I think we'd argued. Can't even remember what about. Anyway, that doesn't matter. Harper knew Pam, so she was there, and we got talking. We just clicked. I don't know what else to say. But then we both decided we loved you and Tom and we ended it after a month.'

'You mean Tom caught you,' corrected Grace.

'How the hell do *you* know him?' demanded Riley.

'Why did you start up with her again?'

He sighed. 'We crossed paths at Paul from work's leaving do.' Grace hadn't gone to that either. 'It was chemistry. I'm weak. But listen, *please*, I don't want her. I never did, not really. I was flattered. There's no one but you.'

Grace went to the window. She stood the picture of her and Riley up, red heart bright about her face. It was dark out, but light from the room fell on the bins outside, overflowing, still not emptied. The darkened bedroom window opposite reflected the sky. No Stacey. No hope. No flower. A police car sat outside her house.

Please God, let there be some good news.

'Stacey is missing,' said Grace softly.

'I know,' said Riley. 'I saw it in the paper. The poor family.'

'That's a *real* tragedy.'

'It is.' Grace heard the sofa squeak as Riley got up. 'Can I come home?' he asked, right behind her, his scent overpowering. How good that would be, not having to fear the dark alone. How nice to have company again, someone to share her worries with. But, she realised, that had to be someone who put her first.

And that wasn't Riley.

Grace thought of something, turned. 'That's why you were reluctant to get a house alarm, wasn't it?'

'What do you mean?'

'You liked it when Harper let herself in with a key and joined you in bed. An alarm would have inconvenienced that.' Anger surged again in Grace's gut. 'She came into our bed while I was caring for dying patients. Can you see how despicable that is?'

Riley's shoulders slumped. 'Yes.'

'You could have gone somewhere else.'

'We did, sometimes, but recently Lights Out meant we had t—'

'Fucking Lights Out, eh?' said Grace, sarcastic. 'Stopping lovers going to hotels.'

'I'm sorry.'

'The fuck you are. You're just sorry I know. You were going to come back here and resume our marriage. And there's one thing I can't forget.' She poked Riley in the chest. 'I can't get out of my head what you said about Jamie – that he was a fussy kid, afraid of his own shadow.'

'I was frustrated with you, I didn't mean it.'

'But it came from somewhere.'

He didn't respond.

'You obviously think it, on some level. That's my son.' She stressed the *my*, knowing it would sting Riley. 'That you would say such a thing as you were going out the door to your lover. Jamie's a fantastic kid, thriving despite an absent father, and you had a nerve.' Grace fought back tears.

'I'm sorry.' Riley looked emotional too.

'Maybe you are, but I don't want you here.'

'Now . . . or *always*?'

'I don't know.' She looked at him. 'It's my turn for space now.'

'But where should I . . .?'

'Not my problem.'

'You want me to go *now*?'

She nodded. She did.

Riley was clearly taken aback. 'I'll give you the space you need,' he said eventually. He waited, like she might change her mind, and when she didn't, he went into the hallway, picked his bags up. 'Can I call you tomorrow?'

Grace followed him. 'No, I said I want *space*.'

She was exhausted now. Was this it for her marriage? Should she be a wreck? She had been earlier, sobbing on the stairs, but now she felt spent. She didn't have to decide today what her future with Riley was.

He opened the door. The light was gentle, forgiving, even if she wasn't.

'I'll probably be at my mum's,' said Riley.

'OK.' What else did he want from her right now?

'Bye then.'

Grace had been sitting in the living room since Riley left, the dark now almost closing in around her. But she was so distracted, she barely even cared. Eventually, she got up again and went to the front door. What she had said to Riley was true: there *were* real tragedies out there.

And she wasn't one of them, she wouldn't let herself be.

She decided to focus her mind elsewhere instead. Opening the front door, she looked out to see if the police car had left Stacey's house. It had. Should she go over, see if there was news? No. Not her place. He had enough on his plate.

She came back inside, shivering, turned all the lights on while she still could – *flick, lit* – and then switched on the TV. Martin on the local news. It was a rerun, she knew, had seen it yesterday, but that didn't lessen its impact. He pleaded for anyone who had seen Stacey to come forward, saying he would give anything for her safe return. 'She's my darling girl,' he sobbed, the words cutting through Grace. 'Please, please, *anyone?*'

She messaged Ben at number seventeen: *Any news about Stacey do you know?*

A minute after: *Not that I know. Hopefully tomorrow?*

Grace felt as though she hadn't slept for a week. So much to process. But eight o'clock loomed. She got the camping lamp and did her usual route, turning the lights off, ending in the bedroom. There was no need to sleep on the sofa tonight. She set the lamp on the bedside cabinet, then opened the drawer and took out the Venus de Milo statue. There was no reason to fear it now, though the absence of arms was creepy. Surely that couldn't be a positive feng shui placing; a woman who couldn't do anything for herself. She threw it back in the drawer.

Though she no longer feared new items or hearing someone downstairs, Grace was still terrified of the camping lamp failing, of waking up to a night that went on forever.

I can help you . . . make friends with the dark again.

God, if only.

If only.

Tonight is different. I've felt different all week. I've been tired. Very tired. I fell asleep in a chair last week before I could begin my time with my latest. I ran. I had to. She came to me and that's not how it's supposed to happen. It's supposed to be this: I go upstairs. I acquaint myself with the house – the smells, the fabrics, the feel – and then I go up and watch them sleeping.

Like I used to watch my mother.

Except I wake them. Shine my torch to startle them. Tie them up. Tell them how despicable they are, like my mother used to tell me. Scream it. Get it out. Burn them if they fight. Strangle them if they fight more.

Despicable, despicable, despicable.

Because I'm not. I leave a gift to show that. I leave it behind because I'm a good man. A good man. I am. It's a gift. A white feather like the ones my granny always kept when she found them on the ground. A gift to say, wish. Wish for all you want.

Like I do.

I'm at the back door. My new victim. She lives alone. They all do. Like me. Like my mother did. I'm going to kill her this time. Because they've been mocking me. This stupid name. The Feather Man. I'm more than that.

More than that. More.

More . . .

HULL LOCAL NEWS

Masked Man Apprehended by Night Watch Man

A man caught breaking into a house in the Garforth area of Leeds just before 3 a.m. today has been arrested. Charley Watson was on Lights Out night duty and apprehended the masked man as he attempted to enter the home of Sarah Pearson, sixty-three.

Charley Watson said, 'I'm glad I was able to prevent a crime. The man was angry that I tried to stop him, put up a fight. He had a rope with him and said that I was despicable. That's when my alarm bells went off. I thought, it's him, that bloody Feather Man. I don't think he was right in the head. His eyes were wild.'

The man remains in custody, where he will be questioned. Superintendent Phillip Waite said, 'Specialist officers are currently comforting Mrs Pearson, who was left stunned but very grateful to Mr Watson. We cannot comment further on the identity of the man, or say if he is in fact this so-called Feather Man. That is all speculation.'

NIGHT SEVENTEEN

46

To Their Final Place

The morning after the cemetery with Grace, Tom found himself on the foreshore. He walked to clear his head. The glass flood defence paralleled the pathway. Choppy water gushed past as though racing him. The River Humber was not the most picturesque of estuaries, except when the sun shone. Then clear sky gave it cinema-esque lighting, made it postcard pretty, especially with the majestic bridge spanning its expanse.

The sun shone now but didn't warm Tom.

There were posters of missing Stacey Reeves stuck to lamp posts, along with bunches of chrysanthemums. Other, dying, flowers were tied to railings and benches, as always. One had a simple note attached, words softened by weather: *I miss you, Dad.*

Had he jumped into the water?

Or had he simply liked this particular place?

Tom wondered how it would feel to stand at the bridge's fence, to look over, then to climb those railings and leap. To know it would all be over soon. After yesterday, talking finally to Grace, he felt empty and exhausted. He had not gone to the police, like the coward that he was. But, really, what would be the point now? He'd admitted his crimes to the person that mattered. Now, he was left feeling like a part of his essence had been lost with that truth. Even the walk didn't lift him.

He reached the old mill, beyond which was the tunnel leading into the country park. The one he had suggested Grace should go into at night to face her fears.

He sat on the bench nearby, beneath a canopy trees.

Knew he wouldn't remain still for long.

329

Hoped his feet didn't take him into the water.

Or up to the bridge.

'You're following me!'

Tom jumped. Grace. Cheeks as crimson as roses, thick scarf pulled up over her chin, eyes angry.

'How could I be?' he said. 'I was already here.'

She appeared to think about this. Looked around, wary. Two ramblers with a dog read the sign near the mill. He knew she was relieved not to be alone with him.

'What are you doing here then?' she snapped.

'Just . . . walking . . . thinking . . . You?'

'Same.' Still gruff. 'I'm also looking for Sta—' She appeared to think again about completing her sentence.

He glanced towards the tunnel entrance. Even on this bright day it was gloomy. It was square, concrete, ugly, with graffiti on the walls and rubbish on the ground.

'That's the place I sugge—' he started.

'I know it is. And there's no way. Absolutely not.' She started back towards the path. Tom wished she would stay and chat. See that he was more than a weirdo who had broken into her home.

'I think it's time for me to go back to work,' he said, unable to think of anything else.

Grace paused. Looked annoyed. Asked with impatience, 'What do you do?'

'I'm a cemetery caretaker. The one where we were.'

'Oh.'

'I maintain the grounds, clean and repair gravestones, do administrative tasks, keep records, etc. I like how varied it is. Peaceful too, though it can feel gloomy if you're having a down day.' He was rambling, but she hadn't left.

'Interesting.' She seemed curious despite herself. 'You work with the dead. I work with the dying.'

'I know,' said Tom.

'You do?'

He looked at her with meaning.

'Harper. Of course. She must know *all* about me.' Sarcasm. 'I see them out,' she then said quietly, more to herself.

'And I see them into the ground, to their final place.'

Grace studied him, not hostile, more thoughtful.

'There are more flowers than usual.' Tom motioned to the three bunches laid by the mill. 'It's so sad. One note over there said: *I miss you, Dad.* I probably prepared his grave. That hits me every time I read a note like that.'

Grace looked emotional. Tom felt terrible. 'I didn't mean to upset you,' he ventured.

She nodded, sniffed, but didn't speak. Eventually she said, 'I should go. I need to get a new fridge. The switch off has wrecked ours so I—'

'You *must* get rid of it today,' he said, urgent.

'*What?*'

'If it's broken, it's terrible energy, and that's your Relationship Area. That's why I put the two candles in there.'

'For God's sake,' she snapped. 'Isn't it obvious that feng shui doesn't work?'

'Only some of it.' Even after everything, it was hard to surrender his hopes for it. 'What about that tax rebate I told you about?'

'That would have happened anyway,' she sighed.

He still wasn't entirely sure. Was everything written in the stars, as the saying went, and they were dragged along, no choices, no control? Or should he have done more about paying better attention to his relationship, giving Harper everything she needed?

'I'm going.' Grace paused. 'Bye Tom.'

And she left.

But she had said his name again.

Such a small thing. But something.

47

Let's Put the Box in a Box

Grace woke after a fragmented sleep where great boxes of snakes blocked the doorway to her bedroom; vicious hissing followed her into the dawn.

She thought of last night. Another search for Stacey. The illumination from numerous torches and lanterns better than any light she might find at home, alone, dwelling on things. Feeling useful thrashing bushes, lifting wheelie-bin lids, calling Stacey's name until her voice was hoarse. Like an echo, others called her name too, a mournful, desperate song in the cold, cold night. Stacey, Stacey. *Stacey.*

Where the hell was she? *Where?*

It had been almost a week. Grace knew from crime dramas and documentaries that the first seventy-two hours were critical, and that after three days the chance of finding a child alive diminished each day. She would not think of that.

Not think of it.

She made coffee and wandered into where Brad and Jennifer frolicked their eternal watery dance. She thought of her mum, as she often had since that evening at her house. She hadn't spoken to her since delivering the sad news about Bailey, but had responded to messages, insisting she was alright. Riley had messaged too, but Grace had ignored it, of course. She had asked for space and he wasn't giving her it. She was supposed to be thinking about what she wanted, whether their marriage was worth saving, but didn't want to.

Instead, she was drawn to the windowsill, to the picture of her face within a red heart, and suddenly wondered if Tom was OK. It was the strangest thing – a man who had broken into her home, scared her half to death, and yet all she could think of now was the odd but kind man who had knelt next to her in the police station, made her think she might share her fears. At first, she had been annoyed to see him on the foreshore yesterday, thought he must be stalking her, which she quickly realised was ridiculous – he'd been there first and couldn't possibly have known she would turn up. She had gone to clear her head, to look – as she did wherever she went now – for Stacey, and to spy on the tunnel Tom had mentioned.

His words came to her.

One note over there said: I miss you, Dad. I probably prepared his grave. That hits me every time I read a note like that.

Grace had thought of Bailey. His funeral would likely be next week. How strange that Tom, if he returned to work, might prepare his grave. The universe certainly had a sense of humour. But this idea, him being involved in Bailey's final resting place, made Tom more . . . *human*. Despite what he had done, he was not *bad*.

Messed up, yes, but not a threat.

Mid-afternoon, she went to the corner shop for milk. She had ordered a new fridge and hopefully it would arrive next week, but until then she would have to buy fresh every other day. On the rack by the shop doorway, the newspaper headline was *Feather Man Suspect Still Being Questioned*. Grace skim-read the piece – though police had arrested an unnamed man two nights ago, and he was still in custody, they hadn't charged him. Speculation had been rife on social media that it *must* be the Feather Man. He hadn't struck since and the man who apprehended him said he'd had rope.

Grace hoped it *was* him, and that women would now be safe.

When she got back home, Tom was sitting on the doorstep.

Grace saw him before he saw her. He wore a thin, dark green

jacket that he must be perished in, his cheeks were flushed from the cold, and his hair was windswept as though he had walked here in a gale.

The red swelling still broke the white expanse of his forehead.

She should have been angry that he was back at her house, uninvited, but she wasn't. She should perhaps have been scared, but she wasn't that either.

'You'd better not have posted crystals through my letter box,' she said at the gate.

He turned; looked nervous. Understandable. He must have wondered how she'd react.

'Just a six-rod wind chime for your chi energy,' he responded, once he seemed to decide it was safe to do so. 'That's a joke,' he added. Still uneasy, then.

'What are you doing here?' she asked, still not prepared to give him a completely pain-free time.

'I'd still like to show you how sorry I am for . . . *it all.*'

Grace didn't respond.

'I thought we could go down to the river . . . when it's dark.'

'*Seriously?* Do you realise how that sounds?'

He smiled; it changed his face entirely. 'I mean . . . I could help you face the dark. In that tunnel. Like I suggested.'

'You want me to trust someone who broke into my home?'

'I know. You're right. As always, I didn't think it through.' Tom looked up the path like he might leave.

Suddenly, bizarrely, Grace didn't want him to. She recalled a young man at the hospice, Billy, who was neurodivergent and had died of brain cancer a year ago. Billy had said that he loved the hospice, despite the horrible reason he was there, because it was so calming and quiet. Everyday life overwhelmed him. He never went to the day room when there were too many visitors, which could occasionally happen if large families turned up all at once. Something about the way he had phrased things reminded Grace of Tom.

'It's not dark for two hours.' She avoided saying whether or not she would go to the tunnel. And yet, it could be a chance. A chance to . . . make friends with the dark.

'Shall I come back later, then?' said Tom.

'I didn't mean that. Can I?' Grace motioned to the door so Tom got up from the step. She unlocked it. It might be a foolish thing to do, but instinct told her otherwise; it whispered that Tom was not someone to fear. 'Do you want to come in for coffee?'

'I just had one, thanks.' He held up a paper cup. 'You sure you want me to come in?'

'Not really. But . . .'

He stepped in before she had a chance to change her mind. Inside, he loitered in the hallway, until she suggested he go into the living room while she put the kettle on. 'You should know your way.' Sarcasm. When she returned, Tom was pacing the room, paper cup in hand. Then he put it on the windowsill next to the picture of her face with a heart around it.

'What's that all about?' she asked.

'What?' He jumped.

'The pacing.'

'I have lots of nervous energy. My dad used to go mad about it.'

She sat on the sofa. 'You can carry on if you must.' She paused. 'You should know, in case it makes you feel any better, that your Harper isn't with Riley.'

'Oh.' Tom slumped into the armchair. 'She told me that, but I didn't believe her.'

'It sounds like she rejected Riley. She apparently wants independence. That doesn't make any of it better, but I thought you should know.'

'I know it's over,' said Tom. 'She wants half of our savings.'

'You deserve better,' said Grace.

'So do you,' said Tom.

She nodded. She knew that she did. Yes. *She deserved better.*

'Anyway,' Grace said, deliberately changing the topic and speaking now like she meant business, 'I don't need to go into that tunnel.'

'Why?'

'Haven't you heard the rumours? Lights Out might end.'

Tom nodded. 'What if it doesn't? What if they start another? This could be our world now. A switch off every time things get rough. Do you want to get into a panic every time?'

'Why do you care so much?' she cried, annoyed.

'I know what it's like to be scared. I hate to think of anyone else being.'

Grace decided against reminding him that *he* had fuelled her fears. He clearly wanted to remedy what he had done. 'You seem like a nice guy, but this is my issue, I'll do things my way.'

'I'm going down there for my walk anyway,' he said. 'You're welcome to come.' He paused. 'Wouldn't you love to be free of your fears?'

'Of course!' She slammed her empty mug on the coffee table; Brad and Jennifer circled the bowl in a whirl. 'But I don't see how going into a dark tunnel will help me any more than extra fish and dragon pictures helped you.'

He nodded. 'I guess I was trying to control my world rather than looking at what was wrong. Rather than taking responsibility. Harper and I were incompatible. I've been thinking about that. I suppose me blaming feng shui, where things were, is like you keeping the lights on instead of looking directly into the dark – at the truth.'

I've heard the truth, thought Grace. *My mother told me it.*

But she still hadn't really looked at it.

She hadn't remembered that day – the day of the box – herself. She had listened to a story. The facts. But she hadn't faced it. *Felt* it.

'A load of classes doesn't make you an expert,' she snapped.

'I know.' Tom stood again and she thought he would pace. 'You're right. I shouldn't have come. I can't force you to do something just to make myself feel better. I already forced my obsession on you,

I've done enough.' He headed for the door. He was leaving. She didn't want him to.

No: she *couldn't* let him. He might never come back.

This might be it.

A chance. He had caused her great fear – could he maybe help cure it now?

'Wait,' she said, the word sharp.

Did she really want to remain afraid? It had affected her life for so long that it was part of it. Did it have to be? Could she overcome it? It had driven Riley mad. It had meant she couldn't go into a dark room at work without switching a light on first, not even for a second. It had meant planning her life around ignoring it, avoiding it, escaping it.

Let's put the box in a box.

Who said that? The words came into her head.

Let's do that, dear.

Her mum? Yes.

A memory. That's what it was. Her mum, eyes teary. The two of them, holding hands. Was it Catherine helping her bury the memory of the box, as she had said she'd done?

'You OK?' It was Tom.

'Yes,' Grace said quickly. 'I'll think about it.'

He nodded.

'I'm hungry. Are you?'

He shook his head.

'I need to eat and then we can . . . *maybe* . . .'

She made some sandwiches and ate them in the kitchen. When she returned to the living room he was standing by the window, lost in thought, a slight figure that somehow filled the room.

'We could walk there now,' he said without turning. 'Wait for the dark.'

It sounded so ominous.

'I . . .' she tried.

'Fear is only fear,' he said. 'Think of it this way – there's no right without left, there's no up without down, and no light without dark. It's part of life.'

'Psychology class?' Grace wasn't mocking but couldn't help it.

Tom smiled. 'We could go there and come back if you can't.'

'I suppose.'

Quietly, she got her coat and scarf again. She tried to imagine how dark it would be near the river after eight. The few cottages there wouldn't offer the usual glimmer of hope with their window lights, and the street lamps would be off. *Don't imagine that blackness or you won't go.* She opened the door; the temperature had plummeted. It would be freezing near the water. She could use that excuse to stay. She started to say it, but quashed the words.

Tom was right behind her.

'Shall we?' he said.

No, she thought. 'Yes,' she said.

They headed towards the river. Grey clouds hid the sun, stealing blue from the river; the wind provoked waves into wildness, spitting spray against rocks and drenching the birds lingering there. They reached the mill, shivering, red-cheeked, and sat on the bench.

She didn't look at the tunnel.

When the sun sank beyond the bridge, walkers departed and the car park emptied. Though the odd light came on, it was dismal.

At eight it would be pitch black.

Don't think about that yet.

As dark as inside a box.

Stop it.

'People used to come dogging down here,' said Tom.

'I guess you'd know,' said Grace. 'Coming here all the time, I mean.'

A small laugh. 'No one bothers much now.'

'Do you honestly come here in the dark?'

'Yes. I love it. There's a peace. I can walk as slowly as I want.

Darkness was here before anything else, and it'll be here when everything has gone.'

'That isn't helping me,' said Grace.

'Do you want to tell me about it?' said Tom.

'About what?'

'About what happened to make you afraid of the dark.'

48

Seven Simple Words

Sitting with Tom on the bench by the river, Grace remembered kneeling on the cold police station floor next to him, fearing that the strange, intimate moment of confession with a total stranger would end if she stood. Now that stranger had a name, was back. And whatever he had done, he was trying to help her.

The incident.

That's what her mother had always called it. Except it hadn't been the true cause of her terror. There had been something before that. Something long buried.

'Tell me what made you afraid of the dark,' said Tom again, more softly.

'*She* should have had me talk about it,' said Grace, shaking her head.

'Who?'

'My mum. But she was old school, buried painful things. Like my dad leaving. What happened that day. Afterwards.'

'Talk about it now,' said Tom.

She could hardly see him. With that lack of visual, his voice took on a strength. Perhaps the absence of light would give her the freedom to speak; there would be no judgement without visibility; she could disguise any weakness or tears that might fall.

'I never have,' she admitted. 'I don't even know if I can . . .'

'It can't hurt you.'

It can, she wanted to cry.

'It might do you good?' he said.

'My dad locked me in a box,' she said.

341

Seven simple words. A sentence that tore out of her, struggling for air, blinking in the light.

Tom didn't speak.

'He locked me in a box,' she said again.

But still she couldn't open its lid and stare inside, share what she saw there.

'I had these Russian dolls – one inside the other, smaller and smaller each one,' said Tom. 'I think by talking about it, you'll get to the next smallest. But maybe you have to go in there – ' He glanced at the tunnel. ' – to get to that last one.' His breath misted the twilight.

'I can't.'

'I'd sit here,' said Tom. 'You've come this far.'

Grace looked towards the tunnel. 'Can you stand outside while I go in?' She knew she sounded pathetic.

'Yes.'

'You won't be able to sit on a bench anyway,' she said. 'You'll start pacing.'

He smiled.

'What time is it now?' she asked.

'Ten to eight.'

The countdown to Lights Out began.

She had no control over anything this time, no camping lamp, no familiar rooms, no bed to escape to. They waited. The wind got up, took crisp leaves scuttling towards the river. Grace concentrated on one of the bridge lights, narrowing her eyes and opening them again so it flashed, flashed, flashed. Tom announced when they had three minutes . . . two . . . one.

'You're not helping,' she cried.

'My mum eased me into tricky things by letting me know how long I had.'

'What tricky things?'

'Going in the bath.'

'The *bath*?' Grace smiled despite it all.

342

'I hated it for a while. Wouldn't go in. It was the . . . undressing. Exposure, I suppose. Even though I went in alone then because I was ten. And our house was very cold. She used an egg timer. To make sure I stayed in long enough to be clean. I got over it because she didn't give in, and I toughened up.'

Suddenly it was black.

Grace gasped.

The lamp above the toilets, and those on the bridge and in the restaurant further along, went out. Grace exhaled. Realised Tom had been talking to distract her. Bedtime stories eased children into the night. And she needed to go into it now without one.

She stood.

'You're doing it,' said Tom. She couldn't make out his features but was comforted by his slight shape on the bench.

'Maybe . . .'

'Yes?'

'Maybe if I conquer it . . . I'll be able to think about . . . the box.'

Tom stood too. 'I'll walk you there.'

'It's metres away,' she said.

'You want me to stand outside?'

'I do.' Grace nodded vigorously. 'I *do*.'

49

The Perfect Place

Grace and Tom walked to the tunnel entrance.

Without artificial light, it was infinite, but Grace knew from experience it only took about a minute to walk through. She could smell dank earthiness, the alien scent of unknown horror.

She stopped. Tom did too. She stared into the abyss. Her feet wanted to run, full pelt, all the way home. Her head said the same. But there was a small part of her nervous, beating-too-fast heart that wanted to overcome this wretched misery, to live a normal life. To be able to tell her mum and Jamie that she had done it. She was no longer afraid of the dark.

The idea made her teary.

'Are you ready?' Tom made her jump.

'I don't know.'

'You can walk in and walk out. You're not trapped in there.'

Trapped. Just the word turned her stomach over.

'Knowing that doesn't help,' she said, edgy. 'Fear isn't rational.'

'I know.' Tom's voice was hypnotic, slow, kind. 'Grace, this is how I feel about it. You can only see properly in the dark. When there's nothing else, no other distraction, no light, you see yourself, in full. And not everyone wants that. But you should, because I reckon you're strong enough.'

'I used to be,' she whispered.

'You could be now.'

'I want to be.'

'I could tell you when half an hour is up,' Tom said.

She took one step into the blackness.

Tom didn't move. She took another. Held her hands out in front of her face but could hardly see them.

She stopped. 'Come with me,' she said. '*Please*. Just five minutes. I can't . . .'

She expected Tom to say no, but he spoke gently. 'OK.'

Then he was at her side.

She took another step. He followed. Was the air different or did anxiety make it difficult to breathe? She stood on something uneven, stumbled, swearing, heart hammering. Righted herself, took another step. Neither of them spoke. There was a quiet weight to this blackness, like a kidnapper had dropped a blanket over her head. But there was no force, no captor; she was her own captor; a hostage only to her fears. More cautious steps, feeling for hidden obstructions. She couldn't see Tom now but felt him at her side. They must be in the centre of the tunnel.

And she was alive. She was OK.

What now?

'Maybe you should tell me about it,' said Tom.

'Not *here*.' Grace sounded five years old.

'Here is the perfect place. You've done it. You're in the centre of your fear.' Tom's hand found hers in the dark; it felt absolutely natural to hold it. 'Tell me about your dad. Tell me about the box.'

Grace found her voice. Slow at first. Faltering.

And then for the first time in over thirty years, she was there. She remembered it all.

50

It Never Happened

The night before the day her dad left, Grace was tucked up in her narrow bed, while he told her a bedtime story. She knew she was too old for this now, and could read well for her age, but there was nothing better than their shared moment, in the glow of the lamp that could be dimmed or turned up as required, stained glass with little stars cut out so a tiny galaxy hit the ceiling.

Dad didn't read from a book; he made the story up. That was what she preferred.

And the darker the better.

It had been the tall tale of Mr Tall, but she got bored of that.

'Tell me a scary one,' she said.

Though she didn't like the dark, it was a thrilling fear, one that made her snuggle into the duvet and shiver excitedly. She was always the first to take a dare at school, the one who others knew could easily be persuaded to climb a forbidden tree or knock on the headmaster's door and run away. She was ten and brave.

'Shall I tell you about Mr Bones, Maisie?' whispered her dad. He yawned, looked sleepy, as he often did these days, but she needed him to stay.

'Oh, yes. Who is he?' Grace was open-mouthed with interest. Her mum often said his tales were 'too scary' so he told them quietly – which added to the drama – and then changed them into something more happy-ever-after when Mum put her head around the door to say goodnight, laughing at their trickery after she had gone.

'No one likes Mr Bones, because he looks very odd, so he hides in wardrobes. He's stooped and bent over so he can fit in all the tight spaces, and his skin glows so he can see his way. He's slimy and snakelike and slithery.'

'Yuck,' said Grace.

'You hear him coming because his bones click-click-click.'

'Click-click-click,' Grace repeated. 'What does he eat?'

'Oh, grubs and worms and . . .'

'And?'

'And *children*.' Dad tickled Grace until she got hiccups.

She knew, even at her young age, that everyone had a shadow side. Life wasn't all sunshine. Her dad was wonderful, but even he had dark moments. Strange moments. Said strange words: *Don't let them in, don't let them in, don't let them in.* There were nights he went out and didn't come back until morning. Her mum would try and make light of his dishevelled appearance, picking out the leaves in his hair and asking about his medication. Grace never knew what medication she meant but she wondered if it was why her dad got so sleepy at times. Anxiety whirled in her tummy at the sight of his ruddy cheeks and his faster words, but she knew the sunshine father would be back.

He always returned.

'Tell me another story,' said Grace now.

'Bailey!' Her mother's voice from downstairs.

'You need to go to sleep, Maisie.' Dad kissed her forehead. 'It's been a long day. We can tell stories tomorrow.'

'Dad,' she cried as he reached for the lamp. 'Please don't turn it off.'

'Just tonight,' he said, though he always left it on. 'Nothing bad will happen while it's on, Maisie.'

And she knew it wouldn't. Which was why, later, when she woke in pitch blackness, she couldn't go back to sleep. Had it broken? It wouldn't switch on. Grace couldn't breathe. Every shape was menacing. Every sound was Mr Bones, crawling closer to the bed, click-click-click. She screamed for her dad. Screamed and screamed. But he didn't come.

347

Her mother arrived, annoyed at having been woken.

'The bulb must have gone,' she said.

'Where's Dad?'

'Asleep. He . . . took something to help him sleep. You won't wake him.'

'Can you get another bulb?' begged Grace.

'You're a big girl, stop fussing.'

But she couldn't. When her mum left, Grace put the big light on, and eventually fell asleep in its full glare. In the morning, her dad was grumpy, as though something heavy hung from his face, pulling his smile and eyes downward. It was a Saturday, so Mum left for her job as a teacher's aide in a local theatre school.

Mid-morning, Dad went into the garden, to his shed. Grace wanted to ask for help with her homework but something in his stance stopped her; he walked like one leg was heavier, scowled like something nasty was trying to crawl out of him. Mum called this behaviour one of his 'bad days'. She knew not to trouble him too much. So she went into his study, sat at his desk and tried to concentrate on decimal fractions.

Suddenly, the door opened, so hard it banged against the wall.

Her dad. Raw terror on his face.

'They're coming for me,' he said.

'Who are?' Grace believed him, grew scared too. He had ranted strange things before, but never as intensely as this.

'They're coming, they're coming, *they're coming.*' He paced back and forth, pulling at his hair.

'Who, Dad?' repeated Grace.

He appeared to remember she was there. 'You're not safe,' he cried. 'You need to hide, and I'll run.'

His panic infected her. It must be someone very dangerous. But who? *Why?* 'Let's ring Mum,' she said, suddenly wanting her.

'No time, they're coming.'

An odour emanated from her father, sweet yet pungent. He pulled her from the chair, looked around, eyes wild. They landed on the trunk in the corner. It was as old as time, dark wood, heavy-lidded, where they stored blankets. Grace knew it had been his mother's, that it had come from a faraway place during the war, once full of family treasures and documents.

'Here.' He opened it, pulled the contents on to the floor. 'In here, no fuss, quickly.'

Grace froze. 'No, Dad,' she said quietly. 'I don't like it.'

'There's no time, they're coming.'

'Who, Dad?'

He grabbed her by the neck; she screamed. His eyes were dead. She could not appeal to the man who left the lamp on. He wasn't in there, no one was. He dragged her to the box. She was no match for his strength.

'Dad,' she tried, '*Please*, I'll hide somewhere else.'

But he didn't hear. He pushed her into the now empty box by the scruff of her neck, banging her head against the wood. Before she could utter another word, slam, the lid was shut. A clinking sound; the key turning in the lock. No. *No.* She pushed at her prison, yelled for her dad to open it.

Was he there? Had he gone?

Trapped in here, she couldn't tell.

It felt as though she had been eaten by a monster. The only sounds were her own breath and the *beat, beat, beat* of her too-fast heart. The darkness was like nothing she had experienced before. She couldn't see anything, not her own hands, not the thick edges of the box. But still those edges felt as though they were closing in, wanting to squeeze the life out of her.

Pressing in and pressing in and pressing in.

And she screamed.

The sound was strange, thick but shrill. She covered her ears and screamed until her throat was raw. Then she called for her dad. Hammered on the lid. Kicked at the edges. Fight was still strong. Hope that he would open it, free her, still there.

He would come back. He *had* to.

Without sight, her imagination was free to go wild. It saw all kinds of things: evil bats with yellow teeth, slithery snakes, ghostly figures in hidden corners, supersized spiders with fangs. These creatures from hell, and the abject loneliness, thinking she might never see anyone ever again, was too much.

Grace began to cry. Between tears, she repeated her favourite rhymes to pass time, over and over and over. When her voice was no more than a croak, she said it in her head.

And then she heard something.

Something else.

'Dad?' she croaked.

But it wasn't outside the box – it was in here with her. A click–click-clicking, soft at first, possibly in her head. Yes. In her head. Like the bats and spiders. Grace covered her ears and muttered, 'No, no, *no*.'

But it got louder. Got bigger.

Mr Bones.

She knew it was him.

He was with her.

Bones click–click-clicking, crawling along the lid, a human snake. A cracking sound and Grace knew he was unfurling, reaching for her, hands clawed and grabby. 'I'm here,' he wheezed, 'I'll join you! We will stay here together forever.' She was dreaming, hallucinating, imagining him.

Yes, yes, *yes*.

But then he slithered to her side, cold and slimy.

'You called for me,' he hissed.

No, I didn't.

'You made me up.'

No I didn't . . . my dad did.

'I'm hungry,' he said. 'I'm *hungry . . .*'

Mr Bones reached for her.

Grace screamed again, shrill, desperate, final.

Then remembered no more.

★   ★   ★

Afterwards, when she was wrapped in a blanket and out of the trunk, shadowy faces loomed over her; voices said she was 'groggy' and 'hallucinating because the oxygen levels were low in there'. Her mum was present, and Grace clung to her, afraid that if her dad came, he would put her back in the box.

Everyone said she shouldn't try to speak.

So she kept silent.

Later, when her father never came home, she was quiet too.

And when the nights were too much, and she couldn't sleep without every light on, her mother told her it *never happened*.

'We're going to put this away in another box,' she said, her words painfully slow, like Grace was stupid.

'No more boxes,' Grace had begged.

'This is a safe one. It's in a special part of your head. We'll put it there, and you can lock it away, and never see it again until you're ready.'

When Grace had emerged from the trunk, the sun in the room was dazzling. She had blinked and blinked and blinked, wanting to drink it in, but unable to keep her eyes open in its sharp glare. It was bright, it was warm, it was safe.

And she never wanted to be without it again.

She would never be ready for that.

51

Facing the Dark

Grace opened her eyes; blackness. She was hunched over, sobs dry, stuck in her throat. It was freezing. But she wasn't trapped in a box. The air was too fresh. A hand held hers. Tom. Still with her, unseen, barely a dark shape, but *there*. They were in the tunnel.

'He's not here,' he said gently. 'It's just your imagination.'

'Who?' she croaked, unfurling from her stooped position.

'Mr Bones. You were telling me about him. Then you got upset, said you could hear him. But it's the bridge clanking outside. It's the trees creaking. *Listen.*'

She did. Sounds that might have been ominous were lessened by Tom's presence.

'You did it,' he said.

'I'm in shock,' she admitted, teeth chattering. 'I can't believe what happened. It was . . . terrifying. But I'm . . . OK.'

'You are.'

'I had forgotten that girl existed,' said Grace quietly.

'Which girl?'

'The one who was brave and messed about at school. That was me, it really was.'

'She survived a horrible ordeal,' said Tom.

Two horrible ordeals, Grace wanted to say. *My dad left me too, and that was worse than the box.*

'You're still her.' He paused. 'I think now is the time for me to leave you here—'

'No,' cried Grace. '*No.* Isn't it enough that I've come down here, that I just went back to a place I've buried my whole adult life?'

'It's enough if you can sleep with the lights off tonight.'

Grace didn't respond to that.

She saw herself going through the Lights Out ritual, camping lamp in hand, nervous, jittery. She saw herself if the switch off ended, letting every bulb shine all night, sleeping beneath their radiance. Nothing had changed. This made Grace want to walk into the river, like one of those poor women the other week, and never come out.

'I'm still scared,' she admitted. 'I might have remembered the . . . the *box* . . . but that's just remembering. That's one part of it. It's like . . . when an injury happens, it hurts. But it heals. Except the scar never quite goes and you pick it and it aches and . . . oh, I don't know, ignore me.'

'Stay,' said Tom. 'Just ten minutes. On your own. You *can*. I'll wait outside for you.'

He let go of her hand.

No, her mind screamed.

But she fought the fear.

Let him go.

Let them all go – Tom, Riley, her *father*.

She would wait. Stay. Endure. For ten minutes. But a minute could feel like a hundred in dark places, she knew that. It was barely the time of respect that dead bodies were given at work. *Don't think about dead bodies, not now.*

'I'm still here.' Tom, farther away.

She inhaled and let it out gradually.

She was tempted to cheat, use her phone's torch.

But she didn't. *She didn't.*

Just stand here. Face the dark. Tom would tell her when ten minutes had passed.

A skittering sound then; dry leaves moving over the ground. Grace knew it wasn't a bony man crawling towards her, intent on devouring her, but still she wanted to scream. It was long-held habit. A natural response. She knew she had imagined him that day in the box. The story had been right in her head, freshly told the previous night. Grace had brought the sinewy stickman to life.

She inhaled again.

She was doing it. She was in the dark, not panicking, not running, not screaming. And it felt exhilarating. She reached out to touch it, grab it, own it. This was her space. She would let into it what *she* wanted; fear was not one of those things. She could think about everything here, see Jamie going about his life, see her dad as he was, lumbering around the garden, farting and blaming the world, see her mum rehearsing her lines, voice confident and vibrant.

Grace made the dark what it was.

After what felt like a long time, but might have been five minutes, she shivered. Her fingers were numb and her toes stiff inside her boots. It had been long enough. The length of time didn't matter so much as the quality of it; that she was not fearful now meant it was time worthwhile.

She headed carefully out of the tunnel.

The dark was less thick there. How bright the stars were. How beautiful and happy. She reached up to them. Then realised.

'Tom,' she said.

Nothing.

'Tom?' she called again.

Still nothing. He had gone. She couldn't believe it. She hated being left.

'You could have said goodbye,' she yelled into the night.

Maybe he had known she was OK, and thought she should walk home herself? That felt right; he would only have left with good intention.

A sound. A shape on the bench. Sobbing?

'*Tom?*' Grace ventured, approaching. 'Are you alright?'

As she got closer she realised the shape was far too small to be a man, even the very slight Tom. A child. A *girl*? What on earth was she doing out here?

'Are you lost?' Grace stopped a foot away, not wanting to scare her.

She sniffed. Shook her head – barely visible in the dark.

It couldn't be . . . *Was it?*

'What's your name, sweetheart?' Grace could barely get the words out.

She whispered the answer in her head as she heard it.

'Stacey,' said the little shape, voice breaking. 'Stacey Reeves.'

52

Out of the Shadowland

'*Stacey.*' Grace whispered the name that had been on her lips, in her head, for almost a week. She knelt down, touched the girl's face, tried to see the features that would be familiar, that straw-blond hair. 'It's me, Grace, the one who knocked you over and gave you the flower.'

Stacey gasped and fell into Grace's arms; she was brittle, ice cold.

Grace squeezed her, said in her head, *We've both been found.*

We've both been found, we've both been found.

'What on earth are you doing down *here*?' She couldn't believe it. *Here.* Right now, in this moment. Had Tom seen her? No, he couldn't have, he wouldn't have gone. 'Have you been here all this time?'

Stacey didn't speak, just clung to Grace, shivering and sobbing.

'Let's get you home,' said Grace.

Stacey pulled back. 'No,' she cried. 'I want to come to your house.'

'Your dad has been worried sick,' said Grace gently. 'We've all been looking for you. Come on, we *must* get you back. Are you hungry? Have you eaten?'

Stacey was mute.

'Let me carry you,' said Grace. *I made you fall – now I can pick you up.* 'We can talk as we go. You *can't* stay here.'

She helped Stacey stand up on the bench and then hoisted her onto her back; Stacey's chill hands clung to her neck, legs snaked snug about her waist. And they headed home. Past dark shapes on lamp posts that she knew were chrysanthemums.

'Where *were* you?' asked Grace.

Stacey's voice was warm in her hear: 'At Billy's.'

'*Billy?*' Grace frowned. 'Who's he?'

'My friend.'

Her friend? How on earth? Wouldn't his parents have alerted Martin that she was there? Surely they would have been interviewed by the police? 'Why didn't his parents let your dad know where you were?'

'They didn't know I was there,' said Stacey.

Grace couldn't believe it. All this time, somewhere safe. The relief weakened her knees for a moment. 'How on earth did you manage that?'

'I hid in the wardrobe – he has a big one that you walk into. When everyone went to work and school, I just stayed there. And in the evening Billy brought me food, and I slept in his bed. I was very quiet. I was a secret mouse.'

Grace shook her head. Stacey was getting heavy but she pushed on, left the river behind them. 'But why here, why now then?'

'They went on holiday this morning. I had nowhere to go.'

'Why don't you want to go home?'

Stacey didn't respond.

'You can tell me,' said Grace gently. 'I can keep it to myself if you want me to.' It didn't matter if she never shared Stacey's response – she was safe. That was all that mattered.

'I hate my dad.'

Grace smiled. Couldn't help it. Didn't most kids at some point? But then she faltered. 'Why?' she asked.

'He wants to move. And I don't. I *won't*. I like it here, I like being near to Billy! I like my school! He doesn't care what I want. He's got a new job in Newcastle!'

'Maybe you can talk to him,' said Grace. 'Tell him how you feel.'

'No,' grunted Stacey.

'Maybe it won't happen.'

No response.

'And if it does,' said Grace, 'someone lovely will bring you a Welcome Pack the way you did me.'

They arrived at their street. It was quiet, dark. Grace had no idea if anyone did Night Watch anymore. Probably not with the end in sight, and after so many reports about assaults.

'I'm going to be in trouble, aren't I?' whispered Stacey.

'No. Your dad is going to be way too happy for that.'

Grace knocked on Martin's door. Stacey began crying in her ear. She patted the girl's leg, told her it would all be alright. It would. She believed that now. Martin appeared, lamp in hand. Grace didn't need to speak. He let out a heart-wrenching sob, clawed at his daughter, pulled her from Grace, into his arms, sank to the floor with her.

'Stacey, Stacey, *Stacey*,' he said over and over and over.

Grace left them. There was nothing more for her to do. She had delivered a gift that no house could have wanted more. Like The Night, Stacey had crept into a house, but hidden in a wardrobe, and kept quiet.

When Grace got back to her own home, it was pitch black.

Was she scared? Did she desperately need the camping lamp? She couldn't deny it came to her, but was it learned behaviour? She couldn't expect that a lifetime of living the way she had would be undone in a moment. It was still next to the bed because she had waited until the electricity was on before getting up.

Could she leave it there?

She could. She *did*. She went into the kitchen, feeling her way, breathing slowly, until the shapes took on more form. She lit the hob, the spark of flame a brief warmth and made black coffee and took it upstairs. Sat in bed, sipping it, camping lamp still off, though her fingers itched to flick the switch.

She remembered one of the patients at the hospice – Annie she'd been called, almost ninety-five – saying that the place between life and death was the shadowland. 'Some pass through it fast,' she said, 'but some linger, get stuck, lost there, afraid to go into the next place.'

Grace had been one of those souls. Stuck in a place where she wasn't living fully, and yet she wasn't dead either. Stacey had been somewhere similar, except in a wardrobe, a secret mouse she had said. Now, it was time to come out of the shadowland. Time to live.

Maybe Grace finally could.

Was the dark her friend?

Maybe they were beginning to become acquainted . . .

Welcome to UK GOV
The best place to find government services and information

Lights On Announcement – 23 January

When we began Lights Out, we intended it to last a few months. We have, however, made the decision to end the switch off Sunday 26 January. On this day, all services will resume.

We made this decision because we put YOU first. Due to the increase in illnesses in the elderly, children and vulnerable, and a rise in road accidents, crime and protests, we must terminate the scheme. For those who have been adversely affected by Lights Out there is help. Click **here** for more information.

For easy and safe disposal of broken refrigerators please click **here**.

Remember: the government's first priority is always the safety of our country.

NIGHT NINETEEN

53

Bruised But Over the Worst

Grace slept like she had been drugged; it was dream-free and she stirred once, aware that the room was unlit, but falling back into oblivion without trouble. When she woke to a watery dawn between parted curtains, she realised that waking in the dark had made it easier to doze off again. She felt invigorated. If this was what sleeping in the dark meant, she welcomed it.

Stacey was home; safe.

Grace said the words aloud, smiled, hugged herself.

They might resume their window waves tonight; their distant but now close, very curious, relationship.

In the kitchen, she made coffee, and plans. A new fridge was coming Monday. It was only Thursday but she would make do. She wasn't at work until next Tuesday, was seeing Jamie on Saturday, and would suggest lunch at some point to Claire. And today she needed to talk to Tom.

Tom.

Had they formed a strange . . . *friendship*?

Could she call it that? Perhaps *relationship* was more fitting. They had only met a few times, and it had all started with a series of break-ins. There was no disputing that Tom committed a crime. Could he be excused by his good intentions? Could they be friends? Was that odd? Did they have more in common than just their duplicitous partners? Every item he had left, and every note he had written, had led to this. To him being there for her hardest moment; helping her overcome the dark. She needed to thank him.

She could use someone kind in her life, especially if she was letting Riley go.

And that was when she realised she was ready to.

She put her coffee mug on the worktop with a clunk. It suddenly felt too heavy to hold. In the last two weeks, she had made meals for one as though it was the most natural thing in the world and had got into bed last night without turning to kiss her husband. Now, hot tears stung her eyes. She *had* loved Riley, and part of her still did, just not in the same way. She had trusted him with her entire heart. And that was the problem. She couldn't trust him now, no matter what he said. He had cheated and then lied about it.

She needed to tell him it was over.

Before that, she needed to thank Tom.

She took her phone into the living room. Brad and Jennifer gobbled the food she dropped into the water. Maybe she should get a third fish. What had Tom said it meant? Protection.

The phone pinged in her hand. Catherine.

Did you see? It's OVER! You must be relieved! Hope you're OK. x

Grace turned the TV on. The strip at the bottom of the screen said BREAKING NEWS, followed by the words *Lights Out will end on Sunday.*

Like her marriage, it was finished.

Grace sank into the sofa. It was over. *Over.* How did she feel? Emotional, the way you are after a long birth, exhausted but now pain free, bruised but over the worst. It was hard to know for sure if the sob that burst from her was about the end of her marriage, or the end of the dark. But she could be proud. She had conquered that darkness *before* the government decided to end it. She would have been OK with or without their decision.

The interviewee on TV was Jane Green, Chelsea and Fulham MP, who argued that it should never have started. 'I warned MPs that the country couldn't take it,' she said. 'We had record numbers in acute poverty. Risking those people with a scheme like this was barbaric. Yes, we need to address the climate issue, but that wasn't what this was about. The prime minister will tell you they're ending it early because the vulnerable suffered but don't believe him. He fears losing the next election if he doesn't.'

Hands still shaking, Grace responded to her mum:

I'm good. Yesterday, I remembered about the box, that day, and I understand why you tried to protect me. We all make mistakes. It gave me peace seeing my dad, now it's time to move on. I'll see you soon. X

She realised how fragmented memories of that last night – the one before the box – had been over the years. She had thought that her mother smoking in the kitchen, telling her they wouldn't speak Bailey's name again, had been the next morning. But that had been days after the box incident. She had thought her dad left the night the lamp went off. But it had been after the box incident. It was like she'd erased whole days of her childhood from her memory in her desperation to feel fine again. In many ways, she still had the job of piecing it all together to form a complete and linear story. She would do that. In time.

Grace paused, phone in hand.

Then she wrote what neither she nor her mum rarely did: *I love you. X*

She waited.

Little typing dots. Pause, restarted.

Then: *I love you too. X*

Grace smiled, touched.

She wandered back into the kitchen for more coffee, found Riley's number while the water boiled. He answered more quickly than she expected.

'I was just going to call you,' he said.

'How are you?' She spooned granules into a fresh mug.

'Not the best,' he admitted.

She felt bad, but not for long. She was going to break his heart but that wasn't her fault. It was his. It would keep though. She would do it face to face. 'I know it's a strange question, but I don't suppose you have Tom . . . you know, Harper's partner . . . do you happen to have his number?' He probably didn't. 'Or could you get it?' she added.

'*Tom?*' Riley said the name like it was the last thing he expected her to say.

'He's been kind. I want to thank him.' Silence. 'You still there?' More silence. 'Look, I know it's an odd request, with you . . . Harper . . . your affair.' She tutted, impatient now. 'Stop being so awkward.'

'There's no point,' said Riley. She couldn't make out his tone – unnerved, cagey?

'What do you mean?' Grace tutted again.

'He wouldn't answer.'

'How can you know that?'

Riley paused. 'He's gone.'

'*Gone?* Gone where?' She half expected him to say Outer Mongolia, a random thought that almost made her laugh. Nothing would surprise her about Tom after his feng shui.

'He left a note,' said Riley.

'A note?' Grace repeated.

He's good at those. Did he sign it from The Night?

'I just got off the phone to . . .' Riley paused, maybe feeling guilty for the name he was about to say. 'Harper.' Grace found she didn't even care that he was obviously still in touch with her. 'She went there to talk about money or something, but the house was empty. And he's left his phone there. She's very worried.'

'Why, what did the note say?'

'That he was done.'

'*Done?*' It sounded so final.

'Yes. That's all. She rang the police because he's been depressed recently but they won't take it seriously until it's been more than twenty-four hours.'

'Are you surprised the poor man has been depressed?' Grace was stunned.

But what if it was down to her? What if he left her in the tunnel because it was too much for him? What if he went home and wrote a final note and disappeared?

'Can I come over tonight?' asked Riley. 'I hate being alone.'

'You're not alone – you're with your mum. Does Harper know where Tom might go?' She paced the kitchen, as Tom would have done.

'*What?*' Riley sounded annoyed.

'She should be looking for him. Is she?'

Stacey had just come back – this was too much.

'I don't know,' said Riley. 'She said he had gone, she was worried, and that was it. Why are you so bothered? You don't even know him.'

'You have no idea,' Grace snapped. 'He's listened to me more these past couple of days than you have in ten years.' She shook her head, paced faster, spoke more to herself. 'I wish I hadn't belittled his beliefs. I was unkind.'

'*I* listened to you.' Riley, still there.

Grace didn't respond.

'I'm your husband,' he said.

'You haven't behaved like one,' she cried.

'*He* scared you to death for two weeks with his weird notes. He's a criminal and we should tell the police it was him wh—'

'Fuck you,' Grace spat.

'I don't get it.'

'No, and you never will.'

Grace hung up and threw the phone on the worktop with a clatter. She clutched her head, hands either side of it, squashing to push the negative thoughts down. A note like that didn't sound good: *I'm done.*

He had seemed upbeat by the river. He had lifted her, encouraged her, helped her face her demons. She remembered his words.

You can only see properly in the dark. And not everyone wants that. But you should, because I reckon you're strong enough. Words so rich in life. But just because he had lifted *her* didn't mean he felt that way himself. This was a man so distressed by his partner's affair that he had developed an obsession with feng shui and broken into her home.

I'm done.

So sad, so final.

Grace couldn't stay here. She needed to get out of the house.

She got her coat and set off, breath ragged, heart racing. A voice. *Tom?* She spun around, hopeful. No – Martin calling from his doorstep. Grace approached, distracted, but keen to check on Stacey's well-being.

'Thank you,' he gushed. '*Thank you.*'

'Oh, it was nothing,' said Grace, which seemed silly. It wasn't. A girl had been found safe after almost a week. 'How's Stacey doing?'

'Good. Very tired, and she's eaten the fridge contents . . . but she's alright.' He paused. 'The police will want to chat to you, just because you found her. I gave them your number. Hope that's OK?'

They already have it, thought Grace. *But they never call.*

She said she was glad Stacey was OK and asked Martin to pass on her love, then let her feet dictate where she went, no idea where they would end up. Only when a cold wind chilled them did she realise there were tears on her cheeks. What was she crying for? The father she had lost? The past she had recently faced? The relief of a child found?

All of it.

She was at the graveyard gates, shivering in the shadow of thick-trunked trees. Rows of headstones rose from the ground like grey ghosts. Tom's cemetery; the place she had chased him, heard his tale. She pictured him maintaining the grounds and repairing graves. Limbs heavy, she followed the curved path to the left, between leafless trees bent over, like elderly men wilting, past their bench and bins full of flower bouquet wrappings. It went full circle; she walked it, again and again, a cycle of death, graves old and new, graves loved and abandoned, graves, graves, graves.

But no Tom.

She stopped, out of breath, near a headstone for a man who had died aged just twenty-seven. It was well maintained, fresh white roses in the vase, photographs in plastic coverings taped to the white headstone. She would do the same for her dad. She and her mum could do it together.

'Where *are* you, Tom?' she said aloud.

She could not cope with searching for someone else.

Cautious footsteps on the path behind her – a woman with a small bunch of yellow roses, who passed with a brief, polite smile, and went on to a grave in the far-right corner.

It was time to go home to her empty house.

That was what Grace had chosen. She would decide who she let in. She had closed the door on the dark, on her dad, and soon would on a husband who had cheated.

But it would be nice to open it and see Tom standing on the step, itching to pace, excited about some new class or theory, full of life and wise words.

HULL LOCAL NEWS

Lights Out Collection to Raise
Money For Child Poverty

Local writer, Sarah Ainsworth, wants your Lights Out stories. The bestselling author, who found the scheme 'brilliant for inspiration', wants your true tales of life, brief as it was, during the switch off. Your contributions can be stories, essays, or poetry. She will curate the collection and release the anthology at Easter. All money raised will go to the local Child in Me charity, which helps children who have been in the care system. 'These kids have suffered more than most these last few weeks,' said Sarah. 'I'd like to make a small difference to their lives.'

Feather Man Suspect 'Confesses'

The masked man apprehended by a Night Watch volunteer four nights ago while breaking into a home in Leeds has confessed to being the 'Feather Man', according to a source. The friend of the unnamed suspect, who wishes to also remain anonymous, said, 'I had no idea about his activities. I'm shocked. But after four days of being questioned, he admitted that he broke into all of the other houses, and tied those poor women up. Lock him up and throw away the key, I say. You can't blame how your mother treated you for such behaviour!'

Humberside Police would not comment at this stage.

54

How's Your Fridge, Love?

Two mornings later – after a third night of sleeping with the camping lamp off – Grace was woken by hammering on the front door.

Who the hell was it at this time? It was eight thirty on a Saturday morning.

She went downstairs, battle ready, having been in a fighty mood since Tom went missing. She wasn't sure if the grief of losing her dad followed by Tom's disappearance was making her angry, but she had been cursing at every news show, bursting into hot tears out of the blue.

In fact, Grace hadn't stopped thinking about Tom. A police officer had called yesterday to interview her about the circumstances surrounding her discovery of Stacey, and at the end of the call she mentioned Tom, said she had seen him the night before he went missing, wanted to help. Sadly, that officer said it wasn't his case and someone else would get back to her. But they hadn't.

Should she speak to Harper, ask if there was anything she could do, anywhere she could look?

Grace opened the door to a burly man in a leather jacket, knowing her face must be thunderous. 'Yes?'

'How's your fridge, love?' he asked.

'Sorry?'

'We're collecting broken fridges.'

'Oh.'

Grace looked into the kitchen. What good was it? Might as well let him have it, save herself the trouble of calling the council or borrowing a van to take it to the tip. A rough voice in the street beyond. Another man driving a van, yelling, 'Bring out your fridges,' the way 'bring out your dead' had been shouted during the Black Plague to let people know the cart for deceased bodies was passing.

The fridge. If it's broken, it's terrible energy, and that's your Relationship Area. That's why I put the two candles in there.

Tom's voice, in her head. She didn't care about fixing her marriage but maybe there had been something in what he believed after all.

'You alright, love?' asked the burly man. 'Can I tek your fridge, or what?'

'It hasn't worked for a while. Let me empty it, not that there's much in there. Are you taking it now?'

'Yes.' He turned and yelled, 'Mike. Over here. This lady's got one for us.'

Grace winced as she removed the few bits of rubbery cheese and limp lettuce from its tepid enclosure and threw them in the bin. 'What are you doing with them?' she called to the burly man, still on the doorstep.

'My mate Smithy's a truck driver. He's gonna tek 'em down to London and leave 'em by Downing Street. His elderly dad died in the dark, first night of Lights Out, only had a landline but with no electricity, couldn't call for help, so he's angry, grief-stricken. We're naming every fridge after someone who died cos of the fucking switch off. Sorry, lady. Bad language.'

'I don't mind,' said Grace. 'I've been sweary myself recently.'

Tom had said she should get rid of this now-dilapidated appliance. She felt sure he would love the idea of it being dumped near Downing Street, making a statement.

Mike arrived then, cigarette dangling from his mouth.

'We OK to come in and get it?' asked the burly one, polite.

Grace nodded and stepped aside.

The two of them huffed and puffed and wrestled the fridge out of its space, half dragging and half carrying it into the hallway, and then outside.

'Mind my things,' Grace cried when they knocked one of Tom's tall, ivory candles over. She put it carefully back in its position. Maybe she would finally light them. Tomorrow, when the electricity came back on in the evening, it would be allowed again.

Today – tonight – was the final Lights Out.

'Anyone you'd like to dedicate it to?' called Burly from the path.

Grace went to the door. 'What do you mean?'

'I don't mean to pry love, or overstep, but if you lost anyone . . . Like I said, we're naming the fridges after folks who, you know, passed away or were hurt during Lights Out. Let this bastard of a government deal with a load of broken fridges on their doorstep and the names of those they wrecked with their bloody scheme.'

'Yes, I did lose someone,' she said quietly.

It hadn't technically been down to Lights Out, but it had been during the switch off.

'Do *I* write the name on it?' she asked.

Burly held out a Sharpie in answer. 'We've had all kinds of dedications,' he said. 'Some of 'em made me tear up, I tell you. You wouldn't think it, would you, so much happening in three weeks? Mind, we were in a state before that. Shows you how much we need warmth and light, doesn't it.'

'Yes,' said Grace softly.

'Remember them poor four women who walked into the river?'

'I do.'

'The sister of one of them gave us her old freezer. Told us to chuck it through the Downing Street window for Debbie – that was her name. But she wrote *all* their names on it. They were mates through a domestic abuse group. Debbie's husband apparently got . . . well, much worse when the lights went out.'

'That's . . .' Grace was too choked to finish her sentence.

She took the pen. What to write? She tried to think. After a moment, she knew.

Dad, I know you did what you thought was best. Rest in peace,
Grace X

Burly looked at it, nodded, as though he understood. Then he and Mike carried the machine down the path and out into the back of the van, its innards clanking and banging furiously. Grace watched them continue up the street, shouting for neighbours to bring out their fridges, and then she closed the door. She went to the square gap left in the kitchen; stood in it. It smelled fusty and needed cleaning, which she did with a wet wipe, but she remained there for a few minutes afterwards too, unsure why.

She headed for Leeds late morning to see Jamie. He hugged her tightly as soon as she arrived at his house.

'What was that for?' she asked, happy.

'I felt like you needed it,' he said.

They went to his favourite coffee shop, and sat in the window. Rain fell hard, flash puddles forming in moments, shoppers rushing to avoid the downpour. The temperature was milder today. When people most needed warmth during the recent chill, they suffered without the heating. Now, when it would be back to normal tomorrow, it was mild again. It was like the weather was making a point – see, I can be kind, but you need to see my dark side too.

When their cappuccinos arrived, Jamie asked, 'How are you, Mum?'

She sighed heavily. 'Yes and no.'

'Yes and no? That doesn't make any sense.'

She laughed. 'I think I meant good and bad.' She paused. 'My father died.'

'Oh.' Jamie put a hand over hers. 'I'm sorry.'

Grace looked out the window, felt tears build, but didn't want to upset her son. She had always tried to keep him from the bad stuff, be the buffer between real life and his heart.

'Did you get to care for him?' he asked.

'I was there when he went. It was . . . gentle. I think he knew it was me, but even if he didn't, I'm at peace.' Grace paused. 'I know now, as an adult, rather than as a confused child, that he *didn't* have a dark side. He wasn't scary or bad. He had a mental illness that made him *seem* that way to the small me. So, I have closure on everything that happened, his leaving, all of it . . .'

'That's good. You deserve that.' Jamie sipped his cappuccino, studying her. 'Did you tell Grandma?'

'Afterwards. When he'd gone, I went to see her.'

'How did she take not knowing until afterwards? I mean, she can be bossy. Likes to know everything.'

Grace smiled. 'She can but she was kind.' She didn't bother sharing about their recent disagreements – there was no point, they were good again.

'I'm glad. She pisses me off how she speaks to you brusquely sometimes.'

'I don't mind,' said Grace. 'She's . . . old school. She's a good soul.'

'I suppose.' Jamie finished his drink, never one to take his time with coffee. He studied her, thoughtful. 'There's something else.'

'What do you mean?'

'You're . . . *different.*'

'Am I?' Grace laughed.

'Yes. You're . . . buzzing. Death suits you well.'

'Jesus,' she said. Then: 'Jamie, there is something else – I'm leaving Riley.'

'*Really?* Why?'

'He . . .' Even after what he'd done, Grace didn't want to speak badly of him. In the future it would come up, but for now she chose a gentler truth. 'We've been growing apart. For a while. The last few weeks have been stressful, and we took a break. He went to stay with a friend. While he was gone I . . .' Grace shrugged. 'I realised I didn't want him back. Do you think I'm awful?'

'Of course not,' said Jamie. 'Why the hell would I think that? I like Riley, but I always felt it had to be him first.'

'Really?'

'You always put him first, but I felt like he never did you.'

At first, Grace was surprised Jamie had felt this way. But then, when she considered it properly, not. He was right. She had adored Riley and let it happen. Jamie and Harry's relationship seemed much more equal; she realised that she had often looked at them, how sweet they were together, and been unable to deny that she was a little jealous. Then she had felt bad – that was her son, she was happy for him. But why didn't Riley look at her in the adoring way Harry studied Jamie? It was strange how now, with hindsight, she saw the flaws in her marriage. She had glossed over them while she was with him.

'Wow,' she said softly.

'You're a powerhouse,' gushed Jamie. 'You'll be fine on your own. You've got me. You've got Harry.'

'I know. Let's not talk about Riley, let's talk about you. How are you guys? What have you been up to?'

Jamie told her about their plans to sell the house and buy some-where bigger, which she was surprised about since they had been doing the place up. Jamie revealed then that they had been talking about looking into having a child via surrogacy. Yes, they were still young, but these things could take time. And they both wanted to be parents. This made Grace happy. She grabbed his hand. There was lots to look forward to. Didn't they always say that new life followed a death?

'Last Lights Out,' said Jamie as the owner took their empty mugs away. 'You must be glad.'

'I've been less scared recently,' she admitted.

She couldn't tell him about Tom because she hadn't mentioned him before. Anyway, how could she explain who he was? The man who broke into her house and left strange items and weird notes was the partner of her husband's mistress, but had helped her overcome her greatest fear. Who was now missing. Had gone. Was *done*. Grace buried the wave of sadness.

'Less scared?' prompted Jamie.

'I was forced to face the dark alone during the switch off . . . I've slept without the camping light the last few nights.'

'Bloody hell, Mum.' Jamie sat back in his chair, head cocked, watching her. 'You really are . . . *wow*.'

'I know.'

'I'm proud of you.'

'No,' said Grace. 'I'm proud of *you*.' She suddenly saw them, long ago, on a beach somewhere, with a picnic because she couldn't afford to buy chips, wrapped in blankets because they had gone off-peak. 'Listen, I'm sorry you never had what other kids did when you were small, you know, a dad, nice holidays, decent house . . .'

'For God's sake, Mum, I had the *best* childhood.' Jamie looked emotional,

'No, but . . .' Grace took a breath. 'I'm sorry I let a man like Steve into your world, even if briefly.'

'*Steve?*' Jamie looked confused now.

'I know how . . . disruptive he was.' That felt like a kinder word than the man deserved, but fitting too.

'I don't remember him.' Jamie's face was blank.

Grace was shocked. Maybe she had managed to keep his behaviour away from her son after all. Or maybe it was because he had only been three, the toxic relationship brief, and memories from that young can be hazy. Whatever the reason, Grace felt intense relief. Guilt at exposing her son to such an unstable man lessened a little.

'I guess he doesn't matter then,' she said softly.

'Don't you realise? I had *you*, and that was all I needed. It didn't matter that my father had gone, or if you had the odd boyfriend; *you* made me happy.'

'Stop it.' Grace shook her head, embarrassed.

'You were always on my side,' said Jamie.

'I always will be,' she said.

Later, after another cappuccino, they walked around a small park, the rain pausing as though to give them a breather. Then Grace drove back.

Eight o'clock did not loom like it had the last few weeks.

It arrived, a natural conclusion to the day.

Grace did not need to count down. Didn't feel anxious as she went on her usual tour of the house, flicking the switches off this last time. At the final one, in the living room, she was ready for the dark. She knew her way. The shadowy shapes were as familiar and safe as the contours of her own face; even the new things had settled in, felt like her own possessions now. She might keep them. The dragon artwork. The heart around her face. And the Tiffany lamp, she wanted back; she would find a way to get it.

They made her think of Tom.

She messaged Riley: *Hope you're OK. Any news on Tom? X*

Immediately, a response: *I'm not OK. Annoying that you only talk to me to ask about Tom. What about me? And no, nothing on Tom.*

She ignored his questions. *Are the police taking it seriously?*

Riley wrote: *They're looking into it. What about us then? When can I come home?*

Reluctantly, Grace wrote: *Come by tomorrow morning, we'll talk.*

He wrote: *OK.*

In bed, with the camping lamp for visibility rather than as comfort, Grace scrolled through local news stories, found a small piece on Tom. She felt sad about its two-paragraph brevity, but so much else was going on. And he wasn't a ten-year-old girl. They called Harper his partner – *ex-partner,* thought Grace – and said it wasn't known what he'd been wearing when he left.

Was it the thin, dark green jacket he wore that night on the river?

She went to the bedroom window and looked out into the endless night. A shivering glow in the opposite window – Stacey, with a torch, hair like flowing strings of gold in its beam. Grace waved, hoped Stacey would see. Hoped she had adapted to being back home; was happier with the changes that might be happening in her life. That was what growing up really was – letting go, facing the unknown, accepting that you still had to follow the current rather than set the pace. Stacey spotted her, smiled, waved.

Grace blew a kiss.

Stacey blew one back.

Grace returned to the bed, turned off the lamp and tried to sleep. Being alone was not as distressing as she had imagined it might be. It was empowering to own her house fully. To own the night.

To own herself.

HULL LOCAL NEWS

Candlelit Walk Proposed to Conclude Lights Out

Hull residents want an event to mark the end of Lights Out, and remember those who died. Local residents have already made big statements, like the fridge sculpture *Close Encounters of the Fridge Kind*. Mayor Teresa Nikolic wants a celebration where families come together. 'A candlelit walk is perfect,' she said. 'We couldn't light them during the switch off so it would be great to walk our streets with a burning candle.'

Others think it's an appalling idea. 'What's to celebrate?' said Lesley Raymond, 34. 'It's been terrible. I want to forget it. My neighbour Shayne got hypothermia and we almost lost her. I won't be celebrating anything.'

THE LIGHT

55

Being Her Own Light

Was the new dawn different?

It felt like the sun woke in a good mood and climbed eagerly over the trees and rooftops to share her joy. The bedroom when Grace woke appeared vivid. She had left the curtains open but still, it was lovely for late January. The first morning of everyday life resuming. Tonight there would be warmth, light, the ability to cook, to watch the TV, devour new shows, not worry about charging anything.

Grace didn't get up for a while.

She knew that things could change in a flash. If there was plenty to be hopeful about, there were always things that tested us, light and shade. Riley was coming over mid-morning. That made her anxious. She was ready to tell him their marriage was over, oh yes, but she knew she would also be compelled to ask about Tom and what if there was bad news? Maybe she should just go to the police station, chase up whether *they* had any news. But there likely wouldn't be time before Riley arrived.

Grace finally got up, made coffee, black, no fridge of course, and waited. Waited for her husband so she could tell him how she felt. Made toast, no butter just jam, and waited to change her life forever.

A message from her mum:

Tickets for my show are on sale now! You'll buy one won't you? Jamie and Harry will come, they must love the theatre, and they'll have loads of friends who do too, won't they?

Grace smiled, shaking her head at the assumption that her gay son and his pals *must* love the theatre. Catherine lived for every moment; she was selfish at times, full on, but kind, and Grace loved her for it. She wrote back:

> *Of course we'll be there for your big moment, all of us. X*

While she was on her phone, Grace messaged Claire, too. That lunch still needed arranging.

> *Are you working today? Why don't I pop in with some sandwiches at noon for your break, we'll eat in the garden. X*

Claire wrote: *Lovely, see you then. X*

When Riley arrived at ten, Grace let him in without a word. He looked a mess. She had never seen him this way, his usually sculpted hair awry, his shirt not ironed, eyes lined. Had he gone to work looking like this all week? She felt sad for him but could not let that influence the decision she had made. He followed her into the kitchen while she put the kettle on.

'The fridge,' he said wearily. 'What happened?'

'Someone took it. Got a new one coming tomorrow.'

'I could've come with you to get it,' he said, as though nothing had changed. 'There's a sale on at—'

'Riley,' she said. "No need. It's all sorted.'

'Oh.' He paused. 'How are you?'

You have no idea, she thought. *You don't know about my dad, you don't know about me going into that tunnel, about my new friendship with the dark. Because you haven't been here.*

'Fine.' She knew Riley was asking how she was so that she then asked how *he* was, and it irritated her. She realised now that he had often done that – got her out of the way so they could concentrate on him. Still, she asked, if brusquely, 'You? You look like shit to be fair.'

'Thanks.' He seemed surprised at her response. Let him be.

She took the drinks into the living room, put Riley's on the coffee table next to Brad and Jennifer. She drank hers in the window, back to him, a position that felt right. 'I'm not going to play games.' She heard the sofa give as he sat. 'I don't want to rehash anything we already said . . . I don't want you back.'

No response.

She turned. He had his head in his hands, was staring at his feet. He nodded. 'I was afraid this was how you felt. I've known, deep down, since we last spoke. But to hear it . . .'

'I want it to be civil,' she said. 'I just don't feel the same now and I don't think that's going to change.'

'I don't know what I'll do,' he said morosely.

Now that she had made this decision, he played the victim. Usually she gave in when he acted hurt. Not anymore. 'That's for you to decide,' she said.

'So I have to move out and you get to stay here?' He looked up, more like the old Riley; thinking of himself.

Grace sighed. 'If you want to stay here, I'll live with my mum for a bit.'

'I don't want to live here without you, Amazing,' he said.

Don't call me that now.

She buried exasperation. 'That's not an option.'

'You stay then.' He stood up, not having touched his coffee. 'I'll come and get my stuff another time. We'll have to sell it, this place, because I'll need to buy somewhere if you don't want our marriage anymore. Neither of us will be able to get much, you know. Splitting the money from the sale, like we'll have to.'

'I don't need much,' said Grace quietly.

As Tom had said, it was the art of where things were in a house that mattered, that made it a home. She suddenly saw a tiny flat, simply decorated, cream walls, favourite things in place, her fish, candles, and the Tiffany lamp illuminating a bookshelf corner. Was it a premonition or a hope?

'Well,' grunted Riley. 'If that's it, I'll go.'

Grace wondered whether to ask about Tom. Should she just go to the police? No, they were never any use.

'Any news about Tom?' she asked.

'Him again. For fuck's sake.'

'*Well?*' Grace stood her ground.

'I have no idea, I haven't spoken to Harper.' He headed to the front door, feet heavy like a sulky toddler. Grace's heart was as weighty. Where was the poor man? Had he done . . . something stupid?

Opening the door, Riley glanced up the stairs. 'Are you leaving that ridiculous dragon there?'

'I am,' she said. 'I rather like it now.'

It'll come to my new place, she thought.

'He was two currants short of a bun, you know.'

'Who?' asked Grace.

'Tom. Harper said he was having some sort of a breakdown.'

Grace wanted to slap Riley's face for the first time in her life, but resisted. 'Is she surprised? She fucked him over, drove him mad with her deceit, and you have the nerve to describe him that way when the poor guy is missing. And *you* – gaslighting me all along. Hiding what you knew about our break-ins! You have a fucking nerve!'

'I still don't know how you knew hi—' Riley tried.

'You think *you* deserve to know that?'

'How do I know you weren't sleeping with him?'

Grace could barely speak. She realised in that moment that Riley's gaslighting was far more insidious than the way Steve had behaved all those years ago. Steve's had been blatant; obvious. Riley hid his cruelty behind charm.

'Get *out*.' Grace found her voice, pushed him now. 'Get out of here. I gave you a chance to be civil, now you can fuck off.'

He resisted, weakly, staggered onto the path. She slammed the door before he could respond. 'This is silly,' he yelled from outside.

'I'm sorry, let's talk properly. I'm a mess, I want you, us. Please, Grace, *please?*'

After a while, he left.

Grace sat on the stairs and stared at the space where he had been.

There were suddenly lots of spaces in her life where people had been, something that she wouldn't have seen coming if you'd asked her three weeks ago. But there was still hope that one space might be occupied again. Wasn't there?

Grace headed to the hospice before noon. She had rarely walked there at that time of day, when the sun was its brightest. It was what she needed after the scene with Riley. She wanted them to be somehow civil, not end up being a former couple who argued over every petty thing. But it took two to create that, and she sensed that Riley wouldn't make things easy.

Before finding Claire, Grace went to the small square room at the corner of the building, its windows with the different views; the place where her dad had taken his last breath. She was mindful that there might be a new resident, and peered through the open door before entering.

Empty. Tidy. The Tiffany lamp, gone.

She panicked. Where was it? Had they assumed it belonged to Bailey? Damn. She must look for it after seeing Claire. For a moment, she thought she heard a voice; her name. She turned. Her *dad*? One last message? One last made-up bedtime story?

But it was someone down the corridor saying *space* or *waste* or something else that sounded like her name.

Claire was in the garden when Grace arrived, sitting on the bench by the snowdrops in large tubs, with a blanket over her knees, eating a sandwich.

'No, I got these on the way.' Grace found the luxury range beef and horseradish ciabatta in her bag, one of Claire's favourites, and then the cheaper tuna mayonnaise for herself.

'Oh, bless you.' Claire put her half-eaten sarnie to one side and took the ciabatta. 'Thank you.' She took a huge bite of it and nodded, happy.

For the first time in a long while, Grace felt able to give Claire the care and attention she needed. 'How are things?' Grace started her sandwich. 'Tell me about the kids?'

Claire smiled wryly, mouth full. 'Full of life as usual, it never stops. Good job coffee exists, eh?'

'You do amazing.' Grace meant it.

'You know. You've been there.'

'Yes, but you do it alone with three, I only had one!'

Claire shrugged. 'It isn't a competition,' she said. 'Work is work.' She paused. 'We really need to make sure lunch is somewhere nice next time. We seem to bloody live here, don't we?'

'You do,' said Grace. 'I feel for you.'

'Can't turn down the money from extra shifts. And you're the nutter who's here on your day off. I should have you sectioned.'

Grace laughed, then spoke seriously: 'If there's ever anything I can do, you would ask, wouldn't you?'

Claire glanced at her. 'Probably not. But your words mean a lot.' She paused. 'Lights Out over, eh? It's good but I think we'll now see the true fallout here, with extra illnesses and deaths. And we'll take care of them because we love what we do, on the same crap wage, with the government telling us we're stars, and then turning the country against us if we strike.'

'Nothing changes, does it?'

'How are you?' asked Claire. 'Any more break-ins?'

Grace chewed slowly. The full story – the one about a mysterious visitor called The Night who ended up being the man who helped her change everything – was not for now. Not enough time. Also, Grace felt surprisingly emotional at the thought of talking about Tom, with him still missing.

'It hasn't happened since I last saw you. The police are still looking into it. Who knows?'

'It's been a strange time, that's for sure,' said Claire.

They sat in silence for a while, finished their food, shared Claire's flask of tea, faced the sun.

Eventually Claire spoke. 'I *know*,' she said softly.

'You know what?'

Grace froze. There were so many things she could have meant, but such words always cause anxiety; you always feel guilt, explore the recesses of your mind for some crime you might have committed when someone says they *know*.

'I know about Bailey.'

Grace couldn't speak.

'The name nagged at me. Then I suddenly realised why. I remembered that you'd once told me it was your father's name.' Claire looked kindly at Grace 'He didn't remind you of him . . . he *was* your dad, wasn't he?'

Grace nodded, feeling eight years old, tears tickling her eyelashes.

'I know I should've . . .' she tried. 'I know it was wrong to—'

'Stop, it's OK,' said Claire kindly.

'Is it?'

'Yes. You didn't disclose it to me, so you didn't put me in a position to have to make a professional decision,' Claire said, pointedly. 'Therefore, now, all we're doing is talking about your beloved dad who died. Come here.'

She wrapped her arms around Grace and let her cry. It was good to let go. To grieve the way others did, no secrecy, no guilt.

'The lamp was yours, wasn't it?' Claire said after a while.

Grace nodded against her chest.

'I put it back in the cupboard so you can take it home.'

Grace could not express her gratitude; it was not only the last thing that had lit her father, but Tom had given her it too.

'I really have to get back,' said Claire, patting her arm.

'I know.' Grace sat up, dried her eyes.

Claire put their wrappers in the bin. They hugged, both saying 'lunch next week and a *proper* catch up'. It felt like they said it every week at this point, but one day they'd get there. Grace went to the staffroom cupboard. The Tiffany lamp was waiting for her; the symbol now of moving ahead, of being her own light.

She took it home and put it back on the hearth where it belonged. Everything in its place. Except Tom. She called the police station but as was the usual now, it rang and rang and rang, and Grace paced and paced and paced.

56

I'll Shine and So Will You

In the evening, eight o'clock approached. Grace imagined people in other houses across the country, old and young, waiting as she was to see if it really happened.

To see if the lights stayed on.

At one minute to the hour, Grace held her breath. Did the whole land do the same? Did a mass inhalation with enough strength to fire a million volts of electricity occur in that moment? They could have lit up the world. She thought of those who didn't wait for it, who couldn't now. Her dad, of the darkness he had forever.

But *did* he? Maybe it was bright where he was.

Maybe it was the brightest of all.

Today, it wasn't because Grace was afraid that she lingered by the Tiffany lamp, but because she was curious. Was it really going to be over? What if it was a trick, a lie? What if – like with the fridges – the temporary outage had caused permanent damage and they were thrust into a new dark age?

Grace closed her eyes to imagine. She would do it. She could now. She just didn't want to. Even though she had made peace with the night, the morning was always good too.

Eight o'clock.

A minute past.

Two minutes.

The lights stayed on.

Grace hurried to the living-room window. All the other house windows were lit too. What a glorious sight. Orange and white and yellow squares, warm waves of encouragement, like shiny gifts waiting under a Christmas tree. The street lamps were rows of festive cheer above. A couple of people came onto doorsteps and gave the light a round of joyful applause too. Behind them, open doors spilled gold promise into the night.

After a while, Grace went in search of gentler rays.

She got Tom's candles from the kitchen and set them on the coffee table. Struck a match and lit each one. Reflected in the fishbowl, they flickered softly, moving in rhythm, swayed by a draught she couldn't see. A ghost? Her dad, sleeves rolled up, face ruddy, ready to take seven-year-old Grace into the garden and pull weeds?

She went to the Shit and Stuff drawer in the kitchen and got Tom's notes.

Read each one, out loud.

I will protect you.
I'm watching over you.
I'm here.
Tiny, but powerful.
Love,
The Night.

She remembered there was one note she had never read; the one Tom had put beneath the Tiffany lamp. She had been too upset. It was still folded over, among the others. Grace opened it now. Read the words there without fear:

I'll shine and so will you,
Love,
The Night.

She couldn't help but think of the one left in his house: *I'm done.* What had he meant? Was it about context? The notes Tom had left with each item seemed creepy when she didn't know his intentions. Now there was something affecting about them. Now the final one felt like a message from a psychic – vague, too brief, not enough.

What on earth had Tom meant?

'Come back and tell me,' Grace cried, angry.

He'd helped her in a way no one else had ever been able to.

Had doing so been too much?

Full of sadness, she put the notes back, blew the candles out, switched off the lights.

And went to bed.

57

The Morning

In the morning, quiet. Like the world waited for her to start things. Like it held its breath. Grace got up to a warm house, to a sun not needed so desperately now. To an empty slot where the fridge once was, to everything as she had left it, to her home.

She opened the living-room curtains.

At the gate, Tom.

She exhaled as though surfacing from a long, painful dive. He hadn't seen her. He looked like he was unsure whether to approach the door. Then glanced up the street. She couldn't let him change his mind, leave.

She rushed to the front door, opened it. '*Tom,*' she cried.

He had found her, just as Stacey had.

'Grace,' he said quietly. He looked exhausted; his clothes hung from his body like they would happily desert him as soon as possible.

'How long have you been there, scaring vulnerable women half to death?' Grace regretted the joke when he might not be in the mood right now, but he smiled.

'I just got here. I was . . . walking.'

'Of course you were.' Sarcastic, but gently so.

So many questions came to Grace: *Where have you been, why did you disappear, are you OK, what did you mean in your note, and what brought you here?* But none of it really mattered right then. Tom was here. That was good.

'You'll be glad to know the fridge has gone,' she said. She hoped that by speaking, he would engage, *stay*.

He nodded. He still hadn't opened the gate. He might *not* stay. Come in. She hoped he would.

'I'm not done,' he said.

Grace nodded, glad.

'I thought I was,' he admitted. 'That night overwhelmed me.'

'In the tunnel?'

'Yes. I waited for you a while but then I couldn't. I had to leave. Come home. It was like . . . like you had conquered your demons, but mine were still there. Still . . . big. Made bigger by your bravery.' Tom shook his head. 'I felt like *less*.'

'No,' cried Grace. 'You should have felt like *more*. What you did for me that night . . . I'll never forget it. I can totally forgive you breaking into my house now, crazy as that might sound to anyone else. You listened to me. And you got me to look at what I never had before.' She wanted to say that she would happily do the same for him, if she could, but he interrupted the thoughts.

'You listened to me too,' he said. 'That day in the cemetery.'

She supposed she had.

'You had every right to drag me back to the police station that day. To make sure they charged me, locked me up. But you didn't.'

'I wanted to,' admitted Grace.

'When I was walking, yesterday . . . I went to the river so many times.' Tom's voice cracked.

Grace felt sure of what he was alluding to, and her heart broke. She opened her mouth to say that she was glad he hadn't done anything but he spoke again.

'Then this morning, just now, I was thinking of . . . going into . . . you know . . . but there was this card stuck to a bench, probably in remembrance of someone.' Tom looked at her. 'Guess what was on it?'

Grace shook her head.

'A dragon. A fucking *dragon*. Can you believe it?' He smiled, wryly. Grace did too. 'And I thought . . . I can't leave a world where there are still dragons on pictures in random places.'

'No, you can't,' said Grace. She paused. 'Tom, why don't you talk to me like you tried to talk to Carole, to the Samaritans? I know you told me about the feng shui, about Harper. But there's more. I know it. There's your history like I had mine. We all have that stuff. Something deeper is overwhelming you, the *real* stuff underneath all that . . .'

Tom nodded but remained mute.

'You can talk to me,' Grace said gently.

Tom still didn't speak.

She waited.

After a while he said simply, 'I'm hungry.'

That was enough. 'You must be. Do you want some breakfast?'

'I do.'

Then Tom opened the gate.

And Grace opened her door fully; made space for him.

Acknowledgements

I wrote this cold, during the Cost of Living Crisis winter of 2022/23, wearing a coat inside and often a hot water bottle on my feet, my fingers chilly as I typed, my breath visible inside the house, afraid to put the heating on during the day.

Many had it much worse. I read stories about children dying in mouldy, damp houses, and the elderly dying of hypothermia. This, naturally, influenced the book. As did what the nurses were going through, with the strikes. These circumstances – much like the pandemic with *End of Story* – had me wondering what it would be like if the lights really did go out.

If it was dark at night, and cold all the time.

Thanks as always to my early readers: Madeleine Black, my sisters Claire and Grace, and John Marrs. Also, thank you to Claire and Grace – a support worker in a palliative care unit and a Nurse Practitioner – for all the help with research on working in end-of-life care. Thanks to Joe for encouraging me to 'keep the things I loved' in it. And to my Katy for being my 'bouncing board' when it came to ideas, and to my Conor for the common sense.

Thank you to all the early readers, reviewers and bloggers, to the book lovers who came to my launches and events, and to the TBC gang, and the many helpful private author groups that kept me going. Thank you to the indie bookstores (the Grove Bookshop, the Rabbit Hole, Imagined Things, JE Books, Tea Leaves and Reads, Goldsboro Books, Beverley Bookshop and Hessle Bookshop, to name but a few) for the endless support. Thanks to the librarians and festival organisers and supportive authors. We writers love and need you all.

Thank you, Lily Cooper, for the incredibly incisive and thought-provoking early edits. You knew what needed pruning, and your vision was spot on. Also thanks to Caroline Hogg for your later, equally helpful edits. And thank you, Lucy Stewart, for making me dig even deeper, making me find those final nuances, and making this the book it is now, one I'm so proud of. Thank you Kay Gale for making it all 'reader ready' with your great copy edits. Also, Kim Nyamhondera for being my publicity girl, and for sending my books (and me) to all the places where they can shine best.

Huge thanks too to my Emily Glenister, for all your love and support, always, unconditionally. I'm so proud to be part of DHH Literary Agency.